About the Authors

Kim Lawrence lives on a farm in Anglesey with her university lecturer husband, assorted pets who arrived as strays and never left, and sometimes one or both of her boomerang sons. When she's not writing she loves to be outdoors gardening or walking on one of the beaches for which the island is famous for along with being the place where Prince William and Catherine made their first home!

Maggie Cox is passionate about stories that can uplift and transport people out of their daily worries to a more magical place, be they romance novels or fairy tales. What people want most, she believes, is true connection. She feels blessed to be married to a lovely man that never fails to make her laugh and has two beautiful sons and two much loved grandchildren.

Amy Andrews has always loved writing, and still can't quite believe that she gets to do it for a living. Creating wonderful heroines and gorgeous heroes and telling their stories is an amazing way to pass the day. Sometimes they don't always act as she'd like them to – but then neither do her kids, so she's kind of used to it. Amy lives in the very beautiful Samford Valley, with her husband and aforementioned children, along with six brown chooks and two black dogs. She loves to hear from her readers. Drop her a line at www.amyandrews.com.au

Red-Hot

COLLECTION

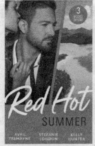

May 2018

June 2018

July 2018

August 2018

Red-Hot Seduction

KIM LAWRENCE

MAGGIE COX

AMY ANDREWS

MILLS & BOON

All rights reserved including the right of reproduction in whole or in part in any form. This edition is published by arrangement with Harlequin Books S.A.

This is a work of fiction. Names, characters, places, locations and incidents are purely fictional and bear no relationship to any real life individuals, living or dead, or to any actual places, business establishments, locations, events or incidents. Any resemblance is entirely coincidental.

This book is sold subject to the condition that it shall not, by way of trade or otherwise, be lent, resold, hired out or otherwise circulated without the prior consent of the publisher in any form of binding or cover other than that in which it is published and without a similar condition including this condition being imposed on the subsequent purchaser.

® and ™ are trademarks owned and used by the trademark owner and/or its licensee. Trademarks marked with ® are registered with the United Kingdom Patent Office and/or the Office for Harmonisation in the Internal Market and in other countries.

Published in Great Britain 2018
by Mills & Boon, an imprint of HarperCollins*Publishers*
1 London Bridge Street, London, SE1 9GF

Red-Hot Seduction © 2018 Harlequin Books S.A.

The Sins of Sebastian Rey-Defoe © 2015 Kim Lawrence
A Taste of Sin © 2015 Maggie Cox
Driving Her Crazy © 2013 Amy Andrews

ISBN: 978-0-263-26697-9

09-0618

MIX
Paper from
responsible sources
FSC™ C007454

This book is produced from independently certified FSC™ paper to ensure responsible forest management.

For more information visit: www.harpercollins.co.uk/green

Printed and bound in Spain
by CPI, Barcelona

THE SINS OF
SEBASTIAN
REY-DEFOE

KIM LAWRENCE

Thanks, Peter

PROLOGUE

Blaisdon Gazette. 17 November 1990

A hospital spokesman this morning said that two babies, believed to be twins, found yesterday on the steps of St Benedict's Church, are now in a serious but stable condition. Police are anxious to trace the mother, who might be in need of medical care.

London Reporter. 17 November 1990

The foundation stone of the hospital's new wing was laid by the late Sebastian Rey's grandson, who was named after his philanthropist grandfather. Stepping in for his father, whose duties captaining the Argentine national polo team kept him away from the ceremony, seven-year-old Sebastian Rey-Defoe is the son of the well-known English socialite Lady Sylvia Defoe. Sebastian is set to inherit the Rey billions and the Mandeville Hall estate in England. He suffered only minor injuries in the crash that killed his grandfather outright.

14 February 2008

'THERE IS A REASON, I suppose, why I am staying in a place called the Pink Unicorn?' Not a name you could say and think of minimalist decor, and not a name Seb could even say without a grimace of distaste.

'Sorry.' His irritatingly cheerful PA pretended she hadn't heard the sarcasm. 'But it is Valentine's Day and there isn't a decent place within twenty miles of Fleur's school that isn't fully booked. The Lake District is considered romantic. Don't worry, it's not contagious,' she soothed. 'And it is five star, so you won't be slumming it, and it has great reviews—people on the website rave about the little personal touches. Your room is… What does it say…? That was it: charming and bijou with beams and—'

'Oh, God!' he groaned. Six-five in his bare feet, he did not do bijou or beams… Was his petite PA punishing him for something?

'Don't be such a misery. You're very lucky that the Pink Unicorn had a cancellation.'

'I've sacked people for less. I'm ruthless, haven't you heard?' The previous month's article in a particular Sunday supplement, even though it had spawned several rebuttal articles in well-known financial journals, had left a public perception of him that suggested his wealth could not have been made without an utterly ruthless disregard for the rules or his fellow man.

'Where would you find someone else who gets your weird sense of humour?'

'You think I'm joking?'

'Or someone who is as efficient as me who doesn't weep when you scowl or fall in love with you when you don't?'

He fought back a smile and, with resignation in his voice, grumbled, 'Who the hell calls a place the Pink Unicorn?'

Now Seb knew—the same people who sat a poor guy with a classical guitar out on a lawn on a zero-degree February evening that neither the heat from a glowing brazier nor the open-sided gazebo affair lit by lanterns offered any protection against. To add insult to injury they'd had him wear some ridiculous Spanish get-up that no real Spaniard would have been seen dead in, while he played a cheesy love song in the candlelight as loved-up couples groped one another.

Sebastian's lip curled. If this was romance, they could keep it!

It was a spectacularly stomach-churning sight, but probably a fitting end, he mused, to a day where the high point had been getting a parking fine from an overzealous attendant.

It *should* have been a good day, a celebratory occasion. His thirteen-year-old half-sister had won the under-fifteens prize at the science fair her school was hosting, and against all the odds their mother, Lady Sylvia Defoe, had turned up in a display of rare parental support.

He should have known better, yet, as she had walked into the room causing conversations to stop, taking the attention as her due, Seb had almost got sucked in by the 'caring mother' act.

Until, that was, she had stepped back from the arm's-length maternal embrace, looked at her daughter's face and delivered some very loud advice on skin care, adding complacently that *she* had never had acne or actually even a spot, and then, presumably because she had not traumatised her thirteen-year-old daughter enough, she had gone on to flirt with every male in the room that caught her eye while her daughter had cringed and wished herself elsewhere. Seb, who had been there, done that, had felt his half-sister's pain as his own anger had built.

The breaking point had come when Seb had found their mother in a classroom in a *very* close embrace with the newly married biology teacher. The doors had been wide open—anyone could have seen—but then maybe that was the idea. His mother loved nothing better than creating a scene.

Offering the embarrassed man a tissue for the lipstick smeared across his red face, he'd then suggested the teacher might like to rejoin his wife. Seb had waited until the teacher had gratefully scuttled away before asking his mother, on whom subtlety was wasted, point-blank what the hell she thought she was doing.

'I don't know why you're cross, Seb?' She'd pouted. 'Why *shouldn't I* have a bit of fun? *Your* father had an affair with that awful…' She'd given a heartbroken sob and allowed the tears she could produce at will to fall.

'I've heard it all before, Mother, so don't expect any sympathy from me. Get divorced, have affairs, get remarried—I'm bored with the entire never-ending cycle—but if you embarrass Fleur again, we're finished.'

The tears had stopped; she'd actually looked almost scared. Even though he'd known it wouldn't last, it had still made him feel like a bastard.

'You don't mean that, Seb.'

On the point of retracting, he'd pulled back. 'Every word,' he had lied. No matter what she did, she would always be his mother, but this was about Fleur, and she needed protecting. 'Do you ever think about the people you hurt when you're doing exactly what you want?' He'd searched her beautiful face for a moment before shaking his head. 'Sorry, that was a stupid question.'

A scowl glued to a face that caused several female heads to turn his way, Seb strode towards the entrance of the Pink Unicorn that had been geared out for the occasion with, surprise, surprise, garlands of dried red roses. If there was one of those damn things on his pillow he would... He sighed and thought, what was the point? The rest of the world was so caught up with the romance fable one single voice of logic would be lost in the brainless babble.

Allowing himself a superior smile, he turned his head to brush the snowflakes that had begun to fall off his shoulder. The night might end with a few cases of exposure, he thought as his cynical stare brushed over the heads of the clusters of couples. The mild contempt etched into his lean patrician features gave way to one of stark shock as his sweeping survey came to a shuddering stop.

As he stared, the scorch of heat that began in his belly spread through his body like flash fire, darkened the intense brown of his deep-set eyes, framed by straight, strongly delineated brows almost as dark as his long, curling lashes, to jet black.

He didn't notice what she was wearing beyond the fact the dress she had on was blue and he would very much have liked to see her without it. She had a sensational body, sinuous curves and endless legs, and the lust that had erupted at the sight of her gave a fresh kick in his belly and lower, where it settled as his hot, hungry stare slid over those delectable curves before he dragged it back to her face.

The sense of recognition was crazy because he had never even imagined a woman who looked like her, let alone met one. Her face was a perfect oval, but it was not the symmetry of her features that held his gaze or caused his stomach muscles to clench viciously, but her expression, as, laughing, she looked up at the falling snow, her head thrown back a little to reveal the long, graceful curve of her throat.

Her lips were full, her eyes big in the light from an overhead lantern, her hair a wild explosion of tempestuous colour, gold, red, then gold again, curls that fell down her slender back almost to her waist.

A whoosh of cold air hit his face, breaking the grip of the spell that had held him motionless for countless seconds. Lowering his heavy eyelids long enough to give his nervous system time to recover from the carnal impact of the redhead, Seb dragged a hand across his dark hair and released the breath that had been trapped in his chest in a long, slow, hissing sigh.

He looked again, already distancing himself from that initial uncontrollable *visceral* reaction. It had been a long day and he'd been too long *without*... There are some things, thought Seb, that a man cannot rely on his PA to schedule... *Like a life...?*

Just as he was making a mental note to free up his weekend and deciding who he might share it with—that part had never been hard for him—the redhead's laughter drifted his way. Low and husky, it had a deliciously *tactile* quality. It felt like a finger running up and down his spine.

Not accustomed to envy, he experienced a twinge of something close to that emotion as he turned his critical, hostile gaze on the man who had invited this laughter... husband...lover...? As the thought slid through Seb's head the man in question turned and placed a hand under his partner's chin, drawing her face up to his.

This time, the sense of recognition Seb experienced

was not to be wondered at: the lucky man was the husband of the local GP. Alice Drummond was a woman Seb had time for. She juggled a demanding career with two children and a husband who, at twenty, had written one book someone had called insightful, which was the sum total of his achievements to date, and he was still living off the kudos.

When he wasn't having romantic weekends with red-heads with endless legs.

It was none of his business if a casual acquaintance cheated on his wife with some little... His jaw clenched, Seb turned away. Then she laughed again, the sound so light, so carefree, so damn sexy that something snapped inside him. First his mother, now this woman... Another selfish, beautiful woman who didn't give a damn about the collateral damage they caused as they went about pleasing themselves, leaving a trail of broken hearts and broken marriages in their destructive wake.

There was a corner of his mind where enough sanity lingered for him to know this was not a good idea, but it was a mere whisper compared to the din of the outrage hammering inside his skull as he strode across the grass, embracing the rage that was colder than the snowflakes that were falling in earnest now.

'So Alice couldn't make it tonight, Adrian...'

Mari struggled to keep her balance as Adrian let her go. No, had he *pushed* her away?

Adrian didn't see her hurt, questioning look; his attention was on the owner of the deep, harsh voice. Mari had to turn her head to bring the man into her line of vision.

Before she absorbed the details of the stranger's tall, impressively athletic frame, expensively tailored suit and face that was combined arrogance and beauty, Mari felt the raw power he exuded.

She felt it like a dark prickle under her skin as he turned his obsidian stare on her.

The tightness in her chest loosened when she managed to break contact with those incredibly penetrating pitch-black eyes—eyes that belonged to the most incredibly beautiful man she had ever seen.

Beside him, dark, brooding Adrian, whom she had fallen for as he read poetry in his beautiful voice looked less of both, almost...*soft*... She pushed away the disloyal thought and waited for Adrian to introduce her. Would he say *girlfriend*? It would be the first time; at college they had to be discreet. Students and lecturers dating was frowned on, though, as Adrian said, it happened all the time.

For some reason the fact she was even more beautiful up close increased the level of Seb's anger by several icy notches. Her eyes, kitten wide, were the deepest shade of violet blue he had ever seen, her mouth was lush and full and her satiny skin was almost translucent...and it turned out husband stealers could have freckles. The detail softened the sultry siren look into a deeply deceptive wholesome innocence.

'Mr... Seb... Well, this is...is...is...'

He let the stuttering loser, for once at a loss for words, suffer for a moment before suggesting ironically, *'Nice?'*

'This isn't what it looks like.' The cheating husband took another step to distance himself from the girl who was standing there, quite beautiful, quite still; she could have passed for a statue.

The music had stopped and everyone around them, sensing the drama, busily pretended not to be listening while hanging on every word. The girl moved towards her lover, who held out a hand as though to fend her off. She froze in response to the rejection, her big eyes radiating hurt and confusion. Seb thought of hard-working Alice, all the Alices out there, and cast out the seed of pity before it took root in his head.

'Is Alice… You know, your *wife*… Is she working, or is she looking after the kids? How does that woman cope?' He shook his head in wondering admiration and drawled, 'A busy medical practice, a mother of two and a husband who cheats on her?'

Mari waited for Adrian to say something, *willed* him to say something, to tell this terrible man who had appeared seemingly out of nowhere like some sort of sleek and dark avenging angel—in a world where angels wore very expensive tailoring—that this was all a mistake.

They'd laugh about it later in bed when they were sharing the bottle of champagne that he had ordered.

But the only sound was the shocked mutters from the other guests. Mari didn't turn her head, but she could feel the hostility and disapproval of their stares like daggers in her slender back.

'I couldn't help myself. *She*… I love my wife but… Well, just *look* at her!'

Her last hope vanished.

Every word that man had said was true.

She was the other woman. She hadn't known, but that didn't lessen Mari's sense of crushing guilt and shame. Her sense of total isolation was complete; she had never felt more alone in her life. Pressing a hand to her stomach, she breathed her way through a wave of intense nausea. When was Adrian going to tell her? *After, stupid.*

Seb, tuning out the rest of the other man's words, followed the line of his accusing finger. The woman standing there represented everything he despised in a female, yet he had no control over the hot hunger that slammed afresh through his body.

While his mind rejected and despised her, his body wanted her. You had to recognise a weakness to control it, and Seb valued control.

Control or not, it was still salt in a raw wound to acknowledge that she stood there looking like a piece of porcelain about to shatter, and there was a part of him that wanted to comfort her.

She could have had any man she wanted, and she had decided she wanted a married loser? When she could have... *Who, Seb? You?*

He ignored the mocking words in his head and launched a fresh invective, this time directed at the woman. 'Do you *care* that he's got a wife and children waiting for him at home?'

Mari cringed under the man's interrogative stare, literally paralysed by misery and guilt.

Her silence whipped his anger to a fresh high as he turned his inner rage on her and snarled contemptuously, 'Is it just a bit of fun?' He shook his dark head, a harsh sound of disgust escaping his clamped lips as he suggested with withering distaste, 'Or just because you can?'

She swayed and Seb heard the catch of her breath above the wind and the litany of excuses that were free falling from Adrian's lips, telling everyone who would listen how this was not his fault, he was a victim.

With an exasperated growl Seb turned his head and dealt the cheating husband an arctic glare. The other man gulped and whined.

'You won't tell Alice, will you? It'll only hurt her, and this will never happen again.'

'Wow, you really are a prize, aren't you?' Seb's attentions swivelled back to the girl. 'Did you think he would marry you, or is this real *love*?' he mocked. 'So that makes it all right?'

'I'm sorry.'

The whisper made Seb's tenuous grip on his self-control slip another fatal notch.

'Sorry...?' he blasted back, six feet five of towering contempt moving in a step closer. 'You think that makes it somehow better, that it makes the people whose lives you trashed happy again? Love or not, sweetheart, what you've done makes you the worst sort of slut... Oh, and just for the record, men take sluts to their beds, but rarely in my experience marry them.'

Every word the man was saying was true; every word was making something shrivel and die inside her.

With a final horrified stare from the swimming blue eyes, she gave a choked sob and turned and ran, her fiery hair streaming out behind her.

'You big bully!' An elderly grey-haired woman voiced what seemed to be, if the glares were any indication, the general consensus.

The hell of it was Seb, who kept seeing those blue eyes, half agreed with them.

CHAPTER ONE

MARI HADN'T EXPECTED it to be this easy, but so far no one questioned her presence in the cordoned-off street where she blended in pretty well with the other women negotiating the ancient cobbles in high heels, worried that any slip or inelegant stumble would be recorded for posterity by the photographers lined up along the other side of the barrier.

She had more things than falling off her heels to worry about!

Relax, Mari. A ghost of a smile touched her lips—she was, after all, only following doctor's orders. Admittedly it was doubtful if the well-meaning medic had had *this* in mind when he had noticed her shaking hand was unable to hold a teacup and banned her from the hospital for twenty-four hours.

'We'll let you know if there is any change. Go home,' he had encouraged. 'Have a meal, get some rest. You need a change of scene and something to take your mind off things. I know it's hard, but you're in this for the long haul and you'll be no good to your brother if you collapse from exhaustion, believe me. I've seen it happen.'

If she'd had the energy Mari might have laughed at the thought of *anything* taking her mind off her brother's situation. But common sense had made her recognise the grain of truth in his words, so she'd not protested when he'd called her a taxi, not that she'd had any intention of being away from Mark's bedside for longer than it took her to shower and get a change of clothes.

After the shower she had sat looking at a sandwich she had no appetite for with the television playing in the background to drown out her thoughts… *If only?* Her brain wouldn't switch off; it just kept going around in dizzying circles. She managed a bite, chewing and swallowing without tasting before her eyes began to close, her chin sank to her chest and she was on the point of drifting off when she was jolted awake by a name. Hate pushed away fatigue as, her expression set in lines of loathing, she reached for the volume on the TV control.

The news presenter on the scene was giving the viewers the life story of the bride and groom in what was being grandly called 'the wedding of the year'.

God, was that today…?

Mari sat there, her hate an aching solid presence on her chest, her thoughts buzzing as she tuned out the woman who droned on while images of the bride looking beautiful somewhere fashionable and the groom—even more beautiful—looking down his aristocratic nose at someone or something flashed across the screen.

She knew all she needed to about Seb Rey-Defoe and his bride-to-be, and as far as she was concerned they deserved one another! When she had seen the announcement of their forthcoming wedding she had laughed.

The bride, Elise Hall-Prentice, was an upper-crust beauty whose claim to fame beyond her wardrobe and her social connections was being the star of a reality show that had involved her pretending to have lost all her money—*would she lose her friends?*

As if anyone cared! The woman had all the sincerity of a fake tan, and the empathy of a reptile, without the charm!

And this was *their* day, while Mark was lying in a hospital bed, and, thanks to that hateful man, if she died tomorrow she'd be a virgin while they'd have the perfect day. Nothing would *dare* go wrong.

It was so unfair!

But then life was unfair, she reflected, reaching for the control as the picture on the screen cut to VIP guests in flowing Arab gowns getting out of helicopters. She dropped the control, her eyes flying wide open... What if something or *someone* spoilt their perfect day? Her laugh was a mixture of fear and exhilaration as she thought— and *why not*?

Why should everything go *his* way? Why should he walk through life immune to the stuff that everyone else had to deal with, cushioned by money and power? Both her and Mark's lives had been touched, and not in a good way, by that man, and he had probably forgotten they existed—maybe it was time to remind him?

Suddenly no longer tired at all but filled with a sense of purpose, she went to the wardrobe and pulled out *the* blue dress and held it against herself as she looked critically at her mirror image. That man had humiliated her in public. *Let's see*, she thought grimly, *how he enjoys it when he's the one on the receiving end.*

'I just have to ask.'

Mari started violently as the young woman touched her arm, stepping back onto the neatly trimmed grass verge as a cluster of well-dressed people, their laughter sounding like a flock of seagulls, went by.

Convinced that her guilt was written across her forehead in neon letters, she waited, breath held, for the axe to fall. *Which it will if you don't start believing in yourself*, she told herself sternly.

'You've got to tell me, *who* are you wearing?'

The comment poked a tiny hole in Mari's grim focus, allowing a ghost of a wry smile to touch her full lips.

Her reply was honest. Honesty was the best policy. She pushed away the stab of unease. There were exceptions to every rule and occasions when breaking them was the right thing to do.

'I'm not sure.'

Another smile almost escaped. The woman's wide-eyed reaction suggested she was seeing Mari walk into a wardrobe crammed with designer outfits. In reality, nothing could be farther from the truth. She possessed one other dress beside this bargain designer second with the label cut out.

The blue silk shift that had excited the other woman's admiration left her arms bare and ended just above the knee. She liked the simplicity of the flattering figure-skimming cut, and the bright cerulean shade echoed the colour of her eyes almost exactly. People who got past her hair often commented on the colour of her eyes, frequently asking if she wore coloured contact lenses to achieve the dramatic shade.

'If I had your hair I wouldn't wear a hat either.' Her eyes on Mari's tumbling auburn curls, the young woman touched a rueful hand to the frothy pink confection perched jauntily on her smooth blonde hair as she responded to an irritable, 'Come on, Sue!' from a tall, grumpy-looking young man, top hat in hand.

He saw Mari, looked far less grumpy and adjusted his tie. Mari, oblivious to the male admiration, attempted to slip away but the young woman moved to block her way.

'Do you mind—can I have a picture for my blog?'

Before she could respond the woman was snapping Mari on her phone.

'Who was that?'

'I think she's that model…or the actress in what was that film, the one with…?'

Under normal circumstances the overheard snatch of conversation as she hurried on would have made Mari laugh, but this situation was not normal, and she couldn't allow herself to be distracted.

What would they say if they could share the joke: not only was she not a famous model or actress, she was not even a guest at this wedding!

She was crashing it!

A thing that a month, a week, even a day ago, she could not have imagined herself doing.

A lot of things could change in a week!

A week ago Mari was listening to her twin brother telling her how his life was ruined, ignorant then of the real life-wrecking disaster that would strike him within the next few hours. At that moment disaster meant being dumped by the woman he loved because her very important brother, with his blue blood and family estates, didn't think that he, Mark Jones, who didn't even know who his parents were, was good enough for a Defoe!

Mari offered her sympathy, while in reality she was dizzy with relief. It was all she could do not to punch the air in triumph. The sick feeling that had been in the pit of her stomach ever since she had realised who her twin's new girlfriend's brother was had gone.

That her happiness came from her brother's misery made her feel terribly guilty, but the truth was, since she had realised that there was a strong possibility that Mark's new relationship might bring her face-to-face with the man who after six years still featured in her nightmares, she had been living with a sense of impending doom.

Crazy, really—for years she'd fantasised about coming face-to-face with him and telling him all the things she wished she had at the time, instead of just standing there and taking every vile insult he'd thrown at her... She had actually apologised!

No matter how many times she tweaked the cathartic speech she longed to deliver, deep down she had always known this was only a fantasy, and the knowledge infuriated her. She had spent her life not only standing up for herself, but also fighting the battles of anyone less able to fight for themselves, but there was no escaping the shameful fact that when the opportunity had arisen for her to defend herself, she'd bottled it!

And run away rather than face things!

She could still remember years ago, how cold the wind had felt as she had dashed across the lawn into the hotel away from all those eyes and the people judging her.

'He was on the news tonight. Did you see him?'

'Who?' she asked, her thoughts still on that terrible night six years ago.

'Sebastian Rey-Defoe.'

The name made her tense and the awed way her brother said it made her want to scream. She could admire achievements, even when money and power were not things she personally felt any desire for, but to inherit a position and money... What was to admire about that? Any more than you could admire someone for being beautiful and brooding, for inheriting genes that gave him sculpted features, spectacular eyes and sensually moulded lips.

'They were talking about the massive deal he has with

some Gulf state. The royal family there are putting up half the capital and one of his companies is supplying the know-how to computerise their health service, sort of a tit-for-tat thing—it could bring over a thousand jobs back to the area where they plan to build—'

Mari gave a cynical snort and cut across him. 'And line his pockets with money, too.'

Mark's sigh was tinged with envy. 'If only I had some money.'

'What's money got to do with it, and what does it matter what he thinks if you want to be together?'

'I don't know why I expected you to understand. I mean, you've never been in love, have you? Oh, I forgot—you go for married men, don't you…?'

Essentially a nice person, this was Mark when he was hurting. He hit out, wanting to share his misery, and he usually succeeded because he knew her weak spots.

He was the only one who did know this particular weak spot. Not the shameful details—those she would never share with anyone—just the basics. Well, knocking on his door at 4:00 a.m., having lost her key during the terrible journey back from Cumbria that had involved trains, buses and multiple changes, had required an explanation of sorts.

'Adrian, he's married!' had been all she'd got out before she had burst into tears and fell sobbing through the door.

It was the past and she had moved on, Mari reminded herself.

Moved on or not, the fact remained that she couldn't think of her eighteen-year-old self without cringing. How had she ever been that naive, that…*needy*? How could she not have seen past the smooth, slick charm and macho posturing of her personal tutor?

'If you're not ready, Mari, I understand you want the first time to be special. I can wait…'

She had almost fallen over herself to assure Adrian that she *was* ready and she *loved* the Lake District. She'd never even had a boyfriend and here was this gorgeous, sophisticated man who looked like one of the Byronic heroes he lectured on falling for her, Mari Jones. Of course she couldn't wait to show him how much she loved him.

And she would have.

If *that* man hadn't appeared when he had…

For a year after the event he had been *that* man in her head, the strong, amazingly handsome lines of his lean face clearer somehow than Adrian's, until the day she had opened a magazine in the dentist's waiting room and there he was on a silver-sanded beach, too beautiful to be real, just like the blonde model he was entangled with.

The man who had humiliated her in front of an audience who had eaten up every word, every insult he had so eloquently delivered, was Sebastian Rey-Defoe: rich, gifted and born with several silver spoons in his cruel, insult-spewing mouth.

He'd made her feel grubby and guilty, his contempt somehow worse than Adrian's deceit; at least she'd got the chance to tell Adrian that he was a total sleaze.

That man had not paused to ask questions, he'd just presumed the very worst. It hadn't even crossed his mind that she might be a victim. Or she *would* have been— he'd saved her from her own ignorance and in the process made her a hell of a lot more cautious where men were concerned.

Done her a favour… Maybe…? That part had been accidental. He hadn't been saving her from anything; he had been there to judge, to serve her up on a platter for public condemnation.

The incident had left Mari unable to trust her own judgement, which had proved an obstacle when some *seemingly* nice guy had wanted to get serious... Yes, she had trust issues.

She'd taken the psych class and she knew a therapist would say her fear of rejection stemmed from being an abandoned baby, which was stupid because Mark shared her history and he tumbled in and out of love at the drop of a hat.

She glared at her brother now. 'You know, Mark, there are times when you can really be a vicious little—'

'Sorry, Mari.' Immediately contrite, her twin got up and came over, enfolding her in a hug. 'You know I didn't mean it. I don't know what I'm saying. Everything was going so great. I mean, I actually made money last month, though the loan was much appreciated, sis, and the weekend was perfect, it was another world, Mari, honestly you've no idea. She never said that her grandfather was a lord, and the house... They live on this incredible estate, Mandeville Hall. It turns out the Defoes came over with William the Conqueror or something and what are we?' His handsome face despondent now after the burst of envious enthusiasm, he sank back down into the chair.

'Lucky—we are lucky to have found a terrific foster family, people who cared about us.'

It had been third time lucky.

Initially there had been plenty of people eager to adopt the cute twin babies whose discovery on the doorstep of a church had captured the public imagination for about five minutes. There had still been plenty of interested would-be parents at the point some months later when the authorities had decided the babies' biological parents were not going to come forward to claim them.

Their enthusiasm had decreased when they had discovered that one of the babies, so pretty as a newborn, had developed a raft of allergies that gave the infant a constant cough and various unattractive rashes, kept under control only by a complicated prescription of numerous lotions and ointments.

If the twins had not come as a package deal, the rosy-cheeked blond-haired boy would have been easy to home, but the authority's policy was not to split twins. So the boy had been left behind with his problematic sister.

There had been two temporary foster homes before they had finally been taken in by the Warings, a marvellous couple who had plastered a wall of their Victorian semi with photos of the dozens of happy children who had lived under their roof over the years, some for a short time, others like the twins growing up as part of the large extended family.

'Yeah, I know, count my blessings,' Mark drawled. 'Don't you ever get tired of counting them, Mari, being so damned *grateful* when our own mother left us on some step?'

'I'm sure she had her reasons.'

'I don't care why she did it.'

It was true, Mari knew it—he didn't care, and she envied her twin this attitude. He never asked himself why. Or, was it something about me...?

'The fact remains she did... Do you know that the Defoes can trace their lineage back to William the Conqueror?'

Mari gave a bored yawn. 'Yes, Mark, you mentioned it.'

Her twin missed the sarcasm. 'Now, *that's* the sort of background to be proud of.'

The envy in his voice made Mari's annoyance grow.

'I'm not ashamed of my background.' That was thanks

to their foster parents; grateful didn't cover her attitude to the big-hearted couple.

'Neither am I,' Mark protested. 'But I was thinking, Mari, perhaps if you could talk to the guy, make him see that we are not—'

The thought would have been laughable had it not been so horrific. 'No, I will not!'

'But—'

'Oh, for God's sake, Mark, grow a pair and stop wallowing!' The exasperated words were out before she could stop them.

Why hadn't she kept her mouth shut?

She pushed away the guilt. It wasn't *her* fault, it was *his*... Her eyes narrowed to midnight-blue slits. She felt lightheaded with the depth of the hate she felt as she walked, confident and smiling, past the security guard and into the cathedral. She'd probably leave through the back door and definitely under escort from one of the numerous security guards, but it would be worth it.

The perfect wedding would have an ugly moment. The rest of their lives might be perfect, but there would be a tiny blemish, a moment when *he* would be the one being judged.

'You sure about this?'

The question from his best man made Seb lift his eyes from his contemplation of the stone floor.

'Just a joke.' Jake shifted uncomfortably under the dark stare. 'Well, it's so final,' he tacked on defensively.

'Not always.'

It was hard to be objective but Seb thought his marriage stood a better chance than many, though his optimism was tinged with a healthy realism—you couldn't ignore divorce statistics—but he had avoided the usual traps that led to break-ups, the most obvious one being starting from the premise that love and passion were a basis for a successful marriage.

He did not have to look far to see the perfect proof of this. His parents had had and presumably still did have both, and their turbulent on-again, off-again union could not by any normal measure be called successful except by them, or the tabloids, whose circulation figures always leaped when the infamous pair married, divorced or decided to tell all.

The only thing the handsome polo player with little interest in the swathe of family acres in Argentina he had inherited had in common with the only child of a titled British aristocrat who knew how to party hard was a total lack of self-control and a selfish disregard for the consequences of their actions.

Not that the pair could be accused of not trying: they had been married three times, divorced twice and had both had several lovers in between. Seb had been born during their first marriage, and *rescued*, as he always thought of it, at age eight by his maternal grandfather during their short second marriage and brought to England to live. Had the loved-up pair noticed? Or had they been just a little bit relieved to have the child that demanded too much attention removed?

His half-sister, Fleur, the result of one of his mother's *in between* affairs, had been born at Mandeville and officially adopted by their grandfather. She barely had a relationship with the mother, who had left a week after the birth.

If in doubt Seb always asked himself what his parents would do, and did the opposite—and it had worked.

When asked what he wanted to be when he grew up Seb had said *not my father.*

Seb's decision at eighteen to change his name by deed poll, adding his mother's maiden name to his Argentine father's, had been his attempt to say thank-you to the grandparent who had brought him up. Though there had been no display of emotion when he had told his grandfather, he knew without being told that the gesture had pleased him, as had his unspoken determination to reclaim the proud family name.

Seb had succeeded. When the Defoe family were spoken of now, 90 per cent of the time it was his own financial success that made the headlines, not the latest instalment in his parents' soap opera of a life. His life was not about to become a spin-off series! His marriage would not be an emotional roller coaster.

He knew that in his efforts to make the name Defoe one to be proud of he had gained a reputation for ruthlessness. But personal insults aside, no one had ever connected his name with anything underhand or sleazy, which was what mattered to Seb.

When people called him proud he did not take it as an insult. He *was* proud—proud of not compromising his principles and of making it work, making the Defoe name synonymous with fair dealing. And the reward had come with the incredible deal that he was about to pull off. A chance like this only came along once in a lifetime and while he hadn't planned this marriage for that reason, its timing had been perfect and probably, he suspected, swung the deal. The royal family were big on family values and believed a married man was more stable and dependable.

The idea that marriage could fundamentally change a man tugged the corners of his expressive lips upwards.

Seb had no expectation or intention that marriage would change him; he saw no reason it should.

Success in marriage was about having realistic expectations; of course, there would be some compromises, and he had thought about them, but he was ready to make the commitment. He prided himself on his control and didn't for a second doubt his ability to be faithful.

His idea of marriage hell was what his parents had.

He just wished his grandfather were around to see today, that he could know that the Defoe name would live on, that he had kept his promise. It had been an easy promise to give, because Seb recognised the attraction of continuity, the opportunity of passing on the values his grandfather had given him.

He and Elise were on the same page. She agreed that stability and discipline were important for a child; they shared the same values, which was essential—in fact they rarely disagreed on any subject. She had even agreed to give up her career to bring up a family. Seb hadn't realised she had one, but he had been touched by the gesture.

Jake began to pace restlessly. 'God, I hate waiting… What if…? No, she'll turn up. You couldn't be that lucky… Sorry, I didn't mean… It's just…'

There was a short silence before the screen of dark lashes lifted from olive skin stretched tight across the angle of Seb's slanted cheekbones. His was a face with no softness in any aspect.

'Just what?'

'It's such a big step being responsible for someone else, being with them every day.'

'Elise is not…clingy.' This understatement caused Seb's mobile mouth to tug upwards at the corners. 'We will both continue on with our lives much as normal.'

With no emotional dramas, no raised voices or tabloid speculation.

'So why bother getting married?' Jake immediately looked embarrassed, adding to it by allowing his doubt to slip through into his voice as he continued, 'Sorry, but you are happy…?'

'Happy?' Seb did not consider himself a naturally happy person, and the constant pursuit of it seemed to him exhausting. He lived in the present. 'I'll be happy when today is over.'

After the warmth of the sun outside, the inside of the cavernous building was cool, lit by hundreds of flickering candles and filled with the almost overpowering scent of jasmine and lilies.

When she paused midway up the aisle the tension that had been building in her chest reached the point where she was fighting for breath. Mari felt as though she were drowning, standing in the middle of this beautiful building filled with beautiful people.

They were here to witness a celebration; she was here to… *Oh, God, what am I doing?* Mari stood there, the adrenaline in her bloodstream screaming flight or fight. She could do neither: her feet were glued to the floor; her limbs felt weirdly disconnected from her body.

'Room for a small one here!'

The cheery cry dragged Mari back from the brink of a panic attack. Breathing deeply, she turned her head to see a woman in a very large hat was waving her hand.

'Thanks,' she murmured as the lady obligingly slid along the pew. She had just settled in her seat when the two men seated in the front pew rose.

'My son, Jake,' the woman said with maternal pride. 'You wouldn't know it to look at him, but he is a millionaire…a computer genius. He and Sebastian have been friends since they were at school.'

Mari wasn't looking at the lanky man with the shock of blond hair who looked embarrassed as he waved to his mother. Her attention was riveted on the figure beside him, her narrowed eyes channelling all her pent-up hate at those imposing broad shoulders, the strong neck and the dark head. He stood with his back to the guests, frustrating Mari's desire to see his face.

When the congregation rose, Mari, hating every hair on the back of his neck, reacted a few seconds later. Her legs were trembling; her throat was dry; she felt like someone standing on the edge of a cliff not sure if she was going to take that leap.

Her chin came up. She'd run once and regretted her cowardice. She wasn't going to run again!

A few moments later the bride glided by in a rustle of lace, satin and the merest suggestion of complacence in her smile—not that Mari saw, as she was the only person who didn't dutifully turn to admire the vision.

'Get on with it, get on with it…' she muttered between clenched teeth.

The big-hat lady moved in closer. 'Are you all right, dear?' she asked, using the big hat as a fan.

Mari managed a ghost of a smile. 'Fine.' The service began and she breathed a soft, 'Finally!'

When she heard his voice for the first time, the cool, confident sound sent a shock wave of anger through her shaking body and burned away her last doubts as the memories came flooding back.

'For better, for worse,' she muttered, thinking, *Pardon the pun*!

When she tried later to recall the sequence of events that preceded her standing in the aisle, she couldn't. She had not a clue of how she got there but she did have a very clear memory of opening her mouth twice and nothing coming out.

The third time it did!

'Yes, I do, I object!'

CHAPTER TWO

MARI FELT ALMOST as shocked as the two-hundred-plus pairs of eyes that swivelled her way; the place had great acoustics.

'A lot, I object.' Aware her voice was fading away weakly, she squared her shoulders and bellowed in a voice that bounced off the walls like a sonic boom. *'A lot!'*

Poor grammar, but it was definitely an attention getter! She had the stage until presumably she was rugby tackled by the security guards, or sectioned under the Mental Health Act. What did it say—a danger to yourself or others? There was only one other she wanted to be a danger to, one other who… *Stop thinking, Mari. You've got your moment—don't let it slip away.*

'He…!' Her second dramatic pause was not intended. The last person in the place, the *only* one who hadn't yet turned did, and as her eyes impacted with the sloe-dark stare of her intended victim her throat dried to dust.

One word slipped through her head—*dangerous*!

In many ways he looked exactly as she remembered: proud, arrogant, actually with that thin-bridged nose, slashing sybaritic cheekbones and sensually moulded, cruel-looking mouth he looked positively pagan! What she *hadn't* remembered about six years ago, before he had turned on her like the jungle predator he reminded her of, was her own humiliating reaction to the blatant sexuality he exuded. Even her scalp had tingled with a sexual awareness that made the muscles low in her belly tighten—that hadn't changed either!

Shamed acknowledgement grabbed her, and for a vital moment Mari lost her focus; she *almost* forgot what she'd come here for. She lifted her chin and ignored the squirming liquid sensation in her stomach. She had come here to give him a taste of his own medicine, see how *he* liked being humiliated.

He didn't seem to appreciate the clever role reversal. The last thing he looked was humiliated. The heavy-lidded eyes that held hers were the eyes of an eagle looking at its prey.

She was no victim!

Not this time, and if he had any doubts... Mari dropped her chin, closed her eyes and exhaled a long shaky breath to compose herself. Then, heart pumping, she lifted her head and stretched out a hand towards him, letting her fingers flutter.

'You can't do this, Sebastian,' she appealed, pressing the hand now to her stomach. 'Our baby, he will need a father.' As she said this she couldn't help but think of her own father. Where was he now?

The woman had had her audience in her pocket from the first throbbing syllable of heartbreak and desperation, and now Seb felt their attention switch to him, not giving him sufficient time to recover from the shock of recognition that had felt like the vibration of a shotgun blast when he'd turned and seen her standing there. While the aftershocks still reverberated in his skull, he schooled his expression into neutral—less damage control and more an unwillingness to provide entertainment for the masses.

He saw her lips move and read, *Do you know who I am?*

Know who she was...?

In other circumstances he might have laughed. The number of occasions when he had lost control in his adult life could be counted on the fingers of one hand, and he wasn't about to forget that particular one, or the woman responsible.

But even if by some miracle he could have conveniently blanked the incident from his mind—it had not been one of his greatest moments—Seb could never have wiped the memory of that primal rush. It had electrified every cell of his body. He had never before or since experienced anything that came close to his response to her innate sensuality.

Did she bring out the same animal response in all men? Men who, unlike him, could not recognise the response as a weakness; men who allowed their passions to rule their lives.

Men who lacked his self-control—without it he might have been a man like his father.

No longer able to fight the compulsion, his eyes dropped, moving in a slow sweep that took in every aspect of her from the glorious flaming head of Pre-Raphaelite curls that framed her perfectly oval face to the length of her endless legs to the sleek, sinuous curves in between. Everything was accentuated by a dress that was probably illegal in several countries...or was that the body?

It was the lust that slammed through him—hard to imagine a less appropriate response in the circumstances—that brought reality like a boomerang rushing back to hit him squarely in the gut. He reacted to the weakness with an explosive rush of anger.

'What the hell do you think you're doing?' As he flung out the question in the periphery of his vision he sensed movement coming from the row that was reserved for the royal party. Hell, this was a disaster. Where was Security and where had they been when she had strolled in?

Her smile, sheer, silky provocation, caused him to take an involuntary step forward, fury for a fatal split second blanking logic.

'Now *you* know what it feels like!' Mari flung with a bravado she was not feeling... Actually she was feeling really weird.

The last thing Mari saw before the dancing black dots joined up and for the first time in her life she fainted was those dark implacable eyes staring with skin-peeling intensity at her.

Before she hit the ground, Seb had been pretty sure that the graceful fainting stunt was just as phoney as the rest of her performance.

But she wasn't moving... If she had knocked herself out, he thought grimly, it would deprive him of the pleasure of making her choke on her words, though not even a full retraction would fix the damage she had just caused.

He had spent years making the Defoe name stand for something, a brand that inspired confidence, and now in a matter of seconds this woman had destroyed it.

Ironic really that he had thought his parents' absence—they had not been willing to interrupt their world cruise for their son's wedding—would guarantee a drama-free day.

Seconds ticked and the entire place collectively held its breath, until Seb lost his fight against the instinct to react—someone had to do something!

Did it have *to be you*? asked the voice in his head.

It was just as well that his grandfather was *not* here.

One arm under her legs, the other around her back, he heaved her into his arms, wondering how many phones were capturing the moment. The action seemed to break the group paralysis in the place, and as people started shifting in their seats it was filled with a low buzz of conversation that drowned out the soft groan of the woman in his arms.

As her head fitted itself into the angle of his shoulder her crazy cloud of fiery red hair went just about everywhere. He spat a tendril out of his mouth and, eyes flat with suppressed fury, turned his head to look at her face, marvelling than anything that looked so beautiful could cause so much damage.

Her blue-veined eyelids fluttered but stayed sealed, and with another little groan she said a name that sounded like Mark.

Another victim…?

Amazingly, unconscious she looked *almost* vulnerable, a million miles from the vindictive drama queen of moments before.

Why the hell had she done it?

'Now *you* know what it feels like' suggested simple payback. Seb understood the attraction of revenge, but who waited *six* years? The possibilities ran through his head as he strode, the cynosure of all eyes, up the aisle towards his bride, the white-hot burning anger he struggled to contain battering at the insides of his skull, his arms full of crazy, delusional or plain evil but definitely sweet-smelling redheaded witch.

'*Keep still!*' he growled under his breath as she squirmed up against him, turning her body so that her breasts flattened against his chest.

When he came level with Elise his iron expression softened. He felt a stab of guilt that he hadn't given her a second thought, which made him a selfish bastard.

Poor Elise—if this was hard for him he could only imagine how she was feeling under her veil. If there was ever a moment when he would have excused a tantrum this was it, but she was conducting herself with a dignity that contrasted starkly with that of the woman who had just smashed the reputation he had spent years rebuilding. A sound of mingled disbelief and self-disgust vibrated in his throat because half his mind was occupied imagining her naked.

'Sorry.' His soft apology coincided with an audible lull in the buzz of conversation. There *might* have been someone in the most distant corner who hadn't heard the word, which would undoubtedly be construed as an admission of guilt, but he doubted it.

His jaw clenched. *Perfect!* Feeling frustration closing in on him, he glanced down at the cause and found a pair of glazed blue eyes looking up at him.

'I'm not sorry,' she whispered before the dark lashes framing them came down in a fluttering curtain against her smooth, very pale cheek. Then with a soft murmur, she burrowed in closer.

You will be, Seb thought, struggling to focus on anger rather than his indiscriminate hormones, which were acting independent of his brain to the squirmy, sensationally packaged softness in his arms.

Even without looking he could feel Elise's dagger stare behind her veil, and who could blame her? Certainly not him. He wasn't always as appreciative as he ought to be of her composure. He sent up a silent apology for ever having wished she'd show just a little more spontaneity, just occasionally. Ninety-nine out of a hundred women in her place would be having hysterics right now.

'Door, Jake…?'

His best man, who had been standing there, blinked as though emerging from a trance and grabbed the door to his right to allow Seb to pass through.

'Look after Elise,' Seb said as he went through. 'Take her…someplace, tell her I won't be long, oh, and send for—'

'Ahead of you there. We have three medics here. Anything else?'

'Any of them a psychiatrist?' Seb muttered, and responded to the handclasp on his shoulder with a nod. 'Is there somewhere, Father, that I can…?'

'This way.'

Seb followed the priest into a small anteroom. By the time he had laid the unconscious redhead on the small couch there, Jake arrived with a guest in tow who he introduced as—

'Tom, Lucy's fiancé—he's a trauma surgeon.'

Seb, who had little interest in the man's credentials, took his eyes off the girl long enough to shake the man's hand. 'Do you mind taking a look?' He turned to his best man. 'Jake, where is Elise?'

'How far along is the pregnancy?'

Seb's attention swung back to the other man, his jaw clenched as he fought for control. *Get used to it, Seb, this won't be the first time.* If he lost control this woman would win…*as if she hadn't already*?

'I really wouldn't know. This woman is—' about to say she was a complete and total stranger, he stopped and finished sharply '—delusional.'

Not hanging around to see if he was believed, he turned to Jake, who responded to his interrogative look

with, 'First left down the stairs, third door on the r...
no, left.'

It was actually the right.

The room he entered was larger and less sparsely furnished than the one he had just left.

His bride, her veil thrown back, was standing looking lovely in front of a stained-glass window. Her mother, a woman he had never warmed to, sat in a chair. She stopped speaking when he walked in, but the word *lawyer* hung in the air.

'Sandra...' He tipped his head in acknowledgement.

'I have never been so humiliated in my life!' she responded in a voice that never failed to jar on him.

Tell me about it, he thought, turning to his bride-to-be. He watched her struggle to produce a brittle smile.

'You're a star,' he said warmly. 'First thing, none of what she said was true.'

The older woman snorted.

'Mother, that is not being helpful.' Elise held up a hand, a pained expression flickering across her face before the smile was back in place. 'Please, Seb, there is really no need for explanations. I thought you realised that. I have total faith in your ability to make this... *unpleasantness* go away.'

'Everyone has their price.'

His glance flickered towards the older woman. 'Thank you for that contribution, Sandra.' His sarcasm sailed right over the woman's head. 'I have done nothing to pay for.'

'Mother, Sebastian is more than capable of dealing with this.'

'He allowed it to happen.'

Seb ignored the shrill accusation from the older woman.

'Do you believe me, Elise?'

Her eyes slid from his. 'I think it's totally irrelevant whether this woman's accusations are true or false, Sebastian.'

'You are taking the possibility I got another woman pregnant and deserted her remarkably well,' he drawled.

'Would you prefer I acted the hurt victim?' A small confident smile curved her lips as she asked the question.

He looked at the hand she had laid on his arm, and after a moment she removed it. The flush on her cheeks penetrating her perfect make-up, she gave a tight smile.

'Look, I know you share my dislike of…messy emotional scenes, but the way you're acting anyone would think you *wanted* me to make a scene.'

Good question. Well, do you, Seb?

'I could but where would that get either of us? I'm a realist—we both are. We need to get back in there, put a brave face on it and show the world that we're a team.'

As locker-room motivational speeches went, it wasn't bad.

'This is about damage limitation, but these things happen. Mother's right, just keep her quiet.'

Feeling like someone who was seeing something that had been there all along, he shook his head as though the action would clear his vision. It didn't.

'How do you expect me to do that?'

The serene mask slipped and she yelled, 'Oh, for God's sake, don't be so dense! Throw some bloody money at her—you've got enough! This is my day, and I refuse…' She took a deep breath and lowered her voice to a soft steely murmur as she clarified it. 'I totally refuse to let anything or anyone ruin it, especially some little tramp you got pregnant!'

'So let me get this straight—you will ignore my indis-cretions and you expect I will return the favour?'

She blinked, her eyes widening in an attitude of exas-perated surprise as she chided impatiently, 'Well, obvi-ously, Sebastian. I didn't think that needed spelling out.'

His reflective smile was filled with self-mockery. 'I think perhaps I did.' He turned to the older woman. 'Do you mind leaving us?'

'I'm not—'

'Get out.' In a business setting the soft menace in his voice would not have surprised anyone—he was preceded by his reputation—but the women he addressed reacted with open-mouthed shock.

He waited for her to leave the room before he turned to his fiancée, searching her face. 'You're not in love with me?'

'Are you saying that I don't satisfy you in bed?'

'I'm not referring to your competence in the bedroom. I'm talking about…' He paused. It was a subject he was even less qualified than Elise to discuss. 'It was not a crit-icism, just a fact, and I'm not in love with you either—that was never a problem—but it turns out I want more than you can give me.' He did not want slavish devotion or mad, undying passion, but at the bare minimum he wanted a wife who gave a damn if she thought he was fooling around.

'Something more… A threesome? Or…I'm very broad-minded, Sebastian.'

And I'm very rich, he thought, his lips curling into a grimace of self-disgust. 'Just what would I have to do, Elise, to make you find me unacceptable as a husband?'

'Why are you acting as though I'm the one who's done something wrong?'

'You're right,' he admitted heavily. He had been

guilty of twisting the facts to fit. On the surface Elise had seemed to be the perfect wife and mother, and he hadn't looked any deeper than the surface. 'This is my fault. I really don't think I'm the marrying kind.'

An ugly look of astonished fury contorted Elise's face as she saw her gold-lined future vanishing. 'Are you jilting me?'

'Yes, I suppose I am.'

Seb had made any number of bad calls in his life but he might, he realised as he closed the door behind him a few painful minutes later, just have been saved making the worst one yet.

In theory a wife who didn't give a damn what you did so long as you kept her in big houses, designer handbags and diamonds was a certain type of man's perfect wife, and he had thought he was that man.

It turned out he wasn't.

Logic told him he had no real right to feel distaste at having her priorities spelled out so starkly. He could accept many things in a marriage or the lack of them, but it turned out mutual respect was not one of them.

CHAPTER THREE

'SEB!' HER HEELS loud on the ancient stone of the narrow corridor, Fleur Defoe hurried to catch up with the tall figure of her brother.

As she got level with him he turned his head to growl an impatient, 'Not now, Fleur.'

His sister caught his arm, breathless and brimming with curiosity and concern. 'What's going on?'

A faint ironic smile touched his lips, lightening the grimness of his taut hard-boned expression as he reluctantly paused and eased his shoulders against the lime-washed wall.

'I wish I knew.'

Had she read about the wedding and thought why not…or had something happened, a trigger of some sort? He did not discount the possibility she was acting for a third party. It wasn't as if he had any shortage of enemies… More than one would not be unhappy if his royal connection was severed.

'People are asking questions, Seb.'

His dark brows lifted as he sketched a quick cynical smile. 'And providing more than a few answers.'

'They're asking if there's going to be a wedding.'

He levered himself away from the wall and speculated out loud. 'Or she might simply be insane.'

'What?' asked Fleur, who was trotting to keep up with him as he strode out, dragging the tie from around his neck as he did so.

'No, there isn't going to be a wedding.'

'Are you all right?' Fleur couldn't decide whether she was relieved or disturbed that her handsome brother looked more abstracted than heartbroken.

'Fine.' Was it coincidental that the Far East deal was at a delicate stage in the negotiations? The royal family were relatively broad-minded and progressive but by their nature nervous of scandal...and half a dozen members of that family had been sitting out there watching that debacle.

He struggled not to replay the scene, knowing that anger was an indulgence he could not afford. He needed a clear head if he was going to at least salvage the deal of a lifetime, and for that he needed the facts, needed to know there were no fresh little surprises waiting... Afterwards he could throttle the redhead, or maybe kiss her, he mused, thinking of that mouth and feeling a strong slug of lust.

An image of her face drifted into his head. It had surprised him over the years how well he remembered it, how deep an impression it had made, though not as it turned out as deep as the one he had apparently made on her...

'How did you meet?'

'Meet who?' he said, only half listening to his sister, who was trying to keep up with him.

'Mari, Mark's sister.'

In the act of dragging a hand across his hair he stopped midgesture and swung back. His sister, two steps behind, dug in her heels to avoid a collision and looked up expectantly at him.

The furrow between his dark, strongly delineated brows deepened. 'Last month's boyfriend Mark...?'

His forehead pleated in concentration as he brought to mind the features of the young man in question. Fleur's boyfriends were pretty interchangeable. This one had been particularly painfully eager to please and say the right thing. Trading on a boyish smile that probably had an appreciative audience, he'd made a pretty inept attempt to sell his latest business venture.

'You make it sound like I— All right, yes,' she admitted with a rueful grimace. 'He didn't last long. He started getting way too serious so I cooled things. She, Mari, is his twin, which is kind of cool.'

'You have met?'

Fleur shook her head. 'No, but he has photos of them, and that hair is pretty unmistakable, but why,' she puzzled, 'are you asking me? You must know that if you're...'

Seb clenched his jaw and bellowed, 'I'm not sleeping with her!'

'Seriously?' She encountered her brother's stony look and held up her hands in an attitude of defeat. 'Fine, I believe you.'

Which might, he reflected grimly, make her the only one.

'Why not?'

He slowed his step slightly and flung over his shoulder, 'Why not what?'

'Aren't you sleeping with her? She is kind of incredible looking.'

'Until a few minutes ago I was engaged and I have only met the mad woman once, six years ago.'

Fleur's eyes widened. *'Six....!* Wow, you must have made an impression! What did you do?'

Not nearly as much as he'd have liked to.

'She acted as though she hated you, Seb.'

'You noticed that, too, did you?'

'It didn't seem likely you were together. She's not really your type, is she?'

The disappointment in her voice struck a nerve. 'Sane, you mean,' he cut back, adding with a satiric bite, 'Are there any mental-health problems in your boyfriend's family?'

'He's not my boyfriend but actually he— *They* don't know. They were found on a church doorstep when they were babies. It was a big headline at the time—he had cuttings.'

'They don't know who their parents are?' He filed away the information; it might be useful but he doubted it.

Fleur shook her head. 'No, they've only got each other, a bit like us.'

The men's voices penetrated the fog that cushioned Mari's thoughts. It was confusing but comforting. She knew that any second it would clear; she also knew that she didn't want it to.

'So she's awake?'

Mari kept her eyes shut, but she could see the flicker of light through the delicate skin of her eyelids. She wished someone would open a window—the scent of chrysanthemums and incense hung uncomfortably heavily in the still air. The man who had spoken had a very deep voice. If it had a colour it would be rich, night-sky blue-black, and the tactile quality in it made the hairs on her nape tingle.

'Oh, yes, it was just a faint, no serious damage. She landed on someone's hat.'

'Thanks, I can deal from here.'

'You sure, Seb? I could stay…'

The rest of the interchange was too softly spoken for her to catch, but the sound of a door opening and closing sent a soft tickling rush of cooler air across her face.

'You might as well get up. I know you're faking it.'

The voice sounded bored. Mari felt her indignation stir lazily; she wasn't faking anything.

'What am I doing here?'

And where was here?

She slowly turned in the direction of the voice, realising her head was cushioned on a hard and dusty pillow thing. Teeth gritted, she prised her eyelids apart. They felt as though she had weights attached to her eyelashes. It took several blinks to bring the face of the man who spoke into focus. The only other person in the room, he was standing in front of a deep window, the sun shining through the stained glass behind him and surrounding his face with a halo of blue flickering light.

Even without the light show it was an incredible face. The combination of the starkly drawn lines of a broad, high forehead, aristocratic cheekbones and sensually sculpted mouth was arresting, but it was the hard, brooding quality in his stare that almost tipped her into panic.

'You took the words right out of my mouth,' he drawled.

Then the panic made sense. It came rushing back in full relentless detail without the protective cushion of adrenaline-heated anger.

She had done it. She really had! *Oh, God!*

Wasn't she meant to be feeling great or at least vindicated? Seeing the villain on the receiving end of the tit-for-tat payback wasn't as satisfying as she'd imagined.

Struggling to channel calm, she moistened her lips with her tongue and cleared her throat. 'Shouldn't you be getting married?' The aura of masculinity he projected was even more pronounced in the enclosed space of this room. It had a skin-prickling quality that was very disturbing on more than one level.

'I *should* be, yes.'

She dragged her eyes off the small V of brown skin where the top button of his shirt had come adrift along with his tie, feeling pretty disgusted with her indiscriminate hormones. 'You mean you're not…?'

'It's called off—wasn't that the idea?' He raised an eyebrow.

She brought her lashes down to shield herself from his hard interrogative stare. *Was it?* Beyond inflicting the humiliation he had not thought twice about subjecting her to, had she thought much at all…? She'd had a vague mental image of sweeping out, leaving him a crushed man…or at least one recognising that he had no right interfering in the lives of the Jones twins. Refusing to acknowledge the strong element of compulsion involved, she moved her resentful blue gaze up the long, lean, muscle-packed length of him.

Yeah, that really worked well!

It was hard to imagine anyone looking less crushed, and it wasn't just his tungsten physique. The man was cold steel through and through. Aware her glance was becoming a full-on stare slash drool, she took a deep breath and pulled herself into a sitting position. Both hands on her hair, she brushed the flaming strands back from her face and swung her legs over the edge of the couch.

'Not really.'

'So what exactly did you expect to happen?'

She shrugged and dodged his stare, thinking, *Good question, Mari.*

A muscle clenched in his lean cheek as he fought to

retain a grip on his temper. 'So you hadn't thought that far ahead?'

'It never occurred to me that she'd let someone as rich as you get away.' She heard his sharp intake of breath and looked up, projecting wary defiance. 'I'm not sorry.'

'So you said, but that could change.' His conversational tone did not hide the warning. Mari hugged herself to ward off the sudden chill in the room.

He had not thought she could go any paler but she did. Her skin had a translucent quality that was fascinating… or was that just him? He pushed away the thought— admitting there were any chinks in his control would have been admitting a weakness. Even in his teens, while his contemporaries were making fools of themselves over girls, Seb had always prided himself on the fact women only pushed the buttons he wanted them to—he was no longer a teenager.

Her rounded chin with the suggestion of a cleft lifted another defiant notch as she met his stare head-on, her dramatic eyes glittering with defiance.

'Is that a threat?'

Seb watched one feathery brow arch. All her features had a clear-cut delicate quality except for her mouth, and that was just plain tempting.

'Oh, that was, by the way, a rhetorical question. I'm not stupid. If you're going to have me arrested just get on with it.'

Seb looked at the hands she held out towards him crossed at the wrists. 'Handcuffs aren't really my style,' he drawled. 'But maybe yours?'

What was his style?

The question and the image that drifted into her head brought with them a rush of scorching heat.

Where had *that* come from?

Feeling the shamed warmth flame in her cheeks, she wrenched her stare clear of his hands and his long elegant fingers that continued to exert an unhealthy fascination for her. Her lashes provided a protective screen of sorts as she rubbed her wrists while the illicit images kept popping into her head—in none of them was she fighting against the imprisonment of those strong fingers.

'You have a disgusting mind.' *It takes one, Mari, to know one.* 'I *knew* you'd be a bully!'

What hadn't been so obvious until this moment was that she was capable of such carnal thoughts. If they'd involved any other man but him Mari would have been quite relieved—it would have knocked on the head her growing conviction that, if not frigid, she had asexual leanings. As it was, a life of celibacy was infinitely preferable to being attracted to men like him... Were there any men like him?

'Being proved right seems to make you happy, though some might call it a lucky break. You might have pulled your little stunt and then discovered I was actually a kind and warm-hearted person. Actually I feel quite flattered that I made such an impression on you six years ago.'

She laughed, a hard, scornful sound, and put her bare feet on the floor. 'I remember you the same way people remember a bad dose of food poisoning.' Her hair fell forward in a rippling wave that caught and held his fascinated gaze as she checked out under the couch, adding accusingly, 'Where are my shoes? I want to go home.'

'And it's that simple?'

Mari struggled to hide the flash of fear that sent a chill through her body. 'You can't stop me!' She caught her full lower lip between her teeth and looked up at him through her lashes, hating the quiver of uncertainty in her voice.

'I think you owe me some sort of explanation at least, don't you?'

'I owe you nothing!' she flared back.

'Do you seriously think you can pull a stunt like that and walk away? Think about it,' he suggested, walking across to the window, where a butterfly was helplessly battering its fragile wings against the glass. He opened it, nudging the insect towards freedom with his finger before he turned back to Mari, whose eyes had followed every move he made. 'Did someone put you up to this?'

The abrupt question made her blink. There was something hypnotic about the way he moved. 'I don't know what you're talking about. Oh, I get it, you're one of those people who see a conspiracy around every corner.' She flashed an understanding smile. 'I believe they call it paranoia.'

'You expect me to believe that after six…*six* years you decided to get your own back just because I spoilt your dirty weekend with your married lover?' He grimaced remembering Adrian, now the *ex*-husband of the local doctor. 'I can only hope that time and experience has improved your taste.'

She loosed a laugh, her chest swelling with indignation. *Experience…* One day she might meet a man who was willing to go at her pace, but that looked about as likely as winning the lottery at the moment.

'Just!' she yelled. 'It'll be your fault if I never…' Appalled by what she had almost blurted out, she closed her eyes. Maybe a better form of revenge would have been sticking him with some bills for the therapy she so obviously badly needed.

I'm so screwed up, she thought grimly, *that the only man I have even imagined myself in bed with in recent memory is him!*

He arched a black brow. *'Never...?'*

She shook back her hair, struggling to force the words past the emotional lump in her throat. 'Nothing. You started this, you acted like judge, jury and executioner when you took it on yourself to humiliate me in front of—'

'Of a handful of people who didn't know you, not several hundred who do know me. If this *was* a tit for tat it was overkill. You may not have liked what I said, but it was the truth.'

'Your truth!' she flared, her eyes flashing. Nothing had changed—he was still the same judgemental creep.

'It's really hard to play the truth-and-justice card, angel face, when you just stood up in front of everyone back there and lied your beautiful head off.' His glance dropped to her flat stomach. 'Are you actually pregnant?'

'How dare you?'

'Dare...?' he echoed, loosing an incredulous laugh. 'You just stood up and told several hundred people that I'm the father of your unborn child...so yes, pardon me for being *crass*, but I do bloody dare!'

'You do realise, I suppose, that a DNA test will prove definitively that I am not the father? If you suggest otherwise I have a team of very expensive lawyers who will sue you to hell and back and issue so many writs that no tabloid will print a word of the story, and I don't respond well to blackmail.'

'And I don't respond well to threats,' she countered contemptuously. 'And I'm *not* pregnant! And if I was,' she added on a horrified afterthought, 'you would be the *last* man in the world I would want as the father!'

The insult appeared to pass over his head. 'There is no baby?' One less complication to be dealt with.

She responded without thinking. 'I don't want children.'

His impressive shoulders moved in the slightest suggestion of a shrug. 'No maternal feelings?'

Mari knew very little about maternal feelings, but she did know there were a lot of children out there who needed homes, and few like her own foster parents who were willing to offer one. She had decided a long time ago that if she was ever in a position to offer a child a home, it would be one of those abandoned children.

'You can't help yourself, can you? You just love to judge.'

'It wasn't a judgement.' At least she was honest, he mused, his expression hardening as he thought of Elise's parting shot—*You think you know everything, but I had no intention of having a baby and ruining my figure!*

The combative silence stretched as blue eyes clashed with dark brown; it was approaching snapping point when there was a tap on the door.

Mari turned her head as the door swung inwards and the girl that Mark loved appeared. The photo on his phone had shown how pretty she was, but it hadn't captured her sheer vitality or the suggestion of mischief in her big brown eyes.

'Tea, two sugars, good for shock, and a sandwich, the best I could do.'

Seb resisted the temptation to mention he was the one who'd had the shock as he took the tray and balanced it on a deep slate windowsill.

'Hi.' She waved a hand in Mari's direction. 'How's Mark these days?'

The unexpected question felt like a raw wound being jabbed with a knife.

'About as well as you'd expect.' A sound half between a sob and a laugh escaped Mari's pale lips as she shivered from a chill that came from within before elaborating with a bitterness born of despair, 'For someone who's driven into a lamp post and been told he might never walk again.'

It was as though it happened in slow motion. The girl's pretty, vivid little face crumpled, but before the tears that filled her big brown eyes could fall she was in the shelter of her brother's protective arms and out of the room. Before he left he turned his head and the look he gave Mari was one that promised retribution and maybe, she thought, biting her own quivering lip, she might deserve it.

The heavy door was only partially closed. Mari could hear the sound of voices, but not what they were saying.

Tears threatened, lying in a heavy clogging lump in her throat as she looked around the room. The stark white walls were bare but for a couple of wall sconces holding half-burned candles. Other than the couch she sat on and a massive dark wood cupboard, the only other piece of furniture in the place was a spindle-backed chair.

She stiffened as the door opened then closed quietly. He did everything quietly, the closing of the door, the crossing the room with the sort of exaggerated care that someone who had had too much to drink uses, but it wasn't the effects of alcohol his slow, measured movements disguised, it was the anger he was holding in… *just*. Nobody under the influence could move like that, she decided, thinking jungle cat as she watched him.

He stopped just in front of her and waited. The silence shredded her already frayed nerves, and Mari lasted about twenty seconds before she felt compelled to break it. The other option by that point was screaming.

'I didn't mean—' she blurted, then stopped. She hadn't come here to apologise again but it was true she hadn't meant to hurt the girl. The only thing Fleur Defoe was guilty of was having a manipulative brother. 'I didn't mean to upset your sister.' She bit the inside of her cheek and fought off a tide of guilt. 'Is she all right?'

Seb struggled to tamp down his anger with only moderate success. How the hell could she pretend to give a damn? 'Because you care so much? Look, have a go at me if you want to. I can take care of myself.' He leaned in closer, his voice dropping to a low menacing purr that decimated any nerve ending his physical proximity hadn't already sent into shock. 'But if you go after my sister, so help me, I'll go after you.'

'Am I meant to be scared?' If so it was working. Only pride kept her retreating from the dark, cold menace in his deep-set eyes. 'I didn't want to hurt your sister. I wanted to hurt *you*!'

Possibly too much honesty at this point, Mari, she thought as she waited nervously for his reaction. The fact he didn't react beyond elevating an eyebrow and looking thoughtful was baffling rather than comforting.

It was hard to retain dignity barefoot, especially in this dress, which had not been this tight across her hips the last time she'd worn it. It was the price you paid when your drug of choice was chocolate. Even in her heels she would have needed to tilt her head back to look him in the eyes; with nothing between the soles of her feet and the stone floor she felt… Well, Mari had once or twice wondered what it felt like to be petite and delicate. Now she had an idea, and she didn't like it.

Ignoring her stomach fluttering and her curling toes, she thought, *What's the worst he can do*? And wished she hadn't because her vivid imagination responded to the invite and kicked in big time!

Seb, his temper cooling, felt an unwelcome stab of admiration. Her regal attitude was totally at odds with her gloriously mussed hair and bare feet but, by God, she carried it off. His eyes of their own accord dropped, following the soft, undulating curves of her body that the blue silk dress she wore lovingly hugged. She had come to play the victim, but looking the way she did she had to have been typecast as sinful seductress.

'I didn't think she'd actually dump you.'

'Is that an apology?'

'No, it's…' She stopped, her eyes widening fractionally as a possible explanation for the bride's reaction struck her. 'Have you done it before…but for real?'

His expression grew cold and contemptuous. 'It must be the company you keep, but a lot of people don't cheat.'

But do you? she wondered, watching as he responded to the imperative hum of a phone, which he slid from his pocket. He scanned the screen before punching something in and returning it to his pocket.

'I haven't got long.' He was not fooled by the polite request; underneath the diplomatic language it was a royal command—he was being asked to defend brand Defoe.

'Don't let me keep you.'

The pert reply caused his attention, which had drifted away, to focus back in on her. 'Was what you said about your brother true?'

She was outraged by the question. 'Why would I lie about that?'

'Why would you lie about me fathering your child?' he countered.

'I've told you.'

'I know, spoil my day, wasn't it?' He tipped his head and gave a slow handclap. 'Well, you succeeded in more ways than you can imagine.' He dropped his hands and subjected her to a scrutiny of skin-peeling intensity.

'What exactly happened to your brother?' Something that had triggered today's stunt?

'He…he…' Hearing the helpless wobble in her voice, she swallowed and blinked back the emotional tears that sprang to her eyes. 'Mark could end up in a wheelchair permanently.' A lot was still unknown, and Mari refused to think the worst. 'Why are you asking? You don't give a damn about him, do you?' she charged, glaring up at him with angry contempt.

'I wouldn't wish that on anyone,' he replied, wondering how he would react in the other man's position. He hoped to God he would never find out.

She gave a bitter laugh. 'Not even someone who doesn't have the right…right…bloodline to marry your sister?'

Seb's dark brows drew together in an astonished straight line above his masterful nose as he looked down at her. 'Back up…'

If only she could have, Mari thought wistfully, she would have responded quite literally to this request. A few more feet to distance herself from his overpowering physical presence would have been welcome but there was nowhere to go.

'Marry?'

Her teeth clenched at this display of unconvincing innocence. 'Don't bother with the act—I know what you did.'

Well, that makes one of us, he thought with a sardonic grimace. Every time she opened her mouth he felt as though he were being led deeper into a maze.

He released a long, slow, hissing breath, controlling his temper and the desire to grab her—and the hell of it was that, whatever his intentions, the moment he laid his hands on her it would change what hovered unacknowledged between them, taunting him, the way her mouth taunted him.

He had known it from the moment he saw her standing there in the church denouncing him to everyone who knew him. He wanted this woman, and if he touched her now that want would wipe out everything else.

Wasn't it supposed to be therapeutic to look into your heart? Not that his heart was the organ involved in this instance. Either way, he didn't feel better—he felt frustrated self-disgust.

'Work from the premise I don't have a clue what you're talking about.'

'They were in love.' She paused, distracted by the muscle that was clenching and unclenching in his lean cheek. 'Y…you,' she stuttered, thinking he should come with a shipping warning to stop females drifting into his magnetic field. 'You put an end to it because you're an arrogant snob who passes judgement on people he doesn't know. You have no heart!'

As the quivering accusation left her lips her scornful gaze slid to his chest. The image of her placing her hand on his warm skin, feeling his heart beat under her fingers, came from nowhere. Severely shaken, she shook her head to dislodge it and the warm feeling it induced.

His brows lifted. She was really rather glorious in full flow with that pouting mouth and those flashing eyes. 'If they were…in love, surely that wouldn't have been possible. Doesn't love conquer all?'

While he was innocent of the charge, Seb privately acknowledged that had there been any actual danger of Fleur marrying the rather insipid young man he had met he would have done his utmost to stop it, but he liked to think he would have been more subtle.

The thought of Fleur's reaction to an outright ban from

him twitched the corners of his mouth upwards in the ghost of a wry smile.

Seeing it, Mari felt her temper fizz up all over again. 'This is just a joke to you, isn't it?' she accused, over-flowing with a sense of righteous outrage. 'You don't even have the guts to admit what you did was because my brother doesn't have the right school tie and has worked for what he has rather than it being handed to him on a golden platter, and don't deny it,' she added breathlessly.

Nostrils flared, he gave a mirthless smile. 'I wasn't about to,' he promised grimly. The idea of him explaining himself to this red-haired virago with a chip on her shoulder the size of a forest offended him on more levels than he could count.

'Before she brought him home to meet you, everything was fine.'

'Relationships end every day.' He cut her off with an impatient gesture of his hand. 'You have decided that I am responsible for your brother's broken heart, I get that part of your delusion, but the rest? I'm a bit hazy where I fit in. He had an accident? What sort of accident?'

'Mark came to see me after he and Fleur split up. He was distraught when he left—if he hadn't been he'd never have been drinking.'

'He drank?'

Hearing the grim condemnation in his voice, she rushed to her twin's defence.

'He was only just over the limit.'

He greeted this weak defence with a thin smile of disdain.

'And there was fog...' Her voice trailed away; she knew there was no excuse. 'He never drinks and drives—normally—and he wouldn't have been doing so that night if you hadn't interfered. You're the reason it happened.'

And if you'd been more sympathetic? Mari closed her eyes and her ears to the voice of self-loathing in her head because she simply couldn't bear it.

He watched, fighting an unexpected flash of concern as she started to sway forward and back on her heels, her eyes closed. Concern he didn't want to feel roughened his voice as he asked abruptly, 'Are you all right?'

Her blue eyes opened. They glittered with unshed tears and loathing. 'Don't worry, I'm not about to faint again.' She sniffed and wiped a hand across her damp eyes.

While Seb considered himself pretty immune to most female tears, the sniff made him feel… *Uneasy* was not the right word, but as he pushed away the suggestion that the prosaic action touched a tender spot he refused to acknowledge he settled for it.

'Sit down,' he urged, coating his concern in impatience, because actually giving a damn about a woman who had deliberately set out to cause chaos in his life would have been irrational, and he wasn't.

He just didn't want her to faint at his feet.

'I don't need to sit down,' she snapped back. 'I'm going home.' She took two steps before a voice said in her head, *Running away*?

Teeth clenched, she swung back. This time *she* would be the one to have the last word. 'Why should you carry on living your perfect life when because of you my brother's life is ruined?'

CHAPTER FOUR

'WE'LL LEAVE THE perfection of my life out of this conversation and while I don't doubt you need someone to blame for what has happened to your brother—'

Mari stiffened defensively and cut in, yelling angrily, '*You* are to blame.'

'What happened to your brother is tragic, but it is not the result of anything I did. *He* chose to drink, *he* chose to get behind the wheel of a car, *his* decision, *his* responsibility,' he intoned with steely implacability. 'It is pure luck that he didn't injure an innocent.'

Gnawing her lower lip, Mari lowered her gaze. He had said it; she had thought it. 'He loved your sister.'

'It was hardly the act of passion,' Seb derided contemptuously. 'It was the act of a weak man who didn't think of the consequences of his actions. It seems to be a family failing.'

'He's lying in a hospital bed!' she cried, wondering if the callous monster even had a heart.

'Which is sad, but he is the architect of his own downfall and I am just glad he has not taken my sister down with him.'

Mari wasn't even aware that her arm had lifted, moving in a swishing arc towards his face until, a few inches short of making contact with his lean cheek, fingers like iron curled around her wrist, forcing it away and back down to her side.

She didn't even give him the chance to release her hand; she started fighting, pulling frantically to wrench her hand free. When he did so she lifted her head very slowly, her wild hair falling back to reveal eyes that were wide and filled with hate, her skin flushed rosy, her lips parted as she panted for breath as though they'd just gone several rounds—everything was out of proportion with her and so, he realised, were the reactions she evoked in him.

He moved in a step, bringing their bodies closer. She didn't move, if anything she swayed towards him as though responding to some invisible cord that connected them. He watched, fascinated, as the blue of her eyes was almost swallowed up by the dramatic dilation of her pupils.

She had the most glorious mouth he had ever seen, the sort of mouth that made a man want to taste. Quite suddenly, despite the deafening peal of warning bells in his ears, Seb couldn't think of a single reason why he shouldn't taste her.

One hand behind her head, he dragged her to him, then, tangling his fingers in the fiery mass of her hair, he hooked the thumb of his free hand under her chin. He dipped his head.

He felt her trembling as he moved his lips across her mouth before accepting the irresistible invitation of her soft, parted lips and plundering the soft, moist sweetness within.

The moment his mouth covered hers Mari's mind stopped functioning and the rest of her nervous system went into overdrive. Then she was kissing him back with combative hunger she had not known existed. Above the thundering of her heartbeat she heard a distant moan and didn't associate the raw, needy sound with her.

From somewhere, some small sane corner of her fevered brain, she found the strength to resist. She pushed hard against his chest and the kiss stopped almost as abruptly as it had begun. She staggered back, her breasts rising and falling in agitation.

'I hate you,' she shot out, wiping the back of her hand symbolically across her mouth.

He stood there looking down at her, managing to look insultingly cool. Could he really turn it on and off like that…?

'So nothing has changed.'

Still shaking while he continued to act as though nothing much had just happened, she smoothed a hand over her hair, appalled, deeply ashamed and most of all bewildered at the wanton way she had responded. 'You kissed me!'

If she'd known that *that* was going to be the price of the last word Mari would have swallowed her pride and bolted when she had the chance!

'I'm not going to get a honeymoon. I think the least you owe me is a kiss,' he drawled while silently cursing his lack of control.

Cursing because she was the sort of woman with whom one taste was not enough, she was the sort of woman who, before a man knew it, he could not function with or without. She was the sort of woman he had spent his life avoiding.

'I wish I *had* hit you!' she fired back.

'The day is young.'

'And you're in a hurry,' she reminded him.

She watched as he turned his cuff and glanced down at the metal-banded watch wrapped around his wrist. 'I am,' he agreed. 'Just one question, I'm curious. Do you think it was worth it?'

'Worth what?'

'Worth what is going to happen next.' He shook his head and looked incredulously at her. 'You really haven't thought your little revenge plan through, have you?' When she continued to look blank he elevated a dark brow. 'You just told people we were an item and you're pregnant. It won't stop there. There will be consequences beyond a bad moment in my *sooo* perfect life.' She carried on looking confused so he spelled it out. 'For you.'

She lifted her chin but he could see the uncertainty she couldn't hide in her eyes.

'What consequences?' she scoffed uneasily.

He didn't reply immediately; instead he left a space for her anxiety to climb.

There was amused contempt in the eyes that brushed her face. 'How many phones do you think caught part or all of your little drama? You have your five minutes of fame.'

A look of horror slowly spread across her face. 'I don't want it.'

'Tough. It's not optional.'

Her pallor exaggerated the sprinkling of freckles across the bridge of her small straight nose.

He remembered those freckles.

'I almost feel sorry for you.'

'I don't need your pity,' she flared back, eyes flashing.

One dark brow lifted. 'I said *almost*. I save my sympathy for those who deserve it. You chose to have an affair with a married man.' He disposed of her historical gripe with a dismissive click of his long fingers. 'You chose to make a spectacle of yourself in public, your brother chose to drink and get behind the wheel of a car. Instead of bleating, perhaps you should both man up.'

Of their own volition his dark eyes dropped. Anything less manlike than her heaving breasts outlined beneath the blue fabric that moulded them lovingly would have been hard to imagine. He didn't waste his time analysing the lustful surge of his body; he was working too hard at ignoring it.

'I *chose*,' she said, emphasising the word, 'to make a spectacle of *you*, and in that I'd say I have been very successful.' Almost mastering her struggle to appear indifferent, she shrugged and took the slim phone from her pocket.

'What are you doing?'

'Ringing for a taxi.' Eyes hard, she sketched a saccharine-sweet smile. 'I think I've imposed enough on your hospitality.'

He strolled to the door, pausing with his hand on the handle. 'Your shoes are on the windowsill, and your hat.'

'I don't have a hat.'

His eyes went to her hair before, face set, he removed his gaze from the fascinating flame-red curls. 'Of course you don't. That would mean you stand the tiny risk of not being the centre of attention when you walk into a room.'

The suggestion that she wanted attention was so unexpected she struggled to think of a suitable response.

'I'd book your taxi for the east gate if you *really* don't want that fame…but you're only delaying the inevitable, sweetheart.'

With that parting shot he left without a backward glance.

The hospital car park was full. Mari drove around three times before she finally found herself a space in an overflow area, or *almost* a space. The one she backed her old Beetle into was so narrow that to get out she had to breathe in to squeeze her way between the car and wall, managing to scrape her knees against the brick wall as she did so.

Without a lot of interest she viewed the damage, the nuisance value of her torn trousers barely registering against the oppressive weight of the real disasters she was dealing with—some of her own making. At times it felt as if she were drowning...but mostly she managed to tread water.

It was two days since the event that had triggered the media storm and by some miracle Mark hadn't discovered what she'd done. That was the plus in what had been a nightmare weekend. Sebastian, with his sinister predictions of *consequences*, had been proved horribly right.

Mari was paying big time for her moment of madness.

She had been horrified when she had got out of the taxi to find a local reporter and photographer waiting. Head bent, she had not responded to the battery of questions or appeals for a quote.

Ironic now that she had thought that was bad—an hour later the duo had been joined by a dozen more from the nationals.

She had closed her curtains, ignored the notes shoved under the doors and turned off her phone, but she hadn't been able to resist the masochistic impulse to go online. There she had discovered the predictable photos posted on numerous sites, and unlike most of the comments, which had been almost universally negative, some had been flattering, especially the one that had gone viral of Sebastian looking impossibly handsome and noble carrying her looking like some sort of ginger Sleeping Beauty up the aisle.

On a lighter note she had discovered an amusingly written piece, which included a detailed, itemised and hilariously inaccurate breakdown of how much her outfit had cost on the—it turned out—much-read fashion blog of the woman who Mari had almost forgotten had admired her outfit on the way into church.

This had spawned several much darker spin-offs that itemised not only how much her clothes had cost but how much she had cost! It seemed that according to 'experts' very few of her body parts were the ones she had been born with! She'd had a nose job, cheek and lip implants... opinion was split on her breasts!

It was universally agreed that Sebastian had footed the bill to turn her into his *perfect woman*.

The phrase had been picked up by a Sunday tabloid that recognised headline gold when they saw it. They had put the words above two shots of her, one in the supposedly ultraexpensive wedding outfit, the other taken Saturday morning when, bleary eyed in her pyjamas, her hair a wild mess and looking slightly demented, she had opened the door and faced a battery of flashes.

But she had taken control and stopped acting like a victim. The turning point had come about two o'clock that morning when she had found herself reaching for the tablet on her bedside table. What else was there to do when you couldn't sleep but to get up to date with the latest vile names people were calling you and what awful things they were saying about you? The tablet propped on her lap, she had stopped and asked herself, *What are you doing, Mari*?

She could not control what people wrote but that didn't mean she had to read it! The light at the end of the tunnel was that presumably there would come a time when people would get bored with talking about her breasts.

Until then she was going to walk around with her head held high.

And that morning, when the number of press outside the building where she lived had decreased, it looked as if she had survived the worst, or so she'd thought.

But the hits kept coming!

She lifted her chin. As tempting as it was to just give up and admit defeat, it wasn't an option. Mark needed her support. She pushed a strand of hair that had escaped the loose plait that hung down her back and glanced down... All dressed up, or in this case down, and nowhere to go.

But that might work to her advantage, she reflected, viewing her typical workday outfit of narrow-legged tailored trousers, teamed with leather pumps and a classic white shirt that she had put on this morning when she'd thought today was going to be a normal workday.

Still the professional look might make the doctors inclined to be more forthcoming with information than when she was wearing a T-shirt and jeans. Either way she needed more information than they had so far given her, and Mark, who had been deeply depressed last night, had responded to all her questions with a defeatist shrug. It hadn't helped that she'd been really late, having changed taxis three times to avoid being followed to the hospital by the press—at least hospital security protected him.

She fingered the knot of the red silk scarf she wore tied around her throat while she dabbed a tissue to the blood seeping through the superficial break in the skin.

Finding herself unexpectedly free, she had hoped to catch the doctors after their morning rounds, but with the congestion in town and the time it had taken her to park that looked less likely. Still, it was worth a try. Throwing her plait over her shoulder, she started to jog.

People stared, but Mari decided that she could cope with a few raised eyebrows after the past few days. She kept up the energetic pace until she was outside the ward, then, consciously smoothing the frown lines from her brow along with the self-pitying thoughts before struggling hard to channel cheerful and optimistic, she advanced, passing the empty nurses' station en route to the side room where her brother had been since he had been transferred from the high dependency unit.

Her mood improved fractionally when she saw a group of suited figures—the doctors were still in the ward. As she approached, trying to identify her brother's consultant the men appeared not to notice her, then one turned and she froze, doing what she later suspected had looked like a 'rabbit in the headlights' impression.

He tilted his head in an attitude of distant recognition and Mari's shaky-kneed trepidation evaporated in a flash of white-hot fury. In a heartbeat she reached the group bristling antagonism and hostility, her decision that if she ever met him again she would be cool and disinterested blasted away in the silent explosion of anger.

'What are *you* doing here?' Possibilities zipped through her mind. Had he assumed that Mark was behind her actions and he'd come to confront him?

The small group fell silent, aware of the undercurrents but politely pretending they weren't.

'Miss Jones, twice in three days. Aren't I the lucky one? How delightful.' He turned to the other men. 'Does everyone know Miss Jones?'

'I asked you a question.'

'I have been visiting your brother.'

Wildly Mari looked past him, just able to make out her brother propped up in bed through the obscured glass panels.

'You know the hospital administrator, Mr Parkinson, and head of—'

Mari, ignoring the other men, cut him off before he made any further introductions.

'If you think you can obviate your guilt by bringing him a bunch of grapes, think again.'

'I do not feel guilty.'

'And that makes you a prize p—' She bit back the insult, struggling to get a grip on her temper. Not easy when every time she looked at this man standing there so elegant, projecting an effortless aura of cool command, so infuriatingly complacent and so sure, so damned *up himself*...! 'I would be grateful if you'd keep the hell away from my brother.'

The words were coated with ice, but Seb could almost see the flames licking just below the surface. Previously he had always discounted the red-haired temper thing as an example of an urban myth.

'Isn't that his choice, not yours?' Was she equally passionate in bed...? A nerve beside his mouth clenched as he struggled to tear his eyes from the plump curve of her lips.

The sort of woman you avoid, Seb, remember.

Mari, who was stabbing a shaky, accusing finger towards his broad chest, didn't notice the darkening of his eyes. She was too busy coping with the tingling aftershocks following the initial electrical charge that had taken away her breath in that first moment of recognition. She looked anywhere, everywhere but his mouth.

On top of everything else she could not deal with that kiss; the fact he'd kissed her or, most disturbing, that she'd liked it!

'If you have upset him so help me...' *You'll what, Mari?* Frustration gnawed at her as an overwhelming tidal wave of helplessness washed over her. Control in every part of her life seemed to be slipping through her fingers like sand.

'He seemed in a pretty positive frame of mind when I left him.'

She willed herself not to react to the provocation she saw in his silky smile as he continued to meet her spitting hostility and suspicion with a pleasant civility that probably made her look totally demented to the watching group—maybe she was! It was hard to call her behaviour over the past few days balanced and rational.

He wouldn't have been human if he hadn't taken a certain amount of malicious satisfaction from the knowledge he wasn't the only one having his life turned into a circus. At least he had the means, the expertise and experience to cushion himself and his family to a great extent from press intrusion, a luxury Mari Jones did not have.

Seb knew how fickle and unpredictable public opinion could be, so it was no major surprise that, by and large, coverage had mostly been pretty negative towards Mari Jones, but the toxic level of vitriol aimed her way had surprised him. He by comparison had for once escaped relatively lightly, partly due to the fact that Elise, who had wasted little time selling her 'jilted bride' sob story to the highest bidder, had chosen to play the victim and given a very inventive account of the woman who had stolen him from her.

His critical narrowed glance stilled on the smudges under her eyes that stood out darkly against her pallor before he looked away, reminding himself that any sleepless night she had she had more than earned—in making him the monster she had made herself the victim.

'How about you, Mari? Are you having a good day?'

Mari lifted her chin. She could hear the malicious mockery in his voice, even if no one else could.

She gazed up at him, feeling a loathing that she had not known she was capable of. 'I told myself it couldn't get worse but here you are…'

Mari hadn't been spared his presence. Even on the rare occasions she had managed to drift off into a light troubled sleep he'd been there every night. She was grateful that the details of those feverish dreams had slipped away but the snatches that lingered left a heavy visceral sensation of discomfort in the pit of her stomach.

'Well, this has been delightful catching up, Miss Jones,' he said with false sincerity designed to aggravate and annoy. The regret he expressed as he glanced towards the suits who had tactfully moved out of hearing distance was equally false and teeth clenching. 'I'd love to stay and chat but I'm afraid…'

Mari watched, a hundred insults unsaid as he calmly strolled away without a backward glance, the message clear in the set of his broad shoulders: she was dismissed. She was unimportant; she didn't even register on his radar.

Do you want to?

Ignoring this unhelpful intrusion from her mind, she stood there fighting a self-destructive impulse to chase after him. As much as she really wanted the last word, she knew it would come at a price.

Even thinking about the price last time sent her pulse racing. She had precious little dignity left, so she didn't want to throw away what she had for the satisfaction of telling him what she thought of him.

Gathering her wits, she stood for a few moments after the group, with Seb's dark head clearly visible above the heads of the shorter men, had vanished through a swinging door.

Hiding her trepidation under a cheery smile, she stepped into her brother's room. 'Hello, how are you feeling?'

The previous day Mark's mood had see-sawed between apathy and anger, so it was an intense relief to see the animation in his face.

'So you look better.' If her voice sounded too bright Mark didn't notice.

'I am feeling quite good… Take a look at this, Mari.'

Mari took a seat and began to flick through the glossy brochure that he handed her.

'Do you see what it says about this place? Just look at the statistics, Mari.' Eagerly he watched her face. 'Impressive or what?'

Mari grunted. She was looking at the fees, and there were numbers there that made her heart sink like a stone. 'Where did this come from, Mark?' She could not imagine that the hospital went around touting customers for this very expensive private clinic.

'Oh, I had a visitor—he left it for me to look at. Fleur's brother.'

Mari managed an expression of surprise, which her brother responded to with a laugh.

'I know, coincidence or what? It turns out he's on the hospital board or something. He said that this place has 24/7, one-to-one intensive therapy, all the latest technology.'

She put down the booklet with a sigh. 'Oh, God, Mark, you know there's no way we can afford this.' And it was hard to think of what had motivated Sebastian Defoe to give Mark this unless it was malice.

Was he really that cruel or vengeful?

And why was she even putting a question mark after the thought? He obviously was!

A determined look that Mari recognised all too well slid into her twin's eyes. 'There has to be a way—*your* credit rating is good…'

Mari, the phone call from the head teacher still very much on her mind, hated bringing her twin back down to earth. 'You know my job doesn't pay that sort of money, Mark.' Nobody went into teaching for the salary. 'I barely make ends meet as it is.'

'We could sell something.'

Mari's heart broke for him. 'Look, Mark, I'll do what I can, but I doubt very much in the meantime—'

'I could ask Fleur. Her family is loaded, and Fleur was always saying her big brother takes the responsibility stuff seriously—giving back to the community and all that.'

'His sister said that?'

Mark, propped up on his pillows, shrugged. 'Yeah, well, it's all about appearances, isn't it? And he can afford it. I thought *you* could have a word, mention how upset I was after Fleur broke up with me… Don't blame her or anything, as I get the feeling he's kind of protective, but—'

'I really don't think that would be a good idea,' Mari, horrified by what she was hearing, interrupted.

'Don't look like that. I'm not asking you to ask him straight out for money—you can be more subtle than that. You know, play up the sob story, flutter your eyelashes, do the weak girlie thing.'

Mari got to her feet; she was feeling sick. 'I couldn't do that.'

'You'd prefer that I end up in a wheelchair for life!'

'That doesn't have to happen, Mark. You know that the doctors have said with hard work and determination…

I know it's a long haul, but I'll be with you every step of the way.'

'Why does it always have to be hard work? I know you're proud to be poor and everything, but I'm not. Why shouldn't I have it easy for once in my life? I have never asked you for anything in my life, Mari…' He saw her expression and stopped. 'All right, maybe a couple of times.'

Mari picked up the brochure. 'I'll see if I can work something out, but I'm not begging for money from Sebastian Defoe.'

'You're too proud to beg?'

'It's not about pride, Mark.'

'Yes, it is!' he flared back bitterly. 'You've always been the same. You can't ask for help. You always have to do things the hard way. Well, it's easy for you to have pride—you can walk out of here.'

Her brother held her eyes for ten silent reproachful seconds before he turned his face to the wall.

'Mark, I'm sorry.'

Almost in tears, Mari left five minutes later, Mark still refusing point-blank to speak to her. He hadn't given her the silent treatment since they were children, and then sometimes he had kept it up for days.

As she walked along the hospital corridors Mari struggled to think past the awful sense of helplessness. She couldn't get the image of the silent reproach in her brother's eyes out of her head and it left her with a sick sense of helplessness that was crushing.

The doctor had caught Mari before she left the ward. She had really struggled to respond positively when he'd pronounced himself cautiously optimistic about her brother's prognosis; he'd gone on to emphasise how important a positive mental attitude was in these cases and how easy it was for patients to become depressed.

Outside she took several deep gulps of fresh air. Mark was right: she could go home but he couldn't.

As much as she loved her twin she was perfectly aware that his impatience meant he always went for the quick fix. Their foster parents used to tell him there was no magic pill that cut out the hard work, but now he was convinced there was a magic pill. A carrot had been dangled and he couldn't have it, but while he knew it was there he'd never settle for hard slog.

Lost in her own thoughts, she barely noticed the drizzle that had begun to fall as she cut across the bay reserved for ambulances, and then across a half-empty area with reserved parking spaces, people who were too important to make the long trek to the overflow parking area for the hospitals.

'So how was your brother?'

Mari let out a shriek as the tall figure vaulted from a low-slung car that had *power statement* written all over it.

Had he been waiting for her? It didn't matter—she had a chance to tell him what she thought of him.

'Are you some sort of sadist?'

The sight of her walking out of the building had shaken loose an emotion that he hadn't wanted to acknowledge. Her body language had been so defeated, her slender shoulders so hunched she had looked as though it was an effort to put one foot in front of the other.

The contrast now as she stared up at him, blue eyes blazing, bosom heaving, her sensational, soft, full lips quivering with emotion as she launched into attack mode, was dramatic.

Seb was a man who valued control and moderation but she really was made for full-blown passionate excess...

She was stunning, but then so was a hurricane, and he had never felt the desire to chase one or throw himself blindly into its path. Encounters with hurricanes needed to be carefully planned.

'I like that in you—you waste no time on pleasantries. You get right to the point. I'm the same way myself,' he drawled. 'It saves so much time.' He held open the door of his car, revealing the plush leather-clad interior. 'Do you want to sit down and catch your breath?'

'You don't make me breathless!' Exasperated that her response had managed to imply the exact opposite, she gritted her teeth.

'Really?'

She stuck out her chin and stubbornly held his eyes. 'Yes, really.'

'I must be losing my touch.'

'Oh, I don't know about that. You seem to be on top form,' she sneered angrily. 'Presumably seeing my brother in a hospital bed wasn't good or rather *bad* enough for you? No, *you* have to raise his hopes and leave me to crush them,' she choked, fighting back a sudden sob and finishing on a shaky quiver of husky despair. 'I'm sick of being the bad guy.'

Catching the thoughtful expression in his watchful dark eyes, she immediately regretted the bitter addition, and you couldn't really compare this situation with all the little things like telling Mark he couldn't ask their foster parents for the expensive trainers he wanted when they were kids.

'Then why do you let him do it?'

Thrown off balance by the soft question, she stared at him. 'What are you talking about?'

'Why do you let your brother play you like…? Whichever way you look at it, it isn't healthy—a grown man letting his sister fight his battles.' He shook his head. 'It's emasculating, not to mention manipulative.'

The casually voiced observation whipped angry colour into her cheeks. 'Are you calling me manipulative?' she asked in a low, dangerous voice.

'No, I'm calling your brother manipulative.'

Immediately defensive, Mari lifted her chin. 'My brother didn't…doesn't know about me crashing your wedding.' She bit her lip and added with a husky question mark, 'I'd like it to stay that way?'

This was not news to Seb, who considered himself a pretty good judge and had recognised the shallow insincerity behind Mark's smile the moment they had met. If the brother had known he had no doubt the younger man would have immediately tried to distance himself from his sister's actions.

'So you're asking a favour from me…?'

She shrugged and said in a flat little voice, 'Stupid idea.'

Experiencing an inexplicable impulse to live down to her expectations of him, he almost asked, 'What's it worth?'

Instead he found himself extending his hand.

Not in the plan, Seb, said the voice in his head.

Mari drew a tense breath but didn't step back. She couldn't—her feet were nailed to the floor. She stood there quivering as he touched her cheek, only lightly with his forefinger, but there was an element of compulsion about the way he drew a line down the soft downy curve of her cheek, his eyes following the action—then he repeated it.

'You think I put a price on everything?'

Hot desire pulsed through her body. Her response to the casual intimacy was frightening, exciting and hu-

miliating all at once. It was so tiring fighting, not just
him but the way he made her feel. For a split second she
let herself wonder what it would be like to stop fighting.

'Don't you?' she asked, her reaction as his hand fell
away ambivalent at best.

'I won't tell your brother about your wedding-crashing
exploits.'

'Thank you.' Her relief was heartfelt, but her worried
frown lingered. He said that now, but what if he changed
his mind?

'Don't worry, I'm considered a man of my word.' He
saw her eyes widen in alarm and gave a low chuckle.
'You really should never ever play poker.' Unless it was
not for money and with him, he thought, warming quite
literally to the idea of a slow striptease.

'I know Mark is bound to find out sometime,' she admitted. 'But it would be easier later. He's not even speaking to me right now.'

'You know, if you're not careful you'll spend your
life—' He shook his head and finished abruptly. 'No, cor-
rection, you won't have a life of your own.' The thought
made him angry.

Confused by the strength of the disapproval she could
feel coming off him in waves, she arched an interrogative brow. 'And you care why exactly?'

A startled look chased across his lean face. 'I don't,' he
denied, and shrugged. 'For all I know you enjoy it. Maybe
it's symbiotic.' Displaying his white teeth in a smile that
didn't reach his deep-set eyes, he leaned in and flicked
her cheek with his finger. This time there was nothing
seductive about the gesture. 'Slice Mari Jones and you'll
find martyr running all the way through.'

She turned her chin away, hating his sneering suggestion and the way her body was betraying her by reacting to the sensual aura he projected.

'Slice Sebastian Rey-Defoe and you'll find sadistic bastard all the way through?' she countered angrily. 'You knew when you gave Mark the details of that place that we don't have the sort of money that it costs—you expect me to believe you did that out of the goodness of your heart?'

Was his cruelty casual or calculated? Mari couldn't decide which was worse.

'I'll pay for the treatment.'

CHAPTER FIVE

HOPE FLARED BUT was immediately swallowed up by a depressing wave of realism. He was no fairy godmother. It would be hard to think of a less appropriate analogy, even if he had been oozing the milk of human kindness instead of a headache-inducing level of testosterone.

'And afterwards,' he continued, 'I will fund any physical therapy and aftercare.'

When things sounded too good to be true there was often a very good reason.

'Why?'

She was unable to stop herself—her hostile gaze slid up the impeccably tailored length of him, but she knew during the journey over dark grey suit, white shirt and narrow burgundy tie that it wasn't hostility that made her stomach muscles tighten and quiver, which was stupid because she had never gone for the 'groomed to within an inch of his life' look. It always suggested a vanity that she didn't find attractive. And he was so groomed he could have stepped right out of one of those glossy ads, the sort that suggested that if you bought the car, the fragrance, the shampoo, you, too, could look like this.

Only you wouldn't. There might be a few pale imitations but Sebastian was definitely a one-off, and in her opinion one too many. All the same, to look at him was… She just stopped herself sighing; the light flush along the high, smooth curve of her cheekbones she could not control… He would have been easier to tolerate had there been a single thing to criticise. Physical perfection when it came with a massive sense of superiority was not attractive.

Tell that to your hormones, Mari.

The suggestion of a smile touched his expressive lips as he studied her face. 'Don't worry, there are no strings.'

She lifted a hand to brush away the heavy strand of dark red hair that a gust of wind had plastered across her face, the same gust that ruffled his close-cropped dark hair up into attractive spikes.

'I wouldn't accept charity from you if my life depended on it!' she told him in a clear, confident voice.

His brows lifted. 'You can pay lip service to your pride if you want, but it's not *your* life we are talking about, is it?'

She flushed at the quiet reprimand. 'We have a more than adequate health service.'

It was irrational to be irritated by her attitude considering his entire plan rested on her stubborn pride.

'True, but it is also overstretched. Taking your brother out of that system would free up a bed and cash to allow another person to be treated.'

'One who doesn't have a charitable benefactor? Thanks but no, thanks.' She shook her head and looked at him coldly. 'We pay our way and we don't accept charity.'

'Then don't call it charity, or are you willing to put your pride ahead of your brother's well-being?' *And now who is being manipulative, Seb?*

Close on her brother's accusation his comment really stung. Mari swallowed, suddenly struggling to force the words past the aching occlusion in her throat. She wouldn't cry, not now, not in front of this man.

'Call it a loan.'

Mari's hope flared and died; she had seen the figures in the glossy brochure. 'We would never be able to pay it back.' But could she really sit back and watch her brother struggle back to health when she could have made it so much easier?

He angled a dark brow. 'I got the impression that your brother has an entirely more pragmatic attitude than you…towards *charity*? I could have been wrong…?'

He wasn't, damn him. If she refused this offer Mark would never forgive her, and if she took it she would never be able to live with herself.

It was a lose-lose situation.

'Why didn't you just make this offer to him? Why did you have to bring me into it at all?'

'I wanted to see if you are as stubborn and proud as I thought you were—you are.'

'So this is some sort of twisted test? Presumably I failed so now you punish both of—'

His voice was gravelled with irritation as he cut across her. 'I have no desire for revenge on your brother, and unlike you I don't think collateral damage is legitimate.' He allowed her guilty flush to develop before finishing softly, 'If I want to punish you I will.'

Looking into the mirrored surface of his dark eyes, Mari had no problem believing him.

'So you're saying that you do want revenge on me.' She held a tight grip on her bravado and fought off the effects of the apprehensive shiver that slid its clammy way down her spine. It would take a very dim person not to realise being the target of this man's revenge would not be comfortable.

'If I did I'd be stupid to warn you, wouldn't I?'

Or very clever. All manner of convoluted double bluffs ran through her mind until she felt not just apprehensive but dizzy!

The rain had begun to fall in earnest. In moments the face turned up to him was wet, a perfect classic oval. The moisture glistening on her pale skin highlighted the freckles across the bridge of her small straight nose and the bluish smudges under her beautiful accusing eyes. She looked delicate, sexy and vulnerable.

The sharp, strong stab of something that came perilously close to tenderness was mitigated by an equally strong slug of more familiar lust that pierced him as his gaze fastened on her shirt, where the buttons were straining against her heaving breasts. The rain that was falling heavier now had drenched the fabric, and he could see the scalloped edge of her bra against her breasts.

She really did have an incredible body, he thought, aiming for objectivity as his appreciative gaze slid over her feminine silhouette. Not hourglass—although her waist was tiny, the flare of her hips was less extravagant and her firm high bottom was taut rather than full, making her long-legged frame athletic rather than overtly lush.

And very, very sexy.

His analysis fell way short of objective. He found her body as provocative as her confrontational attitude. The combination was… He struggled to find the right word. *Stimulating* was a reasonable approximation and one that a man who liked boundaries, who needed control, could live with.

It was ridiculous that he was allowing himself to be

distracted by sex like some hormone-laden teenager, when there were much more important issues at stake. For a time over the weekend it had seemed as if the royal deal was dead in the water; it still might be if this went the wrong way.

'We need to move on.'

'Where?'

His expressive lips twisted in irritation. 'Let's consider the matter closed. I have made contact with the clinic and it is all settled. Your brother is being transferred tomorrow and there is no reason he should know who is footing the bill if that is the way you want it.'

Presented with this fait accompli, Mari shook her head in disbelief, the only response she felt capable of giving. The tension that had sprung up seemingly from nowhere hung heavy in the damp air, and breathing had become something that required conscious effort. It was, she thought guiltily, a sad commentary on her as a sister that she remained so vulnerable to the sexual charge that this man emanated. He didn't even have to try... *What would happen if he did try?*

She pushed the question away, unwilling and unable to deal with the distraction or for that matter the answer it might produce.

The silence that built seemed to have a life of its own and a heartbeat that she could feel pulsing. Her fingers plucked fretfully at the knot of bright fabric at the base of her throat until she blurted with more force than she intended, 'I don't want you in our life!'

Well, that came from the heart, he thought, directing a slow, sardonic, mirthless smile her way. 'You should have thought of that before you put yourself in mine.'

She shivered. It was a comment she felt in wholehearted agreement with; she was living with the consequences of her own actions. The knowledge did not make it easier.

'Why would you help my brother if you don't think you're responsible? You expect me to believe that you're some sort of altruistic saint?'

His rebuttal was immediate. 'My offer is not inspired by guilt.' Not his guilt, but his tender-hearted sister was showing a tendency to beat herself up about things, and if her ex-boyfriend ended up in a wheelchair that situation would not improve. He would do everything in his power to make sure that didn't happen.

Mari remained suspicious of this very expensively packaged gift horse. Though in the equine world, of course, he would be a thoroughbred, sleek and muscled—With a tiny shake of her head she closed down the thought. 'So what do I have to do? What's the catch?'

'There is no catch, no strings. As I said, I have already spoken to the clinic and your brother will be transferred tomorrow once the paperwork is done. My lawyer will send you the details of an account I have set up in your name for the purpose. I think the funds are adequate, but if there is not enough you simply have to let him know. As I said, it is up to you what you tell your brother. If you'd prefer he remains in ignorance from where the money is coming that is no problem.'

'*I* will know!' Mari always paid her debts—how was she going to pay this one? Submerged by a massive wave of sheer helplessness, she lifted her face to the leaden sky, letting the rain wash over her face.

Seb dragged a hand through his drenched hair and gave a grunt of irritation; the rain was now drumming on the roof of the car.

'This is ridiculous.' He wrenched open the car passenger door and walked around to the driver's side, yelling over to the slim figure who had made no effort to take advantage of the shelter, 'Personally I've nothing against the wet-shirt look, but…'

She glanced down and let out a horrified gasp.

A moment after he had slammed the door she slid into the passenger seat and sat there staring straight ahead, her arms folded across her chest.

A grin split the severity of his lean features. 'Very modest, but you see a hell of a lot more on a beach.'

She lowered her hands defiantly. 'I'm not embarrassed,' she lied. 'I'm cold.'

He let his eyes drop. 'I'd noticed.'

Longing to slap the lopsided grin off his too-handsome face, she balled her hands into fists. 'Smutty schoolboy innuendo. I'd sort of expected something a bit more…'

The grin faded and it was replaced by something far more dangerous, far *more*… She felt her insides quiver helplessly in response to that nameless *thing*.

'Is that a request?' he asked smokily.

On the brink of succumbing to the heat of his hypnotic stare, her blue eyes flew wide open. It was definitely time to change the subject or at least remember what it was!

'No, not…' *Definitely not.*

'So no work today?' he asked casually.

Suspicious of his sudden question, she shook her head. 'No.'

'One of those consequences you didn't consider?'

Mari maintained a tight-lipped silence.

'I can't imagine that exclusive school you work for liking the idea of its employees' sex scandals being made public.'

Bristling with suspicion, she turned in her seat. 'How do you know what I do or where I work? Have you had my phone bugged or something?' It was as likely as any of the other wild, nausea-inducing possibilities whirling through her head.

'That would be illegal.'

She gave a scornful snort. 'And you have never broken a rule.' Rules and a thousand hearts, she thought, glad that she was not the sort of woman who had ever had a thing for bad boys.

'I have my resources.'

Seb's *resource* in this instance had been the family lawyer who had witnessed firsthand the wedding drama. It had been the one call that Seb had taken on Saturday night, assuming, wrongly as it happened, that it concerned the possible legal ramifications of the incident.

'I had no idea you even knew Miss Jones, Sebastian. Let alone—!'

The lawyer whose services he had inherited when his grandfather died had sounded as unhappy as Seb had ever heard him, a situation brought about not by any sense of indignation for his client but the disruption to his granddaughter's schooling.

'You do know she's the first teacher that has understood Gwennie? The child actually *wants* to go to school and you know what that place is like—they justify their ridiculous fees by claiming they provide a wholesome learning environment, and they have a very good reputation. Hypocrisy, I know, but from a business standpoint they can't afford a sniff of anything…*sexual*, not with the sort of parent the place attracts. The best the poor girl can hope for is suspension after this gets out.'

Listening to the woman who had lied through her teeth, sabotaged his marriage, dragged his reputation into the gutter and in the process endangered the deal he had worked so hard to pull off being spoken of as a victim, described as *poor*, had been as hard for Seb to swallow as visualising the red-headed virago as an empathic teacher.

Would she be as empathic in the bedroom?

'Your resources?' His cryptic comment sent a shiver through her. 'Well, that sounds suitably sinister.'

She gave a laugh, which missed 'bring it on, I don't care' by several thousand miles. Nonetheless, he picked up on it.

'But you're not about to be intimidated.' Seb felt a fresh stab of reluctant admiration; whatever else she was this woman was not gutless. Right or wrong—actually *wrong*—she had gone out on a very precarious limb to fight for her brother, and, having met the guy again, he doubted that he appreciated how lucky he was to have someone like her in his corner.

If the situation had been reversed would Mark Jones have put himself on the line for his sister? Seb doubted it. Nothing he had seen had given him any reason to alter his initial assessment of Mari's twin.

Mari ignored the comment.

'I have spoken to the head, and he was very understanding,' she retorted, putting a positive slant on a situation that when she allowed herself to think about it looked very black indeed.

'But you're not in work today? He was not *that* understanding?'

She slung him a look of seething dislike. 'All right, you were right. My life is a mess, people who I've never met are discussing surgery I never had and it's my own fault.' Which of course made it worse. 'I achieved nothing and now I'm likely to lose my job, too.'

She closed her eyes, feeling herself falling into the relentless cycle of self-recriminating circles that she had spent the entire weekend trying to escape.

'Self-pity doesn't suit you.'

She opened her eyes with an outraged snap and snarled, 'Go to hell!' Then she closed them again.

Her moment of madness still seemed unreal; when she thought of it now it felt like some sort of out-of-body experience.

It made no sense. It wasn't as if she hadn't been painfully aware of the dangers of reacting in the heat of the moment—two foster families had felt unable to cope with the twins after she had *reacted*.

It was a lesson Mari had learned well. In the short term there was immense satisfaction in making the boy who stole your brother's lunch money cry and walloping the bully who shut a puppy in a telephone kiosk—the black eye had been so worth it—but there were consequences.

There always were, which was why she no longer reacted before she thought—she considered consequences to the point where Mark frequently complained about her lack of spontaneity. But on Saturday she'd not just been spontaneous, she'd been... She shuddered and shook her head, bringing her chin up. She'd done the crime so now it was about taking the punishment—whatever that might be...

'I know of a job vacancy that might suit you.'

She opened her eyes and turned her head, still nestled on the leather headrest, to face him, not bothering to hide her suspicion. 'You suddenly became Santa Claus?'

'No, I suddenly became in need of a wife.'

She struggled to match his flippancy. 'Is that a proposal?'

'Yes.'

The colour flared hot and then faded pale in her cheeks as she sat bolt upright and reached for the door handle. 'I'm assuming this is some sort of joke. Word to the wise—don't give up your day job. Stand-up is *not* your thing.'

'What I am suggesting is a business arrangement.' Only his long fingers silently drumming on the steering wheel suggested he was not as relaxed as he appeared.

Mari's fingers tightened on the handle. 'Hate is not a good basis for a business arrangement.'

'I've factored that in,' he retorted with unimpaired cool. 'In public we would act the happy, loved-up couple.'

A hissing sound left her lips. 'Marriage. You're *actually* talking about *marriage*—it's not a sick joke?' She scanned his face. 'What planet do you live on?'

'In private you can carry on hating me and to a large extent living your own life. Eighteen months, we decided, would suffice before we make our irreconcilable differences public—'

'We...?' Listening now simply because she couldn't believe what he was saying, not because she was for one second buying into his crazy suggestion, she pulled the door she had opened closed with a loud, angry bang that shook the car. 'What is this—proposal by committee?'

Every little girl's dream, Mari thought, repressing a sudden strong impulse to laugh, or was that cry?

'I've had my legal people draw up a contract. It's ready for your lawyer to look at.'

He spoke as if everyone had a legal team waiting at the end of the phone. 'I don't have a lawyer. You'd be surprised by how many people in the real world don't.'

He ignored her sarcasm. 'I suggest you get one before you sign up for this.'

Mari took a deep breath. She had humoured him too long. 'I'm not going to sign up for *this*—you're mad,' she said with total conviction. 'Why the hell would you want to get married? Assuming that you haven't decided I'm your soulmate.'

'This is about damage limitation, not soulmates,' he cut back, ignoring her sarcasm. 'I have spent the weekend trying to repair the damage your stunt inflicted on a crucial business deal.'

His comment stirred a memory. 'The royal thing?'

He tipped his head in acknowledgement. 'Good, you know about it, so I don't have to explain that the royal family are very nervous about scandal, *especially* the sexual kind that involves men getting women pregnant and deserting them.'

'So you told them you didn't know me.'

An expression she could not quite read flickered across his face as he looked at her. 'Strangely, you know, I feel I do, but no, the truth would not have worked. You were way too convincing, angel. I almost believed you myself except I think I might have remembered sleeping with you. No, this was a situation that required some creativity.'

'Lies, you mean. Like the one when you said there were no strings to you paying for Mark's treatment!'

'No, I meant that if you refuse my proposal your brother's treatment will still be funded. The two are not co-dependent.'

'So why would I say yes without blackmail?'

'Because you don't want to be in my debt...' His narrow-eyed scrutiny moved across her face. 'The idea of that kills you, doesn't it?' This thing hung on her stiff-necked pride and his ability to keep his lust in check. This needed to stay business and he needed to retain control.

'*Yes!*' she flung back, hating him so much she could taste it.

'Excellent… In that case you should probably know about us.'

'*About…?*'

'I gave us a history. We had a short passionate rela-tionship, but there was a lovers' falling-out—we can't even remember what the fight was about now. We met up again not long ago by accident, we shared a night of passion, but we were both with other people by then and we went our separate ways. I had no idea you were preg-nant until you appeared. Seeing you again has made me realise that you are the love of my life.'

It was all delivered in the sort of deadpan tone that made a computerised voice sound animated. Mari looked at him, fascinated. 'And they swallowed that?'

'I lack your dramatic talent,' he admitted drily. 'There was no soul baring involved. The reality is they have as much time and money invested in this deal as I do and they are less concerned about me doing the right thing than me being *seen* to do the right thing.'

'They sound as shallow as you.'

'It's called realism. You ought to try it some time.'

'I can see a massive flaw in your plan—the baby—so do you expect me to walk around with a pillow shoved down my jumper, too?'

'That won't be necessary. We will be away on an ex-tended honeymoon when you tragically lose the baby. It's not something we want to talk about and people will respect that.'

'You've thought of everything.'

'If not, I'm pretty good at thinking on my feet.'

'And modest with it,' she snapped back waspishly.

'So what do you say, Mari Jones? Eighteen months

of your life, then afterwards slate clean and a financial settlement to ease your way back into your life? It's negotiable but the figure I suggest is—'

'No!'

He watched as she chewed her plump lip, an abstracted expression on her face, before she settled back in her seat with a little sigh followed by a decisive nod as she looked at him.

'Make it *exactly* what Mark's treatment costs and you have a deal.' She gave him a hard look.

'That would amount to you throwing away several million pounds.'

'I don't care about the money.'

'I assumed you would go away and think about it.'

She gave a slightly wild-sounding laugh. 'Thinking is the last thing I want to do! The only thing is…when you said this was business you wouldn't expect me to—'

'I have never had to pay for sex.'

His eyes trained on the outline of her breasts where the nipples left an erotic imprint against the wet fabric of her shirt. Unable to fight the impulse, he reached across and pushed aside a strand of rain-darkened hair that clung to her cheek.

The touch of his fingers on her skin made Mari tense; slowly she turned her head to look at him. The light contact felt like a brand at every point of contact and her skin tingled and burned.

'Right, I'll marry you but I won't sleep with you.'

A slow smile of satisfaction spread across his hawkish features. 'In my experience it's always a good idea to keep business and pleasure separate, but let's not include it in the vows.'

Mari flinched. Hearing him say *vows* made it seem more real. She felt as if she were living a recurrent childish nightmare of hers—she had stepped on a carousel that wouldn't stop and let her off, it just carried on going round and round while she started screaming.

His smile died as he said softly, 'The next time maybe…?'

She gave a bemused frown and shook her head, parroting in a flat voice, 'Next time?'

'Don't all girls dream of the wedding dress?'

'Not the groom?'

'Let's hope you find a man who hasn't been put off the white-wedding thing by having been previously publicly humiliated by a wedding crasher. Oh, and while we are on the subject it's not the best idea to start looking for Mr. Right or even a little light entertainment until *after* we have split up.'

Struggling to hide her embarrassment behind an air of amused indifference, she shrugged and asked, 'Is that in the small print?'

He did not smile back, and there was a definite warning in his voice as he told her, 'No, that part is in the *big* print. If it's any comfort, you won't be the only one condemned to eighteen months of celibacy.'

What was eighteen months when you'd already done twenty-four years? she thought, swallowing the bubble of hysteria that rose in her throat.

'Still, I suppose eighteen months of abstinence is preferable to a lifetime of regret.'

She lost the battle to allow his cynicism go unchallenged. 'I suppose the trick is to find the right person.'

He gave an eloquent sneer of contempt. 'The trick is to enjoy the party but be realistic.'

His attitude continued to get under Mari's skin. 'So if you don't believe people fall in love forever, why were you getting married?'

A muscle throbbed in his lean cheek as he gave a strange twisted smile. 'Did I say I didn't think people fall in love forever? My parents' passion for one another is as strong today, I would think, as the day they met.' And just as blindly selfish.

The idea of following their example had been the perfect incentive when it came to keeping his own passions under control.

She was bewildered by the aura of anger he was projecting. It had an almost physical presence in the enclosed space.

'Well, that's marvellous.' She looked at him, struggling to read his expression. *Isn't it?'*

'My parents' *love* has not stopped them having affairs, but they always come back to one another. However the divorces were never amicable and the marriages always headline-making lavish.'

Her eyes widened. 'How many times?'

'Married three times, divorced twice…so far.'

'That must have been hard growing up.'

The tentative sympathy was met with a hard look. 'Put your empathy away, Mari. I do not need it. My grandfather brought me over from the Argentine to England when I was eight, up from that point he raised me, and then when Fleur came along he adopted her.'

'Do you spend much time in Argentina?'

He shook his head. 'Not now. After the death of her husband my grandmother moved back to her homeland, Spain. I spend some time there.' He handed her a card. 'My private number—ring me if you have any questions. So where shall I take you?'

'I came in my own car,' she said faintly. 'So what happens…now?'

'We get married. It's not complicated.'

Mari swallowed. 'When?'

'I'll be in touch.'

CHAPTER SIX

MARI WAS PACKING her bag when her mobile rang. Finding it under a pile of underclothes, she saw the caller ID and picked it up. Chloe had been her classroom assistant for two years now. She was one of the people Mari would miss most, along with the children. She had always felt she was one of the lucky ones. She loved her job and never woke up not wanting to go into work—now all that was gone.

She pushed the thought away—no time to look back and have regrets. 'Hi, Chloe!'

'Is it true? Have they really sacked you?' Without waiting for a reply the girl continued indignantly, 'Is that even legal?'

'I'm on a temporary contract. It runs out at the end of the term.' Not long ago there had been some pretty broad hints dropped that she might be offered a permanent contract at that point, but that was not going to happen now. 'They are giving me paid leave until then and a good reference.'

Would Sebastian give her a good reference when their contract was successfully completed? She swallowed a bubble of hysteria and heard the younger girl say, 'Well, I think it's terrible. We all do, Mari—you're the best teacher in the place.'

Mari felt her eyes fill at the tribute.

'So what are you going to do?'

'I thought I might travel a bit, take a trip.' She kept it vague, as she had done the previous day when she had visited Mark, though Chloe showed a lot more interest in her plans than her brother had.

Mark had barely listened when she'd said that she needed to take a trip. All he could talk about were the arrangements for his transfer—his mention of her part in the change in his fortune had been lightly touched on.

'I knew if you could swallow your pride it would be all right. I've no idea what you said to him, sis, but it worked, Seb has done the right thing.'

'I didn't say anything. How do you know it was him?'

'Who else would it be? And don't look like that.' He'd sighed. 'You always managed to ruin things with that guilt thing of yours. It's win-win—he can go around feeling good because he's dug his hand in his pocket for the poor cripple and, let's face it, it's not as though he doesn't owe me. He put me here after all.'

Did he…? Mari's innate honesty could no longer support the deception. She felt guilty for not being more sympathetic to her brother, and when the opportunity arose she'd leaped at the chance to offload that guilt onto someone else.

'I knew you'd come through for me, sis—you always do.'

When his eyes slid from hers she realised that he didn't want to know how. Her twin always had a knack to ignore uncomfortable truths, the ones that made him uncomfortable anyway.

It was an ability Mari envied him.

* * *

She was expecting the knock on the door but she jumped anyway.

She'd been expecting a flunkey of some sort, so when she opened the door and found Seb himself standing there she was too shocked to disguise her reaction. Her jaw dropped and her blue eyes flew wide open. The raw masculinity he exuded hit her like a runaway train.

Like someone coming out of a trance, she blinked and hoped her knees would support her. 'What are you doing here?' It came out a lot more accusingly than she had intended.

In response his dark brows lifted as without a word he stepped past her and into the living room. He subjected the long narrow space to the same sort of critical scrutiny that she'd endured, and from his expression she assumed it had been assessed as wanting, also.

Lucky she didn't crave his approval. In fact she told herself if the day ever dawned that she got it, that was the time to worry.

'I said one o'clock. It is one.' His frown deepened. 'Aren't you ready?'

Trying not to react to his abrupt manner, she gave a curt nod, and, matching his noticeably cold attitude, indicated her bag propped up against the sofa, one of several pieces of furniture in the place she had reupholstered or revamped. She couldn't sew a stitch, but she was a whiz with a staple gun and a paintbrush.

'Of course I'm ready.' Was this about the way she looked? 'Should I go back and put on my tiara?' She tried to hide a sudden flash of uncharacteristic insecurity under sarcasm.

He slung her an impatient look. 'What are you talking about?'

'I thought, you thought that I…maybe should, should I wear something a bit more…?' She glanced down at her slim-fitting jeans and the cropped jacket left open to reveal the silky acid-yellow sleeveless top that showed a tiny sliver of flat midriff.

His eyes moved in an expressionless sweep from her toes to the top of her glossy head. 'You look fine. It's only a register office.'

Wow, he sure knows how to make a girl feel good, she thought, compressing her lips in silent resentment, furious with herself for virtually asking for his approval.

'Actually I wasn't expecting you. I assumed you'd send a driver or something.'

Her calm was only a single cell thick, but it was very important to Mari that he had no idea just how *not* calm she was. She was almost sick with apprehension, and under that there were layers of confusing, conflicting emotions that were just too complicated to acknowledge. On a more practical level she was worried she might actually throw up.

'So how long will it take…?'

He dragged his gaze from that tiny sliver of flat, toned, creamy-skinned stomach and cleared his throat, reminding himself that this was business.

'The flight or—?'

'Both,' she cut in quickly.

'The company jet was available, so not long for the journey. The wedding I've arranged so that we can stop off on the way to the airport.'

'That sounds ideal.' Her voice was clear and cool but Seb could see her hands were shaking as her gaze flickered around the room; she was looking anywhere but at him. She reminded him of a trapped animal.

She accused him of pride, but Seb suspected that Mari's stiff-necked version of that sin would make her walk over hot coals before she'd admit she was nervous. It was an exasperating characteristic, almost as much as her wildly misplaced loyalty to her brother and he was not above exploiting this misplaced loyalty.

Which makes you...?

She was a consenting adult; she knew what she was doing. Somehow this didn't stop his pangs of conscience.

'It's all right to be nervous.'

'I'm not nervous. I'll just be glad when it's over.'

'Is this all you have?' He nodded towards the moderate-size holdall that was propped against a sofa that had *bespoke* and *expensive* written all over it. The open-plan living area suggested that the owner had expensive taste.

'I fit a lot in. I wasn't sure what to bring.' She hurried and clumsily snatched the bag up before him. 'I can manage,' she said with the attitude of someone expecting a fight.

No fight materialised; he simply straightened up and watched as she flung it purposefully over her shoulder, allowing himself a faint smile when the impetus as it hit her hip almost knocked her off balance.

'Fine by me.'

'That's good, then,' she said, knowing the response sounded lame.

Mari lived on the fourth floor in a small nondescript brick building that had no lift, and by the time they had reached the third floor she was regretting he hadn't argued her out of her decision. Halfway down she swallowed her pride and paused to catch her breath.

He paused, too, not breathless obviously, just looking like a Hollywood film star who had drifted onto the wrong set. This peeling paint and worn carpet really wasn't his natural setting.

He looked down at her through the mesh of his crazily long dark eyelashes and nodded to the bag. 'Manage that, can you?'

She gritted her teeth, straightened up and produced a sunny smile. The weight had almost yanked her shoulder from its socket, but she'd die before she'd admit it or accept his help. 'I'm fine, thank you.'

He stood aside as she exited the flat door sideways, not making allowances for the bulk of the bag as she eased past him carefully.

'Sure you don't need help?'

'Yes,' she said shortly, requiring all her breath to negotiate the last flight of stairs. They passed one of her neighbours, whose plucked brows almost vanished into her hairline when she saw Seb.

'Moving on, are we?'

'A holiday,' Mari puffed.

'I don't think she believed you,' Seb said in a voice that echoed spookily down the stairwell.

'Shh, she'll hear you,' Mari hissed as she prepared to swap shoulders, resting her bag for a moment on the step long enough to give him ample opportunity to repeat his offer of help. She'd refuse, but it would be nice to have the option. When he didn't, she gritted her teeth and wished she hadn't packed the books or the pair of boots.

'The reporters knocked on every door in the building. I think they offered money for—'

His lip curled. 'Dirt.'

She turned her head; he was standing two steps behind her.

'I was surprised,' he admitted, stepping down one step and pausing just one above her.

Too close...too close... Struggling to pacify the panicky voice in her head, she took a jolting backward step.

'Really? I thought knocking on doors and buying stories was par for the course?'

'It is, which is why I was surprised when I didn't get to read the lurid details, both fictional and true, of your love affairs in the tabloids. Anyone would think you have a blemish-free past.' The humourless smile that tugged the corners of his mouth upwards faded as his hooded gaze slid covetously over the curves of her athletically slim body. She had an innate sensuality that had to make every man she met think about taking her to bed—he had.

Still was thinking, said the voice in his head.

The difference was he wasn't going to act on it, despite the sizzle whenever they were in near proximity. This might be a long eighteen months.

It didn't matter how hard they dug, she didn't have a past, at least not the sort he was talking about, but Mari was not about to admit her embarrassing lack of lovers to him. She turned her head quickly. Trust issues aside, she had suspected for some time that she simply wasn't very highly sexed. With Adrian she had been in love with the idea of it, the romance of it, which was why having her illusions shattered had been such a big deal.

She'd trusted him and he'd betrayed her and rejected her. She'd prefer to stay single than risk feeling that way again.

'Some of us are discreet.'

'Yeah, I had a grandstand view of your *amazing* discretion in the cathedral,' he drawled, replaying the scene in his head and feeling the acrid aftertaste of anger and humiliation all over again.

Mari clamped her lips together. She was pretty sick of having her nose rubbed in it. It wasn't as if she needed reminding she had set in motion the events that had led her to this place and this moment. 'Are you going to bring that up often? Just so that I know.'

'You're right.' Anger was a waste of energy and an indulgence; he needed to take a less negative approach. 'I'm not in the best of moods.'

Astonished by the admission, Mari didn't say anything.

'After a long absence, my parents have made the news.'

The story dug up from years back by an enterprising hack told of another bride left standing at the altar. His father had been the groom, his mother the 'other' woman, and his father had jilted his new bride just as Seb had done.

The only downside to this story from a journalistic point of view had been that the woman left at the altar had not gone on to lead a tragic life, but instead had been inconveniently happy combining a career as a respected trauma doctor with marriage and four children.

'Today might be better if you remind yourself that a marriage of convenience is a hell of a lot better than one of inconvenience, and there are a lot of those out there,' he mused, fighting the impulse to grab the damned bag off her as she staggered awkwardly down a step. All she had to do was ask, but she didn't, and with a bloody-minded stubbornness she made it to the poky communal hallway where she paused.

He correctly interpreted her hesitation. 'There were no reporters outside when I arrived.'

Still she hesitated, raising herself up on tiptoe to peer through the dusty pane of glass high up on the door.

'Are you sure?' If she was seen leaving complete with

luggage and Seb, she could only imagine how they would spin it. Ironically nothing could be as strange, or crazy, as the truth!

With a grunt of irritation he snatched the bag from her and strode out through the door.

Left with little choice Mari followed him, relieved that no one jumped out of the shadows wielding a camera. He walked straight to the car parked by the kerb. It was an enormous four-wheel drive with blacked-out windows.

'You're driving?'

'I like driving, unless you want to?'

She shook her head.

'So what did your brother think of our arrangement?' Being a brother himself, his opinion of a man who allowed his sister to fight his battles was not positive.

'I don't ask my brother's approval for my decisions.'

Neatly dodged, he thought, observing her neat, peachy behind as she bent, ignoring the passenger door and getting into the back seat.

'Aren't you going to ask me where we're going?'

She had been about to, but she responded to a perverse impulse and said instead, 'One register office is much the same as any other.'

She saw his eyes narrow in the rear-view mirror. 'Life is going to be a lot easier if you lose the victim act,' he drawled.

Not replying, she turned her head and looked out of the window.

'The silent treatment works for me. It's peaceful, but I've never known a woman who can keep it buttoned for more than five minutes.'

Mari clamped her lips over a retort and contented herself with slinging him a fulminating look of dislike in the rear-view mirror.

'Fifteen, I'm impressed,' Seb admitted as he drew up in front of a red-brick building.

She ignored him and looked up at the building. 'So this is it, then?'

He glanced over his shoulder. 'We're five minutes early. I can drive around the block once more if you like?' he suggested, fighting the impulse to apologise.

It was convenient, but had he realised that the office was situated on a road where most shop windows were either boarded up or smashed, he would have added a few miles to their journey.

Mari shook her head and took a deep breath. Not waiting for him to come around and open the door, she flung herself out, gasping, 'No, I'm fine.'

She had actually never been this far from *fine* in her life!

Seb came to join her. 'It's probably better inside.'

It was actually much worse, but Mari barely noticed. It wasn't the place that made her heart feel like a stone; it was exchanging words that were meant to *mean* something. She felt a hypocrite saying them—making a mockery of something that she considered sacred left a bad taste in her mouth.

Mari felt like a cheat.

As they walked through the swing doors, Seb pulled Mari out of the way of a boisterous crowd. At the centre of the laughing group was a bride whose white minidress did nothing to disguise her large pregnancy bump and a groom who didn't look as if he had started shaving yet.

Mari turned her head for one last look as the loud group left the building.

'They looked so happy.'

Seb didn't know if it was the wistful look on her face when she said it, or the fact he had fully expected her to make some catty remark about the other woman giving birth before she got to exchange vows, but as they headed towards the ceremony room Seb found himself wishing he had bought her some flowers.

CHAPTER SEVEN

THE MOMENT MARI got out of the car, even though it was almost midnight, the Spanish summer heat hit her. She focused on the physical impressions and tried not to think beyond them to the lump of apprehension she was carrying around like a stone in her chest for the entire journey.

It was utterly still; the air was heavy and stickily oppressive. For the last mile or so they had driven through what seemed to be a pine forest, and warm air carried the green smell of the trees.

She got out her mobile and texted goodnight to her brother.

'I imagine he is much as he was the past ten times you texted him.' While Seb was exploiting the sisterly devotion, her inability to see that she was being used by her brother was really beginning to irritate him. So was her frigid, tight-lipped silence.

She had not said anything the entire journey; not to him anyway—she had been charm itself to the steward on the flight. The boy had been positively salivating. 'And you've proved your point. Some women can keep quiet.'

He had hardly said a word the entire way, so now he broke his moody silence to criticise her!

'If you'd spoken to me I'd have replied. And texting my brother, that's called caring,' she snapped back, choosing not to inform him that the texting exercise had been pretty one-sided.

He turned his head briefly to scan her profile in the darkness. 'Would he be grateful if he knew what you've done for him?'

'You're the one who is paying for his treatment. This was my choice.'

'So why didn't you tell him?'

'Mark has got enough on his plate without feeling responsible... What's that meant to mean?' she asked in response to his harsh laugh.

'Is it a happy place, this little fantasy world you inhabit?'

Mari shot a look of simmering dislike at his patrician profile. 'I wouldn't expect you to understand.'

'Try me.'

Taken unawares by the unexpected offer, Mari found herself answering, 'I love him. He's my brother.' She could have left it there but for some reason she heard herself say, 'I know he's not perfect but he's not had an easy life, rejected by his mother.'

'Is that the way you feel about it—rejected?'

Too close to the truth. She ignored his interruption.

'Two foster homes that didn't work out, and the children's home—'

'Weren't you in those same places?'

She shook her head. 'You don't understand—he was there *because* of me. He would have been adopted straight away when we were babies if they had allowed us to be split up, but they didn't.'

'Why him and not you?'

'People want pretty babies. Mark had blond curls and dimples—he was adorable. I was not an attractive baby.' It was a matter-of-fact statement with no self-pity he could detect, and all the more poignant because of it.

'Aren't all babies pretty?'

'Not me. I was allergic to pretty much everything. I had asthma, that wasn't so bad, but my skin was awful—eczema. It took hours every day putting on and washing off my treatments…and when it flared up…' She gave a little shudder at the memory. 'People do not want to push around a scabby baby, and not many want the responsibility of looking after a kid with a chronic skin condition.

'Mark got left on the shelf with me, and when we did get fostered my red-headed temper—well, you've seen that—got us sent back both times. So, you see, without me Mark could have had a very different life.'

'Is that how you think of yourself—left on the shelf…?'

'Actually it was a doorstep.' To abandon your own babies that way you had to be pretty desperate…but maybe if there had only been one…?

She heard him swear and then, anxious that he didn't think she was playing for the sympathy vote, added quickly, 'It wasn't all doom and gloom, though, in our teens. We got fostered by Sukie and Jack, and they are the most inspirational couple you can imagine,' she enthused, her voice filling with warmth.

'Are you coming?'

He knew it was irrational of him to be angry with her for not being a person he could despise. It was a lot easier to take advantage of someone when you could say they were asking for it, they deserved it, than someone who literally didn't ask for anything, and as far as he could see had never been given anything either! Mari had worked hard and…ah, hell, she was an adult. If she wanted to spend her life paying an imagined debt, that was her business, he told himself. The story changed nothing.

Mari began to follow and stopped. He didn't even bother to turn around and see if she'd responded, just assumed she would.

And why wouldn't he? She'd been responding like some meek little lamb from the moment she'd allowed herself to be bundled onto the private jet and, yes, there had been a certain amount of novelty value in the unaccustomed luxury, but it had worn off and now... *What the hell are you doing, Mari?*

Mari Rey-Defoe.

Mrs Rey-Defoe.

She pressed a hand to her lips but the giggle slipped past. She was married. She used both hands this time to muffle the hysteria that was locked in her throat.

From where he was standing, Seb, who had walked halfway across the gravel, heard it. There was irritation written in the lines of his lean face when he turned and saw her still standing near the car. All he could make out was the shadowy outline of her slim figure, then the moon came out from behind the heavy cloud cover.

He swore softly under his breath. Nothing, he thought savagely, was easy with this woman. She had set out to make his life as tough as possible, and when she couldn't stage something large and dramatic she made do with little niggling details that added up to a massive and frustrating whole.

The logical thing to do would have been to put her out of his life and erect six walls to keep her out, and yet here he was dragging her in and effectively building walls to keep her there for eighteen long months. Eighteen excruciating months without sex, spent with a woman who could make a sneeze erotic.

At what point had this seemed like a logical next step? It was a means to an end, he reminded himself. This was about saving several thousand jobs and a partnership that in the future could generate a lot more—a means to an end.

Sure it is, the voice in his head mocked, *the end being your bed.*

The illicit thought came with the accompanying image; he had undressed her in his head over the past few days so often that he felt he knew exactly what she would look like.

He ignored the voice and the desire that twisted inside him, and reminded himself this was a business deal. You let business get personal and it never ended well.

'Come on.' The idea of a shower and bed was appealing; the idea of a bed with Mari in it… He saw red hair spread out against the white sheet framing a face that… He clenched his jaw against the thought, but not before his body hardened. 'It's this way. Watch your step.' He jerked his head towards the house.

Ignoring the gesture—did the man think she was some sort of puppy dog to be brought to heel?—Mari shook her head and struggled to maintain her defiant attitude as he crossed the gravel towards her, his long-legged stride bringing him there in seconds.

The resentful words exploded from her before the testosterone he was oozing made her tongue stick to the roof of her mouth, a situation she been experiencing all day.

'You've been pushing me around all day.'

Not in the literal sense. It had almost seemed at times as though he had gone out of his way to avoid touching her. Even at the joke of a marriage ceremony when the registrar had said he could kiss the bride, Seb had barely even brushed his lips with hers, leaving her looking and feeling like a total fool.

The aggravating part of the situation was she had been

letting him, and it was not a good precedent to set for the next eighteen months with a man as bossy and controlling as Seb.

She folded her arms across her chest. 'I've had enough. You're a control freak, and I'm not going another step until you tell me where we are.'

'Don't be childish. All you had to do was ask, but you were too busy playing the victim and giving me the stink eye.'

'I'm amazed you noticed. You haven't looked up from that damned tablet the whole way.'

'Feeling neglected, were we?'

'Not at all,' she retorted haughtily. 'It was an education to see what delightful manners years of inbreeding and the best school can achieve.' It had gone pitch-black again, but his answering hiss made her decide to move on. She'd made her point, although she'd forgotten what it was as he'd taken a step towards her, not touching but awfully close…too close. 'I'm asking now.'

Now that he was close to losing his temper she sounded maddeningly calm. She had accused him of bad manners, yet she had responded to any question with a mutter and barely said a word the entire way here; filthy looks and her ramrod-straight back—he doubted her shoulder blades had made contact with a chair back at any point— were all that had been given him.

'Fine, but indoors.' He glanced up as a cloud drifted like smoke across the moon. 'There's a storm coming.'

'And you can tell that how?'

Before she could pour further scorn on his confident prediction there was a distant roll of thunder. So instead she flung him a disgruntled glare and directed her gaze at the sinister outline of the stone building they stood before. It rose out of the forest, making her think of a haunted mansion in a Gothic romance. Did that make her the spunky but vulnerable heroine…?

She almost laughed at the thought. She was none of the above!

'I think I'd feel safer out here. There is no way that place is a hotel.' The place looked very Gothic, and a little shiver slid a clammy path down her spine.

'No,' he agreed with infuriating placidity. 'It's not.'

'It looks like the set of a vampire movie!'

Despite himself Seb's lips twitched. 'It was a monastery.'

Her voice rose to an indignant squeak. 'You've brought me to a monastery?'

'*Obviously* it is no longer a monastery. It was for a short time, I believe, a school, and now it is my grandmother's home. Her family came from this area of Spain originally and her twin sister still lives close by. After she was widowed she returned here.'

'I don't believe you.'

'I thought you knew all about the special bond between twins, and my grandmother and Aunt Marguerite are identical.'

'You know what I mean—why in God's name would you bring me to your grandmother's house?'

'Because it is her birthday tomorrow,' he told her calmly. 'She has been unwell, she is my last living grandparent and I promised to see her.' In as much as there had been a female influence after he had come to live in England, the tough, outspoken old lady who took a delight in being awkward had been it.

'Oh, God!' The idea of being dropped into the middle of a family gathering filled Mari with utter horror she didn't even try to disguise. 'Is your entire family here?'

What had he been thinking?

What was I thinking? She pushed away the rush of panicked rejection and focused on a mental image of Mark in a wheelchair. After a moment her sense of purpose reasserted itself and the panic receded.

Many people coped with disability—one of her friends had lost her sight and gone on to not only marry and have a gorgeous child but win a medal for her country in the International Swimming Championships. She was an inspiration, but Mark… No, her brother would not react well.

And how, she wondered, was Sebastian's family going to react to her? How was he going to explain the presence of this new wife? God, but that sounded so weird to think. Would she ever be able to say it out loud?

'No, they aren't here.'

'That's something, I suppose.' Before he stepped back into the shadow there was something in his face that made her probe. 'But they, your mum and dad, I mean, they were at the wedding?' And presumably had filled Granny in on the scandalous proceedings, and just when she thought the situation could not get weirder or more awkward.

'My parents are presently enjoying a world cruise. They were not at my wedding and will not be here.'

The undercurrent in his voice made her say, 'I'm sorry.'

He flicked her a look, opened his mouth and closed it again. She was lifting her shoulders and rolling them to stretch the kinks that tied up her spine after the journey. Seb was struck by the almost feline quality in the sinuous way she moved. He took a deep breath as heat seared through his body, as merciless as a blade. Then he launched into a response designed to dampen her empathy.

'My grandparents on both sides played a larger part

in my life than my parents.' He clenched his jaw and taunted softly, 'Aren't you going to say, well, at least you *had* parents?'

'I had parents. Everyone does. The difference is I could walk past them in the street and not know them. They wouldn't know me. I look sometimes and wonder if... When I was little I told people my dad was a war hero and my mother was a nurse.' She stopped, hit by the sheer strangeness and odd intimacy of this encounter, standing in the dark with this man—a man she barely knew but was married to, a man who she had considered her enemy before she knew his name—talking about families.

A subject she knew little of, she thought, ignoring the knot of longing in her chest so familiar she barely acknowledged its presence. She had Mark and he had her; they were a family. Her mother and her reasons for deserting them, which she had trained herself not to think about...*mostly*.

It seemed like a long time before he responded. His voice coming out of the darkness made her jump. 'You stopped.'

'The teacher found out and made me apologise to the class for lying.'

'Sensitive soul. I hope you are a better teacher.'

'I am.' It was not a subject she had any false modesty on. She'd be a better parent, too, than his, who had better things to do than attend their son's wedding.

When her children, the ones Mari dreamed of one day adopting, had their red-letter days she would be there with bells on!

She tilted her head back, squinting, just able to make out the shape of the tiled roof.

'I can't imagine anyone, let alone an elderly lady,

choosing to live here.' Unsure if he had even heard her, she followed the sound of his crunching footsteps because if she lost him she didn't have a clue where she was going.

When he responded Seb's deep vibrant voice came from a little way ahead. 'It is a lot less intimidating in daylight when the bats are asleep.'

Trotting in earnest to catch up, she fought the urge to duck and cover her head. 'That's a joke, right…?'

'Bats are perfectly harmless creatures, more frightened of you than you are of them.'

'Want to bet?'

His low laugh was so attractive that she had to fight a responsive grin. She had to fight a few other responses, too. She was familiar with the notion that opposites attracted and that sexual attraction was indiscriminate, but this was her first real experience of how overwhelming it could be when you encountered the sort of intense physical magnetism that Seb possessed. It made what she had felt for Adrian pale into insignificance.

If he had any redeeming features beyond a fondness for his grandmother she might have been in danger of making a fool of herself and maybe enjoying it, because there was no doubt in her mind that he'd be a good lover. His hands, she mused dreamily, his mouth… Her stomach flipped.

'You can relax.'

Shocked by the direction of her thoughts, Mari realised that was one thing she couldn't do, not around this man with his powerful aura of masculinity.

'My grandmother's home is actually quite civilised, and she is a very young eighty-two. Obviously she doesn't live here alone—a couple live in and there is a gardener and a couple of maids who come in from the village.'

'Cosy set-up,' she murmured, staring at the looming building and not really caring if he got her sarcasm or not, just glad he had no inkling of her previous thoughts. 'I didn't see any village on the way.' Even with her having taken the precaution of turning her back to him, his nearness made the nape of her neck tingle.

'There are two accesses to the place. We took the north road—the village is on the south side of the mountain.'

The geography of the area made little sense to Mari, and her thoughts turned to her brother. What if something had happened? He hadn't replied to her last text.

She slipped her phone out of her pocket, but before she could begin to punch in Mark's number it was snatched from her grasp by Seb before she had even registered his presence.

She turned, eyes blazing. 'Give that back!'

Seb looked at the phone and tucked it into his own pocket. Mari, her hands clenched, watched him and went white with rage. 'Does he always need you to hold his hand?'

Her chin lifted in reaction to the scorn in his voice while in the distance the owl called. 'The support is mutual.'

A slug of anger that on one level Seb knew was irrational slipped past the cool objectivity he struggled to maintain whenever he thought of the man he had judged to be a selfish waste of space. Any sympathy he might have felt for the younger man's present situation was negated by the cynical way he used his sister and played on her irrational guilt.

And you're not...?

Cynical, or using her?

Both. The answer came a second before he closed down this line of internal dialogue.

The situations were not comparable; she was not losing out and this was a fair exchange. Eighteen months with him was preferable to a life spent looking after a brother for whom nothing she ever did would be enough—and that was what would happen if he didn't fully recover.

Recognising a masterful piece of rationalisation when he heard one, he buried the knowledge beneath a layer of anger.

'You'd like to believe that, wouldn't you? But you're really not that stupid, are you, Mari?'

Mari was grateful for the dark when his soft suggestion made her face flame. She compressed her lips over a defensive retort, resenting his insinuation while recognising there was more than a grain of truth in it. While she wasn't blind to her twin's faults, it was something else to hear another person criticise him.

'Didn't you read the literature on The Atler?'

Her face was just a blur, but he imagined her teeth gouging into the soft plump fullness of her lower lip. She'd done that several times on the plane. At one point there had been pinpricks of blood, and he had wondered what she would do if he'd dabbed them away with his tongue...

The question still remained, as did the frustrated ache.

She was grateful for the change of subject, but it took Mari a moment to react to the abrupt question, to connect the name with the clinic that specialised in the rehabilitation of injuries like Mark's—the *expensive* clinic.

She felt resentment she was uncomfortable acknowledging stir. If she had told Mark what she was doing would he have discouraged her? Her resentment was directed not towards her brother but towards the man who had made her think about it.

'I didn't know there was an exam,' she countered,

unwilling to admit that she had read the first page half a dozen times before she had finally given up. She'd had other things on her mind at the time, such as getting married.

Seb, drawn by the scent of her perfume—or was it her shampoo?—fought the sudden strong impulse to lean in closer. Darkness had a dangerous way of bypassing inhibitions.

The air was heavy with an almost audible expectant hum that had little to do with the imminent storm and everything to do with the indiscriminate flare of hormones that escalated the dull ache in his groin.

Sex was always one of those things that defied logic, but not, he reminded himself, his control. He was justifiably proud of his ability to vanquish the primal urges.

'They discourage visitors during the initial assessment period. The regime appears to be as much boot camp as high-tech.'

'It does?'

'When the going gets tough your brother will be begging you to get him out of there…and of course you'll rush to do what he wants, even if that isn't the best thing for him. If you're here with me, you have a legitimate excuse to refuse to ride to the rescue.'

His superior dismissive tone hit a raw nerve. Mari caught his arm and felt the hard muscle under her fingers tense before he swung back his feet, kicking up a shower of gravel that hit her bare shins.

'You don't think a lot of him, do you?'

His response was not ambiguous. 'No.'

'Because he's not been born with your advantages?' she charged contemptuously. 'Well, my brother has got pride, too, even if he doesn't have the required patrician blood to meet your standards!' She glared up at the shadowy outline of his face.

'I thought pride was a bad and wicked thing. Or is that only when it comes attached to me?'

She was attached to him.

Mari's dark-fringed eyelids fluttered in recognition of the contact; she pulled in a tense breath and felt her insides quiver. At some point her left hand had joined her right on his biceps; she was holding on as though her life depended on it. There was no give at all beneath her fingers. He was hard and lean, strong like steel but warm. She could feel the heat through her fingertips, sending pulses of a dark warmth thrumming through her body.

'Your sort of pride comes from an arrogant belief that you are better simply because you are you. Well, he'll prove you wrong.' Forcing a drop of blood from a stone could not have required more strength than peeling back her strangely reluctant fingers; no matter how hard she tried they wouldn't budge. In the darkness with the wind rustling through the trees her heart began to thud in slow, heavy, hard anticipation.

Of what, Mari?

Time seemed to stop. She struggled, feeling things inside her that had built up begin to dissolve like sand. Control was slipping through her fingers… Shaking her head in rejection, she managed to break the contact and the spell. Holding her hands across her chest in a protective gesture, Mari took a lurching step back onto an uneven cobble and in the process triggered a powerful security light.

Without warning, the area was lit up, revealing that they had entered a courtyard. She lifted a hand to shade her eyes. The scent she had been conscious of was more pronounced, and she saw it emanated from the wild thyme growing in the cracks of the cobbles. The illumination after the anonymity of darkness made her feel exposed and horribly vulnerable.

This was her first real glimpse of the building. Its ecclesiastical origins were obvious in the architecture but the severity was softened by ivy on the walls and massive stone troughs beneath enormous mullioned windows that spilled out their impressive floral displays.

But it was not the geraniums that caught her attention, it was the expression in his eyes. Then the first raindrop hit her face, then another and another. The moment gone, she lifted her face to the heavens with a sigh. If ever a cold shower had been providential, this one was.

'This way,' he said, gesturing for Mari to go ahead of him into a wide, open porch made of oak that had silvered with age. 'Not a creaking door in sight.' He lifted the heavy latch on a massive door just to his right.

'What about bats?'

'Creatures with sharp teeth that launch themselves into the unknown with only instinct to protect them. I would have thought that you would feel something in common with them.'

Stepping under his arm and through the huge door that swung inwards as he lifted the latch, she found herself standing in a kitchen. She had barely taken in the room's massive proportions or the latest in kitchen design sitting cheek by steam oven with the original stone flags and heavy oak aged beams, when the niggle in her head solidified into a thought.

'How can this be a standing arrangement? You're meant to be on your honeymoon,' she blurted before she had considered the wisdom of reminding him where he might have been and with whom.

If the reminder had caused him pain, he was hiding

it well. His inscrutable expression told her little, but that could be due to the fact that the dark shadow on his jaw and chin upped the dark, dangerous, moody stakes considerably.

'The plan had been for Elise to fly out to Maldives immediately. I intended to join her at the weekend.'

Her eyes went round. 'She was going on honeymoon *alone*?' Wasn't that taking independence a bit far?

'You have a comment to—' He broke off as two small dogs burst into the room, yapping loudly.

Mari watched as he bent to pat them, speaking to them in Spanish and showing more warmth for the animals than she'd yet seen him display to humans. Maybe he preferred them—she gave a half smile, as she did herself on occasion.

He straightened up just as a larger dog the size of a small donkey padded at a more leisurely pace into the room. The dog wagged its tail and stood placidly while he stroked its ears.

'You were saying…?'

Caught staring and with what she suspected might have been a soppy smile on her face, she glared. 'I wasn't, but, if you must know, if my new husband chose to spend the first few days of our honeymoon with his grandmother rather than me, I'd not be happy.'

'Well, he hasn't, has he?'

It took her a moment to catch his meaning. When she did she flushed. 'This isn't the same. It's business.'

'So you would expect your *real* husband to put you ahead of everything else—work, family, duty…? My grandmother will not be here forever.'

'Well, I'd have come with you obviously… I mean, hypothetically and not you…'

Their eyes connected and she saw a flicker of consciousness in his dark eyes before he bent to stroke one of the animals at his feet who, barometers of his mood, began to yap.

Who said animals and children knew? she thought, watching as the larger dog began to lick Sebastian's hand with slavish devotion.

'What have you told your grandmother about me?'

Before Seb could respond a small bearded figure wearing a dressing gown and slippers shuffled into the kitchen. He carried a rifle, which he lowered when he saw Seb.

Deeply alarmed by the presence of a firearm, Mari had retreated instinctively behind the big scrubbed table. She relaxed slightly as the armed man wrung Seb's hand up and down and addressed him in excited-sounding Spanish.

Seb responded in the same language. He spoke for a few moments and then gestured towards Mari.

'Relax, it is not loaded.'

He said something to the older man, who looked Mari's way, laughed and put the rifle down on the table. He waved his hands, saying something to her slowly.

'Tomas says he is a harmless old man,' Seb translated, saying something that made the man laugh again. 'He says not to be afraid. I contacted him from the airport to say we would be arriving. My grandmother had already retired, but your room is ready.'

She managed a weak smile, which made the man tip his head in acknowledgement before he walked in the direction he had entered. Turning back, he gestured for her to follow him.

'Go. Tomas will show you to your room. If there's anything you want…'

Her eyes brushed his and she knew she was blushing. 'There won't be.'

CHAPTER EIGHT

THOUGH SHE WAS convinced she wouldn't be able to, Mari finally did drift off. She had no idea how long she actually slept, but it was still dark when she woke up, her body bathed in sweat, her heart thudding; only wisps of the nightmare remained. As they slipped away, reality came rushing in.

It was far worse than the creature that had been pursuing her in the nightmare.

'I'm married!'

It had been her secret dream, one she'd never even admitted to herself: her own home, a family and a man who she could drop her defences with, someone she could trust. She saw him in her dreams sometimes, but when she woke, his face vanished like smoke.

What have I done?

On the verge of panic, breathing hard, she sat bolt upright in bed, the crumpled sheets still clutched in her fingers.

She'd made a mistake, a terrible mistake! No, *mistake* wasn't a big enough word for what she'd done. *Eighteen months, Mari, that's all and then you can have your life back, and you'll never have to see him again*.

She flopped back and lay, one hand curved above her head, staring at the ceiling, seeing the shape of the dark exposed rafters against the white. Even though she had left the doors to the Juliet balcony open, the room was totally still, the only noise the soft swishing sound of the whirring fan. The silence pressed down on her like a weight. Her thoughts went round in circles like the fan as she tried to work out what was going to happen next.

She tried to block the negative thoughts. He liked dogs; he loved his grandmother... Oh, God, how had she got herself in this position?

She sat up again and her stomach rumbled. She knew from experience that a glass of warm milk was the only thing that would give her any more sleep that night. How far had it been to the kitchen?

She pushed back the covers, went across to her open case and took out the first thing she saw. It was a lacy shrug, and she pulled it on over the calf-length nightshirt she was wearing.

Outside her room the corridor, with its modern-art-treasure-sprinkled walls, was still lit at intervals by soft light from the wall sconces of beaten copper that had fascinated her when Tomas had led her this way.

Right, she was here, so what next? Right or left?

She remembered a wooden carving of a Madonna at the top of the flight of stairs, but there was no sign of that or, for that matter, the stairs, just lots of doors along both sides of the hallway, all heavy banded oak.

Right, Mari, it's hopeless. Go back to bed.

She ignored the good advice of the voice of common sense, unable to face the thought of lying there for the rest of the night. She was not ready to give up yet. She walked down to the end of the hallway that opened out onto what appeared to be a wrought iron Juliet balcony similar to the one in her bedroom, then with a sigh turned around.

She froze, the feral shriek of fear emerging from somewhere deep inside her… She opened her mouth and it just went on and on. The ghostly apparition screamed right back at her, and when she clamped her hand to her mouth, so did the spectral image that appeared to be floating in the distance.

Weak-kneed but smiling, she gave a shaky laugh of sheer relief, and her reflection, framed in the massive mirror that filled the entire wall the opposite end of the corridor, laughed back at her.

Shaking with reaction, she grabbed the nearest thing for support; it was the big heavy metal handle of the door she stood beside.

'Ghosts don't have red hair.'

Even if he had been asleep the scream would have woken him; the visceral sound of terror made his blood run cold.

'Mari…?' Heart pounding, grim faced, he threw back the thin cover on the big carved oak bed that, had the room not been vast, would have dominated it and leaped out.

Seb hit the ground running, moving as if the devil himself were at his heels. Luckily the room was not in total darkness; a small lamp still burned on a desk in the corner of the room where the book he had abandoned earlier lay open. It illuminated the corner, casting a series of dappled shadows across the vaulted ceiling.

He grabbed the heavy oak door, pulling it hard enough to wrench the ancient wood off its hinges; it held even though it carried the extra weight of someone who was attached to the handle.

Unprepared for the violent lurch, Mari found herself dragged without warning into the room behind the big door. She managed to keep her balance by holding the handle for dear life.

She barely registered the room itself. Her wide eyes developed a severe case of tunnel vision. Spectres were one thing, but flesh and blood and very real Seb clad in what seemed to be a pair of black boxers that hung low on his narrow hips and nothing else was another and far more disturbing proposition!

Her glance moved up in a slow sweeping arc from his bare feet. The farther she travelled, the hotter she got and the more squirmy the feeling in her stomach; her heart was beating harder than it had when she had faced the prospect of a ghostly haunting.

He was magnificent. He looked like some sculptured statue brought to life in glowing golden tones. There wasn't an ounce of surplus flesh on his body to blur the muscle definition of his ridged belly, shoulders and thighs.

Mari had no control over the series of breath-catching butterfly kicks in her stomach; she had never imagined a man could be so rampantly male. Before she had time or the ability to form anything approaching a rational thought, the cocktail of apprehension and excitement coalesced into a heavy ache low in her abdomen.

'I was looking for a glass of milk,' she heard herself say. 'I saw a ghost…' The protective screen of her lashes lifted. 'Not really but—'

'There are probably a few ghosts knocking around the place.' Holding her eyes, he pushed the half-open door closed with his foot.

Mari's glance went to the door and back to his face in a jerky, half-scared movement.

She was nervous. *He* was the one who should be feeling nervous, Seb thought… *Very* nervous. She was the one creeping around the place in the dead of night dressed like… Well, actually if she had not been dressed at all it could not have been any more provocative than the near transparent floaty number she had on.

The thing might be some modern take on Victorian primness, long-sleeved and fastened high at the throat with a little ribbon, but back-lit by the golden light from the lamp the white material became effectively transparent, the fabric so gossamer fine that if he tried, actually even if he tried not to, he could make out the dark perimeter of her rosy areola and the shadow between her thighs.

Mari ran her tongue across her lips to moisten them, struggling for some composure, and missing the resultant hot flare in his hooded glance.

She cleared her throat and turned her head, saying conversationally, 'My, this is a big room.' *Big room—my God, could I sound any more inane?*

He had a cameo view of the classic purity of her profile, her hair a glorious fiery halo glowing under the subdued artificial light in the hallway, appearing dark against the pale and almost transparent whiteness of her provocative nightclothes.

She brought to mind one of the impossibly desirable virgin sacrifices in an old-fashioned horror movie that every dashing hero was determined to rescue and the villain wanted to lay.

As a fist of lust tightened in his groin Seb discovered his sympathies lay with the villain. He dragged a frustrated hand over his hair and reacted to the emotions spilling from her with a sardonic smile. This woman seemed to go from one emotional crisis to another. Did she not understand the meaning of restraint?

He understood it—he valued it because he had seen the sort of selfish excess and chaos that came with it—and yet understanding the meaning of restraint did not prevent his rampant hormones exploding. They overrode his iron control as his dark smouldering stare travelled slowly over her body.

'So what couldn't wait until the morning? Where's the fire?' He struggled to inject some amusement into his voice, but the combination of vulnerability and sheer unadulterated feminine sexiness had got to him in a place Seb had thought he'd hermetically sectioned, sealed off... when...

He couldn't remember exactly what age he'd begun to worry he'd inherited his parents' genes. It had kept him awake nights until he had realised that recognising your weaknesses meant they weren't going to trip you up; it was all about control.

Control, he told himself, struggling to recall the meaning of the word as he breathed his way through the conflicting needs to comfort her and tear off her clothes and sink into all that luscious softness.

'Fire?' she echoed, blinking up at him.

If there wasn't one, there would be—she looked hot enough to ignite anything within a fifty-yard radius, he decided, dragging his gaze from the plumpness of her trembling lips as he reminded himself that she might be as attractive as sin and twice as tempting, but Mari Jones was not destined to share his bed. Even if it hadn't been essential that he kept things on a professional footing, she was not the sort of woman he would have entertained having any sort of relationship with.

Even so, it would have been much simpler if she had been unattractive or, for that matter, had one single flaw physically. His eyes moved from the fabric that had begun to cling with an electrostatic charge to the long shapely length of her legs, drawing his attention once more to the suggestion of shadow at their apex, and he forced himself to focus instead on the many flaws she had personality-wise.

The temper, he thought, sweating now, the mulish obstinacy, but most of all the sheer emotional excess in everything she did. She cried, she laughed, she screamed, she fought, and none of these things she did in moderation—he doubted she was even capable of it.

It didn't matter how pretty the packaging, he pitied the man who eventually tried to domesticate this red-headed witch. It would take a saint or someone equally capable of making a walk in the park a full-blown drama.

The thought triggered an image, a memory he'd thought he'd forgotten. The day his parents had managed to make such a harmless outing a front-page headline. The moment his mother had pushed his father into the lake had been caught on camera for posterity, as had been their making up, but what Seb remembered was the nauseous, churning sensation of shame in his stomach and the desire to vanish.

When he had run away from the scene, his passionately reunited parents had not noticed their three-year-old son was missing until later that night.

The memory enabled him to claw back some semblance of control. He took a step back and stood there waiting.

Her stomach went into free fall as she glanced up at him through her lashes. He looked like the modern-day flesh-and-blood version of some sort of Greek god in his close-fitting boxers that did a very poor job of concealment, his dark hair standing up spikily, his jaw deeply scored with stubble. A primitive thrill shot through her body as she drank him in, in great greedy gulps.

'I'm sorry. It was a m-mistake.'

'Probably,' he agreed huskily. 'Calm down, you're

shaking.' He caught her slim hands and pressed them between both of his.

The action might have been meant to soothe, but it did the opposite. Mari reacted to the contact like a cattle prod, throwing her arms wide to break the connection.

'I was looking for the kitchen. Do I go right or left?'

There was a long pulse of silence. It buzzed in her ears like a cloud of bees. Mari waited until it became unbearable.

'Did you hear what I said?'

He was so still, his stillness projecting a tension that was evident in the skin taut over his face. The tension emphasised each slashing angle and perfect plane. Even at a moment like this Mari marvelled that a man could be that beautiful, not just aesthetically because of the sculpted outline of his lips or the symmetry of his bold features, but it was the underlying earthy quality that charged the air around him.

'This has been a long day. I'll get Tomas to fetch you—'

'Don't wake the poor old man, just tell me how to get there!' She struggled to flatten the panic she could hear in her voice. 'Please, Seb.'

She shook her head resolutely, too stressed to interpret the strange way he was looking at her, wishing he'd put on some clothes.

'You'll get lost. I'll show you,' he said, but didn't move.

'No!'

'Yes!'

They both spoke and moved at the same time, colliding.

Maybe he was a bastard; maybe he was just his parents' son. *You couldn't choose your genes, and why fight nature*? he thought as he reached for her. 'Later,' he murmured as he pulled her up hard against him and, one hand on her bottom, the other tangled in her hair, he pulled her head back and fitted his mouth to hers.

She melted into him, soft and warm, her arms going up to circle his neck as she gave a little sigh into his mouth, and kissed him back.

The hungry kiss went on and on, until with a groan he pushed her away and turned his back to her.

'Get out of here,' he growled. 'While you still can.'

The sudden rejection left her trembling. She could still feel the strength of his arms, the hardness of his erection against her belly. Mari bit her lip, and thought to hell with pride—she didn't care if he knew. She didn't care who knew. She wanted him, and if that meant begging she would, even at the risk of rejection!

'Let me stay, Seb, please. I don't want to go.' She had never wanted anything less in her entire life; she felt dizzy with the sweet hunger that coursed through her veins.

He swung back, took one look at her standing there and with a groan swept her up into his arms and stalked across to the bed with his prize.

He laid her on the bed and knelt beside her, sweeping her wild curls from her cheek and forehead, smoothing them out onto the pillow. The expression of fierce concentration on his face made her stomach flip.

One hand beside her face, he bent down and kissed her softly, running his tongue along the inner surface of her lower lip, tracing the pouting outline before he slid inside, his tongue tasting every inch of the moist interior. His free hand moved to one breast, cupping it through the thin fabric, his thumb running up the lower slope to graze then tease the engorged rosy peak. Then he covered it with his mouth, wetting the fabric and drawing a hoarse cry of pleasure from her aching throat.

Mari arched up to him, tangling her fingers in his hair, feeling his big body curved over her, tensing a little as his hands slid under her nightshirt, up her thighs, then relaxing, her head pushing back into the pillow because it felt so good.

The sensations shooting through her felt like an electrical storm. The frantic feeling escalated until he suddenly levered himself upright.

Her blue eyes flew wide open in protest.

'You're overdressed.' At some point, Mari had no idea how or when, her little shrug had gone, but before she had time to consider how she felt about being naked in front of him he took the hem of her nightshirt in his two hands and pulled. The middle seam parted with a loud ripping sound until the only thing holding it together was the prissy little bow.

Holding her eyes with a wicked smile, he very slowly undid the bow and peeled the fabric apart, then her insides dissolved some more as she closed her eyes and breathed in his scent. Warm and musky, it was intoxicating.

'Look at me.'

She did, her dark lashes parting to reveal the blue languid depths.

Lust slammed through him with a force that threatened to stop his heart, and what a way to go, he thought, drinking in the sight of her gorgeous wanton beauty. Her body was perfect, from the fullness of her high, firm breasts to her long, gorgeous legs that he was imagining wrapped around him.

'Have you any idea how much I want you?'

'I have some idea,' she said, daringly running her hand up his hair-roughened chest and belly.

He gave a low laugh and removed his boxers, drawing an ego-enhancing gasp from Mari.

The first skin-to-skin contact caused a flash of heat within her; the burning continued to build as he kissed her while touching her everywhere until she was on fire. She tensed as he parted her legs, then relaxed as the liquid heat flooded through her body, the pleasure bordering pain, it was so intense.

When he flipped onto his back and fed her hands onto his body she began to eagerly explore his warm, moist skin, fascinated by the overwhelming masculinity of his body, moving across the hard contours of his chest and down over the ridged muscles of his flat belly, while he lay, one hand hooked behind his head, watching her through gleaming hooded eyes.

It gave her a feeling of heady feminine power to curve her fingers around the hard, hot, silky column of his erection and hear him groan with pleasure. So much so that when he removed her hands and pinned them above her head she gave a cry of protest.

'I need to save some for you,' he whispered in her ear. 'Let me give you it all, Mari.'

'Please, oh, please!'

Her frantic plea ripped a lusty growl from his throat as he kissed her.

'I didn't sleep with Adrian.'

He lifted his head, and dark eyes glazed with passion blinked down at her. 'Good.'

'Or actually anyone.'

For a moment he lay above her perfectly still, every sinew strained, then she heard him mumble, low and sounding like someone in pain. 'Too late… Do you want me to stop?'

'No…no…' She trembled in anticipation, relaxing at

the first shallow thrust, no explosion of pain just a feeling of intense pleasure... She let out a moan as he pushed deeper, his tongue sensually mimicking the more intimate movement of his hips.

Instinct made her wrap her legs around his waist as she arched under him, her body rippling tight around him, her fingers clawing at his back.

She clung to him as though he were the only thing stopping her vanishing into the sensual maelstrom that held her in its core as he was in her core, filling her with each stroke, pushing her higher and higher until— When it came, the fierce explosion drew a low keening cry from her throat. She grabbed hold of him and was saying his name over and over as she felt his hot release inside her, then he shuddered and rolled away.

For a moment she felt lost, then he pulled her to him, her head on his chest. She fell asleep listening to the heavy thud of his heartbeat.

He waited for the postcoital sense of *emptiness* that was the trigger for him to leave the warm bed. He never consciously acknowledged it, but if he had he would have considered it a perfectly reasonable price to pay for retaining control, keeping part of himself separate.

Instead Seb felt an utterly alien feeling of peace. Before he had a chance to ponder it another realisation hit: for the first time in his life, not only had he lost control, but he had not used protection. It had not been calculated, but some sixth sense told him that Mari was not going to give him the benefit of any doubt.

CHAPTER NINE

IN MARI'S DREAM someone was knocking on the door and calling…not her…not her name…and they were speaking a foreign language. It was fluid and nice to listen to but growing louder. Mari pushed free of layers of sleep and lay there smiling, feeling good, feeling… She stretched and muscles complained.

'Ouch!' She lifted a hand to smother a yawn and as the sheet, which was the only thing covering her, slid down she realised that she was naked… Naked, and where was she? The rush of recollection coincided with the door swinging inwards and then a woman's voice, the voice in her dreams, calling.

'Sebastian! Sebastian!'

Mari, now fully awake, responded to the emergency in the time-honoured fashion. She buried her head in the literal sense by sliding down to the bottom of the bed and heaving the covers that lay there in a tangled mess up over her unruly curls, tucking in her feet, her knees, her elbows…in an effort to disappear.

And that was it. Too late now to reconsider her actions—she was committed and also very uncomfortable.

In her concealment she held her breath, her heart thudding even faster at the thought of humiliating discovery. The muffled sound of heels on the floorboards got closer and the imperative tapping sound louder and louder. She held her breath in anticipation.

Totally convinced she was about to be discovered, Mari waited with the resignation of a condemned woman, wondering if it would be any less humiliating to reveal herself before her undoubted exposure. Should she test the theory and find out if a person really could die of humiliation, always supposing she didn't suffocate in the meantime?

Her oxygen-starved brain conjured up several versions of the headlines before she decided there probably wouldn't be any. Sebastian would hush it up to spare further embarrassment to the family name.

She was fast approaching the point where she had to breathe properly, even if that meant she was discovered. Just as her autonomic nervous system kicked in and she opened her mouth to gulp in air, the sound was muffled by the creak of a door opening.

'Mamina!'

She huddled down, knees drawn up to her chest, trying to make herself as small as possible, into what she hoped would be mistaken for a bundle of bedclothes by anyone who glanced that way. So long as she didn't do anything like… *Do not think about coughing, Mari*, she told herself sternly.

It was hot. Sweat broke out over her skin, making her situation even more miserably uncomfortable, and still they carried on talking… Didn't he appreciate her predicament? Her teeth clenched, she focused on breathing shallowly while, the longer the conversation went on between Sebastian and the woman he had called Mamina, the worse the skin-crawlingly awful prospect of discovery became.

How humiliating would that be?

Just when she thought it couldn't get worse, the muscles in her calf bunched, and she had to bite down hard on her lip to stop herself crying out. The torture of the cramp became so intense that she was on the point of revealing herself when the pain in her calf that extended all the way to the arch of her foot began to diminish at the same time she realised the flow of Spanish had stopped and the tapping sound was moving towards the door.

A final word from the strong-sounding female voice and the door closed.

'You can come out now.'

The pile of bedclothes moved, the sardonic smile on Seb's face deepening into a broad grin as her head emerged, her hair gloriously tousled, her face deeply flushed a clashing shade of pink. She looked a long way from the sleeping angel with the cut-glass features and perfect profile he had reluctantly left to sleep, and even more touchable.

Indignation aside, Mari felt a lurch in her chest. If he smiled more often she'd be in serious trouble… What was she thinking? She was in serious trouble. She managed to keep her scowl in place as he levered his broad shoulders from the wall.

'My grandmother.' Keeping his eyes on her, he nodded towards the door.

'I figured *that* part out. What I couldn't work out was why you kept her talking for hours. You had to know that I was…'

He arched a sardonic brow. 'Hiding under the covers?'

When he put it like that…

'What was I meant to do?' she fired back. Struggling to retain a modicum of dignity, she held the sheet at shoulder height and eased herself up carefully into a sitting position, keeping her legs tucked underneath. She flexed her toes to ease the discomfort in the leg that had suffered the cramp attack.

'Well, let me see…how about introduce yourself?' he drawled.

'Oh, yes, that would have been fun! I'm your grandson's wife. I didn't know if she knew, or what story you'd told her!' she flung back.

Mari's bitter thoughts mingled with lustful ones as her wilful gaze roamed over him. He'd obviously stepped straight from the shower; presumably that was why he had not heard the knocking from the adjoining bathroom.

He had paused to pull on a towelling robe. His skin, still dusted here and there with moisture, looked vibrantly gold against the black fabric. Loosely belted around his middle, the robe ended midthigh, and Mari's glance lingered a fraction of a second too long on the hard, hair-dusted columns of his heavily muscled thighs, triggering a tactile memory that pressed down on her as heavily and as hotly as his thighs had pressed her down into the mattress last night.

His dry voice cut into her carnal recollections. 'I thought you had a head-on approach towards most situations.'

Mari shook her head, the physical action helping to free her of the last clinging strands of the mind-numbing sensual fog. Adopting a cool expression, she lifted her chin and admitted, 'What seems a good idea at the time can seem a major mistake in the cold, clear light of day.'

An ice age could not have been more unexpected or as total as the frigid hauteur in his regard.

'So you have decided to draw a line under last night and call it a…mistake?' He sketched mocking inverted commas around the word as he bit it out through teeth bared in a hard, contemptuous smile.

Mistake? Wasn't that a pretty good analysis of the emotions that he'd been struggling not to analyse—his own 'head under the blanket' moment—as he'd stood accepting the sharp arrows of an icy-cold shower that had washed the scent of her off his flesh but not the memory of the sex, which seemed to have penetrated to a cellular level?

The light was not cold, but it was clear as it shone on her upturned features.

The fact that calling it a mistake was *exactly* what he'd been doing did not lessen the sense of outrage he recognised as totally irrational.

The confusion on Mari's face lifted. 'No…last night…' Did she regret it? 'I'm not talking about last night. I meant the wedding crashing. Last night was…' Her voice trailed away. She couldn't say *special* to a man who had enjoyed God knew how many last nights… Just sex? For her it had felt like making love. She gulped past a ridiculous desire to weep. She should be glad that her first time had been so special. She knew a lot of people who hadn't been so lucky, and some of the stories had not made her regret her abstinence.

But then, she hadn't known what she was missing; now she did. Oh, God, what had she done? She had no answer, just a total aching certainty that if she had the opportunity to do it again she would.

'One would not have happened without the other.'

Unsure what to read into this statement, she nodded cautiously and eased one leg out from under her.

'And you'd still be a virgin.' Just saying it gave Seb the same gut-punch feeling he'd had last night.

Of course, he'd have been lying if he hadn't acknowledged that the fact he had been her first, that he had taken her to places no other man had, aroused him on a primal level. And though they were damped down, he could only assume that it was those fundamental male instincts that were now responsible for the uncharacteristic possessiveness he felt when he looked at her and the anger he had experienced when he had thought she could dismiss the previous night with a shrug of her elegant shoulders.

In order to hide the depth of her discomfort, Mari rolled her eyes and sighed. 'Oh, are we going to have *this* conversation?'

'I'm sorry if you find this boring, but yes, we are.'

She scanned his lean face and tilted her head in an attitude of astonishment. 'You're mad at me for being a virgin?' The discovery drew a laugh from her parted lips.

'I'm mad at you for not warning me sooner,' he rebutted grimly. He swallowed and dragged a hand over his wet hair, slicking it back from his bronzed forehead. 'I could have hurt you.' Passion was one thing, but to be as full on as he had been with someone totally uninitiated sent a heavy slug of fresh guilt through his body. It should have been gentle and tender…

Tender. Hell, it shouldn't have happened at all!

He looked at the top of her shiny head; it was all he could see. Her chin had dropped to her chest and her hair had fallen in a silky curtain across her face. It made him think of how it had felt. The ends had brushed his chest as she had slid down his body… He inhaled. No, he would not go there, and last night was a one-off. He had not been thinking with his brain, but that would change.

He was totally clear in his mind about this when her head lifted. She parted the hair that had fallen across her face with both hands and looked up at him through the fringe of her long lashes with eyes that shone like sapphires and whispered huskily, 'You didn't.'

As her soft full lips quivered into a slow smile that was both sexy and vulnerable, Seb felt his heart crash into his chest wall like a sledgehammer. Utterly unprepared, he had no protection from the powerful feeling.

'That's...' Without warning, a moaning gasp was wrenched from her lips. The sound pierced Seb like a dull blade as he surged forward in response to the cry of pain.

'What's wrong? What is it?' He sat on the side of the bed where Mari had her knee drawn up to her chest in an awkward tangle of limbs and sheet, and was clutching her calf.

Her lower lip was clamped between her teeth; she was as white as paper. 'Cramp!' she managed through clenched teeth.

'Is that all?' His relief was mingled with sympathy. He knew from experience how incapacitating a cramp could be, especially if you were a mile off shore when it hit; fate in the shape of an off-course kayaker had been on his side that day.

'All?' she choked. If she could have thrown something at him, she would have.

The pain that had earlier been limited to her calf now involved her foot, as well. Her toes had been pulled upwards by the strength of the muscle contractions and she had grabbed them in an attempt to ease the agony.

'Maybe I've got a pathetically low pain threshold but it hurts!' she wailed, ashamed of the weak tears that were leaking from her eyes.

'I know, believe me I do. Let me.'

'I can't.' She shook her head, refusing to release her grip on her foot.

'You can.' He calmly pulled her leg across his knees and began to work on the knots of muscle; the action of his long fingers immediately lowered the level of pain.

'Let go, Mari.'

He'd said that last night and it had worked out okay then; also his air of cool competence was reassuring. Still tensing at every fresh wave of pain, she fell back against the pillows, arms crossed on her forehead, eyes squeezed shut.

His hands on the smooth skin of her calf, he watched the sheet drawn across her chest rise and fall, thinking about what was underneath... He had apparently been taken over by a teenager.

Her eyes opened wide in protest, and she gave a little grunt of pain. 'Hey, that hurt!'

'Just relax.' It was advice he struggled to follow. What the hell had he been thinking of last night...and what was he meant to do today? Pretend it never happened? The memory of his reaction when he had thought that was what she was suggesting was still fresh in his mind.

Relax. *Easy for him to say,* she thought, closing her eyes again as he pressed harder on a knotted muscle, smoothing the kinks.

She complained again with a mumbled, 'Ouch!' But she kept her eyes shut. The compulsion to tense was lessening as his clever fingers worked up and down her calf and into the arch of her foot until her calf was relaxed and the spasms in her toes had stopped.

'That's good,' she breathed. A cupped hand above her eyes, the other now unfurled on the pillow above her head, she forced her eyelids apart and looked at him through glittering blue slits. 'You can stop now.'

He didn't, though. He carried on massaging her legs, his hands running up the silky soft insides in a slow advance-retreat pattern.

Feeling the sigh that rippled through her body, he raised her feet to his lips and pressed a soft kiss to the blue-veined arch of her narrow foot. Who knew that a foot could be sexy?

Who knew, she thought, feeling herself sink into the mattress as delicious tingles zigzagged across her skin, that you had erogenous zones there?

'So how come you've never had a lover?'

She looked at him through her lashes. 'I have trust issues after a really terrible experience when I was being seduced. Actually, I was quite looking forward to it when this man appeared out of nowhere and called me a slut in front of the entire hotel.' She opened one eye to look at him in time to see a look of astonished comprehension flash across his face.

'I suppose he did me a favour, but I found it hard to think of it that way. It's bad enough discovering that the man you had spun romantic fantasy around was actually a sad serial seducer, but to have everyone there think I was some sort of slut who slept with married men...'

Seb closed his eyes and grimaced, seeing her face as it had been, no longer seeing the seductress mankind needed saving from but an innocent victim.

'He sounds a bit of a bastard,' he husked back throatily, as the things he had said came back in painful detail.

'Oh, they both were.'

'But six years, Mari...' he clenched out with a groan.

'Did I not say? I've a low sex drive.'

At her initial explanation his fingers had stilled. They moved again now, and the sound of his deep throaty laugh filled the silence, making the muscles low in her belly quiver.

'Oh, when you put it like that it's kind of obvious.'

She struggled to free her foot...but actually not so very hard, just a feeble kick, because his fingers were sliding higher now up the soft pale skin of her inner thigh, stroke then retreat, each time getting higher, but not high enough to satisfy the throbbing ache between her thighs. Her head turned on the pillow and she released a long, slow, sibilant sigh; the mixture of pleasure and frustration was exhausting.

'What the hell did you see in that creep?'

'I was eighteen, Seb. He singled me out from day one, encouraged me, took a real interest. A man had never done that before and I was flattered,' she admitted. 'And then one day I could see something was wrong. I waited after my tutorial and asked...' She lifted a hand to her head and groaned. 'I asked what I could do to help. It was then he admitted that he'd fallen for me. He'd been fighting it because he was my tutor and so much older. I was totally sucked in, and all the creeping around and secrecy seemed romantic.

'It turned out that everyone else but me knew that at the start of an academic year he had an affair with a new student. It was a big standing joke—I was the joke.' The look she flashed him was rueful.

'You mean he groomed them.' At his sides Seb's hands clenched into fists. If the guy had been there at that moment he would have... He took a deep breath. He wasn't here but Mari was.

He'd taken a virgin bride. *What have you done, Seb?*

'We were all consenting adults, there was nothing illegal and I was pretty stupid.'

'He used his position of authority and trust,' Seb condemned. 'It is appalling that the college authorities allowed it to happen.'

'Well, I don't expect they knew,' she observed fairly. 'And they don't allow it, not now. There was a massive scandal the next year as the girl he singled out for special attention after me attempted suicide. Luckily she didn't succeed, but he resigned shortly after that and I think his wife divorced him. Don't stop…' she pleaded, lifting herself up on her elbows as he swore his contempt bilingually.

His eyes followed the flow of her hair as it settled over her shoulders, but he couldn't push back the hard knot of ice-cold anger that her matter-of-fact retelling of the story had created.

'I'm sorry about the things I said that night. I had just come from a run-in with my mother, who was…well, being herself, and she never brings out the best in me.'

'It was a long time ago,' she said, looking at him curiously. 'And I had my revenge, so maybe we're even?'

'It left scars, and I was partly responsible for that.'

She held out her arms. 'You healed them, too, but there is this little one that I don't think you quite reached.'

A slow carnal smile curved his lips as he pulled her foot, tucking it over his shoulder. 'Now, where would that be?'

'Not sure,' she admitted thickly.

Seb found it, and he took his time about it; he had taken her to the edge twice before taking her over with him.

She flipped over on her stomach to look at him. 'I should go back to my room and get dressed.' She yawned without much enthusiasm. 'I don't know what your grandmother will think.'

'We are married, remember.'

A flicker of a frown disturbed her smooth brow as Mari looked at the ring on her finger, a plain gold band. 'But that's not real, is it? Though I suppose she won't know that.'

'My grandmother is no longer here. That is why she—' his lips quirked at the corners '—stopped by, to say goodbye. She is staying with her sister for a few days. Apparently my great-aunt has had a fall.'

'Is she all right, your aunt?'

'Apparently she was more concerned about the horse.'

'Your aunt was riding?'

'In this instance, falling.' He threw back the quilt that had moments before warmed both their bodies and casually vaulted from the bed, completely at ease with his naked state. Mari was less so, but her glance welded hungrily on his long, lean, muscle-toned frame, and she felt her insides heat.

Their glances connected and she lowered her gaze, clearing her throat. The microsecond of contact sent her nervous system into chaos… *My God, I've become insatiable.*

'You don't sound very worried,' she observed, visualising a scene in her head that involved him crossing the room and slipping back into bed…into her. 'Should she even be on a horse at her age?'

The reproach in her tone drew a laugh, and a look over his shoulder as he moved in the opposite direction to her imagination to the window, which he pushed wider, letting in the smell of jasmine with a soft breeze.

'Marguerite fully intends to die on one, as she will tell anyone who dares suggest she should slow down, but not yet, I think, though reading between the lines it sounds as though she was shaken.'

She glimpsed the concern behind the languid humour and touched the smooth skin of his back as he sat down on the bed to slide his jeans on before standing to zip them up.

'Why don't you hate me, Mari?'

She blinked, astonished by the question. 'Who says I don't?'

She glimpsed a strange look on his face before he turned and stalked across the room, making her think of a panther. 'Because you don't have it in you.' Although what he had to say might severely test that theory.

'I did crash your wedding and nearly cost you a billion dollars.'

'I tricked you into marrying me.'

'There have been some upsides to that,' she admitted, looking from his face to the tumbled bedclothes. At least in bed naked she had no trouble understanding him. 'And I'm not eighteen anymore. I knew what I was doing. I admit I never expected to enjoy anything about these eighteen months.'

Even from the several yards that separated them she could see the lines of strain around his mouth as he began to walk back across the room towards her, looking very like her mental image of a dark, dangerous pirate with his bare feet, rippling muscle, his chest gleaming gold and the stubble on his face giving him a dangerously attractive look of dissipation. In a fair world it would be illegal for a man to be this sexy.

So the world is not fair, Mari—deal and stop drooling! She was dragging her eyes clear of the open fastener on his waistband when he spoke, his deep voice just audible above the blood rushing in her ears.

'Has it occurred to you that the eighteen-month rule might be out of the window?'

Utterly confused, Mari searched his face, looking for a trace of the warm, sensitively passionate lover who had taught her so much about her own body in just one night, and morning…but he wasn't there. Just a sombre-faced stranger, not the man she had fallen… The blood drained from her face as she swallowed and thought, *No, I can't have… It's just sex. Very good sex, but just sex. Love is—*

'Unless you are on the pill?'

Too busy arguing with herself, she still didn't see where he was going with this. 'Why would I be?'

'I didn't use anything. You could be pregnant.' Her comment about not wanting children had not seemed relevant at the time; now it did.

His words hit her with the force of a lightning bolt. She gasped and hit back, fear making her voice cold. 'Do you make a habit of having unprotected sex with one-night stands?'

His dark eyes glittering, the sharply defined contours of his high cheekbones were accentuated by a dull flush as he ground out what she was assuming—no major leap— was a swear word and dragged a hand across his set jaw.

'It was a first. I'm sorry.'

She gave a sniff, feeling guilty now that she had lashed out at him. At the end of the day, she'd become just as caught up in the moment and had behaved just as reck- lessly as Seb had. 'So am I. It's as much my fault as yours,' she acknowledged.

Seb gave a hard laugh. 'I seriously doubt that many people would agree with you, and you are not a one-night stand. You are my wife.'

'For eighteen months…'

'Maybe.'

'What do you mean?' she demanded, gathering the quilt around her.

'I mean if last night results in a baby, that time limit vanishes. There is no way that my child would be brought up by another man.'

When she finally spoke, her voice sounded weirdly controlled, perhaps to compensate for the total chaos rampaging in her head. 'I'm not having a baby.' *And I'm not in love.*

'You're right. It probably won't happen. Why don't we deal with it when or if the time arises?'

She shook her head. 'You really are unbelievable. How am I meant to think about anything else now? It would be a disaster!' she wailed, thinking *disaster* was not a big enough word to describe being trapped in marriage with a man who didn't love you. She had always felt sorry for those people who 'stayed together because of the baby' and she didn't want to be one of them!

His jaw tightened. 'What are the odds?'

Confused by the abrupt question, she shook her head.

'Of you conceiving.'

'Oh.' She flushed self-consciously and did a quick mental calculation and swallowed. 'Pretty high,' she admitted. 'Why is this happening?' She pressed her face with her hands and released a muffled wail. 'I can't have a baby!'

'Calm down.' He sat down on the bed and brought her hands together, covering them with his. 'I know you don't want children but—'

'Who said I didn't want children?' she flared.

'You did.'

'Not my own—there are so many children out there who need homes. I'm going to adopt.'

He pressed his fingers to the bridge of his nose and closed his eyes, wondering if he could feel any more of a total bastard.

'What? What have I said now?'

He shook his head.

'So what now? You're the one who said he was good at thinking on his feet.'

The slow dangerous smile that split his lean face did not lessen the tension that drew the skin taut across his high cheekbones. 'I am thinking, but you are distracting me.'

She followed the direction of his gaze and pulled the quilt up over her breasts, before angling a hot-cheeked look of accusation at his face. 'You're thinking about sex at a time like this?'

'I can multitask,' he promised her. 'How does this work for you? We cut the honeymoon a bit short and go straight back to Mandeville, at least until we know for sure one way or the other. We'll need to consult with an obstetrician. There are probably a few things you should and shouldn't be doing.'

'Stop it. I am not some sort of…incubator!' A short while ago she had been a desirable woman he had wanted to make love to; now she was what…a mother?

A mother… A shiver of reaction worked its way through Mari's body as the words echoed in her head.

At least now she knew the answer to *one* of the questions she had been asking herself on and off virtually all her life. While she still didn't know what made any mother abandon her child, she did know that she never could.

Facing the slim possibility there might be a baby, Mari knew that nothing in the world would make her give it up. She knew, but what about Seb? Would he ask her to? Would he assume she'd have a termination?

'Don't be ridiculous! Look, I didn't plan on having a family now either, but—'

She wanted to cry, but instead she tuned him out. It was ironic really; she had guarded her heart so well all those years, and the first time she let down her guard… God, she had terrible taste in men. At least she hadn't fallen for him.

You keep on telling yourself that, Mari.

'What happens if I am pregnant? What, as a matter of interest, is your grand plan? I'm sure you've got one.'

'Isn't it obvious?'

She tensed. 'Not to me.'

'We stay married.' He angled a searching look at her face. 'You look surprised. What did you think I was going to say?'

She shook her head. 'What about love?'

'We are not talking song titles here, Mari. We are talking about giving our child, should there be one, a secure upbringing.'

'There might not be a child,' she reminded him. The addition was for her own benefit. 'Probably won't be.'

He nodded and looked at her. 'But until we know for sure... Mandeville?'

Reluctantly she nodded.

CHAPTER TEN

THE MOMENT THE private jet landed, Mari's phone began to ping. She fished it out and saw there were a dozen missed calls and twice that many texts, all from her brother.

She scrolled through a couple and found they were all much the same.

Where the hell are you? Come and rescue me, I think I'm dying, the doctors are quacks.

Her finger was poised above Dial when she paused.

Seb was a lying monster, but the law of averages dictated that even lying monsters were right sometimes. He had predicted that Mark would react this way, and she was conditioned to respond as she always did.

Was it time to break the cycle, not just for her but for Mark?

Very slowly she closed the phone and dropped it back into her bag. She knew that Seb was watching her but she refused to give him the satisfaction of knowing that she had followed his advice.

They had hardly said a word since they left Spain. Once or twice Seb had tried to initiate a conversation, but she had cut him off.

On the way across to the waiting limo she stopped and

looked up at him. Despite everything her insides quivered. He looked so incredible.

'I'm sorry I've been sulking.' Actually she had been punishing him for not being in love with her, which, when you thought about it, was pretty pointless. She should be grateful he wasn't pretending.

Seb tilted back his head and dug his hands into the pockets of his well-cut trousers, a smile chasing like a shadow across his sombre features.

'Had you? I hadn't noticed. I'm probably overreacting,' he admitted in return, 'but if we'd stayed in Spain my grandmother would have given us no privacy.' Which had been part of the reason he had chosen to take her there.

The idea that his grandmother's presence would have made it easier to keep her at arm's length, keep his hands off her, seemed frankly laughable now. He could see now that he'd been in denial about the strength of his attraction to her. Logically, taking her to his bed should have diminished that hunger, but if anything it had grown during the short time they had been together.

'*If* there is a child and that remains a massive if, there will be things we need to discuss without ears at doors. You'll like Mandeville. It's a great place for a child to grow up—there's plenty of room.'

The words came back to Mari as she got her first glimpse of the white Palladian mansion with its rows and rows of perfectly symmetrical windows. She snatched an awed breath. Plenty of room? It was the size of a city!

'Ever so humble, but home.'

He covered her hand with his; for a moment he thought she was going to leave it there, and then she didn't. His jaw clenched; the rejection, a small thing, had a sting that was out of proportion to its size.

Mari didn't look at him, just stared straight ahead

as she nursed her hand in her lap. 'This place is pretty daunting, the idea of servants and—'

'You'll be fine. I actually think you could cope with anything, and it is big, but that could work well. You can still have your privacy.'

'So you won't be here? No work, obviously...but when you say *space*, does that mean we won't be sharing a room?' She closed her eyes and thought, *Did I say that out loud*?

'Mari Jones, the first time I saw you I wanted you.'

Mari opened her eyes.

'And I still do,' said the man who was famed for playing it cool. 'We will be sharing a bed.'

He saw a flicker in her eyes and wondered if she wanted to hear something else. He took her hand and felt the zing of electricity shoot up his arm.

'The sex was sensational.' He wasn't in *love*, he was in *lust*. He didn't *need* her, he *wanted* her, and that made all the difference.

It was odd, Mari reflected—she hadn't even known until that precise moment how much *more* she wanted. Much more than what he was offering or would ever offer. It was not until she heard him carefully avoid the word and felt the pain of its absence that she stopped trying to pretend that she had fallen in love with him.

God, could life be more complicated?

Normally Seb could read her expressions, but he struggled to read the look she gave him, and was further thrown by the odd intonation in her soft voice when she spoke.

'How about we just enjoy ourselves?' she suggested easily.

He frowned. That was his line, and he felt irrationally irritated to hear her speak that way.

'Until we know for sure.'

He nodded and struggled to stifle a restless sense of dissatisfaction.

When she had first walked into the place Mari had been utterly convinced that she would never feel at ease in the dauntingly grand surroundings. The ballroom at Mandeville was straight out of a fairy tale, and the walls held the sort of art collection that a major gallery would envy, not to mention the massive leisure suite with a full-size swimming pool tucked away in the lower ground floor, but three weeks in Mari had adapted to the space and elegance with amazing ease.

It might be *unadapting* she had the problem with, she realised uneasily.

It was hard not to compare the life of a child growing up here with one growing up in her tiny fourth-floor flat—not that it was about money. Mari knew, none better, that it was love and security that really counted.

But Seb would make a good father. It wasn't just his genuine desire to *be* a parent; he had a lot to offer. Seeing him interact with his young half-sister, who obviously adored and respected him, made her realise how far out in her initial assessment of him she'd been.

And being around him so much Mari found herself falling deeper and deeper in love with him every day. Sometimes the sheer hopelessness of it all made her seek a quiet corner and weep, although that might be the hormones.

She knew that she was pregnant. She had known for a week now. The little changes—she had no morning nausea, thank God, but she'd gone off coffee completely, and her breasts were painfully sensitive.

She had not confided in Seb, who didn't even trust a

home testing kit. He insisted they have the test done by a Harley Street specialist, totally unnecessary, but she knew better than to try to dissuade him.

He'd been right. It had worked...worked *too* well really, she mused. It was all so *polite*. They hadn't had a single disagreement; there was no sparking off each other; it was all totally *vanilla*, which on the surface sounded good but in reality felt flat and unreal... Yes, that was the right word, *unreal*. There were times when she felt they were actors in a play, performing to an unseen script. She could only assume that was what he thought a good relationship should be.

The only time it felt normal was in bed. That was when the stilted politeness went out of the window, and it got raw and real... It was those nights that kept her going!

She was living for sex—that didn't sound healthy, but it was fun—while it lasted. And that was the point: how long would it last? Then they would be polite or maybe resentful strangers, the only thing holding them together a child.

When the consultant walked back into the office, Seb, who had sat in a chair opposite her trying to channel relaxed, surged to his feet.

'Congratulations.'

He had his back to her, so Mari couldn't see his expression, just the tension in his broad shoulders. It was gone when Seb exchanged a manly handshake with the other man and put a hand under Mari's elbow as she rose, as though she were already burdened by a pregnancy bump.

On the drive back he was unnaturally silent. It wasn't until they turned into the parkland that he slowed the car and stopped.

'Are you all right with this?'

She didn't respond.

'Aren't you excited?' With a frown he searched her face. 'Happy…sad…angry…?'

Crazily, she welcomed the shade of irritation that had crept into his voice.

'I already knew,' she admitted.

He stared at her for a moment before blasting, 'Then why the hell didn't you tell me?'

'Because you wouldn't have believed me!' she flung back, feeling her energy levels rise as she fed off the static charge in the air that had been so absent in the past weeks.

His head went down, concealing his face, but she could see his shoulders lifting as he took several long deep breaths. When he lifted his chin from his chest his expression was *pleasant*… Now, there was a word she had never imagined she'd think in the same sentence as Seb Rey-Defoe.

'You're right…' A muscle clenched in his lean cheek before he added, 'I'm sorry.'

She sucked in a furious breath, the anticlimax sending her spirits into a downward spiral. 'It was probably my fault.'

Hating the dispirited note in her voice, he bit back a retort. He really didn't know how long he could keep this up.

The harder he tried, the more distant she seemed to become. He had turned himself inside out trying to show her that living together did not have to be a constant battle. Did she appreciate how hard he was trying?

He'd have believed that she was indifferent to him if it weren't for the fact that she was so insatiable in bed, and utterly uninhibited. He lived for those nights!

'So I was thinking we're officially married now as opposed to being temporarily married.'

As opposed to what we'd have been if I weren't pregnant, she thought, looking out of the window to hide the hurt.

'There's a dinner at the end of the week, if you feel up to it—the royals are guests of honour.'

'I'm not ill, I'm pregnant.'

'Of course,' he said, reminding himself that he needed to show he could be sensitive to hormones...sensitive, but not mention them—not as easy as it sounded. 'I thought you'd like to officially be my hostess.'

'Fine.'

That word had come back to haunt her on several occasions since.

The brisk walk through the park was not as relaxing as she'd intended. It was hard to forget tonight and relax when you couldn't escape the reminder in the form of the magnificent facade of the house. It wasn't just geography—the gardens had been designed with the vast Palladian mansion as the focal point. Like disapproving eyes, the rows of windows seemed to follow her.

She brushed away the fanciful notion, laughing at her overactive imagination and frowning at her nerves. Under the calm exterior—actually she was no longer so sure her calm, approaching comatose attitude had fooled anyone—Mari was eaten up by nerves. She felt so out of her depth that she was a stumble away from gibbering terror.

'Don't be a wimp.' Above her stern voice the clock in the bell tower pealed out the half hour. With a deep sigh Mari squared her shoulders. She had timed it like a military operation so that she wouldn't be dressed too soon and waiting in the wings twiddling her thumbs while she watched the second hand tick. She quickened her pace—she didn't want getting ready to be a mad dash either.

The massive front door was flung open to allow access for the army of people who were preparing for this 'simple little dinner party'. Everyone had a task, and no one seemed to notice Mari as she walked through the marble-floored hallway filled with light streaming in from the cupola overhead.

The double doors to the formal dining room were still open. As she slowed then paused to watch the hive of activity, she felt more than a little like a child who'd sneaked downstairs to watch from a distance the grownups' party.

The long dining table was as much of a work of art itself as the massive chandelier that lit it. The place settings all arranged with geometric precision, the napkins all perfectly aligned, the glasses gleaming, it groaned with the weight of silver and crystal.

As she stepped into the room, one of the team of florists that had spent the afternoon filling the house with more than the normal quota of massive formal flower arrangements saw Mari and smiled a little nervously.

'Is there a problem, Mrs Rey-Defoe?'

The woman, a girl who was probably her own age, was waiting for her approval. The idea was somehow more shocking than the prospect of hosting a dinner party where the glittering guest list included several diplomats, a Hollywood A-lister, the witty writer of a political column and a scarily famous athlete.

Mari smiled. 'Everything looks marvellous. I wish I had your talent. All I can do is throw some flowers in a vase and hope for the best.'

'Oh, the natural look is very in at the moment.'

They both laughed, and as the conversation progressed

it turned out that the girl had been brought up in a village near to where Mari's foster parents lived. They chatted a while before Mari, conscious of the time, made her way reluctantly towards the curving staircase.

Her hand was on the smooth curving banister when she felt the change in the air and the familiar prickle on the back of her neck. She turned her head and knew he'd be standing there. Seb, already dressed for dinner and looking incredible enough to make her sensitive stomach do a double backflip. He was standing framed in the doorway of one of the many rooms that fed directly off the hallway. Through the open door she could see the book-lined walls of the library, which he used as a study.

Her fingers tightened, knuckles white on the banister. If theirs had been a normal relationship, she would have gone over and straightened his tie, which was of course already straight—everything about Seb was always immaculate, a fact that should not have made her throat ache but it did.

Hormones. The word, she reflected, had become a bit of a mantra. Every time she had a confused thought or feeling she fell back on the excuse. She was saying it a lot at the moment.

Seb watched the animation he had seen in her face as she'd laughed and chatted with the florist fade, replaced with a wariness that she seemed to reserve specially for him.

'I was just going to get ready,' she said defensively.

He shrugged, not concerned that she would keep him waiting, or that she would look anything less than incredible. Most of the women he knew would have spent half the day getting ready for a formal event, but he'd seen Mari step out of the shower, pull on the first thing that came to hand, run her fingers through her hair, gloss her lips with something clear and shiny that tasted of strawberries and look breathtaking.

'It was just the florist lived near the village where my foster parents…'

He dragged his eyes from the temptation of her strawberry lips and cut across her rambling defence with a flash of anger. 'You think I have a problem with you talking to someone who arranges flowers? Do you really think I'm such a snob?'

'Not a snob, no,' she admitted.

He treated everyone the same, which didn't mean he hung out with the staff; apart from a handful of close friends, he appeared to keep everyone at a distance regardless of their social standing. And he didn't seem to notice how hard people worked to please him, and they did. She'd seen it time and time again—they went the extra mile to get his approval.

Had she become one of them?

'So you'd be fine with me seeing Annie socially… The gardener or the cook or the—?' She paused and dragged in a deep sustaining breath thinking, *Calm, Mari, calm.*

'I think they would be uncomfortable with the situation. Whether you like it or not, your position—'

Anger, sudden and hot, spurted up. He didn't have a clue! 'What position?' she blurted, and saw shock in his face but she couldn't stop herself. Weeks of saying the right thing had made her feel like a ticking bomb.

'I've been stuck in this place all week.' Her hand lifted in a graceful gesture encompassing the stately elegance around them. 'The only time I see you is in bed. I miss my work…the children. I'm lonely. I'm bored…' She clamped her lips over the quiver of embarrassing self-pity and steeled herself for his response, fully expecting him to point out that there were no bars on the windows, there was no bolt on the doors.

In her head she could hear him saying, *If it's so bad, what's keeping you here*?

Would she be brave enough to answer him honestly, admit that she stayed for him?

To be near him.

To hear his voice.

Would she ever be brave enough to admit that she loved him?

Well, she didn't find out, because once again she had made the mistake of thinking she could anticipate his reaction.

Lonely—the catch in her voice, all his internal debate, all his endless mental pro and con lists suddenly meant nothing, because he could see himself losing her. As he imagined her walking out of the door, out of his life, the knot in his stomach was fear. He called himself all the insults in his vocabulary, which was extensive, and still they didn't begin to describe what an utter fool he'd been.

His first mistake had been thinking he could take emotions out of marriage; on paper it had equalled no tensions. He had wanted his life to resemble the clear, uncluttered lines of his desk—neat rows, square edges, controlled, no mess—and it could. It *had* been, but as he looked into Mari's stormy, beautiful face, he made a life-changing discovery—he no longer wanted it to.

Love— He had avoided even thinking the word. Love was what had changed everything, had changed him.

He didn't want a suitable bride, someone who said the right things and agreed with everything he said. He wanted Mari. Not the Mari that said what she thought he wanted to hear, but the one who blurted out the first thing that came into her head and argued the hind leg off a donkey just for the hell of it—he wanted *his* Mari back!

'You are totally wrong.'

Hanging on the banister, she took two steps up then, unable to stop herself, one down, but she didn't lower her wary guard as she struggled to read beyond the cool detachment of his manner, to read the expression in his deep-set eyes.

'I am?'

'About me and us… Your position is…' He stopped, his dark brows twitching into a straight line as he framed his suspicious question. 'Has anyone here treated you with less than respect?'

The negative shake of her head lessened the explosive quality of his hard stare; the nerve in the hollow of his clenched cheek stopped jumping.

'We should stay married.'

'I know, because of the baby,' she said dully.

'Because you are you and I am…' He sucked in a deep breath, then let it out slowly before saying in a voice that vibrated with emotion, 'Lonely.'

Mari watched in disbelief as, having dropped the un-exploded conversational bomb at her feet, he turned to go back into the study, pausing to call casually over his shoulder, 'Join me here for a drink when you're ready—tonic, lime and lots of ice?'

The door closed.

CHAPTER ELEVEN

WHEN THE FEELING returned to her paralysed limbs, Mari flew on an adrenaline rush high up the stairs two at a time, her heart thumping against her rib cage.

By the time she reached the bedroom where her clothes were laid out, ready, she had come back down to earth. He had waited to say this until *after* he knew about the baby—was that significant?

And after all, what had he said— *Lonely...?* It might just mean he was at a loose end.

Was she seeing and hearing what she wanted to?

Fingers pressed to her temple, she closed her eyes and willed the inner dialogue to stop before her head exploded, which was not a good look for the perfect hostess.

Her eyes shot wide as she pushed up the cuff of her sweater to see the time.

'Oh, God!'

She stripped off her clothes as she walked across the room. She entered the bathroom, where she proceeded to chuck half a bottle of some expensive bath oil in the bathtub and turned on the taps full. While the tub filled she piled her hair on top of her head, skewering in the pins carelessly before lowering herself into the water.

By the time she had stepped into the black number that managed to be both classy and extremely sexy, Mari had managed to achieve a degree of composure, even if it was skin-deep. Underneath she was so wound up she wasn't sure if she'd be able to wait for him to explain what the hell he had meant. She had a horrible feeling that the moment she saw him she was going to blurt out something terminally stupid like 'I love you!'

Well, he'd either run, laugh in her face or…anything was better than this terrible uncertainty.

Seb took the box out of his pocket. It should have been a ring, he thought, snapping it open to glance down at the string of sapphires that had caught his eye as he passed a shop. He could see them around her lovely neck, the colour a tribute to her eyes. He slid the box back into his pocket and pushed his head into the big wing-back chair that faced the fireplace.

Some inner sixth sense made him glance up just as a figure appeared outside the open French doors. The overalls the man was wearing were emblazoned with the name of the catering company who had been brought in to bolster his own kitchen staff.

The obvious assumption would be that he had lost his way, but his furtive manner told another story. As Seb made these observations, the man looked over his shoulder to check there was no one to see him before he stepped inside the room.

'Very nice,' he said softly as he looked around the book-lined room.

Interesting, Seb decided—the mirror was angled in a way that made it possible for him to watch the man without the intruder being aware of his presence in the room.

The figure in the overalls was moving with increasing confidence now; he even began to whistle a slightly off-key tune through his teeth as he walked around the room picking up objects, turning them over like an expert before replacing them or, in one or two instances—the man definitely had an eye or, as his grandmother would have put it, he knew the cost of everything and the value of nothing—putting them in his pocket.

He spotted the cupboard containing Seb's grandfather's collection of Georgian silver, smiling broadly as he did so, and Seb had his first full-face look at the guy.

A shaft of startled recognition turned Seb's curiosity into something far more personal—something cold, very cold. Ironically at one point the man had picked up the file that told Seb all he needed to know about his intruder and a lot he didn't want to know about George Laxton... Francis...Richie...Griffiths, a small sample of the aliases that this moderately successful conman went by.

The contempt etched on Seb's face gave way to alarm; his eyes went to the door that Mari could walk through at any moment.

That was one introduction he didn't want to make.

If ever he felt a twang of conscience about his decision to keep her in the dark, he reminded himself that if Mari had wanted to know her parentage she would have put the wheels in motion herself, so what she didn't know... *It would hurt her.*

When he'd decided originally to look into her parentage he had debated the ethics of it, but had gone ahead despite his misgivings, tempted ultimately by the idea of producing the loving mother he knew Mari secretly longed for.

When he'd got the information back it had turned out to be no fairy-tale ending: her mother had died from an accidental overdose after she had abandoned her children.

But Amanda was a victim, too, in a way. Her married lover, Mari's father, had served time for bigamy, and was the true villain of the story. So what was that villain doing here in his home?

It was a question for another time. Right now, the priority was to make sure that his and Mari's paths did not cross.

He was halfway to his feet, unnoticed by the figure, who was now efficiently emptying the contents of the silver cabinet into his capacious pockets, when the door did open.

Pausing, Seb sank back down into his concealment. It was hard to watch and wait, but if he wanted this man out of Mari's life forever it would be useful to have a bargaining chip. A pocket full of valuables and the threat of a prison term could be that lever.

Mari paused outside the door. Should she knock? No, she decided, boldly pushing it open, that would be too 'schoolgirl at the headmaster's office'.

'Oh!'

It was a massive anticlimax—the library was not empty, as a middle-aged man, one of the caterers, was there, but of Seb there was no sign.

The last thing she wanted to do was hang around, as she wanted to find Seb, but politeness made her linger. As she did the oddness of this man's presence struck her. Why was he here, in the room that was Seb's private sanctum?

The man, who was staring at her a little too intently for comfort, showed no sign of filling in the blanks without a push.

'Hello, can I help you...?' She stopped, her smooth brow furrowing as she scanned the stranger's face. She was pretty sure she had never met him but...

'Have we met already? You look a little familiar...'
The likeness almost in her grasp, it slipped away.

The man grinned, and for no reason at all a frisson
of unease slid down Mari's spine. Struggling against a
growing antipathy, she smiled weakly back, but also took
a cautious step back towards the door.

'Now, that is nice—early Georgian. A real collector's item.'

To Mari's utter amazement, without even trying to
hide what he was doing, the man slipped the miniature
he had held out to admire into a pocket in his overalls,
one that she noticed was already bulging...with other
stolen items? The bold thief was either mad or... Actually he was obviously mad, but not, she hoped, violent.

'That's stealing. Put it back immediately and we'll
forget all about it!'

'Stealing...?' The man rubbed his hand along the goa-
tee he sported. 'Now, me, I like to call it a redistribution
of wealth.' He bared his yellowy teeth in a cold smile.
'I'd know you anywhere, darling—you're the living spit
of your mum.'

Mari, who had moved towards the door to call for help,
froze; the colour drained from her face as she spun back.
She could hear the pounding of her heart in her ears. It
sounded like the waves crashing on a distant seashore.
'You know my m...mother?'

'Knew. Amanda is no longer with us, sadly.'

'She's dead.' Her thoughts whirled, an unrelenting
flow of question marks running through her head.

Was he telling the truth? What reason did he have to
lie? 'My mother was called Amanda?'

'You're a lot bigger than her. She was a tiny little
thing, except of course when she was carrying you and
your brother.'

For a few moments she'd had a mother. It was crazy to feel bereft, but Mari did. A solitary tear slid down her cheek. While she hadn't known, there was always the hope that one day their mother would come looking for them… She would explain why she'd had to abandon the babies she loved. It had been a childish game she had played, one she should have put away with her dolls, and yet she had clung to the comfort the possibility offered, even though she knew deep down that it was never going to happen.

Now she knew for sure it was never going to happen.

'Don't look so sad, sweetheart.'

'Who are you?'

White-knuckled hands gripping the leather armrests, Seb closed his eyes. Keeping his anger in check was taking every ounce of his energy. He knew what was coming and he couldn't stop it. He had to let it run its course and then be there for her. He ached for her pain—as if she hadn't had enough pain in her young life.

'I'm hurt you don't recognise your old dad.'

Mari's eyes, very blue in her paper-white face, widened. She stood still as a statue, and she shook her head in a slow negative motion of denial; he couldn't be her father.

'I think you'd better leave now,' she said firmly. 'Before I call Security. Just put the miniature down and walk away.'

'My, quite the little princess, aren't we? But you've done well for yourself,' he conceded. 'It has to be said you've really fallen on your feet.' He looked around the room and gave an approving nod.

'If you don't leave now, I'm afraid I'll have to report you to your employer.'

He gave a hoot of laughter; the sound was not pleasant.

'I'm not on the payroll, but this—' he touched the logo emblazoned on his chest with a touch of smug pride in his voice '—made it a lot easier to get in here.'

'You're not my father.' *Say it often enough and you'll believe it, Mari.* Silencing the voice of her subconscious but not the quiver of uncertainty in her voice, she lifted her chin. 'I don't have a father.'

'Look again, my lovely.' He pointed to his face, watching hers, his narrow eyes no longer smiling.

Startled as much by his change of accent as the invitation, she allowed her eyes to rest on the face of the man who claimed to be her father, which was ridiculous. He was nothing like any of the visions she had of her parent. She and Mark had always... Mark. Pressing a hand to her stomach in an effort to counter the sick churning inside, she understood why his face had seemed so familiar. It was no individual feature, nothing was identical, similarities were blurred, but it was there in the slant of the eyes and the curve of the lips, though her brother's was fuller and inclined to petulance and not meanness.

She lowered her lashes in a protective shield, but not, it seemed, before the man—she couldn't even think of him as a father—read her expression.

He gave a crow of triumph.

Pride came to her rescue. She lifted her chin and looked at him levelly. 'Why are you here?'

'To see my daughter.'

'After twenty-four years?' She eyed him warily, struggling not to show the fear that was building inside her, focusing instead on her anger. 'You know *nothing* about being a father, a parent,' she flashed, smiling as she realised that her child would have a father, the sort of father who would give his life for his child.

'Don't worry. I don't want to hang around any more

than you want me here,' he snarled, visibly unsettled by the change in her manner. 'It's just I'm a bit short of cash at the moment and you're... We could call it a loan.'

Mari felt physically sick. This man was her father... She gave a shudder of revulsion and wondered when this nightmare would stop. 'I don't have any money.'

'But your husband does—pots of the stuff.' He rubbed his hands together in gleeful anticipation of the luck that had come his way.

'How did you find me?'

'Saw your picture in the paper, knew you the moment I saw who you were—amazing. You were an ugly little thing when you were born, red and screaming.' He gave a shudder of distaste.

'I have no money,' she repeated flatly.

'But you can get it. I don't think your posh husband is going to be quite so keen if he finds out your dad has a prison record. Can't you see the headlines now?'

This overt attempt at blackmail took her breath away. She looked at him in utter disgust. It was not often that you came across someone without a single redeeming feature, but it seemed that her biological father was one of those people. It was hard to face, but it was the cold, stark truth, and better to face it and move on.

A great sentiment, but at that moment all she wanted to do was weep until she had no tears left.

'Go to hell,' she said conversationally.

'I don't think you quite understand—'

The sound of a chair scraping the floor made parent and child spin around.

'No, it is you who do not understand. How long did you go away for the last time—five, out in two? I think you'll find that the law is less sympathetic to blackmail... With your record what are we talking, fifteen...?'

'Now, hold on, I came here to see my little girl,' he blustered.

Seb took a step closer, towering over the older man not just in his physical presence but his character. 'Not your little girl, *my* woman. You will empty your pockets, you will leave now and you will never come back. Believe me, you'll live to regret it if you don't.'

Looking visibly shaken, the older man began to back towards the door. Once there he raised his fist and shook it at them both. 'You'll be sorry when I sell my story.'

'I'm sorry.'

Seb turned, the pallor of her face causing him a spasm of alarm.

'What if he does?' she said, struggling to control the bubble of hysteria she could hear in her voice. 'The royal deal.'

'Forget him…' he roughed out. It was Mari he was worried about. 'Forget the bloody deal.'

She blinked, misunderstanding him. 'Of course, the dinner.' She took a deep breath. 'People will be arriving. We need to greet them. Don't worry, I won't let you down.'

'It doesn't matter…'

He was talking to air, as she had whisked out of the room and straight into the royal party.

Jaw clenched in frustration and left little choice, Seb painted on a social face and followed her.

Ironically, after dreading it Mari found herself dealing with the dinner without even a flicker of nerves, because she had bigger things to worry about now than using the wrong fork or forgetting the name of a famous guest.

She knew it was only delaying the inevitable, but as far as she was concerned it could go on forever. There

was zero point pretending—she'd seen the seething contempt in Seb's eyes when he had given her father his
marching orders. In Seb's eyes she was tainted. Where
did that leave them?

Nowhere good.

The royal prince seated to her right said something
and she smiled and nodded, not having a clue what he
had said, but glad of the opportunity to look anywhere
but at Seb. Normally at ease in any social situation—she
had always envied him his poise—he had barely said a
word to anyone all night.

'You are a lucky man, Seb.'

Seb tore his eyes from Mari and wondered why the
hell it had seemed like a good idea to have her seated at
the opposite side of the table. This damned meal was just
going on and on forever.

'I know,' he said, thinking better late than never. Gutless, he thought in self-disgust. *I've been bloody gutless.*
His way of dealing with his feelings for her, his solution,
had been to quash them... *Gutless!*

'Give the chef my compliments.'

'Sure,' Seb returned as the waiter took away his un-
touched plate, cutting off for a moment his view of his
wife. His wife sitting there looking poised as a queen
while inside she must be... Pride and love welled up in
his aching throat. While he was eaten up with shame that
he'd not been able to protect her from the truth, at least
he could protect her from anything that waste of space
imagined he could do. The moment this damned thing
was over he'd tell her.

It was not the only thing he planned to tell her.

'A toast to our lovely hostess.'

Seb, fighting a losing battle to control his impatience

and frustration, closed his eyes and thought, *Not another one*!

·   Maybe he said it out loud, because the woman to his right laughed. Frankly he was past caring.

Her scattered wits were dragged back to the moment and the toast directed to her. Mari bowed her head in what she hoped passed for gracious thanks and…there was nothing, just a deep wrenching pain that made her cry out and bend forward, tumbling into blackness.

Mari heard voices but didn't open her eyes. Her head felt as though it were filled with cotton wool.

'Where am I?' She lifted a hand to her head and thought, *My God, I'm a walking, talking cliché.*

Except she wasn't walking; she was lying in bed. The sudden pain in her hand made her lower it; squinting at the drip brought the memory rushing back.

'The baby?'

Seb was there; maybe he'd been there all along. He didn't say anything; he didn't have to. It was there in his face.

'I'm so sorry.'

He took her hand, the one that didn't have the intravenous drip attached, and squeezed gently. She looked fragile enough to shatter, like a piece of semitransparent porcelain. 'It'll be fine.'

He clamped his jaw and swallowed the aching occlusion in his throat. It would be; it *had* to be.

For a time after the nightmare ambulance journey, when they had arrived at the hospital and he had been sidelined as the medical machine had swung into action, he had actually thought he had lost her.

The memory was enough to return the grey tinge to his skin. He braced his hand on the metal bed frame to stop it shaking as he fought his way clear of the expanse of aching empty darkness.

It was a place that he never wanted to visit again.

He never wanted to think of the precious moments they could have had, moments he had wasted because he had refused to accept that there were some things you could not control—like your heart.

Mari sighed and closed her eyes. When she woke Seb was still there, the shadow on his chin was darker and more pronounced and he was still wearing his dinner jacket.

'Why haven't you been home?' Then she remembered it wasn't her home and she wanted to cry. Instead she sniffed.

He smiled and looked beautiful and haggard as he caught her small hand between his. 'I didn't know what you'd get up to if I wasn't here.'

She struggled into a sitting position. 'I'm so sorry, Seb.'

'*You're* sorry?'

'Ruining your dinner. The baby, my father, every-thing, and don't worry, I know what you're going to say.'

He arched a dark brow and looked at her really strangely, but that might be the drugs they'd given her. She did feel a bit…floaty.

'You do?'

'Conman, jailbird father…' She forced back the rush of emotional tears that welled in her eyes by the sheer force of her will, and delivered in a carefully flat voice, 'No baby, the eighteen-month rule kicks in…' Her pale lips ghosted a smile. 'No-brainer?'

The smile just about broke his heart. With her hair pulled back by a nurse into a ponytail she looked so young, so fragile and so beautiful it hurt…*literally* hurt, a physical pain. Was this heartache? Before she came into his life he hadn't even acknowledged he had one; now he could barely think a sentence without referring to that organ!

'Get Sonia to pack my things. I'll go straight back to the flat,' she offered bravely.

'The hell you will!'

Her eyes widened; he wasn't being nice to her. 'I'll miss this,' she sighed.

'What?'

'You being a total jerk. Could you pass me some water? I can…' Despite her protests, he held the glass to her lips.

He sat down beside her, making the mattress give. 'I think we should talk about it, don't you?'

She squeezed her eyes closed and shook her head. Talking about it was the last thing she wanted to do. Her baby was gone, and there was just a big black gaping hole.

'Look, I know you feel obliged not to throw me out because I've just come out of hospital, but I will be fine.'

'You're not fine.'

His loving tone brought tears to her eyes. 'And he'll do it, you know…my father, and it will be much easier for you to distance yourself from the scandal if I'm not here. In fact, if I'm not here there won't be a story.'

'I don't care about a story.'

'You do. My father is a criminal.'

'Yes, he is, which makes him very vulnerable to… *manipulation*.'

'I don't know what you mean.'

'I know, that's what I love about you, but let's just say that I have a feeling your father will be making a new life quite soon in Argentina.'

'He won't go.' But, God, she wanted him to. Did that make her a terrible person? Her own father…?

Seb gave a wolfish smile and kissed her. 'I can be very persuasive.'

'Well, even if he does go, I'm still his daughter, a bastard.' She lifted her teary eyes to his. 'I think our mother… I think she would have kept us if she could have, but he…'

'I think your mother wanted you to have a better life than she had.'

Mari nodded. 'And I have.'

He entwined his fingers in her small pale ones and lifted her hand to his lips, promising fervently, 'It's going to get even better, I promise.'

'There's no baby. You don't have to pretend.'

'The only thing I've pretended is that I didn't love you, but I do. You're my heart and soul, Mari.'

She looked up at him, wonder shining in her eyes like stars. 'You're not saying this because of the mi…mi…'

He squeezed her hand. 'Miscarriage.' He watched her wince and said calmly, 'We'll adopt. I've been thinking about it and you were right. Why bring a new baby into the world when there are so many children out there that need homes? We could adopt two, three if you like.'

'But you want a baby?'

He bent and kissed her lips with a tenderness that brought a fresh rush of hot, emotional tears to her eyes. 'I want you more. For a while back there…' His voice broke and with a groan he squeezed his eyes closed.

Mari watched, her heart thudding fast in her chest as he struggled for control, able to *feel* the intensity of his emotions. 'Seb…?' She stroked his hand.

At the light touch his eyes opened. 'Sorry, but…' He swallowed hard before continuing, 'You had lost a lot of

blood, and I could never… I don't want to run the risk.'
Fixed on her face now, his dark eyes held a shadow of
the fear he had felt as he finished in a throaty whisper,
'I couldn't go through that again, Mari.'

She started to weep in earnest, great gulping sobs that
shook her. 'You really love me?'

'I adore you.'

'But you were nice and polite to me.'

He burst out laughing. 'I promise I will never be polite to you again.'

She took his hand and lifted it to her lips, pressing a
fervent kiss to his palm before spreading his long fingers
around her cheek. 'I love you, Seb, so very much, but I
can't stay married to you.'

Beneath his confident smile there was a hint of wariness as he asked, 'Why?'

'Because you're a Defoe and your name means a lot to
you, you're proud of it and so you should be and I'm—'

'You're stupid,' he completed lovingly. 'I am proud.
I'm proud of having the most beautiful woman in the
universe as my wife.'

'I love you, Seb.'

'We have a lifetime to love. Right now you need to
sleep.'

Mari struggled to keep her heavy eyes open. 'I can't,
I want—'

'Don't worry, I'll be here when you wake up. I'll use
the time to plan our wedding.'

Her tired eyes opened. 'We're already married.'

'I want to do it right this time… You deserve everything, my darling. A church, the dress, flowers, your foster dad to give you away. They were here, by the way,
to see you, and Mark sends his love. Fleur is outside in
the waiting room.'

'How about your parents?'

He shrugged. 'Why not? What is a wedding without a scandal? Though you do realise that no one will be looking at us with them there?'

Mari gave a watery smile; her eyes filled with tears that slid down her face. 'That would all be lovely,' she agreed. 'But all I really want, Seb, is you.'

He bent and pressed a long loving kiss to her pale lips. 'You've had me from the moment I saw you. I was just slow catching on.'

EPILOGUE

'LOOK AT YOUR SISTERS.'

Seb lifted his son, Ramon, up to see the babies sleeping side by side in the crib.

The toddler's eyes were wide.

'Can I touch?' he whispered.

Seb nodded, his heart swelling with pride as he watched his son touch a gentle finger to each baby's nose.

'They look like Mummy,' he said wonderingly as he stared at their golden-red curls.

'They do,' Seb agreed.

'Who do I look like, Daddy?'

Seb swallowed the lump of emotion in his throat. It was sometimes hard to believe how lucky he was. The early months of their marriage had been marvellous. After a fairy-tale wedding and extended honeymoon Mari had returned to her job at the school, which had accepted her back with open arms, scandal forgotten, after they realised she was married to the family who funded ten scholarship places.

But in the midst of their happiness, the shadow of the baby they'd lost had hung over them. It had been the arrival of Ramon, who had been one when they had adopted him, that had chased away the shadows, though not the precious memory of the baby they had lost.

He had been more terrified than he thought possible when Mari had fallen pregnant with twins. She, who had been working part-time since the adoption went through and with typical selflessness, had given up work immediately in an effort to ease his fears. If he hadn't had to keep it together for Ramon, Seb really thought he might have fallen apart. The little boy was a blessing in every way, and now they had two gorgeous daughters.

'You look like your birth mummy, Ramon, who loved you very much.'

'She went to live with the angels.'

'She did,' Seb agreed. 'Now, quiet, we don't want to wake the girls or Mummy, do we?'

Seb pressed a kiss to the forehead of his sleeping wife and left the room hand in hand with his son.

Outside, his brother-in-law, on the crutches he was due to exchange for a stick, stood waiting with his wife—Mark had married his nurse—and Fleur, who was talking to Mari's foster parents.

'You can go in,' Ramon told them all importantly. 'But only if you're very quiet—right, Daddy?'

'Right.'

'And we're proud as Punch, aren't we?'

'We are,' Seb agreed, looking through the window to where his wife slept. 'Very proud and very, very lucky.'

* * * * *

A TASTE
OF SIN

MAGGIE COX

To Karen Middlemiss at the MS Therapy Centre.
Whenever we speak you help me make peace
with this condition and remind me that life
is for living whatever our challenge.
With love and blessings, Maggie x

CHAPTER ONE

ROSE WAS STANDING by the window, mesmerised by the steady rain that hadn't let up all morning, when a gleaming black Mercedes drew up in front of the antiques shop and effortlessly glided to a stop.

It was just like a scene from a movie and she was immediately riveted. Inside her chest her heart thumped hard, because she knew it was the visitor she'd nervously been anticipating… *Eugene Bonnaire.*

Even the name gave her chills. He was one of the country's wealthiest restaurateurs, with an uncompromising reputation for getting what he wanted, and when Rose's boss, Philip, had put the beautiful Thames-side antiques shop he owned up for sale the businessman had wasted no time in declaring his interest.

Not for the first time that morning she wished Philip could be there alongside her, but sadly his already failing health had deteriorated and he was now in hospital. In his absence, he had asked Rose to handle the property's sale on his behalf.

The responsibility was a bittersweet one. Not just because he was ill, and she feared he might not recover, but because she'd nurtured a secret hope to take over the business herself one day. Having spent ten enjoyable years working with Philip, and training as a dealer, she'd honestly grown to love the place. Consequently, she wasn't predisposed to warming to their potential buyer.

Her first glimpse of the man, after his chauffeur had opened his door and he'd stepped out into the rain, was of a pair of classy Italian brogues, followed by a flawless charcoal suit that was no less than stunningly perfect. Rose caught her breath. As soon as she saw his arrestingly sculpted features, the cut-glass jaw and crystalline blue eyes that were frequently described by the press as 'unflinchingly piercing', she had the disturbing sense that she was coming face to face with her greatest fear and—*inexplicably*—her greatest desire...

She irritably chided herself for the thought. Snapping out of the near trance she'd fallen into watching him, she smoothed her hands down her smart navy dress and made herself walk calmly to the door. It was then she saw that the businessman's height dwarfed hers.

Lifting her head to gaze up at him, she said, 'Eugene Bonnaire? Please come in. I'm Mr Houghton's assistant—Rose Heathcote. I've been asked to conduct the meeting with you on Mr Houghton's behalf.'

The handsome Frenchman stepped inside. Charmingly polite, he shook Rose's hand with a slight bow of his head and she immediately sensed the reined-in strength he exuded.

'I am delighted to meet you, Miss Heathcote. But I

have to confess I was sorry to hear that your boss has been taken ill. Might I ask how he is?'

Before answering, Rose pulled the door shut behind him and adjusted the sign that hung inside the glass to read 'closed'. She was glad of the chance to compose herself before she turned round again. Not only had his firm handshake made her far too aware of him as a man, but the deep bass timbre of his arrestingly attractive voice made her skin feel as though he'd brushed it with gossamer. She prayed that the blood that had heatedly rushed into her face didn't too obviously reveal the fact...

'I wish I could say he was a little better, but the doctors tell me it's going to be a while before we see any improvement.'

'*C'est la vie.* It is the way of things...but I wish him well.'

'Thank you. I'll tell him you said so. Anyway, would you like to come with me into the office, Mr Bonnaire, and we can start our meeting?'

'Before we discuss anything I would like you to show me round the building, Miss Heathcote. After all, that is the reason I am here.'

Although there was a faultlessly charming smile on his lips to accompany this statement, Rose realised that here was a man who wouldn't be diverted by small talk, however polite and concerned. Nothing would take precedence over pursuing his goals, and his goal today was clearly deciding whether he wanted to buy the antiques shop or not...

'Of course,' she replied. 'It will be my pleasure.'

Rose led him upstairs to one of the three spacious rooms that, although elegantly arranged, were stacked to the rafters with a mixture of antiques and collectables. The air smelled faintly musty because there was a generous amount of furniture on display, although it was tempered somewhat by the scent of beeswax.

While the sound of the rain against the leaded windows made for a cosy ambience it was a little chilly too, and the dress she wore was sleeveless. Wishing she'd collected her cardigan from the office, she briskly rubbed her arms to warm them.

'The rooms are generously sized, considering it's such an old building,' she remarked, 'which is why we can house so many antiques. I hope you like what you see, Mr Bonnaire.'

Looking faintly amused, her visitor lifted his gaze.

Rose privately attested to spending the most electrifying few seconds of her life as her glance met his. It struck her that she could have chosen her words better. Not in a million years would she invite a man like Eugene Bonnaire to look at her. Did he think that she *would?* He had a reputation for liking exceptionally beautiful women, and Rose knew she was a long way from being in that particular category.

'So far...I like what I see very much, Miss Heathcote,' he answered, not moving his gaze.

Now she really *did* feel hot and bothered. 'I'm... I'm glad. Take as much time as you want, looking over things.'

'Trust me, I will do exactly that.'

'Good.'

Hastily averting her glance, she crossed her arms over her chest, not wanting to draw any more attention. But it wasn't long before she found herself surreptitiously observing him as he walked round, his keen-eyed gaze carefully examining the layout and proportions of the room, every so often dropping down into a crouch to examine the durability and condition of the timbered walls and crevices. It was fascinating to watch him stroking his large but slim hands over the wood and occasionally tapping it with his knuckles.

Whilst Rose understood that it was important the man knew what he would be getting for his investment, he didn't give the impression that the room's contents interested him at all, and she began to be concerned. Philip had told her it was imperative he sell the business as a going concern, because his poor health meant that he now had to retire, as well as pay for his aftercare when he left the hospital.

He had added sadly, 'I'm afraid that pensions aren't worth a light these days…'

The weight of the responsibility she'd taken on in agreeing to make the sale for him hit Rose even harder.

She was still frowning when the preoccupied Frenchman pivoted and remarked, 'Forgive me, but I saw you shiver a couple of times. Are you cold? Perhaps you'd like to go and get your jacket, Rose?'

Even as he asked another small shiver ran up her spine. But it wasn't due to the less than comfortable temperature…it was because it had sounded disturbingly intimate when he'd used her name.

Last night, ahead of her interview with him, she had

looked up Eugene Bonnaire on the internet, and as well as reading about the numerous plaudits he had earned in his career thus far she had also learned that he could be quite ruthless in his dealings and had an insatiable appetite for success. He was cited as a man who went after the very best of everything, no matter what the cost, and his penchant for stunning women suggested he was quite the playboy.

Rose knew she couldn't afford to let her guard down round him for an instant. She didn't want to be persuaded to agree to the sale of the business against her better judgement just because he was so attractive.

Deciding that she couldn't and *wouldn't* let that happen—she knew from bitter experience the danger that men like him could pose—she unwaveringly returned his gaze and said, 'I think I *will* go and get my cardigan. If you want to look at the other rooms on this floor, be my guest. I'll be back in a minute.'

With a polite but inarguably *knowing* nod, Eugene Bonnaire glanced away.

A short while later she returned upstairs to find that he'd gone into the furthest room at the back. This was where the more valuable items were displayed and where jewellery was housed behind secure custom-made glass cabinets. Much to Rose's surprise, she found Eugene staring transfixed into one of the cabinets and wondered if she'd misjudged him. Maybe he *did* admire some of the artefacts and maybe he *would* buy the business as well as the building?

She couldn't help but smile as she stepped up beside him, curious to see what he was examining so avidly.

When she saw that he was staring at the exquisite pearl and diamond ring from the nineteenth century that was the centrepiece of the display, her curiosity was even more piqued.

'It's pretty, isn't it?' she commented.

'Yes, it is. It looks very similar to the ring my father bought my mother when their business first started to take off.' He was lost in thought for a moment. Then, with a heartfelt sigh, he turned towards her. 'But the pearls and the diamonds weren't real. They were just costume jewellery... He couldn't afford to buy her anything expensive back then.'

There was definitely a glimmer of pain in his eyes as he related this, and Rose found herself warming to him probably more than was wise, because he suddenly seemed oddly vulnerable.

'I'm sure your mum loved the ring just as much as if it were the genuine article. Surely it's what it represented, not how much it cost?' When Eugene failed to comment, and turned back to examine the jewel broodingly, she said softly, 'You might be interested to know that this ring was given to a girl who was a nurse in the Crimean War by the grateful family of a wounded soldier.'

His crystal blue gaze meandered interestedly across her features. Then he gazed deeply into her eyes. Rose's mouth went dry as a sun-bleached plain... She was glad she was wearing her navy wool cardigan so he wouldn't see her shiver again.

'Every picture tells a story, so they say,' he mused. 'No doubt it's the same for jewellery. But let me ask you this: do you think the nurse who was gifted it was very pretty and the wounded soldier a handsome officer?'

The roguish twinkle that accompanied his question took her by surprise and all but made Rose's knees buckle. Flooded with heat, she congratulated herself on quickly regaining her equilibrium and not glancing away too soon. Instead, she made herself steadily hold his gaze and her lips curved in a gentle smile.

'Whether he was handsome or not, shortly after they met he died from his wounds. It's a terribly sad story, isn't it? Whether the two of them had feelings for each other we can only wonder, but the giving of the ring was documented in the soldier's family archives. That's how we were able to trace its provenance.'

'I am guessing that you like to imagine the couple *did* have feelings for each other, Rose.' Eugene's expression was suddenly intense.

Feeling strangely as if she was under siege, she shrugged. 'Why not? Who could begrudge them the little bit of happiness they may have had in the midst of such a terrible situation? But the truth is we'll never know what really happened.'

What Rose *did* know was that she had to engineer some space between her and Eugene. She might at one point have felt a chill, but now she was definitely warmer...*too* warm.

'If you've finished having a look round up here we should go downstairs and have that meeting...don't you think?'

'I agree. Perhaps you could make us some coffee?'

'Of course… How do you take it?'

'How do you *think* I might take it, Rose? Humour me.'

If his tactic was to disarm her and lull her into a false sense of security because he'd decided to be playful, Rose couldn't deny that on another day she might have succumbed to his charm. After all, what woman *wouldn't* feel flattered by his exclusive attention? But today she wouldn't be so easily swayed. Not when she had an important task to fulfil. She had to sell the antiques shop on her boss's behalf and secure the very best deal she could. Nothing could distract her from that goal.

Leading the way back downstairs, in an attempt to let Eugene see that she wasn't rattled by his friendly repartee, she breezily threw over her shoulder, 'Okay, then. I'm guessing you probably like it strong and black. But I'm also guessing you like a couple of spoons of sugar to sweeten it. Am I right?'

'I'm impressed. But be careful not to assume you know what I like in any other respect, Rose… You might find that you've bitten off a little bit more than you can chew.'

Even though she'd heard a smile in his voice, Rose didn't doubt the comment carried a warning. No man became as successful as Eugene Bonnaire without carefully assessing anyone who might put obstacles in the way of him getting what he wanted…

When she returned to the office with the tray of coffee she'd made Eugene had his back to her, and she couldn't help but let her gaze linger for a moment on the impressive breadth of his shoulders. In the better lit room she also saw that his hair was a rich dark brown, with dulled gold lights glinting here and there.

As if that wasn't enough to capture her attention, the scent of his classy cologne drifted beguilingly on the air and made her insides turn over. With the tip of her tongue she moistened her suddenly dry lips and placed the tray on the gracious Victorian desk in front of him. Then she walked round to the beautifully carved chair that her boss usually occupied.

Coming face to face with Eugene's features again was not something any woman with a pulse would soon forget... He was chisel-jawed and handsome as a Michelangelo sculpture. But she was perturbed when she saw that his dazzling blue eyes didn't seem as warm as they had upstairs, when she'd met his gaze over the jewellery cabinet and he'd shared that touching story about the fake pearl and diamond ring his father had bought his mother.

In fact, as they swept over her they brought to mind a once sunlit ocean frozen under ice. A little alarmed, Rose sensed hot colour flooding into her cheeks. *Was he assessing the way she looked?*

Having never considered herself a beauty, she was painfully disconcerted at being scrutinised by the businessman so penetratingly. Friends had often remarked that her best features were her eyes and her cheekbones, but other than that she knew she was quite ordinary. Disturbed that she should waste even a second fretting over what the man's opinion of her might be her instinct was to be doubly wary of him.

But the restaurateur's carved lips curved in another disconcerting smile. 'Would you like to pour the coffee for us? Then we can proceed. I have a particularly heavy schedule today, and would like to settle our business as quickly as possible.'

'You sound as though you've made a decision?'

'I have. Having seen the interior of the building, I'd like to make you an offer.'

Straight away Rose noted that he'd said 'the building'—not the antiques business. Her stomach plunged like a stone.

'I'd really like to tie up the sale of the property today,' he added smoothly, bringing his hands together with his long fingers forming a steeple.

His words suggested it was a given that she would agree to the sale. Maybe he didn't think she could possibly refuse him because she was only standing in for the owner? Perhaps he imagined his wealth and status would intimidate her?

If she was right, then his arrogance beggared belief. Biting her lip, she decided to delay commenting and garner her thoughts.

Reaching for the cafetière, she carefully poured out his coffee. 'It's two sugars, isn't it?' she checked, aware that his intense gaze was closely surveying everything she did and resenting it mightily.

'That's right.'

Passing him the beverage, Rose made a particular point of *not* meeting his gaze. After pouring her own drink she sat down, but in truth she knew any hopes she might have had of remaining calm throughout the meeting had fled as soon as her glance had encountered the Frenchman's...

'Can I just clarify something? You said that you wanted to tie up the sale of "the property" today?'

'That's correct'

'Forgive me, but I thought my boss had made it clear that he wanted to sell the business as a going concern, Mr Bonnaire? You can't separate it from the property and just purchase the building. Do I take it that you're not interested in running the antiques shop at all?'

'That's right, Rose—but, please, call me Gene. You may or may not know, but I already run a very successful worldwide restaurant business and I'd like to install one of my most prestigious restaurants here. The location is perfect. And, although I do also have other successful businesses, to be frank with you I'm afraid that antiques don't interest me in the slightest. I'm sure you must have learned from your boss that people just aren't as interested in them these days as they used to be. Anyone in business wants to make money. No interest in the product, equals no profit. Isn't that the reason why he wants to sell?'

Rose felt as if her face had suddenly been seared by an iron. She was both embarrassed and furious. 'You don't have to be so brutal—'

'Business *is* brutal, *ma chère*...make no mistake about that.'

'Well, Philip is selling because he's ill and no longer has the energy to run the business. This antiques shop has always been his pride and joy, and if he was well I can assure you it wouldn't be up for sale at all.'

It was Gene's turn to sigh. 'But I'm guessing the fact is, due to his poor health, he's decided to take the opportunity to make as much money as he can on his asset while he is still in a position to do so. Is that not so?'

She flushed again, and twisted her hands in her lap to still their trembling. She couldn't make a proper decision about anything if her emotions got in the way. But Gene, as he seemed to prefer being called, had guessed right. Because of his failing health Philip *needed* to make this sale. But she knew that he'd fervently hoped to sell the business along with the building, and if Rose didn't manage to do that for him then she would have failed the man who was not just her boss and mentor, but who had been her father's dearest friend…

She came to the only decision that could possibly be right. Now calmer, she met the Frenchman's gaze across the desk. 'It's true that Mr Houghton needs to make this sale, Mr Bonnaire—Gene—but, since you've just admitted that antiques don't interest you in the slightest, and that you're not interested in running the business and only want the building, I'm afraid I can't agree to sell it to you. It just wouldn't be right. I realise it's not the decision you hoped for, but I'm sorry. I hope you understand?'

'No. I do *not* understand. I have told you that it's the building I'm interested in and I'm willing to pay what I know to be the going rate for the property…no question. How many interested buyers has your boss seen since he put the shop up for sale?'

Gene Bonnaire's glare was steely.

'In the current economic climate my guess is not

many… Maybe I'm the only one? If I were you, Rose, I would take my offer on your employer's behalf and congratulate yourself. Trust me…the only regret he would have is if you should be foolish enough to turn me down. Do you *really* want to put yourself in such an untenable position and lose the faith and trust he has obviously accorded you?'

As a helpless tide of defensive anger surged through her Rose set her eyes on the man she now considered to be not quite so charming. He might not be as heartless as she'd first thought—the story about the fake pearl and diamond ring his father had bought his mother demonstrated that he had the capacity to feel things deeply—but she knew that he was determined to secure the desirable Thames-side building at all costs. And he was plainly willing to risk Rose not liking him if he became too insistent.

'I think you've said quite enough, Mr Bonnaire. I've given you my decision and you're just going to have to accept it.'

'Is that so? Do you imagine that any businessman or woman worth their salt who is determined to seal a deal should give up so easily merely because you tell them that they *should*?'

His tone was sardonic, and Gene's glance swept over Rose as if she was a foolish little girl.

Swallowing down her fury that anybody could be so reprehensible, she stiffly folded her arms. 'I wouldn't dream of advising anyone what's best for them, because I clearly don't know. I'm not a businesswoman… I'm an antiques dealer. However, I *do* know my boss

Philip, and how much this antiques business means to him. He's impressed upon me more than once that he wants to sell it as a going concern, so I would be failing in my duty if I didn't adhere to that. On his behalf, I thank you for your interest but our meeting is over. I'll see you to the door.'

'Not so fast.'

As he rose immediately to his feet it wasn't hard for Rose to detect that Gene Bonnaire was more than a little thrown off balance by her refusal to sell. He was holding on to his temper by a thread.

The expensive cologne he wore again stirred the air, reminding her that the moneyed and elite world he inhabited was light years away from hers and that he hadn't expected an argument. But on this occasion, Rose was determined to stand her ground...

'Look, I didn't come here to waste my time or yours,' he went on. 'I came here for one reason and one reason only: to purchase a listed building that I understood was up for sale. If you won't sell the premises to me then perhaps you'd reconsider your decision if I agree to purchase the antiques as well? I don't doubt some of them might be valuable to an ardent collector.'

The comment was hardly encouraging. He might just as well have referred to the collector as misguided rather than ardent. Rose didn't have to guess how appalled Philip would be if he knew that Gene didn't want to purchase the antiques for their beauty and historical significance, or even because he might be considering continuing the business after all, but only because he was thinking about their monetary worth.

'Indeed, some of them are extremely valuable,' she confirmed. 'But unfortunately your remark illustrates to me exactly what you asserted earlier…you have no interest whatsoever in antiques. That being the case, I'm not inclined to consider your offer any further, Mr Bonnaire.'

Extracting a leather wallet from the inside pocket of the impeccably tailored jacket he wore, the businessman took out a card and threw it down onto the desk. The blue eyes that Rose had noted could be icy had turned even more glacial.

'When you've had some time to think things over— meaning when you can make a far less *emotional* decision about the matter, Rose—I don't doubt you'll want to get in touch with me to discuss a sale. In the meantime, I'll say *au revoir*.'

As he spoke Rose found herself yet again uncomfortably captured by his mocking glance, and she thanked her lucky stars that the man was going. Yet as her gaze followed him to the door in truth she didn't know whether or not to be pleased she'd stood her ground— whether the decision she'd made was the right one or not…

Back in his Mayfair office, after the tedious round of meetings he'd chaired that afternoon, Gene asked his secretary to get him some coffee and sank down into his high-backed leather chair to mull over the day's events. He didn't think he had ever felt more irritable and out of sorts, and it was all down to his offer being refused on that damn property.

He'd admired the architecture of the Thames-side building for years, and had often thought it would make the most fantastic restaurant should he buy it. He didn't envisage it as an addition to the more commercial restaurants he already owned, but saw it as the kind of exclusive place that the glitterati liked to frequent. Just like the two esteemed establishments he owned in New York and Paris.

Recalling his meeting with Rose Heathcote, Gene mused that it was beyond his understanding how she couldn't see what a gold-edged opportunity to capitalise on his assets he had given her boss. Most people would have ripped his arm off to take it. But one thing had become eminently clear to him… Just as she had said, Rose was no businesswoman. Her attitude had really irked him. Especially when he'd seen that she wasn't going to be easily influenced by any amount of charm he might utilise. Yet part of him admired the brunette for her determination to stand firm even though he knew she was wrong.

And there was something else about her that had caught his attention. *She had the most startlingly beautiful violet eyes.* Her glossy black hair and ivory-coloured skin made them even more captivating. The passion he'd seen in their mesmerising depths had intrigued him and made him want to get to know her, even though she'd denied him the chance to purchase the property. But, as was his modus operandi when faced with situations or outcomes he didn't like, Gene knew he would immediately work to turn it to his advantage.

Yes…he would step right back into the breach and

make his purchase of the building a foregone conclusion. He wouldn't be satisfied until it was his. Rose could take a couple of days' sober reflection on what a mistake she'd made in turning him down, then Gene would get back to her with an offer that he knew her boss simply *couldn't* refuse.

If he could have some more time with her and assure her that he was respectful of the gracious building's admirable history, had always admired it and only sought to elevate it by housing his restaurant there, he didn't doubt he could persuade her to convince Philip Houghton that selling the building to one of the country's richest entrepreneurs wasn't just a good idea…it was the *only* one that would take it off his hands and make him enough money to see him right for the rest of his life.

But just then, somewhere deep inside him, Gene couldn't help feeling disturbed that he'd so easily dismissed the other man's welfare in the belief that money was the answer to his problems. Even his parents had counselled him on that once.

'Son, you can't always fix someone's pain by throwing money at the problem. No amount of money or good fortune made it any easier for us to endure the devastation of your sister's death. Don't forget that.'

The memory jolted him, and for a few disturbing seconds he felt as if a grenade had been thrown into the room. But now wasn't the time to reflect on how much his sister's death had nearly broken him…

He squared his shoulders. He and his parents saw life very differently. Gene saw practical solutions to adversity while they succumbed to their emotions and

allowed their feelings to dictate how they responded...
The idea of behaving in the same way was anathema
to him. He'd heard his parents' stories about their poor
upbringings, how their own parents and siblings had
suffered terribly when there hadn't been the means to
put food on the table or to have adequate heat and light,
and how many nights they had gone to bed hungry...
From a tender age he'd intuited how essential it was to
have money, and as he'd grown older, having discovered
that he had a talent for making it with ease, he wasn't
about to relinquish it—not for *anyone*.

Pleased that he'd come up with a plan to help him
win the beautiful old property—a plan he was convinced would work because he never, *never* entertained
the possibility of failure—Gene got to his feet, straightened his tie and strode out through the door.

Stopping at the desk of his blonde, statuesque secretary, Simone, whose cousin was an up-and-coming Parisian designer—and frankly that was why he'd given
her the job...because it always paid to utilise his assets—he flashed her a warmer smile than usual and
said, 'Forget the coffee, *ma chère,* and book me a table
for dinner at my club for eight o'clock.'

'Will you be taking a guest with you, Mr Bonnaire?'

'No, Simone. Not tonight.'

'Then I will ring the *maître d'* straight away and arrange for you to have your favourite table.'

'Thank you.'

'You are most welcome. It always makes me glad
when I can do something to please you and make your
life a little easier.'

The woman's glossy pink lips curved in a smile that was definitely inviting.

Gene's fleetingly good mood instantly vanished. Scowling, he said, 'In that case you won't mind doing some overtime tonight, will you? I've left a "to do" list on my desk for you. Goodnight, Simone. I will see you in the morning.'

He was more irritated than usual with the blonde's obsequious manner. She hadn't been working for him for very long, but he didn't need to be a genius to know that she was only too aware of how to use *her* best assets…especially as she clearly thought it was only a matter of time before he would bed her… Just yesterday he had overheard her stating the fact, not very discreetly, to someone on her mobile.

Waiting impatiently for the elevator to arrive, he muttered savagely beneath his breath, 'God save me from predatory women!'

CHAPTER TWO

LONG AFTER HER MEETING, and still stinging from her
encounter with the mercurial force of nature that was
Gene Bonnaire, Rose couldn't help but be interested in
what drove the man to be the way he was. He clearly
hadn't liked her decision not to sell the shop to him. Her
refusal had really grated on him, because he obviously
wasn't used to being denied when he'd set his sights on
something that he wanted.

Knowing that he was a restaurateur, and that he
wanted the building for one of his establishments, that
night she went home and did some more research.

Rose discovered that Gene was one of the richest
men in Europe and had made his fortune by turning
a once small French restaurant in East London called
Mangez Bien into a well-known chain that had spread
across the globe. The original restaurant had been
owned by Gene's parents. They were both French immigrants, who'd settled in London when they were young
and had turned their love of cooking and food into owning a much loved eatery that had been patronised by a
devoted local clientele.

By the time their son had turned seventeen, so the story went, he was already a fine chef whose ambitions far exceeded his parents' own. He had progressed from being Head Chef at one of London's finest hotels to becoming an astute entrepreneur who had started to establish restaurants of his own. But as he'd begun to build an empire of affordable French restaurants he had also acquired a reputation for being quite ruthless in his business dealings.

Rose already knew he didn't like being denied...

Leaning back in her chair, she studied the photograph that her computer had helpfully supplied. It had been taken at a prestigious awards ceremony in LA, and even though the picture of him couldn't help but be flattering, to her mind it didn't depict any pleasure at his being at the event, nor at having received an award. Instead, the man's immense dissatisfaction was clear. It emanated from Gene's steely blue eyes in forbidding icy waves...

He doesn't look even remotely pleased, she mused. And he was probably even less pleased since she'd turned down his offer.

The headline of the article onscreen read, *The man who has everything once again strikes gold.*

'Hmph,' Rose muttered out loud. 'That doesn't mean that any of what he's got makes him happy. *Something* must be bugging him...something he doesn't like to talk about.'

Was it anything to do with his father not being able to afford a *real* diamond and pearl ring for his mother in the early days when they were starting to establish their business? Why else had he told Rose that it was only costume jewellery? Had it made him feel insecure? She remembered the flicker of pain that had accompanied his remark. But surely he wasn't still burdened by the memory? Was he sad that once upon a time his parents had struggled...that not everything had been as easy for them as it had for their son?

Wearily dragging her fingers through her pixie cut short hair, she sighed. Why was Gene Bonnaire at the forefront of her thoughts when she still had to face her boss and tell him that she'd turned down the Frenchman's offer?

She would have done anything to spare him the disappointment and distress the news would undoubtedly bring him, and could only hope he would see that her motivation had been to do what was right by him. After all, he'd been there for her when her father had passed away, staying by his bedside with Rose until he breathed his last breath... The last thing he needed now, when he was so ill, was to be put under pressure to sell the antiques shop to someone who didn't have the first idea about what it meant to him...

Switching off her computer, she stood up and stretched. Annoyed that she'd wasted even more time thinking about Gene Bonnaire, she went into her living room to collect the book she'd been reading. It was a hefty tome all about the Aztecs, with a fascinating chapter on the magnificent jewellery worn by the emperors. There had recently been a momentous find in northern Mexico, and straight away it had fuelled Rose's interest. She'd have loved to go and see the treasure that the archaeologists had uncovered, but she'd have to wait until it finally went on display in a prestigious gallery or museum.

Going to bed, she fell asleep with the book on her chest and dreamt disturbingly of an Aztec emperor who uncannily resembled Gene Bonnaire...

Just like an addict, desperate to buy his next fix, Gene sat in the café across the street from the antiques store and couldn't turn his mind to anything else other than fulfilling his desire to own the gracious building he was staring at... The coffee he'd ordered had long gone cold as he restlessly contemplated going in and demanding that Rose Heathcote came to her senses and accepted the offer he'd made.

It had been three days since their meeting, and no phone call had been forthcoming to tell him that she'd had second thoughts. Maybe her boss had had a better offer from someone else? The very idea made him feel nauseous. He wanted that building as much as he wanted his next breath, and he deplored the notion that he might not get it.

Glancing down at his Rolex, he saw that he'd been sitting in the café for nigh on half an hour, hoping to catch Rose unawares. Catching someone off-guard often paid dividends, he'd found. If he'd seen her then he would have asked her out to dinner, so that they could talk amicably outside of work and get to know each other a little better. If he was able to get her to trust him then he didn't doubt he could persuade her to sell the building to him.

But she hadn't stepped outside even once, and in

truth he was taking an unnecessary risk, sitting in the café in front of the window. Any minute now the paparazzi might turn up—and that really *would* ruin his day, because they were frequently on a mission to expose him as ruthless and uncaring…

Even in the early days, when he'd started to have some success, he'd realised there were more people in the world who were jealous of his achievements rather than pleased. More to the point, they were jealous of his *wealth*… Knowing that, he knew the press was more than eager to take him down a peg or two—no doubt so that their readers could feel a bit better about their own lives.

Suddenly impatient, he glanced upwards at the now darkening skies. Any moment now it would start to rain. He shouldn't waste any more time sitting there, waiting for inspiration to dawn about what he should do. He'd never been someone who *waited* for opportunity to strike. Gene made his own opportunities.

His gaze settled on the old building again. The name of the shop was The Hidden Diamond, and to be honest he thought it a little trite. After all, he reasoned, if it was hidden then what use was it to anybody? Diamonds should be displayed to denote their owner's wealth… not hidden away.

With a jaundiced sigh he got to his feet. The promised rain began to splatter the pavement. He was done with waiting. He was going into the shop to present Rose with a more persuasive offer. If she really cared so much about helping her boss then she ought to be relieved he was giving her a second bite of the cherry…

* * *

Rose was finishing up her bookwork when she heard the doorbell chime. Hurriedly toeing on her maroon leather flats, she tucked her cream silk blouse more securely into the waistband of her smart black skirt and left the office to deal with what she assumed was a late customer.

She should have closed up shop half an hour ago, but she'd been so immersed in cataloguing the dwindling monthly sales and wishing they were better that she hadn't noticed the time.

Her lips automatically curved into a smile, but the gesture immediately melted away when she saw that her late caller wasn't the customer she'd envisaged but Gene Bonnaire. She stared. What was *he* doing here? Forgoing a suit, he was dressed casually today, in jeans and a dove-grey T-shirt beneath a tailored black jacket. But he was no less formidable. It was raining outside, she saw, and the shoulders of his jacket glistened with moisture—as did his hair.

'Do you usually stay open this late?' he asked, clearly opting to dispense with any social niceties.

Tensing, Rose found herself caught in the crystalline spotlight of his disquieting blue gaze. 'Not usually no. But I was busy doing some bookwork and didn't notice the time. What can I do for you, Mr Bonnaire? If you were hoping to persuade me to change my mind about your offer then I'm sorry. I wouldn't want you to waste your time.'

'Don't be sorry. Just let me have a few minutes with you to talk things over.'

'To what end?'

'Why don't we sit down and I'll tell you?'

Rose arched an eyebrow. 'Like I said, I gave you my decision and I see no reason in discussing it any further.' When Gene scowled she got the distinct impression that he was having considerable trouble remaining calm. His next words confirmed it.

'You really have no idea about business, do you, Rose? I'd like to know why your boss, Philip Houghton, has such faith in you... Perhaps you'd enlighten me?'

Now Rose had trouble holding on to her own temper, and she had no hesitation in replying passionately, 'Because I care about him—that's why! I have no ulterior motive other than that I want what's best for him. And what's best for him is to sell the antiques business as a going concern, to someone who will love it as much as he does.'

'That's a nice thought...but hardly a realistic one.'

'Did you come here just to tell me how inept you think I am, Mr Bonnaire?' Incensed, she folded her arms. 'Because if it makes you feel any better, then you should know that I've had sleepless nights about the whole thing. It would be very easy to take your offer to my boss and tell him that he'd be lucky to get another one half as good—remind him that the antiques trade isn't what it used to be and he should just take what he can while the going's good. But I couldn't be so cruel. Not when I know how much the business means to him. If he was just interested in selling a beautiful period building in a very desirable area then he would have done so. But he wants the business to continue... What do you think he'd say if I accepted your offer and then told him you weren't remotely interested in antiques?'

Gene looked thoughtful. Then he smiled. 'I think he'd probably feel that he can't be sentimental about it. At the end of the day, if he believes that his poor health will prohibit his return to work, no doubt he will need the money to help pay for his care. Surely that's the priority here?'

What he said made perfect sense and, suddenly unsure, Rose felt tears of frustration surge into her eyes.

Gene all but covered the distance between them in less than a couple of strides, and as before the air stirred hypnotically with the exotic scent of his expensive cologne.

'You're upset. Is there anything I can do? Why don't we go into the office and I'll get you a cup of tea?'

'I don't want tea. All I want is… All I want is for you to go away!' Her outburst sounded embarrassingly childish even to her own ears… *So much for keeping her composure.* Rose wanted the ground to open up and swallow her.

But the man in front of her didn't go away. He didn't even look remotely put out. The dazzling blue eyes that she knew could turn forbiddingly cold when he was angry were now inexplicably warm…*tender*, even. He lifted his hand to touch her arm gently. Her heart thudded quietly as she felt his smooth skin brush against her own.

'Your boss gave you a tough job when he asked you to sell the business for him, Rose—perhaps *too* tough. I don't mean this as a criticism, but I can see that it's not where your skills lie… I've already learned that it's the *job* you love—being with the artefacts and learning about their history. More than that, you like discovering the personal stories behind them. You're a *people* person, Rose…not a businesswoman.'

She realised the man had an almost uncanny knack of knowing what a person was about. But she didn't want to let him see even for a second that his astute insight perturbed her. Surely Gene Bonnaire had enough advantages without her giving him any more…namely the fact that she could so easily warm to him, when everything in her told her it would be a mistake that would undoubtedly cost her dear…

'That might be the case, and I *know* my forte isn't in the world of business—I told you that before. But my love of antiques and understanding what they mean to people also makes me understand why my boss, Philip, wants to sell the business as a going concern. I think it means even more to him since he's become ill. He's taught me so much about the trade, and that's why I want to get the best deal for him.'

'That's also why you should give me a little bit more of your time and listen to what I have to say, Rose.'

'Why? Are you going to tell me that you've decided to take on the business after all?'

Gene was already shaking his head. 'No. I'm sorry I have to disappoint you, but I won't be getting involved in that side of things. I haven't changed my mind about that.'

'Then how can I possibly be interested in listening any more to what you have to say, Mr Bonnaire?'

'If you'd do me the courtesy of having dinner with me tonight, I'll explain.'

Even as she guessed that most women would be surprised and pleased by such an invitation—not to mention immensely flattered—Rose defiantly lifted her chin to indicate that she wasn't one of them. 'Thank you, but I'm going to have to decline.'

'You have a previous engagement?'

'No, but—'

'You don't want to hear what I have to say, even though it might be to your boss's advantage?'

'How can it *possibly* be to his advantage? You've already said that you're not interested in the business… that you only want the building.'

Gene Bonnaire's steely-eyed gaze didn't waver for so much as a second as he examined her, and it was easy to guess he'd hoped to have the upper hand.

'Like I said, Rose… Have dinner with me tonight and all will be explained.'

Prickling with unease, she sensed herself flush heatedly. 'You're just playing games—and I don't trust men who play games. If you have something to say that you know for a fact my boss will be interested in, then why don't you just come right out and say it?'

'Very well, then, although I'm sad that you won't agree to dinner, and just to reassure you, Rose, I'm not playing games. It's just that it has been my experience that all the best deals are made over a cordon bleu meal and a fine bottle of wine.'

One corner of the handsome Frenchman's mouth lifted in a smile that would make most women—young, old and in between—*ache* to be close to him in the most intimate way... And even though Rose was quite aware that he was using his charm to get what he wanted, she was hardly immune to the idea.

'Is that right? Well, I'm afraid that's not been *my* experience.'

'So you won't even take a risk and try it?'

Unable to glance away from his mesmerising gaze, she felt her breath hitch. 'No...I won't...'

But even as she refused a look of heated longing drifted across his irises and she sensed her resistance indisputably melting. Underneath their polite words, somehow a much more sensual conversation was taking place. Rose couldn't deny it. That impossibly irresistible look of Gene Bonnaire's was captivating her, stirring her own longing into life, and right then all she wanted to do was to fulfil it...

Gene moved to stand in front of her, his mesmerising blue eyes smouldering like simmering fires... In the next instant the businessman had firmly caught hold of her arm and pulled her against his chest.

Rose's blood pumped hard. All she could do was helplessly stare back at him. It was undeniable that he excited her, but his sheer physical presence disturbed her too. It only took a glance to see how supremely fit and strong he was.

Low-voiced, he murmured, 'God forgive me, but...'

The time that elapsed between his words and his next action was brief...*too* brief for her to stop him.

His urgent, initially demanding kiss stole her breath and made her sink against the hard wall of his chest.

Her senses were utterly besieged by him. And as his hot silken mouth moved over hers and became more and more seductive Rose didn't have the faintest inclination to end the passionate caress.

Then somehow it filtered through to her fogged brain just how dangerous her compliant actions were and she came hurtling back to her senses. Shocked and shaken, she freed herself from the Frenchman's embrace and wiped her hand over her already aching lips.

Staring back at him, she declared, 'Your arrogance, Mr Bonnaire, has to be seen to be believed! I don't know what you thought you were doing, but I think you'd better just leave.'

Her heart pumped even harder. The heat from his body and his velvet mouth had seared her indelibly, and she already knew she wasn't easily going to forget it.

'I didn't intend to kiss you, Rose, but somehow the desire overwhelmed me. I am as disturbed by it as you are. I apologise. If you really won't come to dinner with me then I can do no more than tell you about the amended deal I have come up with.'

He paused, as if to take a moment to straighten his thoughts. There was a slight crimson tint beneath his tan that bore out his declaration that desire had overwhelmed him. Rose didn't know what to make of it herself. She was just an ordinary girl, and he was—he was a living, breathing *Adonis*...

'I already know how much getting the best deal for your boss means to you, and I have spent quite some time thinking about how I can make that a reality for you both. This is my new offer.'

His hand dived into the inside pocket of his jacket and he drew out a slim sheet of paper. Unfolding it, he handed it to Rose.

Her jaw all but hit the floor when she saw how much he was prepared to pay for the privilege of owning the building. His initial offer had practically *doubled*. For dizzying moments she was literally lost for words.

'This amount of money can be a real life-changer for Philip, Rose. That being the case, why on earth would you turn down the opportunity to help make things better for him? If you were to persuade him to see the sense in selling to me, then I'm sure he would be nothing but relieved. If he accepted my offer then he would have the worry of the business off his hands and earn himself a more than healthy profit. No doubt *you* would be happy too, Rose, because his ill health would undoubtedly be restored and, last but not least, I don't deny *I* would be pleased, because I'd get the property I've long desired.'

'And the name of the game is always that you get what *you* want, isn't it, Mr Bonnaire? There's nothing altruistic about this scenario, is there? You don't give a fig about my employer's health, or whether I'm happy or not happy. Why *should* you? You know nothing about us! You've seen something you want and you'll do anything…pay *any* price…to get it. Isn't that how people like you operate?'

To Rose's consternation, he chuckled. It was a rich, gravelly sound that sent shivers running up and down her spine.

'*Touché*…you've got it in one. You're a bright woman…'

'Don't patronise me!'

Sighing, he folded his arms over his chest and studied her. 'I wouldn't dream of it. I'd much rather have you on my side than make you my enemy, Rose. By the way, your eyes are an *incredible* colour... I don't doubt you've been told that many times before. What's the shade? I'd say they were violet...'

Rose was hardly prepared for his remarks suddenly to become personal, even though he'd so passionately kissed her, and for several disturbing seconds it threw her. She could hardly think, let alone come back with a retort to put him in his place.

'The colour of my eyes is neither here nor there. This conversation is completely futile. Now, I really need to close the shop and you have to go.'

'Not yet. You haven't told me what you intend to do.'

'What do you mean?'

His eyes narrowed. 'Are you going to talk to your boss about accepting my new offer?'

Rose was still holding the piece of paper he'd given her and she carefully folded it and slipped it into her skirt pocket.

Returning her gaze to his, she said, 'I'll show him what you're offering—of course I will—but if you're asking if I'll try and persuade him to take it, then, no...I won't. Philip makes his own decisions—always has and always will. I neither have nor *want* any influence over him.'

'I don't believe you.' Dropping his hands to his hips, Gene smiled. 'I can sense that you're a sensitive woman,

Rose. I'm sure that Philip must appreciate that. If he knows that you care about his feelings then I'm sure he must respect any opinions you have about the matter and know that you have his best interests at heart.'

'Even so, it would feel wrong for me to persuade him to just sell the building, and some of the antiques, when he dearly wants to sell the business as a going concern.'

'But surely he must know by now that his beloved business clearly isn't viable any more?'

'Do you think I want to tell him that? When I know it's been his life's work and he's lying ill in hospital?'

'You would find a way to put it compassionately, I'm sure. You obviously care about him very much.'

'I do…'

'Then he is a lucky man.'

'*I'm* the lucky one. If he hadn't taken me on and taught me the trade I'd never have found the work that I've grown to love.'

'I'm sure he must have found it a pleasure to teach you, Rose. What sentient man *wouldn't*? Not only does he get a beautiful woman with captivating violet eyes and patrician cheekbones to work for him, but she becomes quite devoted to him too.'

Rose sensed her cheeks flush red. 'I think you've got the wrong end of the stick. Philip isn't attracted to me, if that's what you're implying, and neither am I to him. For goodness' sake—he's an elderly man, past retirement age!'

Gene was instantly apologetic. 'I'm sorry if I've caused offence. I thought he must be middle-aged, but

I didn't realise he was elderly. I'm afraid I confess I
was a little jealous when I heard you talk about him in
such glowing terms.'

Dry-mouthed, Rose hardly knew what to say. The
way he'd complimented her looks just now was un-
bearably seductive, and saying that he'd been *jealous*
of her admiration for Philip was crazy. Coming from
a man who could have any woman he wanted, it was
plainly ridiculous.

Realising that for a dangerous moment she'd been
more flattered than she should, Rose gritted her teeth.
Gene Bonnaire was even more of a threat than she'd
thought...

'Look...I think you'd better just go. I mean it. I'll be
in touch if I get any news from Mr Houghton for you.'

For a surreal moment Gene honestly forgot what he
was about—because he suddenly found himself even
more mesmerised by the brunette. Those violet eyes of
hers were strangely bewitching, and he'd fallen into a
bit of dream staring back at them.

He'd known when he kissed her that he wanted to
seduce her...it was just a matter of *when*...but his sudden fierce attraction was honestly a revelation—because Rose Heathcote certainly wasn't the usual type of
woman he was attracted to. She was not blonde, statuesque or shapely. She was small and slender, with black
hair cut boyishly short. Yet the passionate spark in her
eyes that he'd just witnessed, along with her feisty nature and her determination to protect her boss at all
costs, made her surprisingly alluring.

It was another first, because Gene usually liked his

women to be more compliant. *He* liked to be the one in control.

Quickly returning to his senses, he realised he was just going to have to bide his time and wait for Rose to speak to her boss.

Moving across to the door, he glanced out at the now teeming rain and then back at the diminutive brunette. 'All right, then. I won't press you any further. But tell me… Is there anything I can do for *you*, Rose? Does someone as generous as you are, with your regard for others, ever have her kindness reciprocated? For instance I'd be *very* interested to know if you have a personal heartfelt desire. If you do, then all you have to do is say the word and I'll do my utmost to help you get it.'

'Why would you want to do that? I suspect it's because you have some devious ulterior motive…'

Gene laid his hand over his heart and grinned. 'You wound me deeply.'

'If you could give me my "heartfelt desire" then you'd be much more than a mere man. Has it never occurred to you that not all heartfelt desires are material ones?' Rose challenged him.

He shrugged. 'I can't say I spend much time thinking about it. I prefer to deal with the tangible, not the abstract.'

'So in your world feelings are abstract, are they?'

'Why don't you have dinner with me and we can talk about it?'

She grimaced. 'I'd rather have dinner with a boa constrictor! At least I'd know for sure what I'd be dealing with.'

In spite of his disappointment that Rose didn't seem to believe he might just want to give her something that pleased her, and at not immediately strengthening his chances to buy the property, Gene found her answer undeniably amusing. To his surprise, he also found it indisputably *seductive*…

'I can't say I'm flattered, Rose, but that's *funny*!'

'You should stop calling me Rose. It's Miss Heathcote to you.'

Gene smiled. 'I can see that I've really got to you, haven't I? All right, then—I'll go. But you haven't heard the last of me…not by a long chalk…*Rose*…'

He opened the door and, with a resigned grimace, walked out into the rain.

The phone rang in the early hours of the morning and a brisk-sounding nurse from the hospital informed Rose that Philip had taken a turn for the worse and asked if she could she please come in. Feeling numb with fear, she dragged on her jeans, T-shirt and Mackintosh and practically flew out the door.

When she got to the hospital and was directed to a ward she drew in a deep breath as she saw him. White-faced and fragile, he was lying in bed breathing through an oxygen mask and wired up to the kind of medical paraphernalia that told her this was serious.

All her worst fears crashed in on her at the same time. It hadn't escaped her notice that her boss had been transferred to the same ward that her father had been in when he died. He'd had a fatal coronary whilst in hospital for investigation into something relatively minor, so it had come as the most terrible shock. *Was this how Philip was destined to leave her as well?* Rose could hardly bear the thought.

The doctor on call had diagnosed pneumonia and he told her that it was crucial they stabilised the condition and that he got plenty of rest. To that end they would be keeping him in longer than they'd first envisaged, and would be treating him with antibiotics and extra oxygen.

As she sat by his bedside holding his hand, Philip opened his eyes just once, to acknowledge that he knew she was there, and she gently assured him that everything was going to be all right, that he wasn't to worry. But even as she said the words Rose didn't entirely believe them. Suddenly the man who had been such a firm friend to her and her father looked worryingly old and haggard…and very, very ill.

Having tried so hard to hold back the tears during her visit, as soon as she got home she threw herself onto the couch and the floodgates opened.

They weren't the last tears she cried over the testing week that followed. One day Philip was rallying encouragingly, looking a little better, and the next it seemed he was worse. Managing the shop as well as talking to an array of healthcare professionals about his aftercare, Rose was on a rollercoaster of emotion that one moment had her feeling hopeful for his full recovery and the next fearing the unthinkable…

She had all but forgotten her recent encounter with Gene Bonnaire. But one evening after work when she visited the hospital Philip told her he wanted to discuss

something important. She had an uneasy feeling that
the billionaire's offer to buy the antiques shop was on
his mind. A couple of days earlier she had shown him
Gene's offer. *She was right*. He clearly hadn't felt ready
to discuss it then, but he did now.

'Rose…I want you to contact Mr Bonnaire and tell
him that I'm going to agree to the sale.'

There was a flash of what looked to be deep regret
in his pale blue eyes, and his expression was apologetic.

'I'm disappointed that he doesn't want to buy the
business and that it won't continue as I'd hoped, but in
my present situation beggars can't be choosers. Seeing
as I haven't had any other offers, and I'm advised I'm
going to be housebound for quite some time after this,
I'll need to pay for private care. As you know, I don't
have any family, but at least I have some material assets
that I can realise to help me—the main one being the
antiques shop. The man's offer for the building coupled
with the antiques is more generous than I could have
hoped for. He left me his card, didn't he? Can you contact him and arrange a meeting?'

Fighting to regain her composure at the idea that she
was going to have to talk to the Frenchman again, Rose
replied 'I'll do whatever you want me to do to help,
Philip, but surely you can't meet with him to discuss
things until you get out of hospital?'

Once more he was apologetic. 'I'm afraid I can't risk
waiting that long. I need to sell the place as quickly as
I can to free up some money for my care. I'm asking
you to handle the sale for me, Rose. I've contacted my

solicitor and he'll draw up the necessary papers. This is his name and number.'

He opened the bedside drawer, took out a single sheet of vellum that he'd written on and handed it to her.

'Anything you need to know, he'll explain.'

'It seems that you've made up your mind, then.' Frowning, Rose felt her muscles clench tight at the idea of once again coming face to face with Gene Bonnaire and knowing that this time *he* would be the one who had the advantage and would undoubtedly use it for all he was worth…

'Yes, my dear…I have.'

'Then I'll see to things right away. In the meantime you should try and rest as much as possible. The last thing you need is to be stressed about anything.'

Smiling fondly, Philip patted her hand as it lay on the counterpane. 'I should have told you this before, Rose… I don't know how I would have managed these past ten years without you. Without question, your loyalty, friendship and hard work have been invaluable and if I had been a much younger man I don't doubt I would have fallen a little bit in love with you.'

Feeling her cheeks glow warmly, Rose smiled back—even as she remembered Gene Bonnaire's ridiculous implication that her relationship with her boss might not be just a *working* one. *What she'd give to wipe that self-satisfied smirk off his handsome face when next she saw him!* Only she couldn't. She had to be nice to him because Philip urgently needed this sale. The last thing she would do was jeopardise things just because the man had rattled her.

But then, as she recalled that he'd asked her if other people ever reciprocated her kindness to them, she knew that the man had much more sensitivity than his very public persona suggested and thought that it would be intriguing to discover more…

'It's sweet of you to say so,' she answered Philip, 'but to be frank I think I'm destined to stay single. I've only been in love once in my life and it wasn't the happiest of experiences. I'm not eager to do it again.'

'I'm sorry to hear that. Don't you believe that it might be different the next time? Not so painful, I mean?'

'No, I don't. I don't because—present company not included—I don't trust men. I think I'd be better off on my own.' She shrugged. 'Besides, I'm far too independent, and men sense that. It would take someone pretty exceptional to get me to change my mind and I haven't yet met anyone who fits that particular bill.'

'Not yet, you haven't, Rose, but you will…you will.'

With a knowing smile, the man in the hospital bed closed his eyes and, leaving him to doze, she folded the sheet of notepaper he'd given her, slipped it into her bag and discreetly left…

CHAPTER THREE

Standing in one of his magnificent rooms, where huge plate-glass windows overlooked the ocean, Gene took the call from his secretary informing him that Rose Heathcote had requested a meeting. By the time he ended the call he was feeling more than vindicated. There could only be one reason why the feisty brunette wanted to see him, and that must be to convey the news that her boss had finally agreed to his offer.

He was elated. All his fantasies about owning the gracious building beside the Thames and turning it into the finest restaurant imaginable were becoming a dazzling reality in his mind.

He already knew the people he wanted to hire—both to do the renovations and to create and provide the cuisine that would be second to none. He had the private numbers of some of the finest chefs and sommeliers in the country, and he wasn't above using his money and power to entice them away from their current exclusive establishments. Before much time had passed the place would be up and running and he would be welcoming anybody who was anybody and yet again demonstrating to the world just how far drive and ambition could take a person if they were dedicated enough.

Make no mistake. Eugene Bonnaire was a force to be reckoned with.

His parents had never understood his ambition and drive for more…more money, more success, *more everything…* But they had both come from humble families in France, with barely a franc to keep body and soul together—hardworking folk who had barely eked out a sustainable living.

'Our families may not have always had enough food to put on the table but there was no lack of love in our homes,' his mother had often told him.

But the very idea of not having the most basic requirements had pained their son. No matter how much love they'd had, their lives had been pretty grim when they were growing up. Was it any wonder that Gene wanted so much more, to obliterate the stain of his ancestors' impoverished past?

Yes, his parents had made an admirable success of their East London restaurant, and their teaching him to cook at a young age had been a great platform for him to hone his culinary skills—a fact for which he was eternally grateful. It was that which had led to him becoming a much lauded chef, then a successful restaurateur. Add to that some eye-popping lucrative investments and the sky was his limit… But it had always been beyond him that his parents couldn't see that they could have had so much more for *themselves*…weren't even *interested.*

Breathing out a sigh, he rubbed his hand over his chest. It had been several months now since he'd paid them a visit and he knew they must be concerned. But he guessed that they didn't want to put pressure on him in case he did the unthinkable and cut them out of his life for good. *He would never do such a thing...* God knew they'd suffered enough.

When Gene had been just nine years old they had lost his little sister, Francesca, to a stomach virus. She had been only three. That shattering experience had changed them all. His mother had used to smile so easily—but not any more... There was always the sense that something vital and irreplaceable was missing when they were together, and of course there *was...*

Ever since that time Gene had sought to compensate his parents for their loss. If he became successful, he had reasoned, they would be so proud of him, and in turn he could ensure they enjoyed a comfortable old age. But somehow his success and ambition hadn't seemed to overly impress them. It was the one area in his life where he felt a failure. Consequently, his relationship with them had begun to deteriorate.

Feeling as though he'd lost the ability to properly connect with them, he had turned in on himself to protect his emotions. Inevitably, his other relationships had suffered. Women sensed that he wasn't available emotionally, and now the only women he seemed to attract were the ones who liked his wealth and what it could buy for them... That being the case, he'd decided to keep his liaisons short and sweet. More meaningful and longer-term relationships definitely weren't on his agenda...

But as he crossed the polished parquet floor to the door unbidden he suddenly found himself recalling the incandescent violet of Rose Heathcote's eyes. Without a doubt the woman intrigued and excited him. Gene mused that perhaps she wouldn't be so averse to his company now, when she would in effect be coming to him cap in hand because Philip Houghton had finally seen the sense in agreeing to sell him the shop. In any case, it meant that Gene would have the upper hand, and the diminutive Rose would no doubt have to swallow her pride and be nice to him.

He had no intention of making things easy for her either. Having not long ago arrived at his personal retreat on a remote Scottish island—the one place where he could genuinely enjoy some respite and didn't have to contend with petty jealousies and criticism from press and public alike—he wasn't about to charge back to London to sign the papers for purchase in a hurry. *Not when the tide had just turned in his favour.* No, he would insist that Rose brought them to *him*. Although he had never even invited family or friends to this house, he would make an exception for the brunette.

In that instant Gene knew that he would make it his mission to change Rose's mind about him. He would slowly reveal more of his true nature and let her see that, despite what she might have read and heard about him, he was at his core an *honourable* man.

As he opened the door and went out he felt more than a little pleased with his decision…

Faced with the prospect of spending time in a landscape as alien to her as the moon, Rose gritted her teeth and braced herself as a friendly Scottish boatman guided a sturdy fishing boat towards the island.

As fierce waves lashed at the sides and inevitably splashed her she couldn't help praying that she was doing the right thing in adhering to Philip's heartfelt plea to take the papers to the arrogant businessman and get the deal 'done and dusted' as quickly as possible. Philip had looked so poorly when she'd last seen him in the hospital that the need to arrange some full-time care for him when he went home—at least until he had recovered more fully—had become glaringly imperative.

'This is a rare event,' the young curly-headed boatman remarked cheerfully as he steered the craft towards a landing bay carved out between the rocks. 'As far as I know the Lord of the Manor never has women visit him here… In fact, he never has *anyone*. It's his private hideaway, he told me once. He likes the remoteness of the place. 'It helps him to think straight.' Grinning, he added, 'Must like you a lot, I'd say.'

Grimacing painfully, Rose answered. 'The truth is the man doesn't like me at all. The sooner my business with him is over and I'm heading away from here, the better.'

'Well, the soonest you can leave is tomorrow, lass. The tides dictate when you can come and go. They're a stern mistress to these remote islands.'

'I can't leave until *tomorrow*?' Crestfallen at the news, Rose wrinkled her smooth brow in distress. 'You mean I'll have to stay here overnight?'

'Yes, lass. I'm sure His Lordship will have made arrangements. Here we go—give me your hand and I'll help you out.'

Once on terra firma, although it was rocky and felt less than safe underfoot, Rose couldn't deny she was relieved to be on dry land again. The small craft had negotiated the choppiest of seas on their crossing and she couldn't attest to being remotely excited by it. Give her the ground beneath her feet any day. At least there she felt some small semblance of control.

Arranging the strap of her red leather tote more securely over her shoulder, she lifted her hand to shade her eyes from a watery sun and stared. The wind was groaning with a mournful howl and as far as she could see the surrounding landscape looked relentlessly bleak. She shivered hard.

There was no welcoming party in sight to greet her—but then she wasn't exactly surprised. Although Gene Bonnaire had arranged for a luxurious sedan to pick her up and take her to the airport, and had provided a business class ticket for her to travel on the plane, Rose wasn't resting on her laurels. The two encounters she'd had with the man had been both unpredictable and unsettling, but as she'd made the effort to travel all this way to bring him the documents to sign she thought he might at least have had the decency to meet her and take her up to the house.

'Likely he's forgotten what time you were arriving...' The boatman lifted a broad shoulder in an apologetic shrug.

'Can I get a signal here to ring him on my mobile?' she asked hopefully.

The boatman shook his head. 'Sorry, but we don't have any service. I'd take you up to the house myself, but I've got to make tracks straight away or lose the tide. See that path marked out up ahead? Follow it right to the top and you'll get to Four Winds. You can't exactly miss it. The house is like some huge glass fortress from a sci-fi movie.'

'What about the other people on the island? Where do *they* live?'

'They don't. Live here, I mean. When he's here, Mr Bonnaire is the sole inhabitant.'

Rose took a deep breath in. So, not only did she have to stay on the island tonight, but she would be marooned with one of the most unpredictable and challenging men she'd ever met. Now she really *did* have to grit her teeth.

As she turned to watch the boatman get back into his craft she had a real sense of being abandoned. She knew that wasn't good for her morale. The last thing she needed to feel when she came face to face with Gene Bonnaire again was unsure. The man had too many advantages as it was. And the most disturbing of all wasn't his power and wealth, but his arrogant belief that money could get him anything he wanted—that getting what he wanted was in fact his *right,* even if it meant remorselessly manipulating people to achieve it…

She addressed the young man who'd brought her over to the island. 'Will you be collecting me tomorrow?'

'Aye, it will be me. If you could be here in the morning round eleven I'll come and get you.'

'I wish it could be sooner…'

'You'll be all right, lass. His bark is worse than his bite.'

'You're a lot more confident about that than I am. By the way, I didn't ask your name or tell you mine. I'm Rose…Rose Heathcote.'

'You can call me Rory. It's nice to meet you, Rose. Well, I'd best be on my way. Take care, won't you? Chin up—and don't worry. Just look at His Lordship with those beguiling violet eyes of yours and he'll be putty in your hands! Bye, now!'

With a cheerful salute, Rory expertly steered the craft out of the rocky bay and headed out to sea.

Warmed by his jovial assurance, Rose stood for perhaps longer than she should have, watching the boat. It very quickly disappeared, engulfed by the wind and the rain and the thrashing waves as if it had never been. Offering up a silent prayer for the young boatman's safe journey home, she turned and negotiated some rocks that had been carved into paving stones and made her way onto the path marked out on the hillside.

By the time she'd made the deceptively steep climb to the end, even though on several occasions the icy wind had threatened to unbalance her and she'd had to watch carefully where she stepped, she was surprisingly warm, and she was more than a little out of breath when an impressive glass edifice loomed up before her.

Rory's description had been right on the money. Four Winds *was* like something out of a sci-fi movie. All that glass and chrome was a stunning contradiction, set in the bleak and yet beautiful landscape that embraced it.

Wiping away the sea spray that had moistened her face, Rose stared for what felt like an eternity, trying to make out where the entrance to the building was. Because it was a circular design, it wasn't easy to detect. There was no sign of Gene Bonnaire. How could she be sure he was even *there*?

As tense seconds turned into minutes she had a battle royal on her hands to keep her fury at bay. *What the hell did the man think he was playing at?* What if he'd changed his mind about his offer. What if he'd decided to pay her back for not agreeing to persuade Philip he should sell to him straight away and had made her come all the way out here to this remote Scottish island just because he *could*?

Her heart thumped so hard it felt as if it might burst out of her chest. If this was Gene Bonnaire's warped idea of a joke then it wasn't remotely funny...

'Well, well, well...look who the wind's blown in.'

The deeply gravelled tone almost made Rose jump out of her skin. Glancing up, she saw that part of the glass edifice had silently peeled back to reveal an entrance. Standing outside that futuristic doorway was the man she'd come to see. Dressed in fitted blue jeans that hugged his hard-muscled thighs and a black cashmere sweater, he had his arms casually folded across his impressive chest, giving the impression that it was the most natural thing in the world for him to come outside and find her standing there.

Clearly she wasn't going to receive an apology for his not meeting her off the boat...just his usual mockery. Her warmed hands had quickly turned icily cold while she'd been searching for the doorway, and now she gripped the strap of her tote hard as she fought to counter his cavalier treatment.

'You're lucky I'm here at all. I could have been blown off that hillside into the sea more than once on the way up here and you would have been none the wiser. Is this the way you usually treat your visitors?'

'No… It isn't…'

She had the briefest glimpse of what looked like regret in his fierce blue eyes—almost as if the idea had genuinely hurt him.

'I don't have any visitors here,' he stated. 'This is my private retreat and that's usually the way I like it. I've accorded *you* the privilege of coming here, Rose, because you have something that I very much want… and we both know what that is. However, I'm sincerely sorry that I wasn't down on the shore to meet you—I was busy with some work and simply forgot the time. I trust your journey wasn't too arduous?'

Rose suddenly felt ridiculously guilty. The Frenchman had sent a car to pick her up and take her to the station, and on the plane he'd arranged for her to travel first class. She had no complaints about the journey…

'It wasn't arduous at all. It's not every day that I get to travel business class. It was very pleasant, in fact.'

'Good. Well, you'd better come inside and get warm. And, by the way, there was no danger of you being blown off the hillside.' The corners of his eyes crinkled in amusement. 'You were too far inland for that.'

Biting back an irritable retort, Rose hurriedly moved

past him into a curved entrance hall. A sublime wave of welcoming heat enveloped her. Dropping her tote onto the pristine oak floor, she rubbed her hands together to restore their circulation.

Her reluctant host joined her and the chrome and glass wall behind him slid elegantly closed. She had a disturbing moment of fear, realising she didn't know how to open them again. Were the controls some kind of heat-sensitive mechanism that only recognised the house's owner?

Swallowing hard, she turned round to face him. 'The boatman—Rory—told me I'd have to stay here until tomorrow because of the tides. I don't want to inconvenience you, but I wish you'd told your secretary to tell me that before I travelled.'

'Would you still have come if I had?'

'Of course I would. I'm doing this purely to help Philip, Mr Bonnaire, so I'll do whatever is necessary.'

'Ah, Philip…' His tone suggested the idea that she should undertake what was clearly for her an unwelcome mission only because of loyalty to her boss irked him. 'How is he? Getting better, I hope?'

'As a matter of fact he's still in hospital. He took a turn for the worse. That's what has motivated him to accept your offer.' Rose's heart thumped a little harder as she was suddenly reminded of the precarious nature of her boss's health.

'I'm sorry to hear that. Please convey my wishes to him that he may get better soon. And, by the way, please call me Gene. Mr Bonnaire sounds ridiculously formal, considering the situation we're in. Why don't you come with me into the sitting room and I'll get you a hot drink?'

Rose wasn't so proud that she'd deny that was just what she longed for. The chill on that hillside and in the boat must have seeped into her bones.

'Thank you. I'd like that.'

Pushing her fingers through her short damp hair, she retrieved her holdall and followed her host through what seemed like an acreage of corridor into a wide, spacious living area furnished with state-of-the-art minimalist couches and chairs and a glass table long enough to seat a small dinner party.

The vista through the huge uncovered windows was breathtaking. The rain was pouring from the skies in an endless stream now, and every time it lashed against the flawless glass it was accompanied by the anguished and ethereal sigh of the wind. But nothing detracted from the stunning beauty that surrounded the futuristic building. The wildness of the sea and the terrain were absolutely fitting.

Yet what was a successful entrepreneur who seemed to have an insatiable desire for everything—be it property, land, not to mention beautiful women—doing with a sanctuary in this wild, isolated place with just himself for company? Rose couldn't help feeling even more intrigued.

'What would you like? Tea, coffee, hot chocolate? Or perhaps you'd prefer something stronger?'

She swung her gaze round to meet Gene's. He looked to be studying her with interest. His intense blue eyes suggested he had the capacity to look right inside her, and the idea made her shiver. The planes and angles of his face were uncommonly perfect, yet at the same time undoubtedly proclaimed him to be powerfully Alpha. He was so handsome that she couldn't help wondering what he would look like if he *really* smiled—if he was to drop that arrogant air of his for even a moment and genuinely connected with someone for no other reason than that it was *human*…

Shrugging off the notion because she sensed it was pointless, she replied, 'Hot chocolate sounds wonderful.'

'Your wish is my command. Why don't you sit down and make yourself comfortable? You can watch the storm that's coming, knowing you're sitting inside safe and warm.'

'There's a storm coming?'

'Of course…' He jerked his head towards the skyline. 'See those clouds that look like purple and black bruises? They definitely herald a storm. It's likely to be a big one, so all we can do is batten down the hatches and watch the entertainment. Are you up for watching nature at its wildest, Rose?'

She hadn't missed the provocative implication in his gravelled voice. Nor had she forgotten that scorching kiss he'd given her on his second visit to the shop. More than once the memory had made her catch her breath…

Arching a brow, she responded, 'None of us can control the weather—so why not? Seeing as my stay here was unforeseen, and isn't likely to be remotely pleasurable, it might be a welcome distraction and will help the time to pass more quickly.'

To Rose's astonishment he threw back his head and laughed. It was a full-throated, hearty sound that made her pulse skitter wildly and her blood heat. She'd told him that she didn't anticipate her stay would be pleasurable but in that unexpected moment, as the aloof businessman expressed a response to something that clearly elicited delight, once again she found herself helplessly warming to him.

'Can I ask what you find so funny?'

He dropped his hands to his straight lean hips and stared at her. 'I find your determination not to like me and your desire to leave my company as quickly as possible oddly endearing, Rose. I'm not exaggerating when I tell you that most women have the opposite reaction when they receive an invitation from me.'

'I'm sure it can't be just because of your scintillating personality…'

Gene's dazzling blue eyes narrowed. 'I agree, it's not my personality or even my looks that women are drawn to. Don't you think I *know* that? They're drawn to me because I'm a very rich man. I can buy them beautiful things and take them to all the best places. When they're with me it makes them feel special. It's not hard to work out why they like me. You're frowning. Does it surprise you that I would be so frank?'

Rose shivered as an icy drip of water slid off the ends of her hair and down onto the back of her neck, but her attention didn't waver for a second as she contemplated her host's chiselled countenance.

She sighed. 'More than finding it surprising, I'm disturbed that it doesn't bother you. I mean, can you honestly say that you're comfortable with women who only want to be with you for what you can give them materially?'

Right at that moment a flash of lightning still some way off on the horizon made her flinch, and thunder grumbled ominously. Although she'd deliberately made light of anticipating the 'entertainment' that was coming, thunder and lightning had always terrified her.

'I'm a realist, Rose. At least I don't kid myself. But you might also ask me if people disappoint me when they're so obviously shallow? My answer is *yes*…they do.'

They both fell silent for a while, each immersed in their unspoken reflections about the other…

It was Gene who ended the lull in the conversation. 'Before I get you that hot chocolate I'll show you into a guestroom and you can change out of those wet clothes. Do you have a spare set with you? If not, then I'm sure I can find you something.'

Surprised that he should be so considerate, Rose shrugged. 'Yes, I do. I brought a change of clothes with me in case I had to book into a hotel before I returned. It's a long journey to do in one day.'

'Good. Then follow me.'

As he guided Rose back out into the corridor and into the expansive area that housed the guestrooms—ironically for the guests he never invited—Gene knew a surprising pleasure at being able to help her to feel more comfortable. With her big violet eyes, her diminutive form and the dark hair that had been plastered to her head in the softly falling rain, she'd looked so small and delicate when he'd opened the door and found her standing there.

To his amazement, his pulse had inexplicably quickened at the sight of her. He'd never experienced such an unexpected reaction to a woman before and, disturbingly, he didn't think it was solely because she'd brought him the means to purchase the antiques shop building…

CHAPTER FOUR

RELIEVED TO FIND a hairdryer in the luxurious en-suite bathroom that accompanied the spacious guestroom, Rose sat on the capacious bed drying her damp hair. As the dryer blew welcome heat onto her scalp and neck she stared out through the surrounding bank of windows at the roiling sea and the ever more threatening darkening sky, her belly clenching at the thought of the storm that would very soon envelop them. She'd already witnessed one or two bolts of forked lightning in the distance and couldn't help flinching.

'Get a grip, Rose, for God's sake!' she scolded herself. But in truth it didn't help to engender confidence when she was going to have to sit out the coming elemental furore with Gene Bonnaire. As soon as he saw that she was scared would he mock her?

Recalling that he'd referred to the gathering storm clouds as being like 'purple and black bruises', she confessed to being surprised that he would use such a poetic turn of phrase. When he'd asserted that he had no interest in antiques whatsoever, Rose had wondered why they seemed to leave him cold. Couldn't he see the beauty and artistry in their creation? It had bothered her that he couldn't. Yet why refer to storm clouds as bruises in the sky? Didn't that suggest there was something in him that saw beyond the material? Some innate sense that recognised the incomparable beauty and necessity of nature, knowing that it was the one thing nobody had any control over?

Rising to her feet, she returned the hairdryer to its rightful place in the bathroom. As she turned she caught sight of herself in the generous-sized gilt-edged mirror. Her skin looked white as alabaster and the dark blue sheen in her black hair gleamed fiercely where it caught the light. Most of all, her violet eyes looked big and *scared*.

What was *wrong* with her? Was it just the coming storm she was frightened of? Or was it the thought of spending time with Gene?

Impatient with herself, she returned to the bedroom. After hanging her Arran sweater in a mirrored wardrobe whose doors swished open when she held her hand briefly over an electronic button, as her host had demonstrated, she donned the fresh pink woollen one she'd brought as a spare. Tugging it down over her jeans, she pinched her cheeks to instil a little more colour into them and then returned to the room that Gene had first taken her to.

Rose was amazed when she found it easily. Clearly her sense of direction hadn't let her down.

She found Gene seated on one of the futuristic couches opposite the glass table, his elbows resting against his hard-muscled thighs as he stared out of the windows at the increasingly wild weather. Two steaming mugs were evident on the table as she approached.

Glancing up at her, he smiled. Startled, she fell headlong into his sublime azure gaze and forgot her own name. She'd never seen a man as beautiful... More than that, she had never experienced the forceful sense of a desire so profound that it stopped her in her tracks and—frighteningly—made it hard to breathe...

Gene's heart jolted and plunged him into a reverie of lust and longing that was unprecedented. Transfixed by the sight of the petite and pretty woman in front him, dressed in a girlish pink sweater and fitted blue jeans, all he could do was stare. What *was* it about her elfin features and ethereal eyes that made it hard to think straight when he looked at her? She wasn't a bit like any of the voluptuous women he was usually attracted to.

Suddenly aware that her appearance had rendered him momentarily dumb, he cleared his throat. Then he reached for one of the mugs of steaming hot chocolate and handed it to her. 'I see you found your way back, then? I've made your drink. You should sit down and enjoy it while it's hot.'

'Thanks. You timed it perfectly.' Accepting the proffered mug, Rose moved to the other end of the couch and sat down.

Gene's reaction at the distance she'd put between them was at first amused, then irritated. 'Why don't you come and sit closer to me? I promise I don't bite.'

Cupping her drink, she crumpled her smooth brow a little. 'That sounds like an invitation from the Big Bad Wolf...'

'Do you think of yourself as Little Red Riding Hood, then?'

'Why not? She was a very clever girl. She saw through the wolf right from the beginning. She knew he was up to no good.'

She flushed and Gene sensed his blood heatedly go south. How had he not seen just how engaging this woman was the moment he'd first set eyes on her?

Clearly unfazed by his teasing invitation to sit closer, she took an experimental sip of hot chocolate and licked her lips. The unknowingly provocative gesture had the effect of making his already entranced gaze hone in on the alluring shape of her mouth. The sight inevitably brought back the memory of the kiss he'd stolen at the antiques shop. He tightened as he remembered the luxuriant taste of her satin textured lips and the tide of molten longing that had flowed through him.

'My God, this is so good!' She smiled. 'How did you learn to make it so delicious?'

Once again Gene had to shake himself out of the trance he'd seemingly fallen into. 'My father taught me. He's a connoisseur in the art of making sinfully delicious hot chocolate. "Make this for the woman in your life, son, and she'll love you forever." That's what he used to say.'

'And do you? Make it for the woman in your life, I mean?'

He couldn't take the question lightly. Not when he'd never let a woman get close enough to engage his emotions, let alone make her his mate for life…

Disgruntled, he replied, 'No. I don't have a particular

woman in my life—and neither do I want to. I believe in keeping my options open.'

'You mean you'd prefer to have a selection of women to choose from rather than just one special one?'

He sensed an aggravated muscle jerk in the side of his cheek. 'I suppose you could say that.'

Rose's violet gaze was thoughtful. 'Then I guess I'm privileged that you chose to make hot chocolate for me, Mr Bonnaire, especially when I'm not remotely interested in joining your select little harem.'

'Indeed. And I asked you to call me Gene,' he snapped, unhappy that she should dismiss him so mockingly. It was hardly flattering.

Why on earth had he mentioned that silly comment his father had made? Not only had it highlighted to Rose that he liked to play the field—a fact he suddenly didn't feel proud of at all—but referencing the man who had raised him made him feel wretchedly guilty that he hadn't seen him in a while. It wasn't something he wanted to dwell on.

Pushing to his feet, he moved restlessly towards the panoramic windows and was momentarily captivated by the gigantic waves crashing violently against the rocks on the shoreline.

'Storm's getting wilder…' he murmured.

'Do they bother you…storms, I mean?'

Turning to smile at the woman Gene now realised was innately curious, he felt a frisson of excitement throb through him. What else might Rose be curious about if he were to delve a little deeper? he wondered.

'They don't bother me at all. I certainly don't fear

them, if that's what you're getting at. The more wild and furious they are the better, as far as I'm concerned. As you commented earlier, Rose, the unpredictable quality of nature is an ever-present reminder that people aren't in control of everything…even though some of us might like to think we are.'

His companion looked genuinely surprised. 'Forgive me, but I never guessed you could be so philosophical. You definitely gave me the impression that you're a man who likes to be firmly in control.'

For a long moment Gene contemplated the remark. Rose's deceptively calm demeanour gave no clue as to how feisty she was, or indeed how challenging she could be. Yet again he was taken aback that she dared to be so candid with her opinions. He wasn't used to that. It was true that he prided himself on being in control, but he didn't particularly enjoy it being pointed out to him. It might give his opposition an advantage. He also liked to steer the direction his conversations went in, so that they didn't stray into areas he didn't want them to go. He had a genuine fear of being exposed, of being seen as vulnerable in any way.

Biting back his irritation, he asked, 'And what about you, Rose? Do *you* like storms?'

As she set down her mug of hot chocolate on the table her expression was uneasy. 'Not particularly. To tell you the truth, they scare me. Not so much the wind and the rain, or even the thunder…it's the lightning I don't like. I've always been afraid of it. Once when I was little there was the most terrifying storm one night. Some lightning hit our greenhouse and shattered all the glass. It was like a bomb exploding. I was afraid to go back to sleep in case it happened again. No doubt that event has programmed me to be afraid of it for life. I have occasionally thought of getting some therapy…'

Finding himself intrigued, Gene moved back to the couch and sat down—but this time he deliberately positioned himself a little closer to Rose. 'It's not therapy you need, *ma chère*, but courage.'

'I'm not a coward.'

'Did I suggest that you were? Everyone has something they're afraid of. It's only human. No, what I'm saying is that you have to face your fears head-on. Expose them for what they are.'

'And what *are* they?'

Rose's voice had nervously dropped a little lower, and Gene saw the child she'd once been, too afraid to go back to sleep after lightning had shattered her greenhouse. It made him feel fiercely protective of her.

'They're just *illusions*. Thoughts in your head that don't serve you… Don't let them get the better of you or they'll dictate what you can and can't do for the rest of your life.'

'Is that how you handle *your* fears, Gene?'

For a sensually charged moment he absorbed the prickles of warmth that flared in his belly at the sound of his name on her lips, then he replied, 'Thankfully, they rarely arise for me—but, yes…that's how I handle them.'

'You mean there are no ifs or buts or maybes?'

'I don't let anything stop me from getting what I want, Rose—least of all *doubt*.'

'That's obviously why you appear to be so fearless, then?'

He didn't like it that she'd said *appear*. It suggested there was an element of doubt in her mind—that the confident image he projected wasn't all it seemed. Yet again Rose Heathcote was pushing all his hot buttons and the conversation was definitely taking a direction he didn't appreciate.

It seriously bothered him that he should be so unsettled by a woman, and he quickly sought to reassert his position.

'What you see with me is what you get, sweetheart. I don't need to resort to pretence. If you'd ever read my résumé you'd know that's a fact. My success speaks for itself. Now, as interesting as it undoubtedly is, I think we should bring this little conversation to an end. We'll both need something to eat soon, and I plan on cooking us dinner.'

Surprised, Rose quickly got to her feet. 'I don't want you to go to any trouble. A simple snack will do. I don't need a full-blown meal.'

'Say that to any top chef and they're likely to eject you from the restaurant. Food is more than just essential fuel, Rose… *Great* food is manna from heaven. A "simple snack" is not, and you won't be getting any such thing from me.'

Tucking her hair behind her ear, she felt her cheeks turn arrestingly pink. 'I meant no offence. But if you're insisting on cooking us a meal then the least I can do is help you…'

Gene immediately warmed to the idea. So much so,

he couldn't suppress a grin. 'So your talents go beyond being a devoted and able assistant in the antiques trade?'

She immediately looked stung. 'I'm not just an assistant. I'm a dealer in my own right.'

'Ah… That tells me that being valued and admired for your achievements *does* matter to you. We're not so different after all, are we? Very well, you can be my sous-chef tonight. Let's go into the kitchen and we'll get started.'

Gene handed Rose a white chef's apron and rolled up his sleeves. The tanned skin of his forearms looked silky smooth, and was dusted with a fine coating of dark hair.

As the rain thundered against the roof with increasing force, and the waves at the shoreline spewed icy foam against the jagged rocks, he instructed her on where she could locate the essential items they needed. The stunningly vast 'space age' kitchen didn't reveal its secrets easily. Drawers opened with the lightest touch, or a hand held in front of a discreet sensor, and the refrigerator and freezer looked as if they'd been designed by someone who excelled in writing sci-fi.

Rose's heart knocked anxiously against her ribs at being part of a scenario she would never have envisaged in a thousand years. From their first meeting Gene Bonnaire had challenged her. His too-confident air and superior manner unsettled her more than just a little. Add to that his reputation for acquiring anything he wanted simply because his money dictated that he could, in truth there was little to commend him to Rose.

She had never been the kind of woman who was easily impressed by a man, no matter what his credentials. A good character—someone honourable and loyal— that was what she secretly wanted in a man.

She'd once foolishly fallen for a stockbroker who had professed himself to be madly in love with her and wanted to marry her. But, although briefly dazzled by his declarations of adoration and devotion, Rose had soon found out that it was all a game to him. It had stroked his ego to think that she couldn't live without him. He'd enjoyed the power he had imagined it gave him over her. But his ambition to make money and go much further in his career had been his top priority— not *her*. And when she'd found out that she wasn't the *only* woman he professed to adore Rose had vowed never to make such a painful mistake again and had ended the relationship.

The man her mother had left her father for was also driven by money and status, and he was insufferably ar-rogant. Rose had not had cause to change her opinion in all the years she had known him. All she saw when she looked at David Carlisle was the man who had selfishly charmed her mother with his money and his looks just because it had stroked his ego to win over a happily mar-ried woman and—having won her—destroy her family.

When her mother, Ruth, had left it had been the first time Rose had seen her usually resolute father cry...

Gene Bonnaire was obviously cut from the same cloth as her ex *and* her mother's second husband, and she had plenty of reasons not to trust him. Hadn't he already indicated that he was an uncaring playboy—the kind of man who took what he wanted simply because

his money and position allowed him to be as mercenary as he liked?

Yet here she was in his isolated sanctuary on a remote Scottish island, miles away from anywhere civilised, and until the boatman Rory met her tomorrow
to take her back to the mainland she had to make the
best of things. She'd sleep a whole lot better tonight if
she didn't antagonise the man.

Despite all of that, she couldn't help recalling that
crazily unreal moment when her gaze had locked with
Gene's and molten desire had made her feel frighteningly weak. For a shocking instant there had been the
urge to abandon all reason and surrender to the wild
and wanton nature of it... How was any sane person
able to explain such a thing?

Rose could only put it down to the fact that her guard
was down after all the stress she'd endured recently.
Philip was still in the hospital, and out of the blue he'd
decided to sell the property to Gene.

One thing was certain: she would do everything in
her power to make sure that a repetition of that crazy
moment between them wouldn't happen. In fact she
probably wouldn't rest easy until Gene had signed the
documents she'd brought and deposited the funds for the
sale into Philip's account. Then and only then would she
be convinced that she'd done the right thing in coming
here on behalf of the man who wasn't just her employer
and mentor but her surrogate uncle as well.

Like many people who loved and appreciated crafts-
manship in all its forms, after watching Gene effort-

lessly put the most sublime meal together Rose had to attest that the man was a supreme artisan.

It had been fascinating to watch him work with his hands. Whether it was slicing onions on a chopping board, rubbing spices between his fingers and sprinkling them into the food as he stood over the stove, or working the delicious ingredients he'd put together in a pan with two or three economical stirs, she'd found herself becoming more and more intrigued by the man. With his handsome profile diligently focused, he looked as if he inhabited another world when he was cooking, and the so-called commonplace activity somehow made him seem much more human...

'Should be ready soon—would you like a taste?'

In a near trance where she stood by Gene's side, Rose glanced up at him in surprise. He scooped some food from the aromatic pan onto a metal spoon and offered it to her. *She didn't need to be asked twice.*

His compellingly blue eyes glinted knowingly as she expressed her pleasure at what she'd tasted with an appreciative groan.

'That's amazing! I've never tasted anything so delicious in my life...'

'Haven't you? That makes me want to give you more delicious things to try.'

She felt her skin flame red, and a mixture of embarrassment and irritation throbbed through her.

But then Gene stepped towards her.

'You've got some sauce at the side of your mouth... let me get it for you.'

With the pad of his thumb, he wiped it away. But it

was no simple gesture. The way he lingered over the task made it seem like some kind of erotic foreplay, and as he pressed his flesh against the side of Rose's lips it was as though he ignited a flame that wouldn't easily be extinguished.

There wasn't a single part of her body that didn't feel restless and hot. Trapped by his gaze, all she could do was stare helplessly. But at the same time her intuition alerted her to the danger... *What was she thinking?* Dear God, she was behaving as if she was *enjoying* his attention. One thing she was sure of: Gene Bonnaire didn't need another entranced woman pandering to his already inflated ego.

Stepping hastily away, she grabbed some kitchen towel and dabbed at her lips, unconsciously seeking to obliterate his touch.

Watching her, he released a low-voiced chuckle. 'I hope you're not feeling nervous around me, Rose? I told you I don't bite...' Levelling his chiselled jaw at her, he paused and smiled. 'That is unless you *want* me to?'

Rose's heart thundered so hard in her chest that she wondered he didn't hear it.

As adrenaline shot through her system on a dizzying white water rapid she straightened her shoulders and aimed for a withering glare. 'You know, you might think that *all* women enjoy your insincere flirtatious technique...that they should even be *grateful* for the attention...but I can assure you that *I* don't. That said, I think I should go and lay the table while you finish cooking the food.'

Opening a drawer that she'd learned was full of silver

cutlery she grabbed the necessary knives and forks and closed it again. Not waiting for further comment, she strode out of the kitchen with her head held deliberately high, praying as she went through the door that she'd remember where to locate the dining room...

CHAPTER FIVE

BRINGING A BOTTLE of Scotch whisky over to the coffee
table, Gene poured some into the two waiting glass
tumblers. His reluctant house guest was sitting with her
shapely legs tucked beneath her on the couch, a satin
cushion clutched to her belly, her transfixed gaze focused on the scene that played outside the windows as
if she couldn't believe what she was seeing.

He'd witnessed a few wild storms since he'd built his
sanctuary but never one quite like this. The thunder was
akin to an earth-shattering sonic boom, whose power
shook the walls of the futuristic dwelling he was so
proud of. And the *rain*… The rain was like an enraged
wild river that had burst its banks and was ruthlessly
deluging everything in its wake. It was impossible to
see where the sky ended and the ocean began.

And, like the most magnificent firework display ever
conceived, the lightning had come.

They'd been expecting it for hours now, and had
sensed the atmosphere growing thicker and thicker. It
had grown so thick that *something* had to cut through
it to lessen the tension.

Having arrived at last, the electrifying bolts that ripped through the atmosphere with their eerily bright light did exactly that. But the deafening noise and fury even made Eugene's heart jolt. Sensing a muscle tighten in the side of his jaw, he glanced at his companion. It was plain to see that she was more than a little jumpy.

'Rose?' Feeling an uncharacteristic sense of concern, he leant towards her and pressed a glass into her hand. 'I'd advise you to drink some of this. Not just because it's the best malt whisky in the world, and I only ever drink the best, but it might help calm your nerves.'

Although her hand shook a little, Rose tipped the glass back and gulped down some of the contents. Almost instantly her incandescent violet eyes flooded with tears. Then she started to cough.

Gene reached round to pat her on the back, his lips shaping an amused smile. 'You drank that down a bit too quickly, sweetheart. Make the next sip a little slower, hmm…?'

Returning his wry look, she commented, 'I'll bear that in mind. It's pretty powerful stuff, isn't it?'

'This particular blend is smoky, sweet and smooth. But I don't doubt to a novice it can still pack a punch.'

Even as he was speaking a fierce display of dazzling lightning lit up the room, highlighting everything in full cinematic glory.

'Oh my God!' Visibly shocked, Rose all but threw herself against him.

Even though he knew it was purely a reflex reaction, instigated by fear, Gene was inordinately pleased that in that instant she genuinely seemed to need him. He'd never experienced anything remotely like the feeling before, and it made his heart race a little.

As the gentle scent of her summery perfume made provocative inroads into his senses he draped his hard-muscled arm round her slender shoulders and pulled her a little closer to him.

His beard-roughened jaw glanced against the silkily soft strands of her ebony hair and he murmured, 'It's all right, Rose. Nothing's going to hurt you…I promise…'

At first she stiffened at the assurance, and then she relaxed.

Relieved, Gene was glad she didn't pull away. Despite the storm raging outside, he felt strangely peaceful as he sat there with Rose. He had a distinct sense of being introduced to an aspect of his character that he'd never before suspected. The only woman he'd ever felt remotely protective towards before was his mother. His more intimate female relationships all centred round money and sex. *His* desire for sex and *their* desire for money… Genuine intimacy didn't feature. How could it when he'd allowed himself to become more and more distant from his feelings? Since his little sister had died the spectre of loss and heartbreak was ever-present, and in truth he *feared* it…

The soft weight against his arm grew a little heavier and Rose's quiet, steady breathing made Gene realise that she'd fallen asleep.

It seemed to be a day of shocks and surprises, he thought wryly. Not only had the ferocity of the storm taken him aback, but the realisation that he wasn't just *enduring* his visitor's company but was actively *enjoy-*

ing it really rattled him. His pleasure at being able to purchase the lovely old shop building hadn't dominated his thoughts half as much as he'd expected it to.

He frowned. *Why was that?*

Settling back more comfortably against the cushions, hardly aware that he was doing so, he drowsily let his eyelids drift closed...

The first thing that alerted him to the realisation that he'd fallen asleep was Rose trying to disengage his arm from her shoulders. Eugene cursed...*loudly.* The limb had cramped painfully, and in the throes of sleep he thought someone was attacking him. His primal masculine instinct was automatic.

When he sat up and grabbed his imagined attacker Rose yelped, and the shocked look on her face woke him up to the reality of what he was doing. His hands were tightly gripping her arms through her soft woollen sweater and she looked absolutely terrified. Albeit indignant...

Even as he lessened the pressure of his fingers on her arm he was suddenly mesmerised by the inviting shape of her luscious mouth. Her beautiful eyes were shining like stars. Staring back into that hypnotic violet glance was like falling into another dream...one that he was in no hurry to wake up from.

'Let go of me,' Rose breathed huskily.

Gene heard the words, but even as he registered them he was helplessly bending his head towards her. His body was heavy with desire, and only the taste of those lush tender lips would alleviate some of the insatiable erotic need he was suddenly inflamed by.

'Not yet…' he whispered, and claimed the mouth that unknowingly taunted him as if it were a choice between breathing to live and *not* breathing.

If he'd had any expectations that first time he'd kissed her, then the touch of Rose's lips beneath his had exceeded them all. Now, for the second time, the sensation was beyond wonderful. And the most pleasurable surprise came when she gasped softly, didn't resist his urgently seeking tongue as he thought she might, but instead welcomed the heated exploration as if she needed it as much as he did.

The hot satin interior of her mouth sent his temperature skyrocketing, and Gene's fingers moved through her silky hair to anchor her head and explore her flavours more deeply. Again, Rose showed no sign of protesting. His heart was galloping hard and the strangest feeling washed over him. It was an inexplicable sense that he was diving too deep ever to surface again without some serious damage having been caused…

Rose could hardly believe she was passionately kissing Gene Bonnaire. Had she unknowingly suffered some kind of bump to the head and been transported to an uncanny parallel universe where everything she'd known to be real had vanished? Who could blame her for that conclusion when the violent storm outside was growing ever more ferocious, adding to the sense that she was in some kind of twilight world? Being marooned in this isolated dwelling with a man she'd undoubtedly give a wide berth to if she met him under any other circumstances just didn't make sense. *Yet perhaps it wasn't as unbelievable as it seemed.* How could she have known that this avaricious business-man could seduce her with his unexpected displays of care and concern?

First he'd dispensed advice on dealing with her fears. Then he'd cooked a sublime French dish that had been nothing less than exquisite. And finally...*finally* he'd put his arm around her and held her against him when the lightning had looked to be heralding the end of the world and she'd been terrified.

Was that why she'd found herself willingly kissing him...? Because she was grateful for his protection? Had the feeling awakened some latent desire she'd been burying?

Her father had always sought to protect her from harm and keep her safe, and she'd trusted him more than any other man. Was she hoping to find someone similar in her romantic life? But Gene Bonnaire was nothing like her father had been. The billionaire was known to be utterly ruthless in pursuing his desires, and he had a reputation for letting nothing stand in his way. Yet when he'd held her against his powerful chest as they'd watched the storm Rose had trusted him enough to fall asleep.

How to explain it? All she knew was that she hadn't been able to resist him. Everything about the man seemed to dazzle her...the way he looked, the way he smelled, his sheer indomitable maleness... The reali-sation confused her. It also made her wary about the danger she might be inviting. She only had to remem-ber her ex and the way he'd blatantly lied to her to get what he wanted… Gene was another man who liked the sense of power money could give him…

When Gene carefully separated his lips from hers, his long fingers stroking her hair back, he smiled down at her with a knowing glint in his piercing blue eyes and she knew it was time to end this craziness and return to some kind of normality.

When she explained to him why she'd succumbed to that kiss—she'd been stressed and worried about her boss, and scared of the lightning—hopefully he would understand and not use the minor aberration against her.

Flattening her hand against his chest, she started to move away.

Frowning, Gene reached out to pull her back. 'Where are you going?'

For a moment Rose couldn't think what to say, because his glittering blue eyes were holding her to him as securely as if they'd been bound together.

'I shouldn't have done that. I'm sorry.'

'Why? Didn't you enjoy it?'

'That's not the point. The point is I'm here solely on business. And you're not responsible for comforting me just because I'm scared of lightning.'

'Would your boyfriend have comforted you if he'd been here?'

'What's that got to do with anything?'

His eyes narrowed. '*Would* he?'

'I don't have one.' Rose lifted a shoulder in a shrug, her gaze unflinching. 'I'm not interested in having a relationship at the moment.'

'Presumably that's because you're concerned about your boss?'

'It's not just that. I want to concentrate on my career. When Philip leaves the antiques shop, so will I. I'll have to find another position.'

'Presumably that won't be difficult? You're a qualified dealer, you said.'

She lifted her chin, as if to challenge him to doubt her. 'I am. And if I can't find anything suitable back home I might go abroad for a while and work.'

It was definitely an option, but somehow she didn't feel quite ready to take such a bold leap. She'd like to think she could make things work at home first. Anyway, the thought reminded her of what was most pertinent now.

Meeting the diamond-bright glance that had barely left her since they'd kissed, she said, 'Getting back to the reason I'm here… Don't you think we'd better deal with the signing of the documents tonight rather than leave it until the morning? It's just that I want to make sure I'm ready in plenty of time to meet the boat. The sooner I get back to the hospital and see how Philip is doing, the better.'

'I won't be signing anything until I'm satisfied that everything is in order. Give me the papers and I'll look over them tonight. Then we'll see what the morning brings.'

Dry-mouthed, Rose stood up. Gene's enigmatic comment had left her feeling as though she'd just plunged down a flight of hard-edged stone steps. 'Are you suggesting that there might be a possibility you *won't* sign?'

As he got to his feet his expression was tight-lipped and serious. 'Make no mistake. I want the property. That desire hasn't changed. But it's a policy of mine never to sign anything until I'm sure.'

'You mean you got me to come all the way out here in the *belief* that you were going to buy, but now you're not *sure*? Is this some kind of warped game you're playing?' She shook her head in despair. 'I should have known as soon as I saw you that you weren't to be trusted, but it seems I never learn…'

He moved closer. So close that Rose could see the gentle indentations in his otherwise smooth skin where the dark stubble of his beard had started to grow. His warm breath drifted over her face and made her teeth clench.

'What do you mean by that? Has someone let you down, Rose? Was it an ex-boyfriend, perhaps? If that's true, then I'm sorry. But this isn't a game I'm playing… it's the way I do business. I set out my intentions, believe without a doubt that what I want is going to be mine, and then I take some time to enjoy the realisation before I finally take the prize.'

She swallowed hard as he reached out and laid his palm against her cheek. It was clear that he wasn't just referring to his purchase of the antiques shop building.

Rose felt alternately hot and cold. Did he think that she'd fall into bed with him because she'd so willingly returned his kiss? He'd caught her off guard—that was all.

It was her cue to firmly lift his hand away and engineer some distance between them. Folding her arms over her sweater, she glanced out at the scene before her. Although the storm was still evident, somehow it seemed less ferocious. Sounding more like a subdued grizzly bear now, rather than a rampaging tiger, the thunder continued to rumble but the lightning was definitely lessening. Electrical flashes of cobalt pierced the sky here and there, but they were starting to suggest a once rampaging force now spent and retreating, and she was more than a little relieved.

However, Rose was still anxious that she might not be going home with the business sold and the funds deposited into Philip's bank account after all. A sleepless night was definitely on the horizon, because it wasn't going to be easy to wait until the morning for Gene's decision.

She was quickly learning that the man was a bit of a wild card…a law unto himself. That was a challenge. If for any reason he should change his mind about buying, what could she do but walk away in defeat? The situation might grieve her, but she hardly had the power to make him reconsider, did she? And he didn't look to be the type of man who would be swayed by any sense of compassion.

Rose was dreading taking such demoralising news back to Philip. What if it caused his health to deteriorate even more? The only thing she could do now was stay as calm as possible and not let her host see how perturbed she was.

'Well, there's not much more to say, then, is there? I'll go and get the purchase documents and give them to you to look over.' Glancing down at the pretty platinum wristwatch her father had given her for her twenty-first birthday, she added, 'After that I think I'll say goodnight.'

Turning towards the door, she was stopped in her tracks by Gene's intimate gravel-voiced reply.

'If we have any more lightning during the night and you're feeling scared my room is just down the hall from yours. I'm a very light sleeper, so don't hesitate to knock and come in, will you?'

Clenching her fists down by her sides, Rose prayed for the strength not to succumb to the pure unadulterated temptation the hard-chiselled specimen of masculinity before her exuded with a mere glance…let alone the sexy bass voice that reeled her in like a fish on a hook…

'I'm sure I'll be fine,' she said airily. 'I'll simply use that technique you told me about and remember that my fears are just illusions.'

She swore she heard Gene chuckle in amusement as she walked to the door and went out…

He had another restless night. It wasn't so easy to fall asleep when he knew that Rose slept just a short walk away from him, down the corridor in one of his guest-rooms. Somehow Gene couldn't shake the memory of that inflammatory kiss he'd stolen from her. All night it tempted and mocked him, until the fervent hope of a repeat performance finally lured him into sleep with its promise. But then he dreamt of holding Rose in his arms and making passionate love to her, and he woke at sunrise with his body coated in perspiration and heavy with desire.

Why hadn't she come to him in the night as he'd hoped? The storm had returned round three a.m. and the lightning had once again been spectacular. Surely she couldn't have slept through such a display? Had stubborn pride stopped her from seeking his reassurance?

Even though he admired her tenacity, he had to find out for himself how she'd fared. Quickly showering and dressing, he glanced at the property sale documents he'd examined minutely into the early hours and took them with him into the living room. There was no sign that his guest had been there.

His stomach clenching with nervous excitement at the thought of seeing her, he left the papers he'd been studying on the coffee table then returned to the room he'd allocated to Rose. He rapped sharply on the door. She didn't answer straight away and Gene was immediately concerned.

He was about to knock again when the door opened.

'Morning…' she murmured. Paler than usual, and distinctly bleary-eyed, her appearance suggested that she too had had trouble sleeping. Her black hair was prettily tousled but her skin looked as smooth and delicious as a peach. She was still in her nightwear—a short white satin affair, with spaghetti straps—and one of the straps had drifted down over a slim shoulder.

Gene took a moment to assemble his emotions. Once again he felt concerned and protective. It was so unlike his usual response at seeing a woman he desired that it honestly perturbed him.

'Good morning,' he greeted her. 'Don't tell me you didn't see and hear the lightning last night because I won't believe you.'

Groaning, she was already shaking her head and tunnelling her fingers through her hair. 'I'm not going to lie. I didn't sleep a wink. I wouldn't say no to some coffee if you're making it?'

'Never mind the coffee—why didn't you knock on my door like I told you to?'

Even as he asked the question Gene stepped over the door's threshold and, with no intention other than to re-assure her, wound his arms round her impossibly slim waist. The act was his undoing. The combination of the silky satin nightdress and the warm, shapely body beneath his hands aroused him more than he'd ever been aroused before...to the point where he couldn't help but act on sheer primal instinct.

'I would have held you close all night...protected you...' he murmured.

In between each word of the huskily voiced affirmation he touched his lips to Rose's hair then, hearing her gasp softly, he tipped up her chin and touched them to her mouth. The irresistible fusion was hot, sultry...and almost beyond controllable...

Rose glanced up into his eyes, the flat of her hand resting lightly against his chest. But this time there was no suggestion that she wanted him to leave.

'I—I can't seem to think straight when I'm around you,' she confessed. 'I didn't come to you last night because I was afraid of what might happen.'

'What did you think might happen?'

'I feel like—like I'm under some kind of spell when I'm near you and that makes you dangerous.'

'You think *I'm* the one who's dangerous? You're the one that's cast a spell, you little witch…'

'You should go,' she breathed, but her fingers were curling into his shirtfront and her eyes were full of longing.

Gene needed no further invitation. 'Sweetheart, I don't think so…' he murmured.

Sweeping her up into his arms, without further ado he carried her across to the lavish double bed. As he laid her down against the rumpled silk sheets his heart beat so fast he was dizzy. Rose wasn't looking sleepy any more. She looked wide awake, her flawless complexion no longer pale, but softly rouged pink with desire…

As he started to lower the spaghetti straps of her nightgown down over her shoulders, so that the satin mounds of her breasts were more evident, he couldn't resist a grin. 'If I'd known you wore such sexy nightwear I would have battered down your door and come to you last night. Honest to God, I would have,' he swore.

For answer, she made a helpless little sound of hunger and pulled his head down to hers. As they kissed Gene reached down to his back pocket and drew out the foil packet he kept there. There were no more words after that. There was no need. His whole world had narrowed down to these few heatedly charged moments, to the beautiful woman beneath him and their hungry, *insatiable* need for each other.

When he finally took her, with Rose's strong, slender thighs wrapped round his middle, he honestly thought he'd died and gone to heaven. It wasn't just her kisses and her body that were heavenly—everything about her was divine. Already he knew there was no way on earth he would be satisfied with just taking his pleasure and then setting her aside, as he usually did with the women in his life. A strong desire to *really* get to know her was building inside him.

As she quickly came to her fulfilment her thighs clamped him even tighter and she rode the wild waves that took her. Staring back into her superlative violet gaze, Gene soon followed, issuing a harsh-sounding cry that seemed to emanate from deep inside him. In the aftermath of his climax he was rendered both breathless and speechless for a while before he came back to himself. Then he lay down next to Rose and gently pulled her into his arms.

'*Tu es incroyable...*' he whispered into her ear.

Her pretty cheeks dimpled. 'I like it when you speak French. You can whisper some more to me, if you like?'

'Right now I'd willingly do anything you wanted, *ma chère.*'

'I might hold you to that...' With a teasing but knowing smile, Rose held her hand softly against his cheek...

CHAPTER SIX

ROSE HAD IMMEDIATELY sensed the man beside her tense when she'd asserted that she would hold him to his comment about doing anything she wanted. She hadn't meant anything by it—it had just been a bit of teasing banter. But now, up and dressed, she felt her own tension mounting as she followed him out into the living room.

She could hardly believe what had just happened between them. All she knew was that making love with Gene had made her feel more alive and vital than she'd felt in years... However, as wonderful and exhilarating as the experience had been, she'd better quickly come back down to earth and remember why she was there.

With his straight back and squared shoulders—his flawless white shirt and taupe chinos a little crumpled after his joining her in bed—Gene looked intimidating and officious. That suggested he wasn't going to be as approachable as he recently had been. Obviously he had reached a decision about the antiques store, and perhaps it wasn't the one she'd hoped for...

Would he let her down gently or would he stress that business was business and he no longer saw the building as a viable proposition for his restaurant business? Suddenly Rose was sick with nerves. How would she tell Philip about her failure to bring back the signed purchase agreement if that was the case?

She could already visualise the pain and disappointment in his eyes, even though she knew he would quickly reassure her that everything would be okay—that he would soon find another buyer and all would be well.

Her mind teeming with thoughts, most of them unhelpful, all of a sudden Rose was struck by how bare and austere the white-painted room was. Yes, it had a magnificent view, but how much more beautiful it would look if it had some warmth and personality instilled.

'What a shame you don't like antiques or even beautiful paintings,' she declared. 'The right ones would make this room look even more stunning…it would be so much more homely and inviting.'

Gene turned round. Raising a formidable dark brow, he snapped, 'But this isn't my home. It's my retreat. I don't need pictures or antiques to pretty it up. Besides, no one else is going to see it but me.'

After the intimacy they'd just shared, Rose was more than a little deflated by his sharpness. But she persisted. 'That might be the case, but what's wrong with *you* appreciating them? Surely you would find some pleasure in making your retreat look nice on the inside as well as externally?'

'You're wrong. I wouldn't. It serves a purpose—that's all it does. I'm not interested in getting any pleasure from what the furnishings look like.'

His tone was adamant…not to mention he seemed annoyed that she'd made the suggestion.

'I'm not an aesthetic like you are, Rose. I'm practical and pragmatic.'

'Yet it's important to you to wear beautifully tailored clothing, shoes made by one of the finest Italian designers and the most appealing French cologne, isn't it?'

As soon as the words were out of her mouth Rose sensed her blood throb heatedly through her veins. So hot and heavy did it pound that she was mortified. She'd revealed to Gene that she'd noticed so much. In doing so, she'd foolishly given him another edge with which to usurp her if he chose and, despite their lovemaking, she didn't doubt that he would use it…

She saw that his deliciously carved mouth had shaped a smile. Again the image of the Big Bad Wolf flashed into her mind.

'You're right. I admit that personal presentation is important to me. And to that end I believe in wearing only the very best that money can buy.' He paused, and a muscle flexed at the side of one flawlessly carved cheekbone. 'It goes without saying that my exacting standards are important in my personal life too. For example, I very much appreciate the curves of a lovely woman…the way she smiles…the radiance of a pair of stunning long-lashed violet eyes…'

He was talking about *her*. Rose sucked in a steadying breath as her heart beat double-time. The irresistible magnetism between them which had driven them to consummate their attraction wouldn't have been there under normal circumstances, she was sure. It had probably just occurred because they'd found themselves isolated and alone in this incredible futuristic house, with nothing but the rocks, the sea and the stormy weather to keep them company. Add to that Rose's fear of lightning, and the fact that she'd let her guard down round Gene because he seemed so concerned…

A disquieting thought assailed her. What if his being concerned was just an act and in truth he just wanted to have her in his power because it stroked his ego? After all, he prided himself on having anything he wanted, didn't he? But she still couldn't understand why he didn't seem able to resist her. It just didn't make sense. *Nothing* made sense when she was around him, she realised.

Clasping her hands in front of her soft woollen sweater, she didn't shy away from meeting his gaze. She had come here for one thing and one thing only: for him to sign the documents that would make him the new owner of Philip's antiques store. That was what she should be concentrating on.

'Well, that aside… Have you made a decision about the antiques shop?'

He gave her another enigmatic smile. Yet the charismatic gesture on that too handsome face hardly reassured her. It did, however, make her catch her breath. And the restless heat that seemed to have infiltrated her body because she now knew what it felt like to be intimate with him seemed to increase disturbingly.

His comments just now suggested that he thought her beautiful, and the exhilarating thought affected Rose perhaps more than it ought to. The allure of him was becoming more and more irresistible, and along with the impulse to do what was right and be sensible it had created a war inside her that made it hard to think straight.

Her voice not quite steady, she pressed, 'Well? You need to tell me sooner rather than later, because I have a boat to catch.'

'Do you?'

He was moving closer still, and the faint drift of his arresting French cologne made her stomach clench painfully. 'What do you mean do I? How else am I going to get off this island and return home?'

'I meant does it have to be today?'

Rose widened her eyes. 'Why? Is there some reason I *shouldn't* go today?'

Gene was suddenly standing right in front of her, and his crystalline blue gaze was hot enough to burn her. 'Yes, there is. I'd like you to stay so that we can get to know each other a little better.'

There was a dizzying rush inside her head. 'Why on earth do you think that—?'

Before she could finish what she'd been going to say her lips were captured hungrily, and suddenly there was no oxygen left to breathe—just a heady, seductive heat and the taste of something forbidden…

With a helpless groan Rose found herself responding. The thought *how can something so wrong seem so right?* flashed through her mind. Sexually, the man delivered everything he promised. She found herself strangely weak, with a hard to resist desire to be more reckless than she'd ever been before…

Last night she'd been terrified by the violent flashes outside the window that had lit up her room like every celebratory firework display in the country combined. Yet she'd been more afraid of knocking on Gene's door to let him know because of what might happen if she did. But then in the morning…*it had happened anyway.*

His hands were on her shoulders now, and they moved seductively down her back, the scalding heat from his fingertips feeling as if they were melting the very vertebrae of her spine as they travelled. Then he caught her by the waist and impelled her closer—so close that she was intimately aware of his heat and his hardness again.

He felt so good…so…so *necessary.* The man's kisses were an erotic delight that she could easily become addicted to.

He was still kissing her when he reached for the hem of her sweater and started to tug it upwards. When he lifted it over her head and let it fall onto the floor behind her Rose's heart galloped. She was wearing a sleeveless white vest over a matching cotton bra, and when Gene's searching hand dived inside to caress her breast, his fingertips lightly pinching her burgeoning nipple, she moaned feverishly. Then he carried on kissing her—as if he too was finding it hard to be free of the taste of her.

It felt so good to be wanted and desired. It had been a long time.

Her last and only real boyfriend, Joe Harding, had been a twenty-four-year-old trainee broker, and at the age of eighteen she had lost her virginity to him. At first he had been kind and considerate, swearing that he loved her. But as time progressed he'd become more and more driven by the demands of the City bank where he worked and hadn't seemed to have much time for anything else—including their relationship.

He'd sought to placate her by telling her that he was working hard for *her*…that he wanted to ensure that they had a happy and successful future *together*. But Rose had soon begun to suspect that that wasn't true. One night she had smelled another woman's perfume on his shirt and, when confronted, he had admitted that he'd been having an affair…as it turned out one of many.

She had been horrified and hurt that the man she'd so eagerly given her trust and her love had so blatantly betrayed her. She'd had a short, sharp lesson in the mercenary way some men could behave…and in the lies they told to get what they wanted, not caring who they hurt in the process. Heartbroken, Rose had told him it was over. He hadn't even looked surprised, and nor had he protested. *In fact, she'd never forgotten the look of relief in his eyes…*

After that wounding experience she'd vowed to stay single and focus on her career, and she hadn't succumbed to any soulless liaisons purely for physical release either—no matter how tempted she sometimes felt—knowing it was only because she was lonely.

Yet here she was, in the arms of a man who was the ultimate practised seducer, and she would have utterly surrendered to him for a second time if he hadn't lifted his head right then to examine her with what looked like a knowing smile. If ever a man epitomised the 'cat that had got the cream', *he* did.

Her insides plunged and a deafening alarm bell rang inside her. Rose was suddenly painfully reminded of exactly who Gene Bonnaire was. He was a mercenary businessman who didn't have a single qualm about taking what he wanted—and he was just about to add her body and her capitulation to his self-aggrandising quota of conquests if she didn't take action and stop him.

Breathing heavily, she pushed his hands away and stumbled as she stepped back to collect her discarded sweater. She was still reeling from that too knowing smile. Hurriedly pulling on the garment, she wiped the back of her hand across her throbbing lips in a gesture of disgust.

Startled and disappointed, Gene shook his head.

Rory's boat couldn't arrive soon enough, as far as Rose was concerned. The sooner she was out of there and away from this man the better. However, there was still the important matter of the shop to address.

'You didn't answer my question. Do you still intend to buy the antiques store? If the answer is yes then you'd better get on with signing the papers so I can get ready to leave for the mainland.'

She was still breathing hard as she spoke, unsure of how she would handle Gene's reaction. The feeling brought it home to her how little she knew him. Did anyone *really* know this man who had built a sanctuary for himself on a remote Scottish island?

'Why did you break off our embrace? And don't lie to me and tell me you weren't enjoying it. Or do you get some kind of perverse pleasure from leading a man on?' he demanded.

'I didn't lead you on. I've already let myself down by going to bed with you. I freed myself just now because it suddenly hit me what I was doing. You have a reputation for unscrupulously taking the things you want without giving a damn about the consequences—and I didn't come here to end up as another one of your forgettable conquests. Even though you might call me a hypocrite because of the way I've acted around you, thankfully I've come to my senses. So let's forget what just happened and get on with our business, shall we?'

Stealing a quick glance at the time on her watch, Rose swallowed hard. Although she was adamant she would stay strong, inside she was quaking.

'I've got exactly one hour before I have to be down on the shore to wait for the boat.'

Gene stood perfectly still. As he examined her, his expression was bleak. 'Well, Rose... It seems as if I've misjudged you. I thought you were different from all those people who so avidly believe everything they read in the papers about me...about my less than flattering "reputation"...but I see that I was wrong.'

All of a sudden she felt sickeningly faint. *Was* she the one who was guilty of misjudging?

The usually arresting gleam in his eyes was gone. The burnished light was dulled.

'Did you honestly doubt that I would sign the purchase papers? There was never any chance of that. I still plan to own the property. It's just that I'd hoped I might persuade you to spend some time with me and not hurry to return.'

Rose was in turmoil. Should she believe the desire he'd expressed to spend more time with her was because he genuinely wanted to get to know her, or because he simply saw an opportunity to engage in another sexual liaison? It was so hard to trust Gene when all she had to go on was her bitter past experience of being let down by a man who had put his ambition and desire for money before his desire to have a loving relationship...

Gene smiled—but the blue eyes were chillingly empty now, she saw. He looked as though he expected her just to wait for him to sign the papers and then walk away...

'I can see that you plainly don't want to do that. You'd better follow me into my office.'

He strode ahead of her through the door, the heels of his black Italian loafers echoing loudly against the parquet flooring. Rose had to practically run to keep up with him.

Dropping down into the sumptuous leather seat behind the elongated glass desk that occupied another vast and mostly empty white room, Gene calmly drew the sheaf of property documents towards him. Silently scanning the opening page, he reached for the glinting gold fountain pen on his blotter.

Lifting his gaze, he looked straight at Rose. 'You may as well sit down,' he told her.

Still shaken after hearing his confession that he'd hoped she might stay a little longer, she sat down in the elegant leather chair on the opposite side of the desk. She could still feel the sensation of his hot velvet mouth against hers…still taste him…and she wanted to cry— because after she'd left this remote and isolated place she would never experience such delights again.

'There's one small proviso before I sign,' he declared. Rose's heart stalled. 'What's that?'

'I want your agreement that you'll help offload the antiques for me. I'll pay you for doing it. I've already told you *I* haven't any use for them, but that doesn't mean I want to *give* them away. I can see that some of them are valuable, and that's reflected in the price I've paid for them. You know the market, and I sense you won't let them go for a song. So, do I have your agreement, Rose?'

How could she possibly say no when Philip needed every penny to help towards his aftercare when he returned home? It shouldn't be such a dilemma, Rose thought, but because it would mean she'd still have to have contact with Gene it *was*…

She sat up a little straighter in her chair. 'You know I can't refuse. But at the same time I want you to know that I'm only doing this for Philip. If it wasn't for him I *would* refuse. I shouldn't have succumbed to making our association personal.'

Back in bed, when Rose had asserted that she would hold him to his promise to give her anything she wanted, Gene had had a painful moment of disquiet when it had come to him that she might be just like all

the other women he'd had liaisons with and see him
only as some kind of 'meal ticket' to fame and fortune.
But her words and the inflection in her tone now suggested that she felt nothing but regret in meeting him
and it cut him to the quick.

It was another first for him. He had never known a
woman *willingly* part company with him. Usually the
only sensation he experienced when a liaison ended
was relief. But with her beguiling violet eyes, and the
rare softness that he'd never encountered before, plus
the fact that she could turn his blood to molten fire with
her presence alone, Rose somehow had him spellbound.
So he wouldn't make it at all easy for her to walk away
from him—at least not until he'd had his fill of her…

'Good. Then I'd better sign, hadn't I? And I'll need
you to witness my signature with your own.'

After the documents had been dealt with, Gene
stowed them away in a drawer.

'I'll make sure the money is in your boss's account
as soon as you leave,' he affirmed.

'Does that mean I can check the account when I get
back to London?' Rose asked warily.

Gene expelled a sigh. 'I may be a lot of things that
you don't like, but I never lie about money, Rose. I've
got the property that I wanted and I'm not going to delay
paying what I owe. An agreement is an agreement.'

They both got to their feet.

'It's nearly time for you to meet the boat. Why don't
you go and get your bag and I'll walk you down to the
quay?' he suggested.

His companion's soft satin cheeks inexplicably

turned pink. Was she perhaps not as set on leaving as she had indicated? he wondered?

'That won't be necessary,' she answered stiffly, immediately pouring ice water on the thought. 'I'm quite capable of getting there by myself.'

'Damn it, woman. I'm doing it for my own satisfaction. I just want to make sure you get off the island safely. There'll be a car waiting for you on the other side, like I promised. My driver will take you to the airport, and there'll be another driver waiting for you when you land, to take you back home.'

'I'm going to go to the hospital first—to see Philip.'

'Of course you are.' A flash of what felt suspiciously like jealousy at her unerring regard for the other man ricocheted though Gene's insides. 'I'll meet you out at the front. Go and get your bag.'

A mournful wind was howling as they started to walk down the hillside and, glancing at the ocean, he saw that the surging waves had a chilling bluish tint and were far from calm. The scent of last night's storm still clung to the icy air and he shivered.

Unable to help himself, he hoped that the conditions were too rough this morning for Rory to make the crossing. But then he quickly realised that even if the boatman was able to make the journey to the island there was no guarantee that the return journey would be any smoother.

Suddenly Gene didn't want to let Rose go. If anything happened to her when he could have taken steps to prevent it he'd never forgive himself.

'It looks rougher than usual out there today,' he remarked, coming to a sudden standstill on the uneven stone path to survey his windblown companion.

Her expression impatient, Rose tried in vain to push her fringe out of her eyes. 'It must be because of the storm. I'm sure it will be all right. Rory strikes me as a highly competent boatman.'

'Even the most competent sailors still have to contend with the unpredictable nature of the ocean,' he said dryly. 'Why don't we go back? I'll see if I can contact him and tell him that you'll wait until

tomorrow, when the weather will hopefully be a bit calmer.'

'No.'

Agitated and furious, Rose turned away and started to make her way down the hillside. Her leather tote bumped awkwardly against her side as she gamely negotiated the uneven rocky surface. She'd adamantly refused to let Gene carry it for her.

'The sooner I get off this island the better!' she shouted back over her shoulder.

Too concerned for her safety to let her head off without him, in just a few long-legged strides he had joined her. 'I hadn't realised how stubborn you are, but I'm quickly learning,' he murmured.

'If you mean that I know my own mind, and won't let anyone dictate what I should or shouldn't do, then, yes—I *am* stubborn.' With a flash of sublime violet and a bewitching satisfied smile, Rose forged ahead to the carved-out landing stage in the bay where the boat would dock.

She got there before him, her back straight in her

weatherproof jacket and hanging on to her tote for dear life in the unforgiving gusting wind. She stared defiantly out to sea, as if fully expecting Rory's boat to appear on the horizon any moment now just because she *willed* it…

CHAPTER SEVEN

THE MEMORY OF Gene calling out, 'I'll be in touch soon!' as Rory steered the boat back out of the bay haunted Rose for several nights after she'd returned to London. The exclamation could so easily have sounded like a threat—but it *hadn't*. Instead she'd sensed regret in his tone, as if he genuinely hadn't wanted her to leave.

She'd watched the disturbingly lonely figure he'd made on the shoreline until he had become a mere speck in the distance that had quickly disappeared. It had left a hollow feeling inside her that was hard to explain.

But her spirits had lifted when she'd discovered that Philip had made some definite improvement while she'd been away. And when she'd given him the news that Gene had officially bought the building and the antiques, and that the money was now safely in his bank account, the worried expression Rose had become used to seeing on a daily basis had started to fade. He'd even seemed to breathe a little more easily.

Having returned to work, her aim was to finish meticulously cataloguing the antiques and then to make contact with the dealers and auctioneers she knew who would be interested and hopefully make some sales. There was still the odd 'walk in' buyer that came into the store, and she didn't mind—she'd always loved conversing with customers. But the fact was that her job was swiftly coming to an end and she was now in effect working for Gene instead of Philip.

It was a twist of fate that she couldn't have predicted...not even in her wildest dreams.

She had just got off the phone one afternoon when the bell above the door jangled to announce a visitor. Glad of the distraction, Rose left the office to see who it was. It had been an agonisingly slow day, and she had spent most of her time trying to persuade a wealthy dealer in Paris to visit the shop and view a valuable chiffonier that she knew was right up his street. Sometimes it wasn't enough simply to view an item online. A true connoisseur had to physically see and touch the artefact.

The Parisian dealer was known for his exquisite good taste, and the fact that this piece had originated in the French capital was all to the good. Its provenance was impeccable. Rose had assured him that she would foot the bill for the trip—at the back of her mind she'd told herself that Gene couldn't possibly mind as long as she secured the deal and the chiffonier was sold. After all, wasn't making a profit his main concern?

The moment she walked out onto the shop floor and saw it was Gene himself standing there, his arms ominously folded across his broad chest, devastatingly suited in flawless tailoring as if he was going on to some important business function, her heart clamoured wildly and suddenly her ability to know what to say utterly deserted her.

Clearly not sharing her dilemma, he said smoothly, 'I thought I'd drop by and see how things were going.'

He was acting as if this was the usual way he did business—simply dropping by unannounced. Didn't he have a secretary or some smartly dressed snooty PA to do his bidding? Of course he did. Hadn't Rose spoken to the woman herself when she'd requested a meeting with him? And, yes, the woman *had* sounded snooty...

Clearing her throat, she shakily combed her fingers through her hair. Not since early this morning had she even glanced in a mirror to see how she looked. She couldn't even remember applying any make-up. Telling herself that she shouldn't care how she appeared to Gene, she knew the truth was that she cared more than was probably wise...

'By that I assume you want to know how the sales are getting on? I'm sure you're anxious to have the building emptied and renovated as soon as possible.'

A maddeningly inexplicable smile played round his lips. 'Of course I'm interested to hear how many antiques you've sold on my behalf—but that's not the sole reason for my visit, Rose. I came to see how you were.'

'No doubt you were wondering if I've recovered from my ordeal on the island. It's certainly an experience I'll never forget. That was some lightning storm, wasn't it? Well, I'm still alive and kicking—as you can see.'

'That's not what I meant. We didn't exactly part on the best of terms, did we? I'd hate to think you were still angry with me.'

'I'm not. Tensions were high because of what we'd both been through…that's all.'

'Well, I missed you after you'd left. I came back the next day because the place was too empty without you.'

Rose's heart skipped a beat. *What was he playing at, making such a provocative statement?*

'Isn't that the purpose of having a sanctuary? So that you can be alone and hopefully enjoy some peace?'

Gene grimaced, and it wasn't the reaction she'd expected. It took her aback to see the pain that had momentarily flared in his dazzling blue eyes.

'There's never any peace when you're alone with your thoughts…at least that's been my experience.'

Such a frank and very *human* confession took Rose aback once more. The world seemed to be of the opinion that a man like Gene who had everything—could have anything he wanted at the drop of a hat—was devoid of any human feelings at all. His desire for more went beyond reason, it seemed. Wasn't that how *she* had viewed him? But it had slowly crept up on her that there was far more to him than that. And, in spite of her fears about being used by him, she realised she wanted to know *more* about him…not *less*.

'I know what you mean. Thoughts can drive us crazy sometimes, can't they? Look, I was just about to make a cup of tea before you appeared. Would you like one?'

The frown that creased his indomitable brow immediately relaxed and the smile he gave her seemed perfectly genuine. 'If you could make that coffee and not tea…that would be great.'

'Coffee it is, then. We'll take it into the office.'

Gene couldn't help recalling the last time he'd been in Philip Houghton's office. He winced when he remembered how his meeting with Rose had ended. Had he intuited even at that early stage of their acquaintance that she was going to shake up his world as it had never been shaken before? With her bewitching violet eyes, and the stubborn way she had of refusing to give in to his wants and needs, she was unlike any other woman he'd known before.

The fact that she seemed far from impressed by his wealth and status, and wasn't readily going to succumb to his charms, made her even more desirable. How would she react if he confessed that he hadn't been able to stop thinking about their impassioned lovemaking on the island? That since he'd tasted her soft cherry lips and intimately known her body she'd infiltrated his blood like a contagious fever that bordered on dangerous…at least to his state of mind?

He had even been finding it hard to concentrate on work—and that was unheard of.

Now, as she sat opposite him on the other side of the desk, Gene thought she looked a little flushed. Her short dark hair was mussed, as if she'd been frequently running her fingers through it because she was stressed… or worried… He didn't particularly want to discuss her boss, but he would have to if he wanted to learn what was troubling her.

'How is Mr Houghton?' he enquired, endeavouring to keep his tone as amiable as possible.

'Better than I hoped.'

'You mean he's rallying?'

'Yes. He's by no means recovered, but the doctors tell me he's definitely made some improvement. Knowing that he's sold the antiques store and no longer has the worry of paying for his aftercare when he comes out of hospital has definitely helped.'

'That's good. But what about *you*, Rose?'

'What do you mean?'

'I mean you look like something's bothering you. What are you worrying about if it's not your boss's state of health?'

Breathing out a sigh, she sat a little further back in her seat. 'I'm not *worried*. I'm…concerned. Concerned that it's going to take me quite some time to sell all these antiques and that in the meantime I need to find a new job.'

The opportunity that Gene had hoped would come his way had just landed straight in his lap… Pausing to reflect on his good fortune, he smiled and took a leisurely sip of his coffee.

'You don't need to look for a new job. You're working for *me* now—remember?' he reminded her.

The compellingly beautiful violet eyes widened. 'I know you're paying me to source buyers for the antiques on your behalf, but it's hardly a full-time position, is it?'

'No, it's not. That being the case, I'm sure I can find you something suitable in one of my companies.'

Rose looked at him aghast. 'Like *what*, for instance?'

'Something in the administration area, perhaps… I'm assuming your organisational skills are good?'

'But I'm not an administrator, am I? I'm an antiques dealer.'

Crossly she folded her arms over her very neat crimson sweater. The fitted cashmere garment couldn't fail to highlight her beautifully shaped breasts and tiny waist, and Gene hotly sensed his hunger to make love to her again becoming an undeniable craving he couldn't resist for very much longer...

She lifted her chin. 'In any case, I don't want you to find me a job. I'm quite capable of doing that for myself.'

His thoughts were racing, and he couldn't prevent his growing frustration from spilling over into his tone. 'Do you know how many résumés my offices receive every day? On average about a hundred. Most people would give their eye teeth for the opportunity to work for me!'

'Well, good luck to them—but I'm not one of those.' Lifting her cup to her lips, she took a brief sip of her tea and clattered the vessel against the matching porcelain saucer when she set it down again.

He didn't miss the fact that her hand was shaking. *God, the woman was stubborn!* He longed for her to relent a little. He found himself momentarily lost in the memory of touching her breasts, and of the way her tender nipples had instantly hardened and contracted against his hand...

He stood up, because he suddenly couldn't stay still, and walked round the desk to study her more closely.

'I'd like to let you go so that you can look for a job you really want, but I'm afraid I can't. What I *can* do, however, is double the fee I'm paying you so that you won't have any worries about money until you find a new position. Does that make things easier for you?'

'It's not just about the money…'

'You don't *want* to stay and sell the antiques for me? Is that what you're saying?'

'It's just too awkward…'

'Why?'

'Because I've worked all these years for *Philip*—and you're not him!'

Her upsurge of emotion took them both by surprise. Rose was breathing hard and chewing anxiously down on her fulsome lower lip and Gene's heart was thudding fit to burst. Her meaning was clear. The thought that she regarded the aging antiques dealer over him made his blood boil. He knew he had no reason to be jealous, because she'd made it clear to him that her devotion to the man was purely out of respect and kindness, but he couldn't help feeling the way he did.

Reaching down, he furiously pulled her to her feet. 'You're sorry that I'm not some elderly English gentleman who couldn't give you even *one* night of pleasure if he tried?'

He brought his face down to hers and felt her slender frame tremble.

'That's the most ridiculous notion I've ever heard. If you met him you'd know why. He's the sweetest, kindest man I've ever met and I've already told you I'm not remotely attracted to him.'

Gene heard the heartfelt words but was too far gone to be remotely gracious. He was lost in an incandescent violet sea and in a sweet perfume so seductive that he was helpless to resist the erotic delights it promised. He crushed Rose's luscious cherry lips beneath his without an ounce of remorse and devoured them.

At some point during his greedy exploration he tasted blood on his lips and didn't know whether it was his or hers. But then, incredibly, he realised that she was kissing him back—that she'd freed her hands and was hungrily urging him closer. At the same time she was making breathless little sounds that told him she wanted and needed him as much as he did her...

His blood pounding hotly in his veins, Gene acknowledged that the sparks they'd helplessly ignited together had suddenly caught fire. And there was only one solution to dousing the flames—and that was to unrestrainedly let them *burn*...

With a heated groan he swept aside all the paraphernalia on the desk and papers and items of stationery fell haphazardly onto the floor. His gaze briefly colliding with Rose's, he gripped her arms and, as gently as he was able, helped her to lie back on the mahogany surface.

She was already pushing his suit jacket aside and urgently opening his shirt buttons so that she could touch him. When she ran her hands over his chest and round his ribcage it was an irresistible combination of heaven and hell for Gene. Heaven because being close to her in this way was beyond his wildest dreams as far as pleasure was concerned, and hell because he was so turned on it was painful...

Capturing her mouth in a hard, hot kiss, he dragged up the hem of her skirt to find her panties. When his hands fastened round the skimpy white silk that adorned her svelte hips he eagerly pulled down the garment to mid-thigh and urgently undid his zip. He was almost beyond aching to be inside her.

When Rose clasped her velvet thighs around him he needed no further invitation. He plunged his inflamed sex deep inside her moist satin centre. They both stilled for a moment—not in shock or surprise, but in wonder at the unbelievable ecstasy of their union. Then Gene's ability to think even close to straight disappeared as he was driven to thrust even deeper, at the same time pushing aside her sweater and bra to fasten his mouth on a sweetly distended nipple, nibbling at it with the edges of his teeth.

The taste of her was like the sweetest nectar imaginable and he was already addicted to it. Since their very first combustible encounter Gene had known he wouldn't easily be able to relinquish sampling it again and again…

Releasing a sensuous moan, Rose suddenly stilled beneath him.

Raising his head to glance down at her, he saw that her beautiful eyes looked startled. He saw too that the incandescent violet orbs were glazed with moisture and that it had darkened the fringe of ebony lashes that surrounded them. He didn't pause to wonder why she should shed a tear at such a pleasurable moment because he was already a mere breath away from the climactic fulfilment of his own sensual journey.

In the next instant his desire reached its zenith and his entire body vibrated with the power of it. Releasing a guttural groan that might have emanated from the undiscovered corners of his very soul, Gene lowered his head to rest it against Rose's chest. If they had been in bed together he would have gathered her into his arms and held her for the longest time. Yet again a strong wave of protectiveness had swept over him, and he couldn't help but want to express it.

He was just about to enquire if she was all right, and tell her how beautiful she was, when the lyrical sound of the shop's doorbell made them both stiffen in alarm.

'It must be a customer...' Rose said huskily, her hands already pushing him away.

Even as she spoke Gene cursed beneath his breath, hurriedly got to his feet and tidied his disarrayed clothing.

Red-faced, Rose gave him a nervous glance as she straightened her skirt and tucked in her sweater. Then she dragged her fingers through her mussed hair and went to the door.

Turning, she said, 'If you go through that door you'll find a cloakroom where you can freshen up. I'll tell whoever it is that I'm closing early today.'

'Good idea,' he muttered.

When she'd closed the door behind her he cursed again—not because they'd been interrupted, but because in the throes of a passion that had been as fierce and elemental as the lightning storm they'd witnessed on the island he'd stupidly omitted to use protection...

The unexpected caller turned out to be the persistently cheerful postman, who had once told Rose that his name was Bill. He was making a late delivery, he explained, due to the 'horrendous traffic'.

Rose didn't usually mind a bit of a chat with him, but not today...

Not when she'd left Gene in the office, waiting for her.

The explosion of passion that had erupted between them had made her head spin. There wasn't an inch of flesh on her body that didn't throb and ache, and she was pretty sure she'd inadvertently acquired a couple of bruises. *They'd made love on the office desk, for goodness' sake!* Had she completely taken leave of her senses?

It stunned her that she'd been so reckless. But at the same time, strangely, she felt no regret. In fact she didn't feel like the woman she'd always known herself to be at all...that was someone who always strove to do what was right and act accordingly. She felt like a woman who had somehow liberated herself from the yoke of conformity that had more or less dominated her whole life because of the way she'd been raised—and the feeling was *beyond* exhilarating...

And, although she still found it hard to trust, Gene was the one responsible for her liberation. In his arms she could believe that *anything* was possible.

Bill handed over the pile of letters he'd brought and commented, 'By the way, have you seen that top-of-the-range black Mercedes in the car park? Presumably it belongs to one of your rich customers? It's got a personal number plate...reads EB1. Got any idea who that might be?'

Excruciatingly, Rose felt herself redden. She endeavoured to make her answer sound as uninterested as possible. 'No, I don't. It probably belongs to someone who's popped into the bank. Anyway, thanks for the post. I've got to get on now. I'm shutting up shop early today.'

'Got a hot date, have you?' Bill gave her a playful wink.

Wincing, Rose went behind him to the door and pointedly held it open.

'All right, love, I can take a hint!' He smiled. 'See you next time!'

Breathing a sigh of relief when he was gone, she locked the door and turned the sign that hung there round to read 'Closed'. Then she smoothed down her newly wrinkled smart black skirt and prepared herself to return to the office and face the man who had had no compunction in making her his lover yet again…

CHAPTER EIGHT

WHEN SHE RETURNED to the office it was to find Eugene disappearing through the back door to locate the cloakroom. The papers and stationery he'd swept onto the floor had been returned to the desk and arranged tidily. Anyone stepping into the room would not notice anything remotely amiss. They certainly wouldn't guess that Rose and a well-known billionaire had been making out on the desk!

Walking across the room to her chair, she feverishly reflected on what had happened. She couldn't still her trembling as she sat down. Anguished, she murmured aloud, 'What have I done?'

In the aftermath of the event, shock had set in. Not just shock, but guilt and a generous portion of shame too. *What would Philip think if he knew? What would her father have said if he'd been alive?* Rose felt as if she'd let them both down. But, more importantly, she'd also let *herself* down. There was a good reason why she'd always sought to behave well. When her parents had split her father's friends had intimated that her mother, Ruth, had had a 'wild streak' that her father had never really come to terms with.

Philip had once shared with Rose that her father had told him, 'Living with that woman was like building a house on top of a repository for dynamite. Not a day went by when I didn't anticipate it might blow up in my face.'

Ruth Heathcote had caused utter devastation when she'd deserted him for the wealthy and flamboyant David Carlisle. He'd been absolutely crushed by her leaving and had gone to court to make sure that Rose was raised by him and not her... Suffering the fall-out of those painful events had made Rose determined never to behave as recklessly.

But she was well aware that when nature held sway humans were more often than not powerless to resist. That was why she'd ended up in bed with Gene at the sanctuary. Yet her self-respect was paramount, and she wouldn't jeopardise that if she could help it... *Or so she'd believed.* What she hadn't been prepared for was a man like Gene Bonnaire sweeping into her life and leaving her feeling as though she'd just survived a tornado by the skin of her teeth.

And now there was something else she'd better keep in mind. They had been intimate without even giving a thought to using protection. They'd been so mesmerised by their urgent feelings that it hadn't even crossed their minds. At least Rose knew that Gene hadn't *planned* the passionate seduction. If he had, he would most definitely have brought protection. He might flirt with danger in his business life, but she was certain a man like him wouldn't take unnecessary risks in his personal one…

Although it would be easy to give way to panic, she absolutely refused to. Thankfully, she knew all about the morning-after pill, and before she went home she would go straight to a pharmacy. An unplanned pregnancy was something that definitely *wasn't* in her plans for the future…

Gene returned. The expression on his handsome face was a little shame-faced. To counteract it, a tentative smile lifted a corner of his sculpted lips and Rose's senses were immediately assailed by the seductive scent of him. In her chair, she couldn't help but clench her thighs together. Her heart raced when she thought how desperately they had made love. In his arms she had learned what it meant to be ecstatic, freed of restriction. It had felt like *flying*…

'Who was your visitor? A potential customer?' he enquired.

As he asked the question he was walking slowly towards her, and she had ample time to admire his hard, honed physique in the impeccable bespoke suit. If Gene didn't flirt with danger in *his* personal life, then Rose knew that was *exactly* what she'd be doing in hers if she didn't tell him that turning their association into a sexual one had been a bad mistake. As much as the thought grieved her, the two hot little encounters they'd enjoyed wouldn't be happening again.

'It was the postman making a late delivery,' she told him.

'His timing could have been better.'

Rose flushed. 'He said that the traffic was bad. That's why he got held up.'

'Never mind about that... I'm more interested in what *we're* doing. I want you to come back with me to my apartment tonight. This time I want to make sure I have you all to myself. I don't want to risk our time together being interrupted again.'

He was drawing her to her feet as he spoke and his arms were wound firmly round her waist.

Finding herself once again mesmerised by his cobalt blue eyes and fit body, so soon after the intimacy they'd shared, Rose sensed her determination to hold him at bay and deny him any further intimate contact teeter precariously.

'That might be what *you* want, Gene, but it's not what *I* want.'

'I don't believe you.'

He had the temerity to look amused, and she couldn't help but take umbrage. Flattening her hands against his shirtfront, she pushed him away...or at least she *tried* to push him away.

He wasn't having any of it and held her fast.

'Look, I might have agreed to *temporarily* do a job for you,' she reminded him, 'but that doesn't mean I've agreed to be at your beck and call day and night.'

'Did I say that's what I wanted?' He sighed, and his warm breath fanned her face. 'Neither would I want to be at *your* beck and call day and night, Rose. But if we need to spend some time together that's a different proposition entirely...wouldn't you say?'

Noting that he had said *need* instead of *want* sent a

traitorous warm glow pulsing through Rose. The declaration didn't make it sound as if he intended to use her and then cast her aside so he could go on to the next available woman he took a fancy to.

And yet the memory of her ex Joe's behaviour reminded her that she shouldn't give her trust so easily —she couldn't afford to be lulled into a false sense of security by the dangerous hope that Gene genuinely wanted to have a relationship with her. Didn't his much-documented brief liaisons with various models and actresses prove that he wasn't a man who believed in long-term relationships?

'I just don't think it's a good idea for us to spend any more time together…at least not in *that* way. From now on our relationship should be a purely professional one. I'll do what you're paying me to do as regards selling the antiques, but there'll be no need for us to associate outside of work.'

'I disagree.'

'I thought you might—but that's only because you want your own way. My mind is made up, Gene.'

'And what if you find out you're pregnant?'

He came back at her like a whip and his gaze was suddenly ominously cold. Rose shivered, but he still didn't release her.

'You don't have to worry about that.'

'You mean you're on the pill?'

'No. But there's a morning-after pill I can get from the pharmacy that inhibits ovulation. I'm going to get it on the way home.'

'So I don't have any say in the matter at all?'

'I thought you'd be pleased that there's something we can do. I'm sure you don't want to be tied to me because of a child we created in a totally crazy moment of unforeseen passion.'

For a perturbing few moments Gene didn't know what to say. Everything in him felt as though it had been shaken up and displaced—and, worse than that, he sensed it wasn't likely that the various parts would be returned to their original positions any time soon...

Then he remembered what had instigated their 'crazy moment of unforeseen passion'. He'd told Rose that she was working for *him* now, and she hadn't seemed at all happy. She had finished by exclaiming 'But you're not him!' as if she mourned the fact that he wasn't her boss, Philip Houghton.

His arms locked even tighter round her impossibly small waist. An undeniable sense of ownership and possession seized him. 'Are you intent on taking this morning-after pill because you don't trust me? Do you think I wouldn't take responsibility?'

Rose sighed. 'I haven't thought about anything much beyond protecting myself. We're not in a serious relationship and I'm equally responsible for what just happened. I'm just being sensible.'

'Why? Has something like this happened to you before? You indicated once that you'd been hurt by someone.'

'I was. But he didn't make me pregnant and abandon me, if that's what you were thinking. In a way what he did was worse than that. He fooled around behind my back and then lied about it as if it was nothing.'

Even though she'd endeavoured to make her tone sound matter-of-fact, Gene still heard the pain in her voice. He felt as though he'd been punched. The thought of a man regularly cheating on Rose and then lying to her instigated that primitive impulse in him to protect and defend her honour.

'I'm sorry you had to go through that,' he said, low-voiced, 'but that's not the way *I* behave. You're well rid of the jerk. Getting back to the present situation, I know you're being practical in thinking about a morning-after pill, but what about our feelings? Don't *they* come into the equation at all?'

Gene's heart was galloping as he heard himself asking the one question he'd never asked a woman before. But since meeting Rose he was being more and more drawn to acknowledge an area of his life that he'd long ago become adept at turning away from… *his emotions.*

The matchless violet gaze in front of him reflected her alarm. 'Are you seriously telling me that you have some kind of—of *feeling* about the possibility of me having a baby?'

'I'm not completely heartless. There are some things in life that cause a person to stop and think. A possible pregnancy is one of them.'

'But I've already told you—it's not just your responsibility.'

'I hear you. But I also want you to hear *me*, Rose. I don't know how or why, but we seem to have developed some kind of connection—a connection that's a little deeper than run of the mill. It's not something I want to ignore, and neither do I want to just put it down to experience.'

'I hardly know what to say...'

'In that case there's absolutely no reason why we can't make our relationship more personal, is there?'

'Didn't we just make it about as personal as it can be?'

Rose's comment was clearly meant to be ironic. Unfortunately Gene saw no reason for humour—ironic or otherwise...

He uneremoniously released her. Scraping his fingers through his perfectly groomed hair, he was intensely frustrated that she didn't seem to want to take their relationship more seriously. Even though they'd been intimate, it was easy to sense that she was already putting up walls between them... *He wished he could knock every one of them down.*

Having never experienced a woman spurning him before, he barely knew what to do. Already he felt bereft because she wasn't in his arms... He could flex his masculinity and *insist* she came home with him, but this was the twenty-first century and Rose was an independent woman. He sensed she wouldn't take at all well to his throwing his weight around. In fact, such an action would probably drive her away completely. He would have to mull over another strategy.

Meeting her gaze, he said, 'If you won't come back to my apartment then why don't you let me drive you home?'

'There's no need. I can get the bus—like I usually do.'

'You don't drive?'

'No…I don't.'

In that volatile moment he couldn't contain his temper that things weren't going his way, and he snapped, 'Then go and get yourself ready and I'll meet you out front in my car. Our first destination will be the pharmacy…'

Rose was exiting the pharmacy and heading towards the luxurious Mercedes that waited for her outside when a man with a camera rushed towards her. Pointing it at her, he was taking continuous snaps even as he moved.

'Are you Eugene Bonnaire's new girlfriend? What's your name, love? You might as well tell me. I saw his car. What other reason would he have for parking it there?'

Even as she reeled with shock she saw Gene hurriedly open the door next to the driver's seat. Rose registered the furious muscle that flexed in his hard-chiselled jaw.

He yelled, 'Get in the car quickly and don't tell that idiot anything!'

Rose moved almost without thinking. She all but threw herself into the luxuriously upholstered passenger seat and Gene started the engine as she was still closing the door. The precision-engineered car moved smoothly away from the kerb.

'That's exactly what I *don't* need,' he murmured.

Placing her bag down by her feet, she glanced up. 'I wouldn't have said anything, you know. I certainly wouldn't have given him my name. Does that kind of thing happen very often?'

'A little too often for my liking… I never thought I'd miss my anonymity, but it's funny how things change.'

Genuinely surprised that he should share such a personal reflection, Rose relaxed a little. Perhaps Gene didn't seek the limelight as much as the press made out that he did? Could that be the reason he'd looked so unhappy in that photo she'd seen of him at the awards ceremony? The idea of having your every move stalked and being photographed by paparazzi must be a living nightmare. There was nothing about his life that she remotely envied. In fact she suddenly found herself feeling genuinely sad for his lack of privacy...

'I never thought I'd say this, but I feel for you, Gene...I really do. I'm glad I said we should keep our relationship on a professional footing rather than a personal one. In light of events like *that* happening, it's probably best if you stay away. We can communicate by phone.'

Turning his head towards her, he scowled. 'I won't be dictated to by anybody—least of all the media.' He returned his furious gaze to the road. 'Just give me your address and I'll take you home.'

When they pulled up outside the neat semi-detached house in the pleasant cul-de-sac where Rose lived, Gene switched off the engine and turned to gaze out of the window at the building. Rose saw him glance at the newly mown lawn and the tidy window boxes that were full of colourful perennials. It was late autumn, and she loved the fact that they were still in bloom. But he was probably thinking how ordinary the place was, she reflected.

'Have you always lived here?' he asked.

Even as she nodded, she hated the feeling that he

might be judging her in some way because of where she lived.

'It's the house I grew up in with my parents. When my father died he left it to me.'

'Not your mother?'

She shook her head. 'No. They weren't together any more.'

'You mean they were divorced?'

Expelling a jaundiced sigh, Rose replied, 'Yes. She ran off with a rich unscrupulous businessman who promised her a better life.' She couldn't hide the bitterness in her tone and sensed her cheeks flush red.

Gene's brow puckered interestedly. 'And *did* he…? Give her a better life, I mean?'

'Depends what you mean by "better". As far as I know she's happy. They live in a swanky place in Paris and she doesn't want for anything. Apparently she's got the kind of life she always dreamt of…the kind of life that my father could never have afforded to give her. But she broke his heart when she left him and he never really recovered.'

'I'm sorry to hear that. But her desertion must have been tough on you too?'

Rose felt the backs of her eyes sting. 'It was for a while. But then I got over it. I had to deal with what was in front of me. In any case, who needs a mother who'd rather have the material things in life over the people that really love her?'

She thought she saw Gene wince.

'What did he do for a living? I mean your father?' he asked.

'He was an accountant…a very good one, as a matter of fact.' She was quite aware that she sounded defensive. 'But he was never as ambitious as my mother wanted him to be. Instead of seeing what a loyal and devoted husband and father he was, she saw the fact that he put spending time with his family before rising in his career as a weakness.'

'You said that your mother and her husband live in Paris? Can you tell me where?'

Again Rose sensed her face heat. She didn't doubt that Gene would know the place. She hadn't forgotten that he was French. 'It's a suburb called Neuilly-sur-Seine.'

'If they can afford to live there he *must* be rich. It's got some of the most prime real estate in the city.'

She shrugged and unbuckled her seatbelt. 'I wouldn't know. Nor do I care.'

Before she could turn and open the car door she heard the soft snick of Gene's seatbelt being freed. Leaning towards her, he captured her hand and held it fast.

'Before you go I think we need to have a serious talk, don't you?'

Like a moth drawn to a flame, she fell headlong into the dangerous fire of his glittering blue gaze and sensed herself sizzle. At the same time the sensual musky scent of him made her insides melt. Shockingly, all she could think about was the silkily hard, hot sensation of him inside her… It stunned Rose just how much she ached to experience his intimate possession again.

She bit down hard on the lower lip that was already contused from his passionate kisses. 'What kind of a talk? If it's about the sale of the antiques I told you I'd stay in touch.'

Even to her own ears her voice sounded distinctly shaky.

'You know damn well it's not about the antiques. We need to talk about what just happened between us at the shop.'

Rose forced herself to stay strong, not to let him suspect how deeply his passionate attentions had affected her. 'We had sex on my boss's desk…that's what happened. I told you I was going to take the morning-after pill to make sure I don't get pregnant, so you don't have to worry. What else do we need to talk about?'

'I don't believe for one second that's *all* you think we did, Rose.'

Suddenly Gene was lifting her hand towards his lips with strangely purposeful intent…

'We made *fire* back there—that's what we did…a fire that burned us both right down to our core. And if you deny it I won't hesitate to call you a liar.'

Even as he made the assertion he was inserting her slender forefinger into the silkily hot cavern of his mouth and sucking it…

She gasped. 'What are you…? What are you doing?' She snatched her hand away even as she wished that she was brave enough to keep it there.

His lips formed a lazily knowing smile. 'I was reacquainting myself with your taste, Rose. It seems that I can't get enough of it.'

'Well, you're going to have to learn to do without it— because I can't and won't continue with this stupidity!'

The feeling that she was about to burst into tears was overwhelming. Because she didn't want to make an even bigger fool of herself than she'd done already, she snatched up her bag and opened the door.

As she stepped out onto the pavement Gene's inscrutable handsome features gave not the slightest clue as to his feelings, but he remarked, 'You might call it stupidity for us to spend more time together, Rose, but I don't happen to share that view. Whatever the outcome of this situation, I personally have no regrets. Be assured that I'll be in touch.'

Rose didn't reply. Instead she slammed the car door shut and headed straight for the house. Even as she heard him pull away, and as the tears she'd tried so hard to hold back started to stream down her face, she made sure not to turn and follow his progress...

CHAPTER NINE

GENE HADN'T BEEN lying when he'd commented to Rose that he couldn't get enough of her taste. It wasn't just her taste he was addicted to either. He couldn't get enough of *her*...especially since that wild episode in Philip's office. His blood rushed and his heart pumped harder every time he thought about it.

The realisation that she was becoming more important to him than he'd ever envisaged threatened everything. Dear God, the woman had him in such a tailspin he'd barely even given the ownership of the antiques shop building a thought. How could that be? he wondered. Wasn't possession of the listed building supposed to be the icing on the cake, crowning yet another successful year of his restaurant chain as well as the other numerous lucrative investments he'd made?

It didn't feel like that. It made him realise there was a big difference between *being* successful and *feeling* successful—and right then he didn't feel successful at all. He felt strangely empty...as though everything he'd set such store by in his life had suddenly become meaningless.

Rose's story about her mother's desertion of her for an 'unscrupulous rich businessman' had definitely hit a nerve. It was evident that she despised her stepfather. Without a doubt Gene could probably find at least a dozen parallels with himself and the man, and it was quite possible he even *knew* him. The business community *he* was a member of only welcomed the 'elite of the elite' into their ranks...the wealthiest and most powerful of men and women...and Rose's stepfather might even be one of Gene's competitors.

Yet it wasn't that that perturbed him. It was the knowledge that he'd behaved exactly like her mother when he'd turned his back on his loved ones, believing that the simple life his parents enjoyed wasn't enough. He'd become greedy and ambitious, and hearing Rose's story had made him aware of some of the more negative consequences his desires had wrought.

He'd purchased a beautiful Georgian house for his parents a few years ago and had sensed their deep unease at accepting it.

His father had told him, 'It's a wonderful gift, son, but in truth your mother and me would rather know that you're happy and content, and have your company from time to time, than have you buy us a house. We're quite happy with our simple little terrace. All our memories are here...it's where we raised you and your sister.'

Gene had felt crass and insensitive. He'd never even considered what *they* wanted. Yet it hurt him deeply that they'd never understood how much losing his beloved sister, Francesca, had affected *him*. Knowing that life was so precarious and ephemeral had really shaken him. And the need to protect his remaining family at all costs had driven him to become more and more successful in the world. Yet he had never been able to share his feelings with them about it.

After the disappointing reception of his well-meant gift of the house he had retreated to lick his wounds and had distanced himself from them even more. Gene had numbed his discomfort and pain by acquiring even more restaurants and playing the stock market. He had been employing the only way he knew how to protect himself from further hurt.

He had been as devastated as his parents when illness had so cruelly taken Francesca from them. From time to time her beautiful face would come into his mind, and it was like a knife in his heart that he would never see her grow into a woman, would never see her fall in love, maybe marry and have children of her own...

They'd all been like ghosts after she went...alive, but not really living. And now Gene feared he'd lost his parents' respect and regard. They might tell him that they loved him, but too often when he visited he saw pain and disappointment in their eyes because of the path he'd taken. They had no idea what drove him to pursue success and money so relentlessly and probably never would. They no doubt believed it made him happy. How could they know what a high price he paid for being so driven?

Every night when he went home from his day's work—to his apartment in London or either of the desirable residences he owned in New York and Paris when he was there—more often than not he went home alone. Eugene didn't have relationships. He had joyless liaisons that were usually conducted in some luxurious hotel that was utterly devoid of anything remotely homely or comforting. It made him secretly despise the women he entertained, because they were more interested in his money than in expressing even a passing interest in the real man behind the wealthy and polished veneer...

He might have been kidding himself that that was okay, but deep down he knew it was a *lie*. Seeing Rose's house today, in an ordinary suburban cul-de-sac, with its well-tended window boxes and tidily perfect lawn, he had been almost *envious* that she clearly didn't feel the need for something grander. The mere concept of being satisfied with your lot in life was a million miles away from the world Gene inhabited. And, although he couldn't envisage himself in a similar situation to hers, it had surprisingly instilled in him a longing for some of the comforts of a real home.

And it wasn't just that that he longed to experience.

There was a deep yearning inside him to be with someone who really cared...someone who didn't just want him for what he could provide materially but who genuinely wanted to get to know him and likewise would let him get to know *her*...

He headed for the kitchen. Whenever he was troubled and—yes—sometimes *sickened* by the relentless desire for more that had set him apart from so much that was true, he returned to the one thing that was guaranteed to give him pleasure...*cooking*. And while he gathered together the pots, pans and ingredients that he needed to make a meal his thoughts inevitably turned to Rose and the meal he'd made for her on the island.

Already it had become one of Gene's favourite memories. But thinking of her was bittersweet, because he'd left her on her own to deal with the possibility that he might have made her pregnant. *It wasn't right*. He hated the idea that she might be feeling scared and upset. Having the presence of mind to think about taking the morning-after pill might denote that she was a practical woman, but he knew she was a sensitive one too.

Frustrated that he couldn't be with her, he reached for his mobile and dialled the number of a trusted business colleague who was the owner of an exclusive jeweller's in Bond Street. After that he contacted an equally prestigious florist. If he couldn't have the pleasure of Rose's company tonight at least he could do something to show her that he cared about the compromising situation he had put her in…

The next morning Rose was roused from a restless night with very little sleep to take unexpected delivery of the most beautiful bouquet of white roses. Even as she carefully transported them into the kitchen to put them into her favourite crystal vase the scent of the flowers filled the air like a soporific hypnotic balm. Had Philip sent them to thank her for dealing with the sale of the antiques store?

With their exotic scent and lush, velvety petals, even in her sleep-deprived state they couldn't help but make Rose think of Cleopatra, Queen of the Nile. The legend went that the queen had regularly bathed in a bath of milk scented with rose petals…

Gently laying the bouquet down on the table, she bent to inhale the scent a little more closely. It was then that she saw the card that accompanied them, and tucked in amongst the flowers she saw a narrow red velvet box. Frowning, she opened the card and studied the inscription. With her pulse racing she read it.

To the Hidden Diamond I never expected to find.
Gene x.

Gene had sent her the flowers? To receive such a message from him was so unexpected, so exhilarating, that Rose felt quite intoxicated by it.

Pulling out a chair from the table, she sank down into it because her legs suddenly felt as though they might not support her. Her mind was racing as she strove to find an explanation of what he might mean. Then she reached into the bouquet of buttery roses for the glamorous presentation box. She opened it.

Lying on a bed of sumptuous cream silk was the most dazzling diamond bracelet Rose had ever seen. Set in white gold, the square-cut gems were flawlessly pristine and glinted up at her like brilliant sunlight radiated through a prism. What had Gene meant by sending her such an amazing and valuable gift?

Lifting the bracelet out of the box, she tried it on. It was blissfully cool against her skin and yet her whole body felt drenched with heat, just thinking about the man who'd sent it. But it was the words he'd written on the card that had taken her aback the most. *The Hidden Diamond…* Was Gene saying that *Rose* was the hidden diamond he'd never expected to find? Was the sentiment a heartfelt one or was he merely flattering her?

She suddenly felt like crying, because more than anything she wanted to believe that Gene meant every word…

The telephone rang. Rose rushed to answer it in case it might be the hospital. As far as Philip's health was concerned he was by no means out of the woods yet.

But it wasn't anyone from the hospital.

It was Gene.

'Rose? It's me.'

The seductive bass voice that never failed to raise gooseflesh on her skin made her instantly tingle. She hadn't yet taken off the diamond bracelet he'd sent and the glittering gems winked back at her as if daring her to remove it…

Dry-mouthed, she answered, 'What's up?'

She wanted to sound nonchalant, as if she didn't care that he should be ringing her so early in the morning, but as soon as she heard his voice her insides were deluged with a swarm of agitated butterflies.

'Tell me how you are this morning.'

'I'm—I'm fine…'

'I still wish that you'd come home with me.'

'I did the right thing. I was very tired. It's been an emotional time.'

'That's the reason why we shouldn't make any hasty decisions.'

Rose heard him take a deep breath in and remembered the comment he'd made about considering their feelings. It had knocked her for six. It certainly hadn't followed his infamous pattern of brief, 'take it or leave it' liaisons.

'I was worried that you might be upset about what happened yesterday and regret it,' he went on.

The comment made her burn as she recalled the sheer power of the elemental forces that had driven them to make love with such wild abandon in her boss's office. In the cold light of day it was hard to believe she'd behaved so recklessly.

'I'm not upset. We did what we did and I don't regret it. But, like I said...it's not going to happen again.'

She sucked in a breath and released it slowly in a bid to calm her nerves, but even as she'd said the words she'd been wishing she could take them back...

'By the way, thank you for the beautiful roses and the gift you sent.'

Frowning, she lifted her arm once again to examine the elegant diamond bracelet that adorned her wrist. The apricot silk dressing gown she was wearing, which she'd bought from a vintage clothing sale, couldn't help but complement the jewellery. The sensuous feel of the garment next to her skin made her feel like a million dollars.

Wearing both the bracelet *and* the gown, she felt like a whole other person...someone much more stylish and beautiful than the unremarkable woman she thought of herself as.

But her pleasure quickly died when she caught herself. She didn't want to give herself illusions of grandeur or to feel different or special just because she'd been given an expensive diamond bracelet. She wasn't like her mother, whose craving for the finer things in life had made her leave her loyal, dependable husband to be with a much wealthier man just because he could indulge her material desires...

'I'll keep the roses...but I'm afraid I won't be keeping the bracelet.'

There was a significant momentary silence at the other end of the phone. It was soon filled with an exasperated, 'Why not? I know how much you admire beautiful things and I wanted to give you something beautiful—so what's the problem?'

'It's a *diamond bracelet*, Gene. That's the problem. The clarity, cut and carat of the stones is amazing, so it's by no means a simple gift. Do you think that men give women gifts like that every day? They might in your exalted world, but they most definitely don't in mine. And it—it makes it hard for me to trust your motives. My ex used to give me pretty gifts when he was seeing other women behind my back and wanted to divert me from finding out. I know we're not serious, but if that's what *you're* going to do, Gene, then I'll save you wasting your time and your money by giving you the bracelet back. At least then we know where we stand.'

By the time she came to the end of her impassioned speech Rose could just imagine Gene dismissing it with a shrug of his impressive shoulders...more than likely encased in his usual impeccable tailoring. It was hard not to break down and cry... He might have talked about having feelings, but that didn't mean he'd honestly meant it.

'It sounds to me as if what happened yesterday *did* upset you, Rose. Why don't you have lunch with me today and we can talk?'

'About what a colossal mistake we made?' Even as she made the comment the churning emotion in her gut made a liar of her.

'You really believe that? A mistake suggests we had a choice in the matter and had time to think it through. If you recall, Rose, *thinking* didn't come into it. We were drawn together by an overpowering force of nature that we couldn't resist.'

And she had the sore spots on her body to prove it...

Feeling her face flame red, she replied, 'Anyway, I can't meet you for lunch. I have far too much work to do.'

'Do I have to keep reminding you that you're working for me now? You can have the whole damn day off if you want to.'

'But I don't *want* the day off.'

He made another exasperated sound and Rose was glad he couldn't see the tears that welled in her eyes.

'Meet me for lunch and let that be an end to it,' he ground out. 'I'll give you the name of the restaurant and you can meet me there. I'll pay for a cab.'

She sniffed and wiped her eyes, then stared blankly at the shimmering diamond bracelet that had slid down her slender-boned wrist to rest elegantly against her hand. 'I can pay for my own cab.'

'I might have guessed that you'd say that. Did I tell

you that I think you're the most stubborn woman I've ever met?'

It was Rose's turn to shrug. 'More than once… But it probably does you good to not have your own way all the time.'

Gene chuckled, and the sound elicited a burst of warmth inside her that made her want to count the minutes—no…the *seconds* until she could be with him again…

As Rose followed the smart, straight-backed *maître d'* to the table Gene had reserved she was sure that every single diner in the exclusive little restaurant watched her progress. As soon as she'd mentioned what seemed to be the magic words 'Eugene Bonnaire' she would have sworn that every one of the stylishly dressed customers seated at the tables had turned to see who was enquiring.

The table was in an intimately cordoned off alcove, tucked away at the back of the restaurant, and Rose's heart clanged hard as Gene stood up to greet her. He was wearing a slim-fitting charcoal suit, and the single-breasted jacket hung open to reveal a navy shirt and an azure silk tie. But it wasn't the colour of his shirt or tie that transfixed her. It was the arresting glint in his incredible blue eyes…

Every single muscle in her body stiffened and contracted at the undeniably voracious glance he gave her—because he was shamelessly undressing her with his eyes. That intense examining glance left her with nowhere to go…nowhere to run and hide…

He huskily murmured, 'Hi…' but she couldn't seem to find a single word with which to respond.

The discreet *maître d'* smiled, saying he would give them a few minutes to look at the menu. Then he politely left them alone.

Despite her see-sawing emotions Rose couldn't deny she'd been looking forward to their lunch date. That being the case, she'd decided to wear what was perhaps her most eye-catching outfit. She'd bared her shoulders in a top the colour of metallic silver, and had teamed it with a black chiffon mini-skirt with ebony tights and long leather boots.

She'd wanted Gene to see that she could look chic and classy and didn't need to dress in haute couture to prove it… Showcasing what she thought of as some of her best assets for their date—namely her tiny waist, slim arms and shapely legs—made her feel good.

In fact she was beginning to realise that she felt more womanly and attractive than she'd ever felt before when she was with him, and she wanted to let him see that— however their relationship *did* or *didn't* progress.

'You look sensational.'

His low-voiced compliment confirmed that she'd opted for the right outfit.

'I definitely heard an admiring gasp when you entered the restaurant. I'll bet everyone wants to know who you are.'

Although Gene's effusive compliments had stopped her in her tracks, confidently holding his gaze, Rose murmured, 'Thanks. You scrub up nicely yourself.'

With a gravel-voiced chuckle he moved round the

table to be closer to her. Then he made an elegant bow, like a gentleman from the upper echelons of society in one of those classic novels, and politely brushed the side of her cheek with a kiss.

Immediately the cool touch of his lips rendered Rose dangerously weak. *The reaction was definitely starting to become a habit.*

'Come and sit next to me…' he breathed, and it didn't once cross her mind to refuse. 'I haven't been able to stop thinking about you,' he confessed, his piercing cobalt eyes practically consuming her with their electric glance.

Rose set her handbag down on the chair next to her and twisted her hands together. 'I don't know whether that's a good or not so good thing. We're work colleagues now, remember?'

His sculpted lips shaped an amused grin, 'So our relationship is purely a working one, is it?'

'I didn't come here to talk about what's happened between us. I want to put that behind me and concentrate on doing a good job of selling off the antiques for you.'

'You can still do that…but it doesn't mean that we can't see each other outside of work.'

'Where are you going with this, Gene? I've already told you that I'd prefer it if we kept our association a professional one. Like I said before, I'm not interested in becoming one of your short-term little liaisons. In spite of what's happened, my decision hasn't changed.'

Gene sighed. As he pushed back his hair the eye-catching gold watch he wore glinted against his wrist. The bracelet was made unusually of rose gold, as was the intricate dial, set in relief against an ebony back-drop. Surely only the most confident and assured of men would be able to wear such a watch? And not only that, but wear it with enviable panache.

Rose didn't need to see the maker's name to know that it had been made by one of the most esteemed watch designers in the world. Her stomach lurched as it was brought home to her yet again just who Gene was and what he represented...

'I don't see our liaison as being a short-term one,' he told her, his tone etched with frustration. 'In fact I want us to have a *proper* relationship.'

Reaching for the water jug on the table, Rose poured a glass and gratefully swallowed some. She was almost lightheaded with shock. 'That's impossible. I know you don't do "proper" relationships, so why would you make an exception for me?'

His expression was serious. 'Why? Because I'm tired of denying the fact that I want something more, that's why. I'm tired of isolating myself from people. I haven't seen my family for months now, and it's near killing me.'

'Why haven't you seen them?'

'Because I'm too busy working.' Looking agonised, he shook his head. 'And because all I seem to do is hurt them when we're together.'

Rose caught his hand and held it. The heartfelt con-fession had utterly shaken her.

'Whatever has happened between you, there's always a way to make things better.'

'Maybe there is in your world, Rose...but not in mine.'

'Have you even talked to them about your belief that all you do is hurt them? That might not be the case at all. What if they're just waiting for you to come and talk things over?'

He glanced down at her slim hand, covering his, and his faint smile of acknowledgement twisted her heart.

'Maybe they are. I just haven't considered it.'

'Then you shouldn't waste any more time in going to see them and reconciling…that's my advice.'

'See how good you are for me? *That's* why it doesn't make sense for our relationship to be purely platonic.'

Rose sighed and carefully withdrew her hand. Again the fear arose that she was lulling herself into a false sense of security. 'Yes, it does. Just look at the facts. We're oceans apart, Gene. It doesn't matter how attracted we are to each other physically. The fact is we inhabit very different worlds. An association like ours is never going to work unless we keep things purely platonic.'

'You must be joking!' His lips twisted grimly. 'You might not want to admit I'm right, but our relationship is never, *ever* going to stay platonic. That would be like touching a lit match to some dry tinder and expecting it not to catch fire. Because that's what you do to me, Rose…you make me catch fire.'

Even as he finished speaking she knew he was going to kiss her. And what was more worrying was that she knew she wasn't going to try and stop him…

CHAPTER TEN

As Gene's mouth claimed Rose's in a hotly voracious kiss the depth and power of his desire genuinely scared him. It scared him to want and need a woman this much because it gave her a power over him that he wouldn't be able to repudiate easily. It wasn't just about the intense attraction he felt towards her either. The realisation that he might want something deeper was territory he'd never encountered before, and potentially it made him dangerously vulnerable.

But he simply couldn't leave her alone.

It would be like depriving himself of life-giving oxygen not to see her.

As his silken tongue danced with hers he heard her moan softly with pleasure and he gathered her into his arms. The sensation of her shapely and slender body pressed close into his chest inevitably made him tighten. *Why hadn't he suggested she met him at his apartment instead of at the restaurant?* At least then they could have tumbled into bed and continued what they'd started on the island and yesterday…

Intimately possessing Rose in the office might have

been the most red-hot sex he'd ever experienced, but it had fanned the flames of Gene's desire even more—despite his not using protection and the potential consequences.

But he didn't want to raise the topic of the morning-after pill right now...

Lifting his head, he glanced down into his lover's prettily flushed face and smiled. '*Now* do you believe me when I say a platonic relationship hasn't got a chance in hell of working? Not between you and me, Rose.'

Even though her beautiful eyes were drowsy with need, they also reflected unease. This was confirmed when she immediately extricated herself from Gene's embrace and moved further down in her seat.

'Well, we'd better not have *any* kind of relationship, then. We shouldn't have been intimate. Sex just confuses things. It always leads to trouble of some kind.'

Her words reminded him that Rose had been badly let down by an ex-boyfriend and that it wasn't just her mother running off with her rich lover that had made her so mistrustful of men...

'I told you that that's not going to happen between us. I may have played the field a little, but I've never lied to any woman about my intentions. That's why I've come clean with you and told you frankly what I've been feeling. I'm not like your ex-boyfriend and I won't let you down like he did. Can't you trust the connection we have and just be open to seeing where it goes?'

She glanced away for a second. 'I could... But it's

difficult when my ex had many of the same traits you have. I don't need to go into details—all you need to know is that he put work and ambition before everything else and basically did what he liked, because he thought it was some kind of inalienable right. Our relationship came very low down on his list of priorities, and if I dared complain he'd tell me he was only working as hard as he was for *me*. Then, finally, I found out that he'd regularly been cheating on me. I felt like such a fool. That's why I can't trust my feelings—and I can't trust men like *you*, Gene.'

'Just because he had similar traits to me and hurt you, Rose, it doesn't mean I'm going to behave in the same way. The least you can do is to give me a chance to prove myself.'

'It's a risk I can't afford to take, Gene. In any case the point is that I need to focus my attention on getting a new job, and you need to…you need to—'

He might be hard, hot and frustrated, but Gene couldn't deny he wanted to hear what she had to say. Raising an eyebrow, he murmured, 'Go on. What exactly *do* I need to do, Rose?'

'Forget it. What do I know? We lead very different lives.'

'You obviously have an opinion, so you may as well share it.'

Trapped, she heaved an annoyed sigh. 'Okay…but you're not going to like it. It's never going to work out between us, whatever our relationship. The way you live your life is totally alien to me, and I think it would do you good to check in with the *real* world from time to time.'

Gene suddenly sensed that he wasn't going to enjoy hearing what else she had to say, but still he invited, 'Go on…'

'Well…you have a reputation for being able to get anything you want, and you like the power that it gives you. I sensed that the very first time I met you. There was beauty all around you but you barely even saw it. What you saw was a desirable property that you were desperate to acquire and you would do anything to get it. But let me ask you this: Don't you have enough property already? You probably don't even register what you own because you're always looking for more. It must be hard for the people who care about you because your focus can't ever be on nurturing those relationships— not if you're always so dissatisfied with what you've got. You've told me yourself that you haven't seen your parents in months, and I can see how much that hurts you. Perhaps you ought to try and heal that relationship first, before you think about having one yourself. In truth, I genuinely feel sorry for you—because I can see that your wealth has stopped you from seeing the things in life that really matter.'

Gene had never before been stunned into silence but he was now. Rose's impassioned words hadn't just unsettled him—they'd honestly disturbed him. He felt as if he'd been put under a magnifying glass in the hot sun. He was in pain and he was *furious*…

Reining in his temper, he countered, 'What do you mean I should get in touch with the "real" world? Do you think I was born with a silver spoon in my mouth and have no notion of what it's like to have to work hard for my living? My parents were immigrants and they both came from poverty-stricken backgrounds. They came over here, worked hard at various restaurants, then started up their own restaurant with minimal money and no help from anyone but each other. When I was old enough I started to help them and they taught me how to cook. When I realised I was good at it I discovered what I wanted to do in life and was determined to be a success. I've spent my life working hard to make my dreams into a reality…that's why my family and I will never be poor again. Do you think I'm going to apologise for that? Like *hell* I am!'

Rose's smooth brow puckered. 'It's commendable that you made your dreams come true, and of course I don't expect you to apologise for what you've achieved. I'm sure your parents must be very proud of you. But all I'm asking is haven't you ever thought about appreciating some of the more valuable things in life that are actually *free*?'

Gene glared irritably. 'Like what, for instance? It's been my experience that nothing is free. Fortunately I've always understood that the name of the game is money.'

'What about the ability to nurture and enjoy good relationships and—and to experience love? Do you think you have to pay for those too?'

He scowled. 'Love is a fool's game. It's too easy to lose. I prefer things that are more tangible.'

The look on Rose's face instantly conveyed her dismay, and Gene knew he would come to regret his cynical response.

'So that means that you would never risk loving someone?'

'Let me ask *you* a question, Rose. Is your mother a pretty woman? I'll bet she is. Your rich stepfather probably saw her as another desirable possession and she saw him as a better bet to take care of her than your dad because he was wealthy. Love doesn't have anything to do with it. You probably despise the man, but there was a mutually satisfying pay-off in that they both got exactly what they wanted.'

Stung, Rose shot up and grabbed her handbag. 'I don't despise him. I hate the fact that he used his wealth and fancy lifestyle to persuade my mum away from my dad. Yes, I know she wasn't entirely innocent. But I'll never admire *anyone* who uses their wealth in such a devious way—not even caring that they helped break a man's heart.'

Clutching the neat black leather bag she'd brought with her tightly against her chest, she used it as if it was a shield.

'Anyway, you can think what you like. You barely know me…much less my family.'

Rising to his feet, Gene folded his arms. 'You're right. But how can I *get* to know you when you don't trust people enough to let them get close? Going by what you said about your ex, it's clear that you have no intention of ever trusting that I might act honourably towards you.'

Her crimson-painted lips quivered and she looked

as if she was about to burst into tears. As much as he wanted to comfort her and take her in his arms, he elected not to.

This time her comments hadn't just touched a nerve—they had genuinely wounded him. It had stung to hear her suggest that his desire to keep on acquiring things must end up separating him from the people who cared about him... It stung because he knew it was *true*. It made him reflect uncomfortably on what he had done to his parents—on how his quest for 'more' and 'better' had indisputably hurt them and forged a chasm between them that was growing ever harder to bridge...

'I don't think I should stay for lunch after all,' she murmured.

'Why not...? I never had you down as a coward.'

Lifting her head, Rose stared. 'I'm not. I just think it's a case of wrong place, wrong time for us—and what's the point in us both being unhappy?'

Unable to make sense of anything much right then, Gene answered. 'I agree. There clearly isn't any point.'

'Anyway, there's one more thing before I go...'

Even as he fought to gain control of his pain and disappointment that she was leaving and, yes, the undeniable sense of loss that had engendered, he stayed grimly silent as Rose drew out the red velvet gift box from her handbag and laid it down on the table.

'I'm sure you meant well, but I can't accept this,' she said softly.

Then, with her pretty violet eyes glistening, she turned and walked out...

* * *

By the time Rose got to the hospital to see Philip it was already late and there was just half an hour left of visiting time. As she approached the bed and saw him intently perusing an antiques catalogue it hardly signified that he was looking so much better, because her heart was painfully leaden at the way she'd left Gene at the restaurant.

She'd told him some unpalatable truths and he would have had to be made out of stone not to be affected by it. She hadn't meant to be cruel. But neither had she wanted to lead him astray and let him believe she was happy to have a meaningless fling with him. Her feelings for Gene were far from meaningless.

That was why she'd returned the bracelet. It might be his habit to buy women expensive gifts in payment for sharing intimacy, but Rose knew she would never take anything from him that wasn't given freely or because it was important to him. If they had a real relationship it wouldn't be one that he had to *buy*...

'Rose...how lovely to see you!' Philip couldn't hide his delight when he saw her.

She bent down to kiss him. 'You too. I'm sorry I didn't get here earlier but I lost track of the time. I've been canvassing as many dealers as I can to get them to buy the rest of the antiques. I did quite well this afternoon, I'm happy to report, so all the time and effort was worth it.'

When she pulled out the grey utilitarian chair next to the bed and tiredly dropped down into it her smile wasn't as animated as she would have wished. But, quickly gathering herself, Rose delved into her bag for the generous carton of plump red grapes that she'd brought.

'I know you'd probably prefer some of your favourite Belgian chocolate, but I thought I'd better not lead you astray.'

'Why on earth not...? Even an old fogey like me can use a little of what they fancy from time to time, can't they?'

'Well...perhaps next time I'll smuggle some in. How are you? Any news on those other tests you had?'

The time seemed to pass in a flash, and most of the other patients' visitors had left when Rose finally plucked up the courage to share what was uppermost in her mind...*Gene.*

'Philip?' Nervously smoothing her hand across the crisp white hospital counterpane, she leant towards him. 'Can I talk to you about something? It's a personal matter.'

'Of course you can, my dear. Is it to do with the shop? Are you perhaps finding it too much of a struggle to sell off the antiques as well as dealing with everything else that needs doing before Bonnaire comes in and takes over?'

Even the mention of Gene's surname had the power to make Rose ache with longing. She couldn't help wondering if she would ever see him again after their heated exchange at the restaurant. What if he sent his secretary or some minion to oversee things at the antiques store, just so he wouldn't have to come face to face with her?

It was like a dagger in her heart to think that he might so quickly forget the staggeringly powerful passion that had driven them to make love in Philip's office and treat it as though it was nothing important. Look at the risk they'd taken.

But the declaration he'd made at the restaurant that he wouldn't risk loving someone—that love was 'a fool's game'—couldn't help but fill her with more sorrow. If Rose had privately nursed an impossible hope that somehow he *could* learn to love her, his searing admission had obliterated it.

'I'm fine organising the sale of the antiques and everything else. That's not what I wanted to talk to you about. It's much more personal than that.'

Not commenting, Philip leant back against his plumped-up pillows and waited patiently for her to continue. Meeting his infinitely kind gaze, Rose assured herself that it would be all right—that he would understand and wouldn't judge her…

'I—I've fallen for someone…' she told him, even as her privately anguished feelings threatened to overwhelm her.

'Are you telling me that you're in love, Rose?'

Nodding miserably, she sensed her lip quiver.

Philip smiled. He couldn't have looked happier. 'But that's *wonderful* news. Who's the lucky man?'

'You don't need to know his name… I—I'd rather keep that private for now, if you don't mind. All I can tell you is that he's someone completely unsuitable.'

'But that hasn't stopped you from having feelings for

him?' he observed gently. Her comment clearly hadn't fazed him.

His reaction genuinely surprised her. 'No, it hasn't. But he's the absolute antithesis of me,' she insisted. 'It's hit me like a ton of bricks that I should feel this way about him.'

Philip was thoughtful. 'Falling in love can happen in a myriad different ways, Rose. For some it's a slow progression as they get to know each other…with others their eyes can literally meet across a room and they know instantly that he or she is the person they want to spend the rest of their life with. For others still it can knock them flat when they're simply going about their business, convinced that everything is under control and that nothing can possibly make them deviate from the path they're set on. It sounds to me, Rose, as if you fall into that category.'

'It's true. I never even *wanted* to fall in love. I schooled myself against it…especially after Joe cheated on me. Do you remember? But now that it's happened it's threatening everything I believe in. Doing what's right, I mean—the tenets that my dad taught me and stood by. Loving this man *isn't* doing what's right. I feel so guilty and I'm ashamed that I've let everyone down.'

Philip frowned. 'Everyone? Who do you imagine you've let down, Rose?'

Twisting her fingers restlessly together, she sighed. 'I've let *you* down, Philip. You've done so much for me and you deserve better'

'My dear…'

She found her agitated hands captured in his frail ones and subdued.

'You're behaving as though you've committed some heinous crime. Since when has falling in love been a criminal offence? Your feelings are no concern of anyone else's. Yes, the people who love you only want the best for you—but how does anybody know what's best for someone else? It's surely better to risk all for love than to turn away from it because of your fear of letting people down and living a life filled with regret and "if only".'

More than a little shocked, she stared. 'You sound as if you know exactly what that's like. Have you ever loved someone you turned away from because of what other people thought?'

The distinguished man nodded slowly, and his pale blue eyes couldn't hide the sadness that his memories must have aroused. 'I didn't just turn away from the lady because of what people thought, Rose... I turned away from her because I chose to focus on my career rather than go with her into the unknown. She was an artist...a rather wonderful one. She was ten years younger than me and she wanted to travel the world and be inspired by the vistas she saw to do her painting. She had no time for what she called "the safe option"—having a career, marrying someone and living what she used to call "a conventionally stultifying life of suburban boredom". She was a free spirit.'

He coughed a little and glanced away for a moment—but not before Rose spied the glint of moisture in his eyes.

'Her name was Elizabeth and I loved her more than life itself.'

'Do you mind if I ask…is that the reason why you've never married?'

Nodding again, he released her hands. 'There was never anyone for me but *her*. I could never even contemplate it. That's why you must follow your heart, Rose. There's no need for guilt and shame. Don't be like me and live a life of regret, imagining what might have been. I'm sure if your father was still here he would tell you the same.'

'And what about Elizabeth…? Did you ever see her again?'

'Sadly not… She said she thought it best that we didn't stay in touch. I just pray that wherever she is she continues to enjoy her travels and paint her pictures. It makes me happy to think of her doing what she loves.'

Leaning towards the bed, Rose affectionately brushed the side of his weathered cheek with her lips. 'Bless you, Philip. What you've just told me means more than I can say. I feel as though a great burden has been lifted from me. I feel lighter and—and more hopeful that whatever happens it will all work out. Although I'm still scared the man concerned might not feel the same…'

'I don't think you need have any fear about that.'

'Thanks. You're good for a girl's ego—you know that?'

Glancing towards the door, she noticed there was a stern-looking nurse pointing up at the wall clock to indicate that visiting hours were over.

Turning her gaze back to her boss, she said, 'I'd better go. I'll keep in touch by phone as often as I can, and let you know how I'm getting on with selling the antiques. And if there's anything you want me to put by for you, I will. One more thing: please let me know if you get a date for when you can come home, won't you?'

'Of course I will. Now, go and see your mysterious man. Maybe one day soon you'll feel able to tell me his name? In the meantime, tell him from me that the gods of good fortune smiled on him the day he set eyes on you, Rose.'

The first thing Gene saw when he opened his eyes the next morning was the red velvet jewel box. On his return from the restaurant he'd dropped it onto his dressing table as though he despised it.

Did Rose have any idea how much she'd humiliated him with her vehement little diatribe about the way he lived? And—more to the point—the way she'd all but thrown his gift back in his face? Hadn't the message he'd written meant anything to her? He was sick to his stomach that she'd scorned him.

Because he'd been so agitated, and hadn't been able to face returning to his office, he'd gone straight to his apartment and started to work from home. Deliberately focusing on his plans for the new restaurant, he'd sought to distract himself from thoughts of Rose by contacting as many of the professionals he'd previously courted who worked in the high-end hospitality business to remind them about the new Thames-side restaurant he was planning.

As Gene had confidently expected, there was plenty

of interest about coming to work for him and he'd been able to get quite a few people to commit.

After imbibing a couple of glasses of the rare Bordeaux he'd brought over from his cellar in Paris, he had talked and planned and made arrangements into the early hours. And finally, when sheer exhaustion had got the better of him, he'd kicked off his shoes, pulled off his tie and fallen into bed fully clothed.

But even as his burning eyes had drifted closed Gene hadn't been able to banish the memory of Rose's beautiful face, her mesmerising violet gaze, and the realisation had hit him that for the very first time in his life he was madly, head over heels in love.

The knowledge should have filled him with joy—but not when the sobering thought that the object of his affections was a woman who neither wanted nor regarded him had quickly followed it...

He had been utterly despondent. And that was why this morning, when he saw the red velvet box containing the diamond bracelet, he was painfully reminded that Rose had given it back to him without a qualm. She wasn't remotely impressed by his wealth or his ability to acquire whatever he wanted. In fact she definitely saw it as a negative rather than a desirable attribute.

She was refreshingly different from any of the women who moved in his so-called 'elite' circle. She wanted nothing of him other than that he start to look around and see the things in life that were important— the things that came in abundance just by dint of being born human...the things that came without a price tag, like nature and beauty and the possibility of being close to someone special…

Nothing that Gene could buy her or give her was ever going to convince Rose that underneath all his wealth and acquisitions had once been a genuinely good man who had somehow taken a wrong turn.

His understandable drive to make money and help secure his parents' future and his own after losing his sister had become insatiable… He'd started out doing it for all the right reasons, but the desire had long since become an addiction. He knew no peace and had no decent relationships to speak of. *All he did was work*. It took far more energy than people realised to maintain a position like his, and that was why he'd had no time to build relationships.

He'd had his sanctuary built in the hope that as well as not having to contend with the day-to-day bombardment of the press there, the isolation might one day help him deal properly with his grief so he could start to heal the out-of-control compulsion for 'more' that plagued him.

If only he had the courage to confide in Rose and explain *why* he had become so addicted. Gene would tell her that he'd thought it would protect him from the spectre of loss that haunted him… He would tell her about his sister and how she'd died unexpectedly and cruelly when she was just three years old. She had been the family's 'bright star' and they would never forget her…

Dropping his head into his hands, he thought hard. The only solution that would restore any hope for him was if he came up with a realistic plan to win Rose back—because suddenly the idea of living without her was too unbearable to contemplate...

CHAPTER ELEVEN

ROSE HAD RESISTED making her all-important call to Gene's office until she'd finished work, telling herself that he would no doubt be working late himself. Yet the truth that lurked beneath her delay taunted her, and all that day her insides were tied in painful knots because of it. She was terrified that he might not want to talk to her…that after she'd walked out on him at the restaurant he had mulled things over and decided he just didn't need the grief of a woman who perpetually liked to speak her mind.

When she finally picked up the phone and rang him she'd worked herself up into such a state that she felt physically sick.

'Mr Bonnaire is not in the office today,' his snooty secretary informed her, her imperious tone suggesting that a nonentity like Rose was wasting her time.

Immediately that put Rose's back up.

'Well, if he's not in the office can you tell me where I can reach him? He's not answering his mobile.'

'No. I'm afraid I can't.'

'But this is important!'

The woman expelled an irritated sigh. 'If Mr Bonnaire had wanted you to reach him he would have left instructions, Miss Heathcote. All I can tell you is that he doesn't want to be disturbed by *anyone* today.'

'But—'

'Goodbye, Miss Heathcote.'

The receiver was firmly put down to signal the end of the call and now Rose really *was* worried. The thought that she'd lost her chance to make amends with Gene was agonising. Why had she left it so late to ring him? What if he was out of the country on business somewhere and wasn't going to be back for days—or maybe even *weeks*?

Unable to sit still, she found herself restlessly making tea in the kitchen as she thought hard about what to do. She was taking her first sip of the hot beverage when the answer came to her. She knew *exactly* what she had to do…

The idea so excited her that she felt dizzy. Gripped by a steely determination and a newfound daring that she hadn't known she had in her, she emptied the mug of tea, grabbed her coat and bag and turned out the lights. Then, locking the doors of the antiques shop behind her, she hailed a cab to take her to the station…

Nearly drowned by the sea spray on the turbulent crossing, Rose smoothed back her plastered hair and turned up the collar on her raincoat with damp, icy fingers. Any conversation with Rory the boatman was impossible above the eldritch mourning of the wind and with the craft's constant leaping over the waves and its rollercoaster dive back down into them.

The young man had warned her when she'd boarded. ''Tis a rough crossing you'll face today, Rose. Sure you want to risk it?'

With her heart thudding fit to burst, she'd answered, 'If you're willing to risk it, then so am I. But I don't want you to cross if you honestly feel it's too dangerous.'

In answer to that statement Rory had grinned and said, 'I've crossed in worse seas than this and lived to tell the tale. But the message you're taking to His Lordship must be powerful important if you're willing to risk life and limb to take it to him, Rose. Did you let him know you were coming?'

So her instincts about Gene going to the island had been right.

She'd breathed out a relieved sigh and climbed into the boat. 'No…I didn't. Let's just say I want to surprise him.'

'Doesn't strike me as a man who likes surprises much…but I'm sure he'll make an exception for this one. He's a good man—in spite of all the rubbish the press say about him.'

True to his word, the boatman delivered Rose safely to the island. He even insisted on waiting for her to start negotiating the climb up the hill towards the house before leaving, calling out that he would bring the boat back one more time that afternoon 'just in case'.

Although she was chilled to the bone, and her damp clothing was clinging wetly to her body as she climbed the rocky incline, Rose hardly registered the discomfort. She was too tense to worry about it. But as she approached the futuristic dwelling that loomed out of the landscape the strangest sense of coming home washed over her, and she hugged the feeling to her as if it was something infinitely precious.

Glancing down at herself, she couldn't deny she wished she looked better. But then what did that signify, as long as Gene was pleased she'd made the journey? Because if he wasn't…

'Don't even *think* it…' she muttered crossly.

Remembering where to locate the dwelling's entrance, she moved her hand over the sensor and to her profound relief the curved doors slid opened. As she stepped onto the flawless parquet floor she heard the doors swish closed behind her. Swallowing hard, she nervously smoothed her hand down her damp raincoat. How was she going to let Gene know that she was there? Should she call out? Or simply just go and find him?

Still unsure, she kicked off her shoes, firmed the strap of her bag more securely over her shoulder and set off towards the living room. Even as she walked she detected the warm and tantalising scent of the Frenchman's cologne, and the provocative trail made her feel weak with excitement and longing.

'Well, well, well. Look who the wind's blown in.'

The tall, broad-shouldered Adonis with golden lights in his otherwise dark hair was staring out at the crashing waves through the panoramic windows. He turned slowly. There wasn't even the briefest acknowledgement of surprise in his piercing blue eyes. *It was just as though he'd been expecting her.*

Rose felt the strap of her bag slide off her shoulder and didn't move to stop it from falling to the floor. 'You said—you said that to me once before,' she answered, her teeth helplessly chattering.

'Did I?' Moving towards her, Gene smiled. 'I can see I'm going to have to find a new repertoire.'

'You don't look a bit surprised. How did you know that I would come here to look for you?'

'There are some things that are hard to explain…particularly when it comes to feelings. But that will have to keep for later. More importantly, you need to get out of those wet clothes and into a hot shower right now.'

Rose wasn't going to deny it. 'Yes, I do… But what about you, Gene? What do *you* need?'

His blue eyes mirrored his surprise…his pleasure too. 'What I need, sweetheart, is to join you,' he said huskily. 'You okay with that?'

Transfixed, Rose silently conveyed her agreement.

He stepped closer and his strong, muscular arm confidently encircled her waist. Feeling as though she was in a dream, it was as though her feet didn't even touch the floor as she let him lead her into the corridor and straight to his private suite.

In the state-of-the-art bathroom with a mosaic tiled floor in dazzling azure and wall-to-wall mirrors, Gene turned on the water in the spacious shower and soon the whole room was filled with hot, perfumed steam.

Even as she tried to take in what was happening the vehement desire that surged through her body easily took precedence over what was in her mind. When he came to her and helped dispense with her raincoat she was more than happy to let him.

After laying it on a nearby chair he came back to her, and his handsome face was a study of intense concentration as piece by piece he started to remove Rose's clothing. She was still shivering—but this time it wasn't from the cold.

'Together we make fire,' he'd told her once, and it was true.

Placing his big hands either side of her hips, he expertly removed her skimpy underwear, and she felt every touch and stroke of his flesh as though she couldn't bear to be without it.

Then he drew her towards him and, gravel-voiced, commanded, 'Kiss me.'

Rose had no intention of denying him and hungrily complied. Their mouths opened helplessly as soon as their lips collided and they were reunited with the molten heat that seemed to be generated so effortlessly whenever they were together. Now that heat intensified and burst into full scorching flame, and as their kisses became ever more urgent, with Gene's deliciously velvet mouth all but devouring her, Rose's hands started to tear desperately at his clothes.

When he was naked, for the very first time she had a true 'up close and personal' look at his magnificent body. As well as being muscular, fit and toned, he was heavily aroused, primed to take her, and she could hardly wait until the moment when they would join together...

Feeling deliriously weak and hungry, she wrapped

her arms round his neck and begged softly, 'Take me into the shower...*please*...'

Lifting her against him effortlessly, so that her slim thighs clamped tightly round his lean waist, Gene stooped down to his discarded jeans and extracted a strip of slim foil packets. When he stood again, with his indomitable brow furrowing, she noticed his smile was a little self-conscious.

'I don't want to put you in the same position I put you in last time and have you worrying about getting pregnant,' he confessed.

'Would you be shocked if I admitted that I actually thought about *not* taking that morning-after pill?' Rose asked him softly.

'Why? Why would you do that?'

'Perhaps we'd better talk about that later...' She smiled.

Gene immediately concurred. 'All I want you to think about now is the sweet, unadulterated pleasure I'm going to give you, sweetheart.'

Bending his head, he stole another incendiary, open-mouthed kiss and Rose's body all but melted as he carried her into the hot, steamy shower.

The first time he took her hard and fast, and she gasped her need and pleasure out loud as hot rivulets of water deluged their naked bodies. They ran down her hair and face and streamed over her breasts as Gene claimed her again and again, and finally Rose couldn't hold back the elemental force that threatened to take her over the edge any longer... *In his arms she came undone.*

Rapturous with the hot tide of sensual feeling that overwhelmed her, she felt tears of joy flood into her eyes and mingle with the water from the shower. Her lover released a deep guttural groan and grew still as he climaxed.

For a while both of them couldn't speak. Then he looked down at her and carefully eased her back onto her feet. Even in the steam that enveloped them she saw his blue eyes shine as she'd never seen them shine before...

'We've been together for half an hour at least, angel, and I haven't yet told you how beautiful you are.'

Sighing with satisfaction, he pulled her against him and covered her eyelids, nose and mouth with infinitely tender kisses that made Rose catch her breath and stare at him in wonder.

'I promise I'm going to make up for that, sweetheart—starting now, by telling you that you're one gorgeous, sexy woman. I don't know what I did to bring you to me—only that I'm *beyond* grateful that you're here.'

Rose's smile was warm and loving as she stroked a strand of glistening wet hair back from his lightly ridged forehead. Her heart was so full it was hard to put her feelings into words.

'I couldn't have stayed away, Gene. Did you think I *could*?'

Shaking his head, he captured her hand. 'When you left me in the restaurant after saying those things about the way I conducted myself... I won't lie to you and tell you that I didn't resent it—because I *did*.' He paused to lift her hand to his lips and kissed it. 'But I knew I was angry because you were the one person who had dared to tell me the truth.'

'I didn't mean to hurt you.'

'I know you didn't. But it had to be done, Rose. I was in a hell of my own making and you came along and set me free. Maybe now I have a chance to redeem myself?'

'Let's dry each other off and go to bed, shall we? I want to hold you in my arms and tell you exactly what I feel about you, Eugene Bonnaire...businessman *extraordinaire.*'

Her smile was teasing and unashamedly seductive, and she revelled in the new sensation of feminine power that she'd discovered—no holds barred.

The second time he took her Gene deliberately slowed things down. In the lavish double bed, with its satin and silk sheets, he took his time and savoured every incredible, joyous moment of making love with Rose. She was the most giving woman in every respect, and she took just as much delight and pleasure in exploring him as he did her.

Her sweetly shaped breasts, slim hips and silkily smooth thighs perfectly complemented his hard, lean physique when he took her in his arms and caressed her. And when he gazed at the stunning revelation of her bare body lying on his silk sheets he saw that she was the perfect 'pocket Venus'.

He found it hard to understand how he had ever thought any other woman beautiful. How could he have when there had always been one vitally important missing ingredient? The heart-to-heart connection that now made him hopeful and helped him look forward to a truly *joyous* future instead of one that he'd feared would bring only more sorrow.

Rose was lying atop him and had been teasingly nipping at the soft flesh of his lower lip. As much as he was enjoying it, in one deft motion Gene had manoeuvred her to lie next to him. Turning towards her, he cupped her small jaw in his big hand and for a long moment was lost in the beauty of her radiant violet gaze.

'You said it crossed your mind not to take that morning-after pill. Will you tell me why?'

Rose didn't shy away from meeting the intensity she saw in his glance and said, 'I couldn't help wondering what a child we made would look like. And for the first time in my life I realised I wanted children. I wanted a family of my own.'

'Do you still feel like that?'

'If the right man came along I wouldn't hesitate.'

Trying not to give way to a delighted grin, Gene eased out a long slow breath. 'And has he?'

'What do *you* think?'

He answered her, leaving her in no doubt, with a lingering hot kiss.

When they both came up for air he asked, 'Out of interest, how did you know I would be here on the island?' His breath hitched as he waited to hear her reply.

Rose sighed. 'How do you think? I *sensed* that you were here…that you would be waiting for me. I didn't even stop to pack. I just jumped in a cab. My only worry was that you wouldn't forgive me.'

'Forgive you for what?'

She grimaced. 'For taking it upon myself to tell you where you'd been going wrong, that's what. It's not like I'm some kind of expert. I've made plenty of mistakes too.'

Unable to resist teasing her, Gene made himself look serious. 'Oh? What kind of mistakes?'

'Funny enough, always trying to "do the right thing." Not allowing myself to really live...to trust that if I listened to my heart it wouldn't lead me astray. My dad found it hard to trust too. He was a wonderful man, but he could be unforgiving about making mistakes. And he was so afraid I was going to turn out like my mother if he didn't make certain rules about how I should behave. The thing is, she isn't a bad person—but he probably forgot all the reasons he'd once loved her when she left him and he was worried that one day I might replicate her behaviour.'

'You mean he was afraid you might run off with some unscrupulous billionaire who, after he'd seduced you, would make you fall in love with his wealthy and essentially empty lifestyle?'

Feeling the bitter bite of regret, Gene couldn't help his sardonic tone.

Immediately concerned, Rose put her hand on his shoulder and lightly stroked it. 'It's not your rich lifestyle that I fell in love with...it's the man I always sensed was beneath the aloof and polished façade. It's *you* that I love, Gene. You and no other.'

Somehow Gene's breath felt as if it was trapped inside his chest. His heart was racing so hard he could scarcely think straight. Then he realised that he was hearing the words he'd thought never to hear. Not in *this* life anyway…

'You *love* me?'

Rose looked perturbed. 'You sound as if you might doubt it?'

'It's not that I doubt you mean it, Rose. I'm just surprised…*delighted* and surprised. The truth is I don't think I'm a very lovable person. My own parents probably have trouble even *liking* me. Don't think I'm feeling sorry for myself—I can't help but be a realist.'

'I don't believe that your parents don't like you. And I certainly don't believe they don't *love* you. A parent's love is unconditional, isn't it?'

He shrugged. 'They tell me that they care, but it was my sister they adored.'

'You had a sister?'

'Yes…'

Instead of pushing the feelings of grief away, as he usually did, Gene let them come. He remembered the fierce joy he'd felt whenever he was with Francesca, and the sense that he would protect her with his life if he could. To his everlasting regret, he hadn't been able to.

Swallowing hard, he smiled painfully. 'Her name was Francesca. She died when she was just three, after a short and painful illness.'

Rose's hand stilled against his shoulder. 'Gene, I'm so sorry. How old were *you*?'

'I was nine.'

'Your poor family… You must have all been utterly devastated.'

'We were. We still are. That's why I was determined

to do everything I could to make sure my parents at least never had to worry about money. Unfortunately things didn't go exactly as I'd planned. My desire to secure their future got rather out of hand. I became addicted to the pleasure of seeing my bank balance grow larger and larger—and to the kudos of being successful… I thought it would protect me from the spectre of loss that had haunted me since losing Francesca. But I lost sight of my reasons. As you said to me at the restaurant, Rose…I just didn't know when enough was enough. And along the way, when I saw that my relationships—especially with women—weren't fulfilling, because they were mostly meaningless, I think I lost a little bit of my soul.'

'Oh, baby…'

She kissed him tenderly and it was then that Gene sensed the truth in her touch. His heart leapt.

'I love you too, Rose. The thought of not being with you for the rest of my life is torture.'

She wrapped her arms firmly around him and kissed him again. When she glanced up she was grinning. 'The last thing I want to do is torture you, my love. I want to spend the rest of my life making you happy. And I'll tell anyone who cares to listen what a good and kind man you are. The kind of man who always makes the people who love him proud.'

'On that subject: I'd like you to be with me when I go and talk to my parents, Rose. I want to tell them how I've been feeling, why I've grown more and more distant from them. I also want to share with them the way I felt after we lost Francesca. And lastly…'

'Tell me?'

'I want to tell them that I've met the woman of my dreams.'

Rose dimpled. 'Now you're going to make me cry…'

'There's something else I'd like you to do for me.'

'What's that?'

'I'd like you to take back the bracelet I gave you. I meant what I said on the note I sent with it. You *are* the hidden diamond that I didn't expect. If you accept my gift, and the heartfelt intention that it was given with, I'll know it means that you love me for the *real* Gene Bonnaire—not the ruthless businessman that the world sees, but the very fallible and ordinary man who doesn't mind admitting that he's made quite a few mistakes in his life. However…the one mistake I'll *never* make is to walk away from the woman who is far more precious and valuable to me than anything material I could ever acquire or achieve… The woman who I hope will one day be my wife and the mother of my children.'

Rose was crying…crying inconsolably.

All Gene could do was to hold her lovingly against him until she grew quiet, all the while telling her how much he loved and adored her.

Then he asked her to marry him.

When she looked up at him she answered, 'Yes! Of *course* I'll marry you!' And the happiness that shone from her beautiful violet eyes shimmered like the most exquisite diamond of all…even though they were drenched with tears…

EPILOGUE

ROSE HAD WANTED to make her afternoon visit to her husband's Parisian office a surprise. She'd agreed beforehand to meet him at a sumptuous and classy restaurant in the city, to have a late lunch with his parents and her mother and stepfather, but in the end she'd made the decision to meet him at his office first, so that they could travel to the restaurant together.

She wanted to pinch herself at the way things had changed. Not only had Gene been reunited with his family, but Rose had also started to rebuild her relationship with her mother. And, to top it all, just a few short weeks ago she and Gene had been married in the most exquisite Gothic church in Kensington. Even the presence of a flock of paparazzi hadn't spoiled the day. Unbelievably, she was now Mrs Bonnaire.

Walking down the richly carpeted corridor of what she teasingly referred to as 'the presidential suite', she felt her tummy deluged with butterflies. She couldn't help being nervous at the prospect of seeing the man she adored. Their passionate relationship had been nothing less than a dream come true. Every day when she woke up next to him Rose told Gene that he took her breath away.

Today she'd donned one of her prettiest dresses underneath a stylish designer jacket, and she was particularly hoping that he would notice.

'Mrs Bonnaire. How nice to see you. Is Mr Bonnaire expecting you?'

His new smartly attired middle-aged secretary, Martine, was genuinely pleased to see her, and had made no secret of the fact that she was pleased and delighted that her handsome boss had found the woman he declared to be 'the love of his life'.

Rose sent up a silent prayer that her husband wasn't with a colleague or a client. She was literally *aching* to see him.

'No, Martine. He's not expecting me. But if he's free can I just go in and see him?'

'But of course.'

After knocking briefly on the panelled oak door, she walked inside. Gene's office was not just stylish, it was bright and beautiful too. Rose loved the way that sunlight never seemed to fail to be pouring in from the large plate-glass windows that looked out onto the busy city whenever she visited.

Today was no different. As her avid gaze fell upon her husband she saw how the light reflected burnished lights in his immaculately cut dark hair.

He turned to welcome his visitor. 'I knew it had to be you, my love.' He smiled. 'I think I'm psychically attuned to that polite little knock of yours.'

Rose moved swiftly towards him for his embrace. 'I know I said I'd meet you at the restaurant, but—'

'Is something wrong?'

Seeing his worried frown, she hastened to assure him. 'No, there's nothing wrong. I just couldn't wait to see you. Do you mind?'

'You may as well ask me if I need to breathe.' Gene chuckled. 'Not only have you decided to surprise me with an impromptu visit, but you've worn that very pretty red dress that I love on you.'

He nuzzled the side of her neck and the heat he exuded along with the seductive scent of his cologne made Rose instantly weak.

'I'm just wondering if I should lock the door and lower the blinds. And if I have time to take it off you and make love to you before we go to the restaurant.'

'Ordinarily I'd agree it was a good idea, but we're meeting both your parents and mine for lunch—remember?' Her cheeks dimpled and she gently touched her palm to his cheek. 'And not just that—I have something I need to tell you before we leave.'

Lifting her hand away, her husband pressed his lips in a briefly tender kiss against hers. 'That sounds ominous…' he remarked teasingly.

'But only in a good way, I hope?'

'Depends what it is you're going to tell me.'

'I'm pregnant. We're going to have a baby, Gene!'

His blue eyes widened, glinting in the sunlight. 'This is true? I mean, you know this for sure, Rose?'

'I took a pregnancy test this morning and it came out positive.' Her heart was hammering as she spoke, but there was no need for anxiety. Already she could see the joy in his expression.

'*Mon Dieu*… I'm going to be a father! We are going to be parents. This is the most wonderful thing I've ever heard, my love!'

Gene caught her to him and passionately kissed her. When they came up for air he pushed a button at the side of his desk. The lock on the door firmly clicked shut and the cream-coloured blinds at the windows started to lower smoothly.

He turned back to Rose and gently divested her of her jacket, and then he expertly pulled down the zip at the side of her pretty red dress.

'I've decided we definitely have time to make love before we go to lunch…' He smiled. 'Our parents won't mind if we're late… Not when we tell them that they're going to be grandparents.'

Rose's eyes moistened as she gazed up at him. 'Have you *any* idea just how much I love you?' she breathed.

For an electrifying moment Gene looked serious. 'If it comes anywhere near to the depth and breadth of the love I have for you, Rose, then I know I must be the most blessed man on earth.'

* * * * *